PARADOX LOST

ARLAN ANDREWS, SR

WOODS
PUBLISHING

CONTENTS

OF TIME AND THE YUCATÁN

Distant gunfire rattled somewhere outside, but that was not his first concern: it was *hot* in Valladolid, and Zed Wynter wanted some ice for his drink. "*Hielo, por favor?*" he asked the bartender. The Mexican behind the bar just looked at him without responding. Damn, wasn't he pronouncing it right?

"Ice—*ee-aay-low?*" Zed pointed at the warm glass of rum and coke. The bartender just shrugged and turned up his hands in mock (or was it actual?) despair. "*No hay hielo, señor.*" As if in explanation, he waved a hand toward the door. Humid air wafted in through that open puerta, not so much a breeze as a shrug of a wearied wind, bringing with it hints of the odors of war—oil and engine exhausts, burning organics, unidentifiable but acrid smells. *Disgusting!* As a kind of exclamation point to Zed's feeling, dull thuds of artillery drowned out the nearer rifle exchanges. The cantina shook, causing dust to fall from the cracked ceiling.

Yeah, Zed thought grimly, *I know there's a war on, Pedro. The same damn war that's been going on down here for four years, only the sides and the borders keep changing.* He took a sip of the warmish mixture and hoped that his meeting with Filemón—*El General Filemón Garcia, gringo, and don't you forget it!* he told himself—would be worthwhile.

At least worth the trouble to get here, he thought. As the unsmiling bartender came over to top off the decidedly unwholesome brew in his pitcher, Zed thought back upon his journey to the war zone of the Yucatán.

IT HAD ALL STARTED BACK IN HIS OFFICE IN Dallas. "Future Perfect—*The MetaZine of Personal Robotics,*" the business card said aloud, in Zed's somewhat augmented voice, "Zed Wynter, Editor, at your service." Zed smiled as his own visage appeared on the card and continued the sales pitch. The picotronics features were simply amazing but cheap enough to pass out as video advertising. He went back to admiring his not-too-handsome face and blond hair. *Too bad I didn't opt for a full figure image. Maybe some female clients would like my tall frame and skinny body.* He laughed silently.

"Doris," Zed spoke to his androbot secretary. "Please pass on my congratulations to the fabber." Doris nodded, then rocked and waddled out to the front of the office. She — his androbot — was an expensive affectation, but his job was to write about robots and robotics, so having a physical one in the office was appropriate, and a deductible expense item at that. At times, "she" was a welcome presence in his otherwise rather sterile office environment.

Zed spread out the stack of cards in a fan shape across his wide oak desk. He finally made it to his new office in the Dallas New America Center—success! He loved it when the business card recognized that human fingers were touching it at both ends. *My own design, that, and a nice touch if I do say so.* In a humorous mood, he thought: *Wonder if I could get the fabber to make me one that listens and transmits as well? Now* that *would be some business card—one that spies.* He'd mention it to his nanofab supplier at the first opportunity. Donne Enterprises was first rate.

Absently, he wiped the card over his wrister for a scan, then watched the entire spiel. "*Future Perfect* is the metazine of *now robotics*—with minute-by-minute downloads for all your wristers, comps, minibots and electronic pets, and the very latest in Developing Intelligence Analyses. In your home business or your large corporation, can you afford to be without your personal link? And advertisers—special rates apply for personalized markets, for metastimos and for royalties of downloaded sales." The sales pitch droned on with an appropriate musical accompaniment chosen by the algorithmic analysis of the preferences of the client holding the card.

Followed by a freebie download, if they listen all the way to the end! Otherwise it deactivates in an hour. Zed smiled. *The smart ones get the better deals,* he thought. *Even the pricing information scales in real time.*

Zed's metazine had flourished even more than the personal robotics market itself, and he was extremely lucky to own a share of *that* market. He hadn't been so fortunate ten years before, back when he was a designer of personal robots: a near-bust in that market back then, caused by consumer liability lawyers handling a multitude of cases where mutilation of degenerates having unauthorized (and impossible) sex with their androbots. That had put Zed and thousands of other engineers out of work.

A Ph.D. in mechanical engineering wasn't worth a lot when everyone was looking for puffware geniuses with Nobels in their pockets. He'd survived for a while by working with his British ex-pat friend, Mark Donne, in a seedy part of a Dallas suburb. Mark and Zed made some small money for a few years, developing adjunct devices for laser tooling in a small niche market in the industrial robot industry. But Zed could write—a by-product of his long years of reading science fiction and then writing his own stories in response. As the personal robot industry rose again, he used his funds to found his robotics metazine.

Zed had enjoyed the past five years or so, even though robots were still not totally practical for home use as maids, butlers, or babysitters. But he was already making a steady, if not lucrative, income from his long-held shares of *Teddy Toys* and *Living 'Lectronics*—his contingent payment for helping save the company that produced them, a desperate Third China conglomerate that had needed a native English speaker to write defensive copy and advertising for them. *I'm so happy I was not born in Quebec!* he often thought.

Doris broke his reverie with an irritating buzzing signal on his antique intercom. "Phone call, Mr. Wynter. Satellite Service, voice only." Wondering why his wrister hadn't received the call, Zed wrinkled his forehead at the ancient telephone receiver on his desk. *Another affectation*, he mused. *Why am I so stuck in the past?* That antique device came on, responding to switches invisibly tattooed on his brow, one of Mark's nano-apps. He wondered if his arms might atrophy if he used this new gadget too much. At least he would have strong forehead muscles!

"*Señor Wynter, por favor?*" The crackling, wavering voice signal and the loud background noises did not sound like the typical business call. He answered the inquiry in Spanish. "*Si, aquí. Pero mi Español está muy mal,*" he apologized.

Laughter at the other end. "Yes, Zed, your Spanish *is* still terrible!" The unknown voice changed to a friendlier tone. "Zed, *compadre*, you still have a German accent in Spanish, did you know?" For an instant, Zed didn't recognize the caller. The crackling grew louder and the background noises were like firecrackers in a barrel. Who...?

Then recollection came. His last night in Juárez. The *White Cave.* Migod, it was Filemón! But he was a guerrilla leader in the Yucatán! What—?

"Hey, *Jankee*," Zed recognized the joking pronunciation of his old-time friend, "it's been *mucho años*, but we had a time in Chihuahua, didn't we?" Zed heard a noisy, static filled pause, then more firecrackers chattering in a larger barrel.

"Sorry, Zed," the voice now spoke in perfect English in a very sober tone, "but we have just taken this central office in Pisté, in the Yucatán. We think the *Federales* will cut the trunk lines soon. All satellite phone service is shot to hell, so no wristers are up. I'm depending on these old phone cables. I want you to come down here with me for a very important reason."

Zed was dumbfounded. This old friend, this People's Movement revolutionary leader, wanted him to come to the war zone for some "important reason"? *No damn way!* "Listen, Filemón, I—" Zed realized his reply channel was cut off. He could hear only the one-way message from Filemón, who suddenly spoke very fast. "Zed, you are a good writer and I think sympathetic to justice. I have a discovery to share with you..." Crackling, wavering. "...don't you think?"

More interference, then "... tonight at 1900 hours … your secure home DI system ... more information. *Por favor* ..." More crackles, more firecrackers. And then silence.

Zed sat back in his chair, the myomassagers sensing his stressful muscular condition and beginning their programmed massage of his tensed muscles, the aromatherapy incense adding in its soothing calmatives. Still, he remained in mild shock. What in the hell was going on? Zed and Filemón Garcia had shared a dorm room at New Mexico State University back some fifteen years ago, had known a few women together, and had partied entirely too much. They had often philosophized about the various Latin Peoples' Movements, but never shared any common beliefs in the ultimate destiny of the region. Zed remembered Filemón's sloganizing and revolutionary rhetoric, uncommon in an engineering student.

"Hey, *Jan-kee,*" he would say, "if I'm gonna rule *El Sur,* then I gotta know all about electronics and satellites and robots and shit, right?" After Zed had sputtered most of his beer out of his mug, Filemón had continued. "Else, how I'm gonna be able to train *mis hombres* in ultra-tech weapons?

"Besides, once I am *un enginero,* I'll be cultured in the ways of the world, and WorldNet interviews will be as important as bullets in my coming revolution." Zed remembered Filemón's sober repetition of those last three words: "My coming revolution… *my* revolution..." Those memories trailed off into nights of carousing in nearby La Mesilla, and the fragments finally dissolved into misty recollections of dark eyes and silky thighs and other familiar pleasures under the arching black velvet skies of New México.

All Zed knew about *General* Garcia now was what he'd seen on the metaweb—how an unknown agricultural engineering student, educated in the U.S., had led student riots at a university in central México, aided peasants in the decades-old fighting in Chiapas Province, and became a libertarian-anarchist guerrilla leader in the civil war raging in the Yucatán for the last four or five years. *God knows*, Zed thought, *that place needs some kind of revolution, what with the cartelero terrorism, the over-population, the famines, even the incessant police brutality of the official but corrupt government against hungry, unemployed mobs in the choked cities.*

He was glad that northern México, at least, had been spared the disasters of the central and southern regions. The *maquiladoras,* the co-operated Mexican-American border factories, had been the source of the prosperity and stability in Chihuahua and the other border states of México after some of the more prominent *carteleros* had been violently but effectively squashed. And were still peaceful. So far.

But for the last year, the media had been displaying only negative images about Garcia, primarily his campaigns against Cancun and

Cozumel, on the Turquoise Coast of the Caribbean side of the Yucatán. *For good reason,* Zed thought, *since Filemón destroyed Cancun, San Miguel, Playa del Carmen, and most of the other tourist areas in Quintana Roo province. Not occupied, just destroyed.* The media most often overlooked the fact that those cities and towns had been home to the remaining drug cartel leaders, the *carteleros,* whose vast sums of money had bought both political and media influence. So Filemón was fighting both a criminal empire and an unresponsive Federal government. Who knew which of those forces was stronger? Filemón had quite a set of challenges!

Zed sighed, remembering romantic walks with señoritas in the moonlight on the albino beaches of Cozumel, the incessant songs of the swallows, and the transparent waters. *So sad that the place is now a ruin.*

For all the painful remembrance, Zed's thoughts raced, *Filemón was once my friend, and that I owe him. I really do owe him ... my life!* The reverie misted away and clearer thoughts returned. Regardless of the media bias, Zed knew that Garcia was not one of those old violent revolutionary firebrands, not after the last few decades of neo-Marxists in South America had brought disaster to their respective nations. He hoped that the more libertarian-leaning stirrings that Filemón represented would help lift Latin nations out of their centuries-old burdens of corruption and superstition.

Garcia's pronouncements, as far as Zed had been able to find, put him in line with the new People's Movements around the world. These groups wanted to bring real reform, real freedom to the peasants, and the one proven way to do that was through the pragmatic free-market solutions that flourished in Nordica and the USA. (He hated to dwell on the suicidal disasters that befell the old European Union.) And so far, even though a few South Americans used the old fashioned terminology of bygone populists, the libertarian economies they had established were as free and prosperous as those of three of the Four Chinas. *Like Hong Kong used to be*, he mused.

The cross-Caribbean attacks against dying revolutionary Cuba by heretical Christian Marxists had provided the death blow to that decrepit police state some years ago. He was certain that Garcia was one of the new Latin firebrands, using the old slogans just to bring back some fervor to his band of peasants.

And now, he thought, *after years of war and destruction, Filemón calls from out of nowhere—where is Pisté?—to drag me into his battles? Don't think so ...* An important advertising client called on his wrister, interrupting his worries, and Zed did his best to forget Filemón's call until he arrived at his apartment that evening.

"Mr. Zed, sire," Brighton, his home Developing Intelligence (DI) system, addressed him in a perfect Etonian British accent.

"On the priority channel, outside normal wrister comms, two urgent messages arrived tonight. The first was rather strange, from someone named Ms. Marina Tanner, who said she would try to call you again, later. That you would not be able to contact her."

Zed frowned. He had never heard of any Tanner, Ms., Mr., or whatever, and he was troubled that some stranger would have his priority access code. He'd have to review Brighton's security systems. It was odd that the woman hadn't left a video image, and even more odd that he could not contact her back. With wrister communications, no one was out of reach unless they overrode with a Priority Zero. Zed regretted he'd done just that on the way home. *But business is business,* he told himself, *and privacy is privacy.* He shrugged; everything had its price.

"And the second call was from México," Brighton volunteered, having paused until Zed's facial expression registered completion of his thoughts about the first message.

"Out with it, Brighton," Zed said, somewhat irritated about having blocked off his wrister. A fuzzy image appeared on the nearest wallscreen. Garcia himself spoke, his voice slightly ahead of the slow-scan image, almost a caricature of the ancient English-dubbed Mexican movies.

"Dirty capitalist, Zed, you are not at home. Nevertheless, a plane ticket to Cuba awaits in your electronic mail, and connections to my headquarters will be made in person when you arrive in Havana."

Garcia became very serious. "*Amigo,* there is much at stake, and I know you love a mystery. My only hint to you is this: what kind of robot can you build of copper and stone?" Slowly the image smiled and Garcia's arm came up to his forehead in the friendly mock salute they had always used with each other. "Come to my México, my friend. Come and find out!" The panel screen faded, paused, and the next message, a Priority Two, came up: a porno ad.

"I told you to stop that crap, Brighton. How did it get through?"

"Sire, I really don't know. I can assure you it had the proper IDs and passwords." The DI sounded contrite.

Damn, some hacko is breaking all the codes now! Twice in one night! Better gin up another one if I want to keep some privacy. Watching the intriguing calisthenics in the ad, however, Zed decided to review the rest of the intriguing message, just to see what kind of advertisers he was working against.

THAT WAS A NICE TRIP TO HAVANA, ZED THOUGHT, *but the submarine trip back across the Caribbean was not much fun at all!* The Chilean Navy, for all that it was nuclear, was not noted for luxurious accommodations. *One hell of a way to get down to the Yucatán!* But the peninsular war zone was strictly quarantined by Mexican authorities, and the Havana-to-Yucatán connection was well-oiled and well-traveled by revolutionaries, weapons dealers, journalists, and even a few respectable people.

Finally Zed arrived on a dark night near the ruins of Cancun, its battle-scarred, abandoned high-rises visible in the darkness only as ragged silhouettes against a star-strewn sky. The gaping vertical crags reminded Zed of the stark, unfriendly ruins not too far away over at the ancient site of Uxmal: Nazi-like, he remembered thinking, possessing none of the human spirit, none of the friendlier ambience of Teotihuacan or Chichén Itzá.

Eventually he was transported in a covered, bouncing vehicle through scrub jungle for several hours, to God-knows where. From his previous visits, Zed assumed he was halfway to Chichén Itzá and its nearest town, Pisté—he had checked out Filemón's calling location. From Pisté, the next most important goal of any revolutionary army had to be the provincial capital of Mérida, and he was sure Garcia's PRY—Revolutionary Yucatán Party— would besiege it next.

The next morning Zed was driven into Valladolid, the present rebel stronghold, and was told by a sour-faced *commandante* that *El General Garcia* himself would see the *gringo* in a day or two. Meanwhile, Zed was to enjoy himself, see the local sights, and relax.

Enjoy? Sights? Pock-marked buildings, a cathedral lying in ruins, mud-filled streets strewn with surly peasant soldiers and battle-damaged vehicles? Relax? Zed had sighted the one remaining open bar and determined he would await his "message from Garcia" in the most civilized manner he could arrange. The decrepit building where he was lodged smelled of mold, and the occasional hot breeze from the countryside brought with it odors of gunpowder and worse.

Two long, hot, humid days Zed waited and sweated. Then the ice ran out, and the sounds of battle grew closer, and Zed could swear that those jets continually *vrooming* overhead were not Filemón's. Was Garcia losing? No one spoke to the *Norteamericano* except for the briefest of acknowledgements to his requests, so Zed talked to himself a lot to break the silence. The Mexican bartender ignored the crazy *yanqui's* mumblings.

"So there's no ice, the *Federales* are winning, and I'm stuck in the rebel headquarters, liable for execution as a civilian spy, if my friend the guerrilla leader, loses. Maybe even if he wins! What a situation! Wish there was some ice!"

After an unsatisfactory lunch of thin soup and incendiary chopped jalapeños, mixed in debatable concert with dark beans inside a stale tortilla, Zed ordered a warm *cerveza Superior* and waited some more. Occasionally he dictated notes to his wrister, but the suspicious glares of the armed men at the cantina door made him somewhat reluctant to appear to be spying. He made mental notes about the city, recalling the mysterious conversation with Garcia.

Robots of copper and stone? What the hell did Filemón mean by that? The Greek god of engineers, old crippled Hephaestus, was the first person in legend to make a mechanical man—a robot. Zed remembered from reading Homer that Hephaestus' most famous creation, the giant man of metal called Talos, was fashioned of brass. The legendary warrior and brigand Ulysses had killed the robot by draining its life-fluid from a plug in its ankle. Zed had always wondered if that story was a vestigial memory of ancient technology. And there were lots of stone idols around the world; Zed had seen his share in Egypt and in South America, but *stone robots?* Not likely.

Sweating miserably in the hot early afternoon breeze that fairly crawled in the door and out the window at his back, Zed Wynter concluded that a Wynter in the Yucatán in July had a snowball's chance of surviving, much less of achieving anything useful. *Garcia knew I couldn't turn down such a cryptic invitation. And he also knows that I owe him.*

Suddenly the street outside clattered with loud, repetitive booms. *Oh God, they're shelling the town!* He thought in panic, throwing himself to the floor. But then the sounds stopped, and laughing guards pointed their rifles at him, motioning him to come outside.

"Scared of a backfiring jeep, *Jankee*?" someone yelled as Zed stepped out, blinded, into the bright sunlight. "Hey, you're going to hear louder things than that where we're going!" The voice was deep, throaty, Spanish-inflected—Filemón Garcia!

El General en jefe Filemón Garcia stood in the middle of the street, just disembarking from his coughing, sputtering, muffler-less jeep. Bandoleers crossed a sweat-soaked khaki shirt, and a large gold and white sombrero incongruously perched on his head, shading a handsome face and a drooping Pancho Villa moustache. Filemón Garcia stood only five-foot-six; not your typical revolutionary hero. *God!* Thought Zed, *If he's not a stereotypical Mexican* bandido!

Amidst good-natured laughter of the street filled with armed rebels, Zed and Garcia embraced and pounded on each other's backs. *I'm surprised at myself, but I am glad to see this guy*, Zed thought. *Even with the showmanship, the disarming comic appearance, he is so real compared to the pseudointellectual puffware artists and single-minded engitechs I deal with. Why, with the leadership abilities he's shown down here, he could even make a good sales rep!*

Zed smiled at his own parochial thoughts.

Looking around the street while his eyes adjusted to the incredibly bright sunshine, Zed thought he would not make such a suggestion to Garcia just yet. He could sense the camaraderie, the fanaticism, of the Garcista armed men, many of them only children, some of them in bandages hiding stumps of arms and legs. Filemón was a general, he reminded himself, and something of a god to these people. His old friend had a lot of war to go, even if he ever could win. But maybe someday, they could talk of other things.

"Zed," Garcia said quietly after they retired back inside the relative coolness of the cantina, "I'm happy to see you here." Miraculously, *hielo* appeared out of nowhere and found its way into premium mescal drinks delivered to the table by a smiling bartender. Both men drank the cool liquid gratefully. Wiping his dripping moustache with a dirty sleeve, Garcia said, "Brings back old memories of school in New Mexico, and the fights and the girls." He stared directly into Zed's eyes with no trace of humor.

"And Juárez, too, *amigo*. What we did there." He took another drink and whispered, "Zed, someday I'll take Juárez, too, you know?"

"I don't doubt that for a moment, Filemón," Zed replied evenly, sipping the delightfully cold mescal. "If you want to do it, I'm sure you will. But please don't do to Juárez," he said, his voice suddenly rising, the stress of the situation showing in his abrupt gesture toward the cantina door, "what you've done to Valladolid and Cancun and San Miguel and the rest! What will you gain if you destroy so much?"

The bartender drew down a rifle and aimed at Zed. Garcia tensed visibly, motioning the man to point the gun away. Garcia sipped mescal, chewed the ice momentarily and said quietly, "Old friend, I'm glad to see you. We never did agree on politics, and we may never. But just one more thing." His dark eyes grew cold and narrowed, unblinkingly. "Do not ever say such things in front of my men, ever again, or it will be a bad situation." He signaled for more drinks, which came in seconds, ice and all. No one else came inside the cantina, and the bartender stayed quietly in a corner of the bar, showing no signs of life, awaiting only the snap of his General's fingers.

"Trust me, Zed. My country's history is just one long struggle, one continuous battle, and it will last until the people finally win against the old corrupt aristocrats and the new *carteleros*. The destruction will be paid for by the fat ones—*los gordos*—when I am victorious. They have enough funds in Swiss banks to make every Mexican wealthy. I plan to confiscate all of that and settle accounts for the poor here, once and for all.

"But forget all that for now. You are not here to fight battles—for me or against me." He emphasized the latter choice with a frown, his eyes half visible under weary eyelids. "I asked you to come down to Yucatán for another reason. You remember?"

Reaching into his bulging shirt, down between the crossed bandoleers, Garcia smiled and tossed a rectangular metal plate, about one inch by three inches, onto the table. The bartender reacted quickly to the tinkling noise, but Garcia waved him back. Zed was getting nervous about that guy's hair-trigger finger!

"This is what I wanted you to see, Zed."

The American picked up the small thin piece of metal, examining it in the late evening sunlight that glared through the cantina window. It was a nameplate—a robot manufacturer's nameplate.

Wetting his forefinger with some mescal, Zed wiped off enough dark, thick, syrupy tarnish to read the engraving. Model Romeo-14, Serial Number 002-35-101RR, it read, followed by nearly incomprehensible technical data. When he saw the logo at the bottom, Zed was so surprised he said aloud, " Manufactured by QuanTonics, S. A., Hecho en México."

"Filemón, it's an OEM nameplate." Seeing Garcia's puzzled look, he added, "That means Original Equipment Manufacturer— an OEM takes parts from other people and builds a final product, as opposed to the factories that build quantum circuit chips, or micro-gears, or whatever, for others to use.

"What are you doing with one of these Romeo-14s, anyhow? At last month's Robotics Conference, QuanTonics was saying that the 14 models wouldn't be out for a year or two—parts problems or something." He looked at Garcia with sudden apprehension, forgetting his friend's admonition from minutes before. "You're not going to attack their factory, are you, Filemón?" His voice rose in pitch and volume, and the bartender was fetching the assault rifle one last time.

Garcia pointed at the man, shaking his head vigorously. The bartender scowled, but kept the gun across his chest at an angle, ready for immediate use. Zed cringed, but stammered out a whisper, "Filemón—the *maquiladoras* like QuanTonics—they keep the border economy stable. The jobs, the benefits..."

Garcia shook his head slowly, both at friend and to disarm the nervous barkeep. "Sit down , Zed," he said to his friend. He turned to the bartender, *"Por favor, la comida por mi amigo aquí."* The bartender finally deposited the rifle onto the bar and went to prepare Zed a meal.

"No, Zed, Juárez is not the problem right now. We are over a thousand kilometers from Chihuahua and my victories will be many before I arrive at the border of your country." He smiled again, then reached back into the same shirt pocket, pulling out more nameplates. He laid them all on the table, quietly this time. "Zed, these nameplates, they are highly unusual. My men found them on the battlefield after we blew up a Federal highway near Chichén Itzá. I had a sympathizer at the Technical University analyze them in his lab."

He whispered to Zed, "They were found in an ancient Mayan tomb, Zed." He paused. "They are over a thousand years old!"

ZED SIMPLY STARED AT GARCIA IN DISBELIEF. THEN he took another drink

"Filemón," Zed began slowly as the mescal stabilized his reaction, "*I'm* the one who writes science fiction, *compadre.* And I'm the one who knows you can't date metal plates. How do you expect me to believe these are a thousand years old? How do you know they didn't just fall into that old tomb before or during your battle?" He shook his head, chuckling, while Garcia poured him another full glass of mescal over the precious ice cubes.

"Zed, that tomb had never been opened. The entrances were all sealed off. It looked like there were some explosions a long time ago down there, but except for our hole, it was closed up tight." Garcia reached into yet another pocket and pulled out a crumbling piece of ancient cloth, which left a comet-like trail of musty dust that settled onto the tabletop. "And this, Zed, is the piece of cloth the nameplates were wrapped in. It has been Carbon-

14 dated, and it is indeed over a thousand years old!"

Garcia sipped his own drink and studied Zed's face. He knew that his *Norteamericano* friend was interested, and furthermore, that Zed believed him. He sat in awe at the adaptability of Americans. No wonder they ruled the world. But soon they might have to share.

Garcia continued, "And we know, don't we, Zed, that the only technology these old Mayans had was based on copper and gold and stone, right?" He stared as Zed's gulping acknowledged the Yanqui's acceptance of the facts. "And so I ask again, what kind of robots did they build here a thousand years ago?"

THE SUMMER MEXICAN SUN WAS BROILING HOT AS Filemón Garcia rousted Zed Wynter out of a pile of hay in the back of a flatbed truck.

"We're here," the guerrilla leader said, waving his hand out toward the stepped pyramid that dominated the skyline. "Chichén Itzá, the most spectacular reconstructed ruin of the Mayan civilization."

Zed rubbed his eyes and patted the pockets of his guayabera shirt, trying to find some sunglasses. The sun's brightness seemed a stark contrast to the dimness of his brain. *I'll never drink mescal again! What a kicker.* Through his diminished senses, Zed could tell that his military friend showed no signs of their all-night mescal bash. *So that's just one more reason he's a real-life General.*

Jumping down from the truck bed, Zed saw

Garcia walking toward the pyramid, and he ran to catch up. *El Castillo,* "The Castle", it was called. *I was here—when was it?—in the 20s, I think. Long before the destruction of the cities in Yucatán. Long before my friend destroyed them.* he thought sullenly. *I hope he hasn't ruined anything at this beautiful place.* He walked slowly, scanning the buildings and pyramids, comparing them to memory. He smelled ancient mold, more recent urine, heard the cooing calls of ubiquitous *quetzal* birds, saw the swarms of small yellow butterflies. *At least those things haven't changed,* he thought. Garcia sat in the shade at the base of the stepped pyramid, next to a three foot-high snake head carved from a single stone. The serpent's visage seemed to emerge from a stairwell that climbed to the top of the sixty-foot structure. A matching head defined the other edge of the wide stairwell.

"Zed, over a thousand years ago, my Mayan ancestors planned this staircase so that at the equinoxes, its shadows would make the rays of the sun appear to crawl up and down the steps of this pyramid. That shadow-snake was the feathered serpent, *Kukulkan.*" He chomped on the short Cuban cigar and asked, "Do you know why?"

"I didn't know you were Mayan, to start with," Zed replied, "And no, I don't know why they did it. What does any of this have to do with our visit here?"

"*Compadre,* they did it to demonstrate their understanding and control of supernatural events in the sky." Garcia drew in a deep breath of smoke and slowly let it dissipate in wispy curls through pursed lips. Zed immediately responded to the odor, and his body craved a smoke.

He still doesn't look like a killer, Zed mused. The old-time Villa moustache, the dark glasses, didn't add up to a menacing appearance in his old friend. And with the sombrero off, General Garcia could have been just another professor at Juárez Tech or New Mexico State.

"Even today, my people worry about Venus," Garcia continued, ignoring Zed's comments, "The bearded star they called *Kukulcan* or *Quetzalcoatl* still scares them–sometimes the old ones shut the windows and doors and board up the chimneys when the Evening Star appears." He stood up, tossing the smoking stub toward an interested bird on the ground. "I always wondered why they invented advanced mathematics just to keep track of where Venus is all the time. Some kind of primeval fear, but a fear that drove them toward civilization." He stared off into the jungle thoughtfully. "There are many old stories that affect the daily lives of people around here, and nobody really knows the reasons behind them."

"Sounds like old von Daniken stuff to me, Filemón. Weird things in the sky. Maybe Velikovsky, even."

"Close, maybe, Zed. Something sure as hell made these people spend all their time and talents calculating Venus' orbit. We may never know why." He smiled, patting his American friend on the shoulder. "All of that can wait. Now let's drive over to Pisté and I'll show you evidence of a *real* mystery, maybe one you *can* solve. Have you thought any more about those nameplates?"

My God, Zed swore to himself. *Then that part of the nightmare was not a mescal dream!* He searched his pockets and came up with several of the metal plates.

"Still surprising, eh Zed? Even in the bright

sunlight of morning they remain a mystery. Reality is what remains when dreams are gone."

Zed sat quietly as the old truck bounced over the cratered, nearly non-existent road. After about a kilometer, the driver stopped and motioned toward guards in the scrub brush near the roadway. In the distance Zed saw the rubble of several buildings, the scorched carcasses of half a dozen automobiles and the gutted remains of an old Chinese tank. One of the old Nicaraguan ones, undoubtedly, left over from one of the several revolutions down there and probably sold to the Mexican rebels—Garcia's—on the black market. *What a waste, what destruction.* Zed couldn't make himself accept such consequences. But then, he hadn't had to live under the iron fist of a corrupt dictatorship or the worse reign of the *carteleros*, either

A few gun-toting guerrillas came over to investigate and snapped to attention as Garcia got out of the cab. Zed hurriedly jumped off the truck bed when Filemón called his name: he wanted the Mexicans to recognize him as a friend. Quite a few light-skinned journalists had already been killed in this war and Zed didn't want to be mistaken for a foe.

Garcia and his men led the American a few dozen yards off into the bush and the soldiers began to remove a pile of brush. One of the men told him that an artillery shell had impacted here without exploding, during the battle for Pisté. When the ammunition-short guerrillas had tried to recover the shell for re-use, it had exploded and left this six-foot deep crater in the ground. While searching for remains of their unfortunate comrades, they had found an opening into an old underground Mayan tomb, just a few feet below.

"Zed, you are the first person outside my army to see this tomb," Garcia said as he slid down into the crater. "I want you to use your wrister and record what you see. As Lord Carnarvon to my Howard Carter, I want you to witness everything. But Carter's old King Tut never had anything like this!" He laughed and dropped down feet first into a two-foot diameter hole at the bottom of the crater. Zed followed down the six-foot deep shaft, one armed man right behind him. The others stayed on guard aboveground.

Garcia's wide-beam flashlight lit up the scene: a breathtakingly large room, it must have measured a hundred feet by eighty feet, at least, with a fifteen-foot ceiling height. Dust-covered tables lined up in straight rows like silent crypts—at least a hundred of them. Though covered with dust and various animal droppings, they were recognizable to Zed, but he couldn't believe what he saw.

"Looks to me like assembly-line workbenches, Filemón. This had to have been a factory!" In amazement, he picked up a dusty hand-sized assembly from the nearest table and turned it over. Some kind of plastic packaging fell apart in his hand, small metal cylinders falling into the thick dust. *Rivets!* And next to the table stood—

"A chair, Filemón! This was a chair for assembly workers! How could that be?" He quickly brushed off table after table, refusing to believe, yet slowly accepting the evidence of his own eyes, his touch, his experience. "And if these aren't soldering irons, and rivet guns, and..." He stopped talking and swatted a spider off a pile of tiny rectangular chips, blowing the dust off them.

After coughing at the dust cloud he had raised, he said, "These things are quantum chips, Filemón. They weren't even invented until this century, so there's no way this place is a thousand years old!" Shaking his head at the General, he stuffed his pockets with the components.

Garcia just smiled as his friend, bemused. "Let's go to the next room. Tell me if you recognize anything there."

The wide-beam flashlight played upon the palpable darkness as Garcia led them down a staircase into an even larger room, perhaps two to three times the area of the first one. This one had what appeared to be fluorescent lighting fixtures hanging from the ceiling.

"Filemón, this place was abandoned a while back, I'll admit, had to be years ago. Probably after your revolution started. Sure, QuanTonics just didn't want anyone to know about their Yucatán operation. Saves a lot of headaches when you aren't sure who's going to be running the government. After you started winning, they must have pulled out and sealed the place up." Zed felt satisfied with this explanation. Then he realized that QuanTonics hadn't even come on the scene until five years ago. But what else could explain—?

"Very good reasoning, but would you look down this hallway, please?" Garcia pointed the flashlight, narrow-beam this time, down a long hallway.

Zed saw where the ceiling had been cracked and ground water had seeped in, probably from a nearby well, a *cenote*. Although there was no dampness now—water had not run for a long time —clinging to the mottled roof like slender, pointed holiday decorations, hung two beautiful limestone stalactites, each over two feet long.

When he caught his breath, Zed whistled long and low. Garcia looked at him with relief. "Now, my friend, do you see why I asked you to come to Yucatán?"

"All right, Filemón, I do believe you now. This *is* a factory." Swallowing, he played his own flashlight around, illuminating metal cabinets labeled in English as containing electronic parts and subassemblies. "It appears to be centuries old, with those stalactites. Even though QuanTonics, S. A., is only five years old, I believe you did find their nameplates down here somewhere."

He turned and shouted to the bare walls, the dusty workbenches, his tremulous voice echoing off ancient metal cabinets marked with the drippings and droppings of a millennium. "What the hell is going on? If somebody's got a—" the word choked him, he could barely speak it, "—a *time machine*, why would they set up a factory down here in the jungle? Why go to the trouble? Why not just go back in time and steal gold? Platinum? Jewels?" Zed looked at Garcia. "Why screw around with all of this?"

The Mexican just shrugged. *Quien sabe?* Zed read in his face.

The other inhabitants of the "tomb" did not respond, either. Spiders, snakes, frogs, insects, all carefully watched Zed's flashlight etch out brilliant cones in the near absolute darkness, but they remained quiet while his frustrated shouts reverberated down ancient hallways. Their secure hideaway was being disturbed, but they were silent.

Garcia nodded his head slightly. "Zed, there is a lot more to this factory. Four levels in all, the bottom ones cut out of solid limestone. There must have been thousands of people working here for years to cut this place out of rock." The flashlight beam traced out the perimeters of the enormous factory floor. Overhead conveyor belts and other apparatus hung from the ceiling like twisted tendrils of petrified plants, some dangling from the ceiling bare, others encrusted with limestone stalactites long since dry.

A silent, high-tech jungle.

"So this is what factories look like after a thousand years," Zed said to Garcia as they kicked away piles of debris, causing multitudes of crawling creatures to scatter in panic. "I never thought this much would survive."

In the next hour, the three men inspected remains of power generators, assembly tools and equipment, assorted robot sub-assemblies scattered on the floors, and fallen shelves of electronic parts. There were three elevators, long since fallen to the bottoms of their shafts, and the explorers decided to put off any excursions down into the lower levels until they had rope ladders. Zed found a bank of file cabinets, each drawer half full of disintegrated papers. "Must have been sulfur-based," he observed. "The old Mayan parchments would have lasted until now. A couple of their Codices are still on display in México City." Garcia nodded solemnly.

There had been running water, judging from the corroded copper pipes they found. The electrical outlets hadn't fared much better. Some doorways had been blocked, apparently by explosions from within. One set of steel doors was still locked.

"Here, Zed, is the biggest mystery of all."

Garcia's flashlight revealed steel doors ten feet wide by twelve high, their aged factory-gray appearance married by the new blast-marks of futile attempts to open them.

"We only had some grenades, and tried to blast them apart," Garcia said quietly, stroking the doors as if his touch might magically open them. "It didn't work at that time, and we were in a hurry." A few quick words in Spanish from Garcia and the other soldier disappeared toward the surface. "He will bring back some shaped charges that your submarine delivered to me. We will soon see what is on the other side of these mysterious doors, *amigo.*" He lit up another cigar and offered one to Zed. The American gratefully took it; his nerves needed steadying.

In fifteen minutes, a blasting crew of several soldiers arrived and set the charges on and around the steel doors. All of the men retreated to the safety of the large adjacent room, putting two thick walls between them and the blast to come. The crew chief flicked a small remote control button, and the whole factory shook with the roar of the explosion, the massive doors clanging as they ripped from their fixtures and fell back into the room they had hidden. When the dust settled, the men went back in.

The room behind the doors was small—about twelve feet square—and entirely featureless: no outlets, no tunnels, no other doors. Only a corroded instrument panel of some sort hanging loosely from the wall next to the door openings, obviously shaken loose from its wall mountings by the blast. It looked to Zed for all the world like an elevator. *But an elevator to nowhere!* Zed thought.

"Filemón," he began, "I don't understand it.

The only way into this place was by those stairs we used, and the 'Down' elevators are on the other side of the factory. There is no way to get materials down into this place, whatever it is…or was. Whatever they built down here had to be carried up the stairs." He shook his head. "Doesn't make sense."

Garcia rattled the nameplates as if in answer. "*Compadre*, we know what they made down here. How much do these 'Romeo-14s' weigh? Or what will they weigh when they are built? A hundred kilos, two hundred?"

Zed did a mental conversion. "Yes, I would guess that 440 pounds wouldn't be too heavy, if they're anything at all like the earlier models. But no one, especially small Mayans, could have carried four hundred pounds up those narrow stairs. Couldn't be done." Zed rubbed his bearded chin and pondered the implications. "Are you sure no one has found any ramp down from the surface?"

"I'm sure," Garcia replied.

"Then I just don't understand it. A nearly sealed-off underground factory building robots a thousand years ago. What do you make of it?"

Garcia waved for his group of guerrillas to leave. As he and Zed walked, he pointed out scenes for Zed to record on the wrister's microcorder: a closeup of an outlet here, a pile of rubbish there, some overhead fixtures, colorful but meaningless graffiti on the walls. He spoke in serious, measured tones. "I would like for you to find out for us everything you can, Zed. Go to this QuanTonics in Chihuahua, and talk to them." He narrowed the flashlight beam to a small cone and shone it up a ventilation shaft, pointing out that Zed should record that, too.

"I want to know why they were here. If it was a thousand years ago, I want to know why and especially, *how.* I'm sure you would like to know too, but..." Zed watched his friend's eyes narrow and his jaw clench on the stub of the mangled cigar. "This is my country, my new free territory, and it is my duty to protect it, present, future, —" Zed's gaze followed the flashlight beam as it quickly sliced the blackness in a wide arc emanating from Garcia's hand "—or past."

The two men climbed back up through the shell crater. Garcia barked orders to his men to fill in the hole and erase all evidence of activity around the spot. As the men began carrying out the command, Garcia and Zed walked back to the truck, where a meal of sandwiches and cold *cerveza* awaited them.

"Be careful how you approach the QuanTonics people," Garcia was saying between bites. "If they have some secrets down here, no telling what else they may want to keep from prying eyes. And since the mystery revolves around robots, my friend, you are the logical man to be investigating it!" He laughed and swigged some *Superior*, then changed moods to serious. "Myself, I think the factory was making warbots. And I do not want to have to fight machines." He laid back languidly on the grass and thoughtfully gazed beyond the scattered clouds. "Chile will provide me with warbots if I want them, Zed; all I have to do is ask. But I want this revolution to be won with brains and *blood,* not hydraulic fluid." In a whisper, he added, "Blood is a strong bond between men, right, *compadre?*" He winked.

Zed was taken back in memory, almost against his will, to a late night street scene in Juárez about twelve years before. The painful recollection re-staged itself in minute detail: hot breezes blowing across baked dirt streets in a disreputable section of the border town, fine dust swirling in tight eddies around the corner, just barely visible in the erratic illumination of sputtering streetlights. And everywhere, a smell of desperation.

Zed and Filemón were just leaving the White Cave brothel, each totally satiated from their marathons with the *señoritas.* Woozy from sex and drink and appearing to be easy targets, they were still alert enough to sense two hoodlums erupting from a night-black alleyway, coshes in hand. "Rolling" drunk tourists provided a living for increasing numbers of desperately poor immigrants from farther south, but Zed and Filemón did not wish to contribute, and so made a stand. Zed was the first to see the attackers coming at them head-on. He stepped back, shouting to his friend, "Filemón! *¡Ayudame!*"

"Help you, Zed? What?—" Filemón said, automatically taking a backward step with his friend. He spun his head around to see what Zed meant.

Surprised by the shouting, the thugs lost their well-practiced timing. As Zed lashed out with a pointed boot toe, he gave his closest opponent a wound in one-half of a sensitive pair of male organs. Screaming, the man dropped to his knees, hands covering his groin.

Filemón crouched and took the full force of the other attacker's charge, holding the bludgeon at arm's length. Both men fell to the dirt, still stunned by the suddenness of the assault. Zed took a few seconds to get to his feet, grateful for his nearly-autonomic defense response. He felt the rage flow, tried to control it, allowed the adrenaline to charge his body for the counterblow. In all the years that followed this night, he had alternately blessed and blamed the mandatory U.S. Army ROTC guerrilla training for that response. *Keratsu* fighting was the deadly culmination of computer-enhanced training and Eastern martial arts. (It had also been the least expensive way to train a reserve army that was suffering from massive budget cuts following the end of Cold War Two.)

Falling into a tense crouch, Zed spun on his right foot just as his injured attacker regrouped enough to unleash a switchblade. He caught the man's right arm in a heel kick, hearing the bone crack upon connection. As the man fell, Zed chopped his opponent's neck with a sharp hand blow. The man dropped his left hand from his crotch and gasped for breath, convulsing, then falling over quietly. Zed stood in shock momentarily, then turned to help Garcia.

The other thug lay limp under Garcia's chokehold. "This *cabrón is* out cold. Thanks for yelling, *amigo*!" He stood up, rifled the unconscious man's pockets, threw away a pistol and a knife, keeping a wad of bills. Smiling, he walked over to Zed, waving the money. "Let's go out and do some more partying with these ill-gotten gains." Then he saw the still body of Zed's attacker. Bending down to take the man's pulse, he whispered loudly, "Holy shit, Zed! You killed this one!"

"I knew that when I chopped him, Filemón," Zed said in measured breaths, bringing his anger back under control. "I *wanted* to kill the bastard for attacking us. What do I do now? Turn myself into the police?"

"Never, dumb *gringo*!" Garcia said through clenched teeth, rubbing his bruised jaw. "Down here, the police are seldom your friends, and we don't have enough money to pay them off for mur—*killing* somebody." He shook his head. "Especially a *gringo* killing an *hermano*, a brother of the homeland!" He spat on the body.

"Look, let's throw this one into the alleyway and put the live one on top of him. When the police come, they'll think it was a fight and won't come looking for us until after we're on the other side." He shrugged. "Who's going to believe a cheap crook like this, anyhow?"

They dragged the men into the alley and Garcia strewed the wad of money around the two, stuffing some into the dead man's pockets. "We'll call the Juárez police, my friend, but only after we get across, and from a burner phone." Acting like tipsy tourists, the two made their way back across the Chamizal Bridge without incident. Although Garcia never mentioned this particular night again, Zed had often thought about the dead man and the other thug, and wondered if he should have held back just a little against his outclassed opponent. Not an everyday guilt feeling, but an occasional pang that he found impossible to purge entirely. He had never killed anyone before, and he wished that the dramatic occasion could have been in defense of some better cause than simply saving his wallet.

ZED THOUGHT ABOUT THE INCREDIBLE SIGHTS HE had just witnessed here in the Yucatán. Was a 'time machine' any more incredible than the unknown means by which materials and products had been transferred into and out of the underground factory? And a few other items didn't add up, either.

"*¡Aeroplanos! ¡Federales*!" The guerrillas were screaming, as Zed came out of his thoughts completely, he and Garcia hitting the ground simultaneously. Jet fighters split the sky just above the treetops, their strafing fire chopping up the remaining highway. Phosphorus bombs blossomed white hot just across the road, spreading their gruesome pollen to screaming bodies that waved wildly and disappeared into the jungle.

Everybody ran into the bush.

The aircraft—Vietnamese manufacture, Zed noted, roared back to work on the other side of the highway, destroying the guerrillas' flatbed truck and killing two unfortunates who were still closing the entrance to the factory.

"*Chingasos!*" Garcia screamed, grabbing a shoulder-launcher from one of the cowering soldiers. He sighted one of the jets as it arced in the sky, turning back for another run.

Garcia fired.

The shoulder launcher kicked back and its rocket blasted the jet out of the sky. Parts of the plane and pilot continued downward at several hundred miles per hour, deadly shrapnel zapping the treetops. All the other men, Zed included, dived for protection behind tree trunks. At that speed, even bone fragments could kill.

"Damn, Filemón!" Zed shouted as the other jet

peeled off and disappeared over the jungle, "I didn't even *see* that rocket! What did you use?"

Garcia, who had stood his ground the whole time, patted the firing tube. "Our Chilean friends make superboosters, too, my American friend. They can even knock out satellites with the proper aiming mechanisms." He smiled at Zed. "And we have those, too. We do have those, too." Zed didn't like the menacing tone, but attributed it to the man's battle adrenaline. Garcia glanced at his wrister. "Time to go, Zed. Let's find some other means to get you back to Playa del Carmen for the pickup tonight. Rendezvous with a submarine there. Our *troca*," he pointed at the smoking rubble of the flatbed, "*¡Esta frita!*" He stopped smiling as soldiers brought back the four dead men, two of the bodies still smoking from phosphorus wounds.

After a solemn burial ceremony, they all walked back to the base of the stepped pyramid where a radio call brought them fresh transportation in the form of a decades-old Jeep. Sorry to be in a hurry, Zed had wanted to take another walk around Chichén Itzá, especially to look over *El Caracol*, "The Snail", the ancient observatory. He had a disquieting premonition that the recently-restored Mayan constructions might become obliterated ruins, since his rebel friend insisted on camping nearby, making the site a target for the Mexican government air force.

That night, Garcia and a few other guerrillas wished Zed an emotional "*Adios*" as a Chilean naval crew motored their small Zodiac dinghy out to the waiting submarine. Zed wondered if he would ever be back to this beautiful "Turquoise Coast" again. "Not *adios*, *amigos*, but *hasta la vista*," he said softly over the lapping waves. "Until we meet again, Filemón."

In his pocket, a sackful of ancient nameplates jingled, tinkling.

"FBI, Mr. Wynter," Doris said over the old intercom speaker. "Shall I let them in?"

"Of course, Doris," Zed Wynter replied with irritation, "The FBI is always welcome at our magazine." Inwardly he groaned. *Now what?* Outside the office a bright blue August day greeted his bloodshot eyes. *These guys have to show up on my first day back? Damn Filemón anyhow!*

Nothing's gone right since...

Since he'd left the Yucatán coast: a nightmare voyage in a noisy diesel Chilean submarine, barely surviving depthcharging by Mexican vessels, followed by a surface firefight as he was landed ashore on the Isle of Pines. Between the dead Mexicans and Cubans, and the damaged Chilean submarine, there were all the ingredients for an international incident, but fortunately one that the affected governments were keeping quiet. Somehow, an Anarchist connection had gotten him aboard a hydrofoil that sneaked him back into the U.S., to SoVI, the unfortunate but official abbreviation for the State of the Virgin Islands.

But now, the FBI was into the fray and Zed was worried. *What has Filemón got me into? I've got a metazine to run, and I haven't been able to sleep for the whole week since I left Yucatán. Wonder if these guys will just take a statement and leave?* Zed recalled that he had read somewhere that back a few decades ago the FBI had been a highly respected institution, back before the political scandals. *Hard to believe that, now!*

The two of them, Zed noted, were conservatively dressed, red shirts with softly glowing green phosphor ties, three smart-rings per hand, and orange-soled hydroshoes—fairly reactionary fashion standouts here in the more leisurely-dressed society of Dallas.

"Agents Grant and Farrar, Mr. Wynter," the taller one said, imposing himself past the human Doris into Zed's office. "I'm Grant. Want to ask you a few questions."

Zed started to motion for them to sit, but they were already down and comfortable before he could move his hand. He recognized the standard intimidation technique. Sure enough, each sat down in an opposite corner, so that their prey would have to turn to address them in turn. Zed shuddered to think what other interrogation methods they might have, but he smiled politely. "Certainly, gentlemen, make yourselves at home. Ask away." He walked behind his wide desk and adjusted his chair to a higher elevation. *We all can play these Personal Warfare games.*

Agent Grant, his dark face gleaming in the heat—(Zed's foot switch had turned up the temperature with infrared heat lamps hidden behind dark panels)—held out a large hand, offering Zed a thick manila envelope. Zed, recognizing the gesture, refused to yield Personal Warfare points and waited until the frustrated agent got up from his chair and walked over to deposit the envelope on the desk in front of Zed.

My point. Zed chortled to himself.

"Mr. Wynter," Agent Farrar said from the

opposite corner of the office. Zed refused to face him, and the agent coughed loudly.

My, aren't we impatient: two points for me!

The FBI men collected themselves, standing in front of Zed's desk. One opened his coat to show the thin outline of a flechetter in his shirt pocket.

Oops! Lots of points for them. Getting really serious now. Time for me to kiss their feet, or whatever! "Gentlemen," he said, leisurely slicing the envelope with his tiny laser-blade opener, "I'll be happy to help you. What is the question?" He thoughtfully shuffled through the textprints and the photographs that had tumbled from the package when he shook its contents out.

Garcia's picture!

Grant spoke. "We want to know why the Mexican guerrilla leader, General Garcia, called you last week. Our monitors of your apartment gave us only cryptic information." Grant leaned over the desk ominously, the weight of his flechette pulling down the shirt pocket.

"We know you were roommates in college in New Mexico. We know you traveled to Mexico many times together." The FBI man punctuated each statement with a gentle tap of his large fist on the desk. "And we believe that you went to the Yucatán war zone last week to see him."

Grant stood up, sweating and trembling, his "bad guy" routine done for the moment. In a more relaxed tone, the "good cop", Farrar, blond and slight of build, asked, "Mr. Wynter, are you a revolutionary? LibArk or red?"

Flechette or no, Zed had had enough. He stood and gazed into each agent's eyes with determination. "I would laugh out loud, gentlemen, but I doubt if you have much of a sense of humor. But no, I am not a revolutionary, not a capital-L libertarian, not an anarchist, certainly not an old Marxist. If you must know, and I'm sure you do, I am a libertarian, small L, and I'm not convergent with violence. And, outside a few professors on American university faculties, I don't know that *anyone* is a Marxist anymore.

"I am an American, a laissez-faire libertarian. And you'd know *that,* if you've searched my files, as I'm sure you have." Zed began to suspect that what he had taken as an innocent hacko attack on his home DI system had been deliberate microtapping by his own government. Maybe even those mysterious calls from that mysterious woman—Tanner? She'd kept trying Zed's home number while he was in Mexico, not his personal wrister, and had refused to leave any messages with Brighton. "But I am indeed a friend of General Filemón Garcia, whom I was indeed proud to visit in the Yucatán Free Territory last week." Agents Grant and Farrar dropped their collective jaws at his admission.

Zed was a bit worried. *Whew! Was that being honest enough? Now, how do I cover my real reason for that trip? Quickly, now, a half-truth, told loudly enough, works as well as the whole truth!*

"Filemón is interested in starting up a robotics factory when he takes power in México," Zed lied, hoping he was being convincing enough. He had to be careful; undoubtedly they would continue to monitor his DI and wrister systems, and he didn't want to contradict any coded information that Filemón might want to pass on.

"And General Garcia wanted me to scout out likely sites for operations there, probably in a couple of years, after he is running Mexico." He watched the agents' reactions. From their body language, they probably believed most of the story. He continued, "If they win—*when* they win—Filemón wants me to be his industrial agent, using my contacts in the robotics field to bring investments to that war-torn province." Zed smiled widely, knowing he had won this particular battle with the FBI. "Pure libertarian capitalism. Anything wrong with that?"

Agent Grant was smoothing back his jacket and tie, still perspiring from Zed's hidden heat lamps. Zed smiled at the man's discomfort.

Farrar, also sweating, nodded. "Mr. Wynter, I want to let you know that we will be expecting you to tell us of any more contacts with General Garcia." The agent took up the envelope and reinserted its contents, careful not to touch certain areas.

Don't they already have my fingerprints? Zed wondered.

AFTER THE AGENTS LEFT, ZED TURNED OFF THE heat lamps and restarted the air conditioner until he felt the cool breeze blowing across his face. Undoing his tie, he thought furiously. *I don't think I've violated any laws. I mean, even the government trades with more radical revolutionary groups than Filemón's.* Zed knew there were rumors that some old-style American monopolists loathed the new libertarian countries, but surely the FBI wasn't one of their tools, notwithstanding those scandals of the '20s.

Of course, there could be some problems with the Mexican government, Zed conceded, but the U. S. wasn't really on speaking terms with Mexico

City any more. Nuking their own oil fields to keep them out of rebel hands a couple of years back had not gone down well with most civilized governments. México was lucky that the Yanquis even allowed the border to stay open anymore, much less continuing the *maquiladora* factories. No, Mexican relations would not be involved.

Then why was the FBI interested? Just keeping tabs on all potential enemies? Or something else? Zed couldn't figure it out. He did know one thing: in about a week or so when the metazine was running smoothly again and he could hand over the computer files to his assistants, he was going to find out more.

"QuanTonics, S. A.," Brighton was droning, "is a privately-held corporation, chartered in México to develop and to sell personal robots. With primary manufacturing plants in the State of Chihuahua, Republic of México, QuanTonics also has offshore facilities in three of the Four Chinas and in Singapore, Ltd."

"Very good, Brighton," Zed replied. "Now tell me something about its founders and present owners." He sipped some Scotch and flicked on the latest ads that had been downloaded while he was away at work. He had seriously considered having only a telecommute office at home, but he found his magazine office's near-hysteria environment stimulating, and he believed that human contact was still a necessity for creative work. Only a few straggling newsletters used home offices anymore.

"Right, sire." The wrister's telescreen lit up with photos of two men. "To your left, is Michael

Frost, founder and President of QuanTonics." *The man was so young!* Zed was astonished; he'd heard how the robotics company had started in a garage in a place called Fabens, Texas, but that was five years ago and Frost couldn't be past his mid-twenties now. That meant he was only about twenty when he founded the company.

Zed wondered how he could have missed that story and he texted Doris to initiate a DI freelancer on the backgrounding right away. His wrister beeped in response. *Good!* His request was on file and Doris would act on it, first thing.

Brighton continued, "And the man on the right is Samuel Baleen, Vice-President." At least Baleen looked the right age to run a company—about forty-five, in Zed's estimation.

"The other officers are not shareholders. In fact, the only other shareholder of record is one Stephen Daviess, a Scottish national." Zed knew that name: a world-class physicist, famous for the orbital and lunar experiments with crystal growths that had led to semimorphous technology and a Nobel Prize. Dr. Daviess was also the developer of the controversial Sidespace mathematics which predicted the existence of extra physical dimensions wrapped tightly around something called a "Corkscrew."

So far, Zed hadn't heard of any physical implementation of Daviess' Sidespace theories, but the concepts were intriguing if not easily comprehended. Funny that such a mathematical physicist would be associated with a commercial robot firm, the fields being so widely removed. Zed asked Brighton to access further connections between Daviess and QuanTonics, and told the computer also to drop hardcopies of all of

QuanTonics' public records into his office mailbox in the morning; he would review them at leisure. Right now, he wanted more information on their not-so-public records.

He instructed Brighton to call up certain password algorithms he had invented and collected over the years, and then to hack as many corporate memoranda as possible from the robot company's computer files.

"Always stay at the misdemeanor level, Brighton, as usual. No felonies, please." *Not with the FBI looking on, my friend!* Zed's own personal interest in codebreaking, plus occasional discreet inputs from hacker friends on the various WorldNets, meant that he could usually infiltrate any system, given time.

Up until the porno ad and the call from that Tanner woman, Zed had doubted that Brighton's systems could be compromised – now he wasn't too sure. It was time for a new entry scheme. While Brighton assaulted QuanTonics' systems, Zed reprogrammed the computer's access codes, using a complex interactive feature that required the active participation of his wrister. Now, only an exact timing sequence match between his wrister's picoprocessor and a seemingly innocuous circuit in Brighton's control panel would gain access to his innermost databases. Plenty of lower-level data, mostly business-related, would crop up first, and he hoped it would throw off any serious hackos.

Reviewing his daily financial statement, Zed noted with satisfaction that his Developing Intelligence program, ##INVEST##, was proceeding quite nicely. He had profited significantly during his trip to México. *Might be able to sell this one, hackos tend to pay for software they really respect.* He added more codes to allow Brighton to pull out the original nest egg for investing whenever the probability factors were favorable. Zed never knew when he might need more traveling money, and an extra ten thousand could conceivably be useful in an emergency.

A WEEK LATER IN THE LATE AFTERNOON ZED landed at El Paso International Hyperport. He had set up appointments with the management at QuanTonics over in Juárez, ostensibly to do a story about their personal robot lines. Checking into the Airport Hilton, he refreshed himself with a shower, then strolled along the airport's roof walkways.

A small, pretty sidewalk café caught his eye and he ordered a *margarita grande*. Looking out from the veranda, his view took in the rugged, barren Franklin Mountains. To his left, looking south toward Juárez, Zed could see the haze of evening-meal cooking fires beginning to obscure the *sarape* colors of the sunset. The overcrowded city hosted hundreds of thousands of immigrants, refugees from the civil war going on in the South. To his right the barren peaks of the Franklins gleamed in the sunlight like golden castles in a fantasy movie. He hadn't been in the area in years, and he felt a twinge of nostalgia. One thing was quite different though this time, a discordant note. Though he couldn't see them from his location, he knew that the *colonias,* the overcrowded Resettlement Camps housing millions of Undocumenteds in squalor, took up a hundred square miles of desert north of El Paso, east of the golden Franklins. He ignored that thought; there were lots of sad problems in the world that he couldn't solve.

If I have the time, I'll drop in at Las Cruces, he promised himself. *I want to see the old school, and check up on the Cobblestone Pocket Tokomak they brought online there last month.* He felt there was another story there, too, maybe the ultimate power source for really efficient robots: a fusion reactor in a six-inch diameter sphere.

Zed's thoughts faded with the sun and he almost yearned for the youth and innocence he had taken for granted back in his college days. *I lost something in Juárez once*, he recalled with a painful grin, *but I guess I gained something, too.* The margarita finished, he went to bed early. He dreamed of Yucatán, of El Paso, of beautiful *señoritas*, and somehow, of Filemón Garcia and of long, winding, darkened streets in dusty downtown Juárez.

"Buenos días, Señor Wynter," THE MEXICAN engineer said in greeting. "Welcome to QuanTonics. We are most happy for you to publicize our robots." Smiling, the small attractive woman ushered Zed into a spacious lobby and signed him in, pinning a visitor's badge on his jacket.

Zed followed the engineer to an escalator that carried them to a long, carpeted hallway. A pedelator scooted them quickly down that hallway and through sliding doors into an office larger than the lobby, decorated in colorful photos. The engineer excused herself and left Zed standing, facing an empty desk. Various robot models stood guard around the room, Zed recognized most of them, and speculated that a few were meant only for industrial spies to see. *Including me?* he wondered.

What he took to be space probe photos on the walls turned out to be even more intriguing: a full set of Jupiter views, original Bonestells. *Priceless*! Several other pictures were videos, long shots of someone flying microlight aircraft, others of ultragliding. Some were very professional holos: a multi-hued ultraglider over a background of low jungle, reminding Zed of the Yucatán bush country where he had been just weeks before. At the sound of another sliding door, Zed interrupted his visual tour and turned to meet two men who approached him, hands outstretched to shake his.

The older man, Samuel Baleen, was actually in his mid-fifties, dressed in a tricolor suit, looking the part of financial and legal advisor. Zed noted his expensive cologne, probably the most desired fragrance available from *Santiago de Chile*, which had long surpassed Paris as the *parfum* capital of the world. The more reserved, much younger man, blond and balding, in a conservative cream-colored suit with a glowing-emerald bolo tie, was Michael Frost. *This one smells of grease and sweat*, Zed observed.

"Welcome to our factory, Dr. Wynter," Baleen said cheerfully. "We are proud that a publication such as yours has chosen to visit our facility here." Gesturing for Zed to sit, Baleen was all charm. Zed noticed that Frost casually strolled to the chair behind the large desk, listening.

Weird character, that kid, Zed thought. *Some kind of emperor complex, I'll bet. Ties in with Brighton's accessed information.*

"...most competitive organization in the

robotics field—industrial and personal robot models," Baleen was saying, as Zed tried to shift his attention to the spiel. "Why, we hope someday to be the Tesla of robots."

Zed would have sworn that Baleen expected to be applauded. He studied the man more closely: Samuel X. Baleen, born in the old Soviet Union, son of emigre parents who'd arrived in the US some years ago, right after things started falling apart over there. With only wisps of gray hair above prominent ears, Balleen's slight Russian accent could have made him a fixture in any of thousands of small shops in New York or Dallas. Zed was glad he'd brought some of Donne's telltale electronics along, he wanted to know more about *Señor* Balleen.

I can record their voices and skin responses and analyze them with my wrister when I'm safely back in El Paso, Zed thought. *I'll be able to tell if these guys are lying.* He would have to maneuver them into it, playing the dumb media man.

"May I record these interviews and photograph your offices, Mr. Balleen, Mr. Frost?" They nodded assent and Zed held up his wrister. *Honesty throws them off the track, and gives me a better quality picture for the metazine layout, too.*

"And why did you wait until now to come visit us, Dr.Wynter?" Frost asked, suspiciously in Zed's estimation.

"My magazine is only three months old, Mr. Frost—"

"Michael, please."

"—Michael, and my travel budget's been too low until recently. But after hearing your reps talk at the Personal Robotics show last month, I thought it was time to come out to see things in person."

"And what part of the operation did you wish to see?"

Balleen interjected. "We have twelve plants, all over Chihuahua. You are now in the Administrative offices. Here in Juárez we have the final assembly facilities for the Romeo-12s, and—"

Zed interrupted with a smile and turned up his hands. "How about those Romeo-14 models? Your rep said you'd been having some developmental problems. Anything you'd like to say to clarify things for potential customers?"

Did Zed notice a quick glare from Frost to Balleen. "Er, well, yes," the older man stammered, "We have had a few *issues* down in our *Ciudad* Chihuahua factory, but ..." he mumbled to a halt as Frost interrupted.

"I'm sure Dr. Wynter is not really interested in the details of our developmental problems, Sam. Those can get awfully boring."

He turned to Zed."Zed—may I call you that? —as you've probably guessed, we're trying to expand the state of the art in Developing Intelligence. Our DI personnel are all cloistered down in Chihuahua City, busting their asses to implement some electromagnetic interference protection schemes for our Romeo-14s. I have personally been involved, and there are some avenues I've asked the sci-techs to investigate before we start production."

He walked around the desk in an amiable mood. "Now you know we can't let out such information to any of the Chinese or the Chileans or Singaporeans —they'd steal it in a minute." At this point, Zed did smell cologne, some super expensive pheromonal, he guessed, but obviously triggering only to females. But at first he had smelled of sweat and grease. *Some kind of programmable cologne?* At the thought, Zed held back a grimace.

Frost took Zed by the arm and led him into the long hallway again. "Let's go down to the video room. We'll show you an overview of all our operations, and you can pick whichever other ones you'd like to see starting tomorrow."

Balleen followed them, and the afternoon dissolved into pleasantries and drink. At an impromptu after-hours party in his honor, Zed again met the QuanTonics female engineer who had signed him in. She surprisingly arranged a second private party for the two of them that night in his room in El Paso.

THE NEXT TWO DAYS OF TOURS BEGAN TO WEAR ON Zed's nerves. What he was shown was interesting enough: industrial robots that built personal robots, personal robots that did manual labor, and glimpses of research laboratories. But never again did the subject arise of a visit to Cd. Chihuahua or of the Romeo-14s.

In fact, Zed puzzled, *none of the Romeo models are built in any of the facilities that I've visited. Wonder why?*

That night, back at the Hilton in El Paso, he reviewed all of the recorded wrister data. He was right. No Romeo models to be seen, even down hallways and assembly areas he'd been whisked past. He hadn't forgotten—he simply hadn't been shown any.

Taking advantage of his first extended time

alone since arriving at QuanTonics' Juárez office, Zed prompted the wrister to evaluate the Donne telltale scans. Not many people knew of the TT technology and Zed hoped that it would stay that way. Mark Donne, a good friend who owned a semi-legal weapon shop and an advanced security lab, had sold him a wrister-compatible TT that evaluated voice stress, perspiration rate, skin reflectivity, and numerous other truth or lie detection parameters.

Zed smiled at the results. *What good this gadget hath wrought!* When he compared the evaluations for Balleen and Frost, his suspicions were confirmed. They were both lying: Balleen under some duress, but Frost willingly.

What a pair! Both weekos, but one a cool creep and the other a wimpy one. Now what do I do? I can't ask again about the Romeo models, but I damn sure ain't going back home without a trip to Chihuahua City!

Zed laid under the air conditioner's breeze and tried to plan his next moves. He would travel to Las Cruces tomorrow, to allay any suspicions from Frost and Balleen, while he planned his visit to Cd. Chihuahua. Within an hour he had a call from the Mexican lady from QuanTonics. It was another great night!

"The Cobblestone Pocket Tokamak is just one more step toward the universal use of fusion power," the pretty young guide was saying. "First proposed here at New Mexico State University by an Emeritus Professor of Mechanical Engineering decades ago, this compact device promises to revolutionize energy production for all mankind."

She led the tour group into a demonstration laboratory.

Zed Wynter was an alumnus of this school, (an *Aggie*, he reminded himself) but had not returned in years. Sure, he paid his annual pledges toward engineering scholarships, but he hadn't found the time to come back. He often looked down longingly at the brown terrain as his jet crawled across the vast New Mexican sky, en route to one coast or the other, but forty thousand feet was as close as he had been until now.

After another dragging day in QuanTonics' crowded factories in Juárez, he had thanked his hosts and then driven the seventy miles up to Las Cruces. He made one quick automobile stop under an Interstate bridge en route, as if to relieve himself.

Using the excuse that he had to do another story, this one about the Cobblestone Tokamak, he visited old haunts in the Mesilla Valley. At a centuries-old restaurant and bar in nearby La Mesilla, he renewed his love for *chiles rellenos*, Rio Grande style; he'd never found anything comparable since leaving New Mexico. And with several margaritas and a dessert of honey-filled *sopaipillas*, his nostalgia for his college days returned. He would definitely return sooner, next time. With an innocuous stroll around the plaza square, reading various historical signs, he also hoped to throw off suspicion by anyone who might have followed him, QuanTonics or FBI.

Zed looked up an old co-op buddy who had stayed here, working at White Sands Space Development Area, while Zed and the other graduates had worked their way into the high-technology companies around the world. "And a couple of us Aggies work on the Moon, too!" his friend revealed. Zed shrugged; the succession of the recent landings—and findings—on Mars were exciting, but the Moon colony with its hundreds of people was old stuff.

Zed and his friend fondly remembered other late evenings in La Mesilla, as they watched the sun sink over old adobe buildings. Zed recalled the Sixteenth of September dances in the streets, the dark eyes and flashing teeth of the girls, the throbbing music. *Damn!* He thought, *maybe I should come back more often. Wonder if they still do all of that here?* His friend assured him that those important things remained the same, only the traffic was worse! And now, a day later, Zed was touring the Engineering Complex to see the world's first soccer ball-sized package of fusion power in operation.

"I won't go into the technical aspects of the Cobblestone tokamak," the guide said, "because it involves Daviess matrix technology that is still classified by the government." She smiled. Zed wondered again what connection the Nobel laureate Daviess had with the wackos who ran QuanTonics. In response to a question from a lanky man in cowboy clothes, the tour guide said patiently, "Yes, I could explain it to you if I were allowed. I have my M. S. in energy engineering and a minor in energy matrix mathematics. And yes, I did help build this model." She shook her head slightly as the cowboy blushed in embarrassment.

The Cobblestone looked like a larger version of its namesake: a spheroid of roughened metal, suspended in a magnetic field. Enveloped with an intricate web of wiring, tubing, and connectors, the ball continuously burped segmented pulses of green laser light in all directions, neon-like particles instantaneously traversing the few inches to the waiting power receptacles. The effect was of a dynamic, living pincushion of green, a nova spewing out its emerald lifesblood to waiting parasites. Zed thought of a new term for these receivers: *powersites*. Seemed appropriate.

"The pinprick pulses of light around the tokamak constitute the new mechanism by which the Cobblestone delivers its power to the distribution system," the guide was saying. Zed felt another kind of power surge when her eyes met his.

Efficient medium that, light!

ZED HAD FOLLOWED THE DEVELOPMENT OF DAVIESS Sidespace mathematics in the technical journals. Still, he found it amazing that a nanoscopic laser-etched topology, as utilized in the Cobblestone, could be developed that allowed the dissipated waste heat to interact with itself to cancel phonons, the heat-carrying subatomic particles. *Where did all that heat eventually go? Into Daviess' theoretical or imaginary Sidespace?* he wondered. Entropy would just have to increase faster, once the Cobblestones were in operation. He'd have to ask the guide about the Daviess topology, among other things.

After the tour ended, Zed approached her, "Miss...er..." he looked closely at her nametag. He'd arrived near the end of the tour and had missed her name. "Miss Serna, is it? I enjoyed your presentation."

She was lovely, mid-twenties, he guessed. Her Mexican heritage was beautifully evident in her full figure and olive skin. She answered quickly, as if slightly embarrassed. "You are...Dr. Wynter," she said, reciprocating by inspecting his crookedly-adhered nametag. "Press?" she asked laughingly, "Is that an ID tag, or a command?"

Zed blinked, then understood the joke. "Well, I can promise you much interesting information if you push my button, or," he laughed, "I'll attempt to get information from you if you'd rather interpret it as a request, not as a command."

They walked together back up the slight rise toward the parking lot where Zed had left his auto. When he said that he was an old alumnus—"not that old", she replied with an interesting smile—and also a metazine editor, she was impressed.

"A Ph. D. in engineering, and you would rather be an editor?" Serna asked as she accepted his invitation to visit La Mesilla as his tour guide there, too. "How could you give up research? Won't your career suffer since you don't publish technical papers anymore?"

Zed told the car to start. "No, Ms. Serna—Sylvia, right?—I don't miss engineering, if that's what the question is." The engine delayed slightly, started, and he instructed the car onto the westward street. "I've always loved to write, and I guess it was probably a mistake not to have been a writer all along."

As they drove the few miles toward La Mesilla, he told Sylvia about his years in research and development, in writing science fiction, working with DI computers and personal robotics. "Yeah, I think that it was always the romance, the adventure of science and engineering that appealed to me, more than the hands-on hard work."

The car pulled itself into a tiny parking space

behind a painted adobe wall. Zed sat and talked a few minutes more. "The actual practice of engineering wasn't as much fun as I had dreamed it would be." He pointed eastward to the jagged Organ Mountains. "If I had stayed at White Sands, or had gone into space activities, the romance would have gone on longer." He turned to her thoughtfully. "But after the robot industry crash a few years back, before I got on my feet again financially, I decided that writing about new and exotic technology was more enjoyable than the work and the risk that it takes to actually make that technology happen."

He got out and started to walk around to open her door. Sylvia was already standing outside of the car when he came around. But she did take his hand as they walked away.

"But don't you think the Cobblestone technology is exciting in and of itself? And Daviess' contributions? Sidespace phenomena are so—so *unique*!" Her eyes lit with excitement. "I mean, I've never read much science fiction, but I stay enthusiastic about my work," They went toward an older place called Billy the Kid Bar —1878.

"And I want to go on to get my Doctor's," she continued. "I'm already getting offers from energy research centers in Chile. Free tuition and a paid stipend." When she looked up at him, electricity in her eyes and a determined smile on her lips, Zed saw evanescent glimpses of his past self, somewhere deep in that innocence.

And he saw more: *God, she was beautiful!*

They passed the afternoon in the genuine leisure of a genuinely sleepy town, and later Zed kissed her softly as the Rio Grande trickled under the pedestrian bridge near the dark lava fields. He slept alone that night, not having made a move toward anything else because of the brevity of the encounter, but the softness of a New Mexico sunset, made lovelier by the evening's company of his new friend, left wonderful memories. He slept soundly.

THE NEXT MORNING, ZED DROVE BACK TO EL Paso. This time, he could see the experimental solar cell farm on the west bank of the Rio Grande —a Federally-funded project being pushed through by Congress, in direct competition to the mostly privately-financed Cobblestone. The radical basis of operation of the "Solar Sea", as the grandiose project was sometimes called—it now spanned forty square miles with its hundred-foot high support towers—was that sunlight would be collected on Earth, converted to microwave energy, and transmitted to space.

Zed never had understood the economics of that mode of operation, but it was quite the latest thing among the renascent Sustainability Movement of the twenty-first millennium. Zed knew there was no arguing with politicians, especially by mere sci-techs like himself.

From space, the microwave energy would presumably be sent down to areas of need, and converted into electricity. *And of course, no one has ever considered its capabilities as a weapon,* Zed mused. He could foresee ecological and political problems, if the pilot farm worked as advertised. A vision of the entire American Southwest covered by the Great Solar Sea darkened Zed's vision of the future. He liked the Cobblestone tokamak better, it left the countryside in its natural state. Plus, it had much more attractive advocates.

ARRIVING AT EL PASO, ZED WENT ACROSS THE border, obtained a three-day temporary tourist permit, and headed toward Chihuahua City.

It was a long drive for Zed—some seven hours of manual driving, with no autonomic systems available in this part of México—and the desert was hot and dusty. "Dust devils"— small desert tornadoes—danced among the greasewood-anchored sand dunes. Zed watched the vortices form, suck up brown sand and small vegetation, and thrust their swirling forms a thousand feet into the clear sky. He was nostalgic once more, thinking of a fishing trip he and Filemón and a gang of other guys had made down here many years ago. They had caught little, but sang and drank a lot, and chased dust devils across the boondocks with their jeeps. Those were great times for Zed. *And safer times*, he thought.

Toward evening he stopped at a motel, checked in, and parked inside the barbed-wire-tipped security fence. He left a request for a wake-up call. After a quick dinner, he decided not to go to the bar that night, but called room service for a small bottle of tequila and some margarita mix. He spent the next hour checking out his room for bugs and preparing the door with alarms, should anything unplanned occur.

Suspicious after he had left Juárez the first time two days before, he had stopped en route to New Mexico and checked out his car using a Donne bug-scanner. He found two tiny transmitters. *It's a treat to have these new detection gadgets for the wrister*, he told himself. *I'll have to thank Mark, the next time I see him. Maybe give him some free subscriptions or something. He certainly wouldn't want free*—or any—*advertising!* Zed had driven the car under an Interstate overpass where hopefully any transmissions to satellites would be thwarted, and then attached the transmitters onto a truck heading toward Phoenix via tony disposable drones. *Let them figure out that one!*

THE FIRST NIGHT AT THE HOTEL WAS UNEVENTFUL. After room-service breakfast the next morning, he found a telephone booth with a primitive landline connection and called Brighton. He left a few innocuous and a few seemingly-coded messages with Brighton, then hung up. Back in the car, windows down and radio blaring mariachi music, Zed actuated the tiny neurophone in his wrister strap and caught up on the latest news.

"Mr. Wynter, sir," Brighton's voice came through by bone conduction, "QuanTonics, S. A., has been attempting to gather information from your databases, both in legal and coercive ways. Doris and the office staff have received mysterious threats that I have traced to QuanTonics employees. My own intercepts of QuanTonics datastreams indicates that they are aware that your visit is not above board. They seem to have some worry that you will discover that they are building military robots for the Mexican Federal government. At least that is the story that I have determined at this time. Please keep in contact, sir."

Good old Brighton! But that story about the military

robots is a bit strained. I think they're hiding something beyond that. Seems they use levels of security similar to mine.. But that damned abandoned underground factory is something I just can't get off my mind. Surely there has to be some reason the place looks a thousand years old. I was just kidding Filemón about a "time machine"; no way would anyone as dumb as that QuanTonics crew use a time travel device.

The QuanTonics facility in Cd. Chihuahua was right downtown—Zed couldn't believe his luck. Only problem was that the entire place was behind a five-meter-high security fence topped with razor wire. He parked at a fenced hotel lot, tipped the guard, and walked around the four city blocks that comprised the factory, certain that the company's facial recognition sensors were identifying and tracking him. *That's OK,* he thought. *Let them worry.*

Through the factory's fence he could see incoming trucks delivering bales of components, and other trucks apparently taking out the finished products. Later he sat in a small, smoky cantina and drank cold *cerveza Superior* and pretended to be a tourist.

Zed then visited the hawkers in a nearby marketplace, bought a leather briefcase and a carved onyx chess set. At the factory's quitting time, he estimated the number of workers who left the plant—about a hundred. As he had arranged, Zed's hotel room was on the second floor, directly across the plaza from the QuanTonics factory.

Great location! He mused, photographing the whole place in as much detail as his wrister's added zoom lenses would allow. Using a small Donne-designed pack that served as an adjunct to his wrister, he also did a thermoelectrical survey of the factory's emanations in the invisible spectrum.

Ciudad Chihuahua wasn't too attractive from his window. The population boom that was strangling México, evidenced by an early-evening smog from the wood fires of the several hundred thousand miserables in the nearby refugee camps. Zed thought of his last visit to México City. A lot worse than this—like Filemón says, "Thirty million people in one city means a lot of shit and a lot of smoke. If you don't handle those two things, *compadre*, you can't call yourself a government." *By the looks of the sky and the smell around here, Chihuahua City is losing its grip, too, Filemón. Just don't bring your war here.* Zed shuddered to think of the impact of another ten million Latin refugees on the American economy. The initial waves resulting from the last decades of miniwars had severely affected the American Southwest. He shrugged mentally and continued his analysis of the QuanTonics factory across the dingy plaza. A menacing haze wafted in from the campfires.

Better finish this before the smoke gets too thick, he sighed.

The Donne instrumentation pack evaluated the data and outputted the integrated graphic results to the room's television set, via Zed's data cable. *Only a low-res two-D*, he regretted, but at least usable. He didn't want to use the VR metascreen unit in his briefcase until necessary, its EM signature might warn some QuanTonics detection system. On the screen, the wrister pack painted isotherms, lines showing the temperature distributions of the factory walls and ceilings. This information, when compared to the next morning's scans, would tell him where the hottest equipment was located. Presumably these areas would be run by robots and not by human operators. These would be foundry-related activities. Analyses of electromagnetic isopotentials and radio emissions would show him where the more exotic processing occurred. Once he had absorbed all of that data, he would decide his next moves. Zed looked at the information he had analyzed and concluded that he was a decently competent industrial spy. *Not for nothing had he been a voracious gadget collector—and science fiction writer*, he added cheerfully.

A sudden "Burp!" from the wrister pack made him turn away from the television set. *Damn! The thing was smoking! What could have happened?* There it was, still pointed at the factory wall. *Could it have been overloaded?*

Zed glanced back at the image on the television screen; it too had shrunk down and then come back to full size. *What the hell?* He picked up the instrument pack. Its red "overload" LED was flashing. The wrister analysis streamed onto the television screen. Indeed it had been a large EMP, large enough to fry the sensors. *My God*, he thought as he tried to calculate the intensity of that pulse, *what are they doing over there?*

To the naked eye, the factory's adobe walls and tin roof gave no evidence of any high technology. Small wisps of smoke began to rise from near the guard shack, as the armed men made coffee outside their hut on a small fire.

The plaza became quiet as the cantina's last customers left. A very peaceful scene, Zed observed. *But what the hell is going on inside that place?* He spent a restless nightin the summer heat, which was not at all dissipated by the overhead fan. Aas it squeaked in slow rotation, the city's smoke smell tinging the air, Zed finally slipped off to sleep wishing that the Cobblestone's Daviess topology could be used to cool his room.

He awoke to the sound of dogs barking and trucks backing up to the loading dock at QuanTonics. Through the window he watched the ninety-five employees—(he counted them, this time)—walk through the one main entrance. The day before he had ordered for all his meals to be delivered by room service, giving a story that he was ill from "*la turista*"—Montezuma's revenge—and tipped the room boy with an extra ten dollars. The boy, Guillermo, caught on quickly and made sure that his patron was not disturbed by anyone. The story was debatable, but the money was very real. Guillermo would protect his *gringo* friend.

There was a knock at the door. "*Señor.*" A young voice spoke out, softly. It was Guillermo. "Señor, I need to speak to you, very quickly!" Zed did have the presence of mind to look through the peephole first. The boy was alone. Zed opened the door and Guillermo came in, seating himself on the unmade bed. *As if he owns the place,* Zed thought.

"*Señor* Gringo, someone is here. To find you."

Zed put on his pants and wished for a cup of coffee. "And what makes you think that, *muchacho*?"

The boy went to the window and pointed out a man lounging in the plaza, directly between Zed's room and the QuanTonics factory.

"That's the one, *Señor*. He was asking questions around the cantina last night."

Zed looked closely at the man through the wrister's zoom optics. He was strangely familiar. He turned to Guillermo. "Keep a watch on him, kiddie." He handed the kid a ten dollar piece.

With smiles and movement faster than Zed thought possible of the boy, Guillermo was gone. In a few moments, Zed saw him playing with some stray dogs near the lounging man.

Zed smiled. *Worth a few bucks, that kid! Hope he's dependable!* He chuckled and went to take a bath in the dubious facilities of his tiny bathroom.

"Damn! What's happening to me?" He couldn't believe what he saw in the dim bathroom mirror, as he shaved—his pale skin was darkened! "Am I becoming a Mexican?" he asked aloud. The stuff wouldn't rub off. "And my hair! It's getting dark, too!"

He wandered back to the single chair and sat, dazed. *What could I have done? Certainly not radiation, not sunlight—that wouldn't account for the hair. What, then? The food? Has that damned kid fed me some kind of poison?*

BUM, BUM, BUM.

Someone was at the door. Zed looked out the window: the lounging man, and Guillermo, were gone. Another knock. *What do I do?* He had no weapon—he wanted no excuse for the Mexican authorities to imprison him. On the other hand, he had not stayed in training for hand-to-hand *keratsu*. As usual, guilt stemming from that night in Juárez would not stay in the background. With no other options, Zed answered cautiously and stood flat against the wall, hoping for the best.

"Quien es?"

"It's Guillermo, *Señor Gringo*," came the boy's voice. "Guillermo and a friend." With little choice, but still ready for action, Zed slowly opened the door. In came the lounging man and the boy. The man was obviously Mexican, about twenty-five years old, with a few days' growth of whiskers and a haunted look about his eyes. A faded blue work shirt competed with pale jeans for lack of color, for evidence of wear. He was short, thin, and dark, but a tenseness in his motion was enough to convince the American that this was a very dangerous man.

"I'm sorry, *Señor* Wynter," the man said, extending a hand to Zed. "Filemón asked me to come see you. He thinks you may need help. I am Hilario Cardenas." He tossed Zed a metal nameplate. Filemón had a real sense of the dramatic.

"Are you becoming a Mexican?" Cardenas laughed as Zed stared in puzzlement. "I took the liberty of putting additives in your food the last day. Our little revolutionary here helped." Guillermo beamed at this. "A variant of nano-carotene. Filemón said you would appreciate the humor."

"I would like to have been asked," Zed said with a smile as he shook the man's hand. "Is it permanent?"

"No, *Señor* Wynter. General Garcia does not require permanent conversion"—he chuckled at his pun—"just temporary obedience to his orders. There is an antidote, another nano-drug." He walked to the window and looked out toward the QuanTonics factory.

"You see, Zed, Filemón thought you would need some muscle, some help. He knew that you would arrive here eventually. So he sent me to assist you in our mission."

"*Our* mission? I'm doing everything I can right now." Zed pointed at the Donne instrument pack, the isotherm plots, and other notes scattered around the room. "My equipment got fried and now I'm limited in what I can do." Looking at Cardenas with a sudden frown of realization he asked,

"Unless...unless General Garcia has something else in mind?"

Nodding, Cardenas lifted the curtain slightly and pointed at the factory. " Filemón has orders: you and I are going to penetrate the factory, tonight."

DAMNED IF I DON'T *LOOK LIKE A MEXICAN*, ZED told himself as he examined his reflection. He had acquired much darker skin and hair, courtesy of Filemón's nanochemicals, dark eyes by way of Hilario's contact lens kit, and cheap *peon* clothing from Guillermo's shopping along *Calle de Sueños. Street of Dreams indeed! I just hope it doesn't become a nightmare!*

Cardenas engaged the night guards in friendly banter while Zed kept quiet, his own accent could not be easily masked. A bottle of mescal completed his costume, and as long as he handed it over when asked, grunting "*Bueno*," no one seemed to notice his presence. Zed could not imagine such lax security around a high-tech installation like a robot factory.

"Filemón's sympathizers inside have surveyed the building, Zed. Aside from patrolbots and perimeter volumetric sensors—microwaves and the like—there's nothing protecting the place. Except," he laughed, pointing out the coffee-drinking guards, "the ready guns of my countrymen over there."

A night watchman inside, a *Garcista* friendly, would escort them through the detection screen once they were past the guards.

"Friends," Cardenas said in soft Spanish as the foursome sat near the guard shack, listening to the cantina music that drifted across the plaza. "Is this not a good night? Is not God good to grant us such delight?"

Each man took another swig of mescal and nodded in answer. A woman emerged from the cantina and slowly walked toward them. "And is that"—Cardenas pointed the bottle at her—"is that not one of God's delights? *¡Hola mamacita, ven aca!*"

As requested, she came closer. About nineteen years old, she was a daughter of her race, dark hair flowing to her waist, dark eyes promising sensual fulfillment, flared nostrils and a throaty voice promising ecstasy. She was dark. She was voluptuous. She was beautiful.

God, Zed thought, *I almost wish Filemón would bait me with as much temptation as he does these guards!* A few moments of sharing their bottle and the beauty led away one guard into a nearby alleyway. Zed was envious, bemused.

Next she led Zed away, but while the first guard related his excited tale of extemporaneous amour to his anticipating friend, Zed slipped behind the guard shack and ran across to the waiting night watchman. The man rushed him inside.

Maybe I should have gone first, Zed thought.

Running away from her was definitely not a good idea. But I do need my strength, he sighed inwardly.

The girl returned, saying that the tall one had left after his fun, and that she needed a more grateful lover. The other guard agreed and left with her, groping drunkenly at her wrinkled dress. Cardenas easily slipped behind the shack while the first guard began to doze off from the effects of sex and mescal. Inside a minute all three of the conspirators were briskly walking toward the center of the factory.

The watchman provided each of them with a coded badge that would allow them to pass anywhere within the building. As they moved on, Zed saw no other people inside the factory. Once or twice a patrolbot wobbled past but took no notice of them.

I begin to understand, now, Zed mused. *After a few years of superefficient patrolbots, I guess any security force would grow a little lax. Without these badges, those bots would just grab us and hold us. Or kill us.* He was glad that Filemón was so thorough. *Guess that's why he's a General, and I'm a simple foot-soldier.* He smiled.

The factory is fairly open, he thought. Over here, the assembly benches where nimble-fingered Mexican women would assemble intricate electronic configurations that were destined to become nearly-conscious matrices of semimorphous crystals. Over there...

Wait a minute, Zed thought, *There's not nearly enough space inside this factory for the quantity of robots they ship!* He accessed the wrister that was taped inside his shirt. *The trucks leave every day with at least twenty machines*, he calculated. *Made at these few benches?* Stopping at a representative bench, he looked at a subassembly in progress. His mind raced. *Damn! This is just make-work! These people are not making any robot guts, or any semimorph braincases*! He asked the watchman for a quick tour of the other assembly areas. The results were the same —no serious assembly work was going on anywhere.

In a low voice he counseled Cardenas. "Hilario, what we see around here is enough to fool anyone who's not familiar with robot assembly. Even the workers, I suppose."

He saw the thoughtful look on his comrade's face. "In each area, there's enough make-work assembly going on to make it appear that the factory is turning out product. But even a hundred workers, or ninety-five as I counted yesterday, is not nearly enough." He picked up a partial braincase assembly and rotated it to show the kaleidoscope of semimorphous circuitry inside. Cardenas shrugged; it meant little to him.

"Hilario, this work has to be done by human hands—no robot can yet build such a sophisticated braincase. It must take at least a thousand assemblers to make twenty of these heads every day alone. And there are tentacles, arms, macrotronics." He put the braincase down. "This is what's been bothering me ever since I came to Chihuahua City." He was deadly serious. Cardenas and the watchman listened intently. "The robots that they ship out the door every day are not built in this factory!"

Even Cardenas was surprised at Zed's conclusion. "Where, then, Zed?" Turning to the watchman, he asked, "*Compadre*, do the *hombres metallicos* come out of this building each and every day?"

The watchman nodded, speaking in extremely

fast Spanish to Cardenas. Zed didn't catch his meaning.

"Back there, Zed," Cardenas said, pointing to a large set of locked metal doors that looked familiar to the American. "*Los metallicos* come out of there every morning. Our friend here clocks out right after those doors are opened." He frowned, realization suddenly dawning on him. "And every day there are twenty robots in the little room beyond."

As they cautiously approached the metal doors, Zed whispered, "Hilario, these doors are just like those Filemón and I saw in Yucatán."

Cardenas was puzzled. He said that he didn't know about any doors in Yucatán. Zed wondered why Filemón hadn't told him. A few discreet questions revealed that Cardenas thought he was assigned to help Zed infiltrate a factory, maybe to steal some plans, or to arrange for future sabotage. He knew nothing about underground factories anywhere. General Garcia took few chances.

Zed decided not to enlighten Hilario at the moment. *Maybe when we find out more here, I can give Cardenas information to take back to Filemón. What a way to run a revolution!*

The watchman was telling Cardenas he had no way to open the doors when suddenly the man became agitated, pointing at his watch.

"We've got to hide, Zed", Cardenas said quickly. "He says some people are coming in tonight at twenty hundred, and he had almost forgotten. We've got about ten minutes."

The two men were inexpertly sequestered in a small engineering office, and the watchman promised to retrieve them after the visitors left. Zed was hoping for something of importance to happen. So far, the mystery was only becoming more strange.

HALF AN HOUR LATER, FOUR MEN ENTERED THE hallway leading to the "robot room" as Zed now thought of it. Two of them carried luggage, including briefcases, and the other two lugged in several trunks of heavy equipment. Zed recognized Michael Frost and Sam Balleen—the owners of QuanTonics.

But what were they doing down here at this particular time? Zed turned to Cardenas, who was nodding at two small photographs he had taken from his wallet. He noticed Zed's surprise and smiled. Both men were thinking, *Filemón is very efficient.* Zed could barely believe that Garcia could have anticipated this encounter. *he must plan for every eventuality.*

As they watched the two men, they could not hear well enough across the assembly area to tell what the men said, but soon the two porters left. Frost shut the hallway door behind them and began to rearrange the trunks. Balleen stood by, nervously wiping his hands together.

Did he always look so unhealthy? Zed recalled the man's waxen appearance several days before in Juárez. He looked even worse today.

Frost opened a briefcase and manipulated a touchscreen device. Balleen made some remark, and Frost snapped back. The older man rubbed his face and stayed quiet. He was obviously becoming more upset. *Why?* Zed wondered. Cardenas, too, could not understand the men's actions and made a rotating finger sign toward his temple indicating his opinion of the situation. *Loco?* Zed shrugged.

Frost walked to the large steel doors and

touched his palm to an indicator plate. The doors slid back into the walls, revealing a twenty-foot-square room, its concrete block walls showing signs of heavy use: tire tracks of forklifts, scratches and gouges on the walls, and faded signs warning of overloading.

Overloading what? Zed wondered.

Frost inspected the room, made a few verbal inputs to his wrister, and then walked back into the hallway. The doors slid closed. Frost said something to Balleen, who was growing more discontent with each moment. Frost shrugged in disgust, walked over to a wall panel, opening it with a palm press. He looked at his wrister and touched several fingerprint sensors simultaneously.

The large doors began to glow and the hallway was flooded with the smell of ozone. Zed and Hilario watched with jaws agape: the doors wavered for a moment, as if seen at a distance through the hot air of the desert. And for one second, Zed could have sworn that the doors were *distant*, distant in a way he had never before perceived.

Cardenas had no comment. Both men breathed hard.

Within thirty seconds, the doors returned to their normal dull finish, and Frost walked over to them and pressed the actuation plate. The doors opened.

Cardenas and Zed drew in breaths of surprise. The room was filled with robots!

"Que paso?"

"What the shit...?"

Both men sat back in total disbelief, shaking their heads as if to reinforce each other's observation. When their shock dispelled sufficiently, they eagerly turned back to watch what other magic might occur in that strange room.

Frost shouted for Balleen to help him, and the two began to roll the robots out into the hallway. Zed counted eighteen.

"Romeo-12's, a dozen and a half," Zed whispered into his wrister. He swallowed and continued, "They just appeared out of nowhere, after Frost operated some kind of control panel down the hallway." He wanted the report to give enough specific information that Filemón—or someone—would be able to understand what had just happened. These events were too strange not to be shared.

Ten minutes later Frost and Balleen had the Romeo-12 robots lined up in the hallway for the next morning's pickup. Then they began to load their luggage and other crates into the robot room. Zed heard Frost swear several times, yelling out orders to Balleen, his arrogance evident enough although the words were not totally distinguishable. Zed thought, *What an asshole punk!*

The loading finished, Frost and Balleen came walking over toward the engineering office where Cardenas and Wynter were hidden. Their conversation became audible.

Sam was groaning as usual. "But Mike, why do *we* have to go back this time? You know that my heart won't take many more of these trips. And we don't know all of the effects, do we?"

Uncharacteristically, Frost laughed softly and put an arm around the older man's shoulders. "Sam, look at me—a hundred trips so far, and I'm healthy." He jokingly beat his knit shirt with both fists. "The trips make you healthier!"

From his frown, apparently Sam was not convinced, but nodded anyhow.

"Sam, Chichén Itzá is a milk run. Don't sweat it. Besides," he laughed, sarcastically this time, "*you* of all people need the trip!"

Zed crouched low around the base of a drafting table. Cardenas, against the wall but shielded by the partially closed door, simply pulled his flechette and waited.

Violence loomed large in Zed's view: if the two men stepped through the door, he would have to make a decision. He himself would prefer not to fight, though he would attempt an escape to prevent being arrested. He didn't have much chance of making it back to the U. S., no matter what. If Cardenas fired his gun, there would be no real problem. Just two bodies! The look on the Mexican's face told Zed that the *Garcista* was not having any problem deciding his actions.

Frost reached his hand inside the door to turn on the light switch, but Balleen reiterated some complaint. A moment of indecision, and the hand withdrew, Frost going back to reassure his partner once more. One more second and Cardenas' fletchetter would have hamburgered the young man.

Zed let out a sigh of relief. Cardenas put the weapon on safety and slid it back into his belt. As the unknowingly lucky pair left the office area and walked back toward the robot room, the two hidden intruders stood up to stretch in the relatively dark office.

"Hilario," Zed whispered, "You would have killed him if he'd turned on that light, right?"

"Correct, Zed. My orders were specific—first help you get inside this factory, and second, to ensure that any opponent witnesses would not talk afterwards." The Mexican eyed Zed quietly.

Zed thought, *And undoubtedly, you have order for my own disposition too, don't you, Hilario? I'm sure General Garcia doesn't overlook anything.*

Cardenas' expression confirmed the thought. *You, too, Señor, if you betray Filemón.*

Zed shuddered. *What a way to run a revolution!* He was reminded of the comment of a particularly notorious criminal revolutionary of the previous century: "We do not have a revolution to make friends!" That particular murderer of children had died crying like a little girl, begging for his life, somewhere down in Bolivia, if he remembered correctly. *No friends for him,* Zed thought.

The spies crouched near the door again to observe what other magic the robot manufacturers might be doing. Those two were checking over the stacked crates of equipment, and Frost was making more verbal notes into his wrister.

Wham! Wham! Wham! Three tremendous explosions rocked the world, knocking both Zed and Hilario to their knees.

Zed scrambled up, in shock. "It's okay, Zed," Cardenas said. "My associate Gallegos is right on time. Bombs outside in the parking lots, not in the factory here, no danger to us."

"What was it?"

Cardenas didn't answer, put pointed down the hallway at the robot room. "Look, the bad guys are leaving." Frost and Balleen were running away, presumably to the outside to see what had happened. Zed and Hilario looked at each other, grinned, and nodded.

"The same thought, *gringo? Vamanos*!"

Let's go, indeed, Hilario. How opportune! With

Cardenas' flechette at the ready for any sign of trouble, the two ran down into the robot room and lay down behind the shelter of equipment crates.

"I told Gallegos to create a diversion if we were not back outside in one hour," Cardenas said. "And of course, he did." Zed shrugged again. He would never get used to this intrigue, this casual violence, necessary though it might be to their plans. *Not my plans. Filemón's. The Revolution's.*

A staccato chorus of small firearms rattled through the factory windows, followed by the banshee wails of fire engines. At least Chihuahua City still retained some rudimentary social services. Zed wondered what the shooting was about. Suddenly an ominous silence permeated the cavernous building.

Zed took a minute to relax, meditating to calm his nerves, but at the same time recalling some of the *keratsu* techniques to prepare himself for the reappearance of Frost and Balleen.

The two Americans returned.

"Mike, I told you we shouldn't have built his joint down here. There's a war going on! Just tell me, why can't we take it over into New Mexico, where it's safe? We've got land near the Gila Wilderness. Hell, we could rent Federal park lands. Why here?"

"Sam, the nexi are right on this spot for several more years. It would take hundreds of millions to set up artificial nexi anywhere to the north," Frost said, exasperated.

The young man walked around the room, checking some crates. Zed and Cardenas heard them approach, and the Mexican pulled the gun once more, ready to kill. Frost didn't come around to their side of the crates, once again unknowingly saving himself. "But you're right about the war here. I didn't expect that damn Garcia to be blowing up hotels in Chihuahua so soon."

Hotel? Shit, my recordings of the wrister pack outputs were in my room! And Guillermo—! Zed frowned in disgust and horror. Though he couldn't see Cardenas' reaction, he could see the flechette at the end of his companion's hand, the fingers trembling.

Balleen said, "At least they killed the son-of-a-bitch sapper. Too bad about the cantina, though. They had good women in that place, Mike." He laughed, a hollow chortle. Zed couldn't tell if it was for the memory of the women or the death of the sapper. Cardenas' hand jerked in response, and for a moment Zed thought that Balleen was a dead man. Was Hilario sorry for his compadre, or for the innocent civilians? Zed wondered if he would ever know what Cardenas really thought, or even Filemón for that matter.

"We'll be back there in two minutes, Sam, get a grip on yourself," Frost commanded. "I'll send a message to ask Steve to calculate some likely alternate sites, maybe back in California. If the war is spreading here so fast, we wouldn't want to be in a border area swamped with wetback refugees again." He chuckled and leaned against the wall panel, pressing his palm flat against a colored plate.

"Stand by, Sam, we're on our way!"

Zed smelled ozone again. The strange blue glow permeated the room and penetrated through his own tightly closed eyes, too.

He was sucked into a black hole

In a maelstrom of tensive limbo—not a passive void, but into something worse than nothingness,

Zed lost his soul, his identity. He tried to scream, but couldn't. He had no body.

After an eternal moment, the void *wavered* and the blue light returned. Zed found his body and his voice; he was screaming. Opening his eyes, he saw Cardenas, too, reacting to the incredible experience. The Mexican was standing, one hand over his face, the flechette pistol dangling from one shaking hand.

Across the room, Frost swayed back and forth briefly, then opened his eyes. Clambering over crates, he raised his own flechette inches from Cardenas' face.

"Drop the damn gun, wetback!" he screamed, the spiked gunbarrel wavering dangerously in front of the Mexican's eyes. Cardenas hesitated, carefully considering his chances, then just as coolly handed his weapon to Frost, handle first, as the man stepped back. Hatred filled Cardenas' eyes as Frost tossed the gun to Balleen. The pale young man sneered, "Watch this one, Sam, I don't want another Alamo."

"Look who else has taken a trip with us!" Frost waved Cardenas over toward Zed. Sam stood rubbing his eyes, trying to aim the pistol at the stowaways. "Although he looks like a darkie spic, this must be the famous editor, Dr. Zedediah Wynter," Frost pointed his pistol by way of introduction. "Our Dr. Wynter must be catching some Mexican disease—he looks pretty greasy. The real spic here must be one of Garcia's peasant soldiers."

Cardenas remained tense, as if he would attack the insulting gringo at any moment. Zed felt as much anger as fear. Unaffected, Frost laughed at both of them.

"And right now you two guys have no idea in hell where you are. Are you in for a shock?" He chuckled again, walked over to the control panel, slapped the palm press. The doors opened.

Zed prayed, *Please don't let this be what I'm afraid it is.*

It was.

THE FACTORY OUTSIDE OF THE DOORS LOOKED much like Zed remembered, but this time it was new—bright fluorescent lighting, humming conveyor belts, ultra-tech assembly line equipment—a vibrant, living, productive factory. Hundreds of workers—Mayan men and women—were soldering, assembling, cleaning, inspecting, brazing, drilling, forklifting, computing.

As Frost escorted his prisoners down the hallway, some workers turned toward the group, bowing in reverence, then went back to their work. *This is not happening,* Zed told himself. *Not all of this, not just to make robots!*

A contingent of brightly-dressed Mayan warriors. (*Aluminum armor and aluminum spears?* Zed wondered) greeted Frost and Balleen. At Frost's barked orders, the armed men surrounded the two spies and prodded them not too gently. Frost left, returning in a few minutes in an expansive mood.

"Gentlemen, welcome to QuanTonics' Yucatán operation. We are underground, in the vicinity of Chichén Itzá." Frost smiled at Balleen, who seemed to be sharing his partner's mood. "Sam, don't you think it's appropriate for Dr. Wynter to be here?"

Cardenas glared at Zed, suspiciously. Zed just

raised his eyebrows, puzzled. "I mean, Dr. Wynter, editor of *Future Perfect*, meet the *Past Perfect!* Welcome to the Yucatán, 903 A. D.!"

Zed shuddered, closing his eyes at the confirmation of his worst fear, finally believing the unbelievable. He wanted to vomit, but held back. Cardenas, however, didn't.

Even machismo has its limits, Zed noted.

Frost growled out more commands, presumably in Mayan, and the guards took Cardenas away. The stunned Mexican went quietly, still wiping vomitus from his face. A Mayan woman quickly mopped up the mess from the floor. Zed began to protest the separation, but Frost cut him short with a wave of the pistol. "Don't worry, Zed, I'm not going to hurt your friend, just as long as he behaves himself. He's a little confused now, and fairly amenable to suggestion. I'm going to hold him in a comfortable cell for a while. For now, you come with Sam and me. This way."

Zed followed the two Americans into a conference room, where Sam motioned for him to sit. The overstuffed chairs, the long wooden table, reminded Zed of the typical prosperous Dallas business office. Much like his own. Certainly not Mayan!

Slipping the flechette into a shoulder holster, Frost poured drinks for the three of them. *With those spear-toting goons outside, Frost must feel fairly secure. And I guess he is at that,* Zed thought. I'm *sure not going to attack him.*

Not yet... Zed sipped the sweet wine, a flavor he hadn't tasted before, fruity and dry.

"Dr. Wynter. *Zed,*" Frost began, "I don't really know what to do with you now. You've seen entirely too much—you've come too far." Smiling at his own joke, he continued, "Much too far. Only the sixth person in history to travel in time." Zed saw Balleen shoot a glare at Frost, shaking his head slightly.

"The sixth one who counts, that is," Frost corrected himself. Zed didn't know the meaning of the abbreviated communication between the other two men. Zed's opinions of them hadn't changed a bit: *Still weeko-wacko zanes, both of them.*

Frost was pacing the thickly carpeted room, pointedly pausing to scrutinize an exquisite Mayan codex that stretched the length of one wall. "Sam and I don't kill people—that's for nuts like General Garcia and his *pedros.*" Balleen's body language was drumhead-taut; Zed couldn't figure him out.

Frost came close to Zed, sipping his own drink, suddenly becoming serious. "And with the FBI on your tail—"

How did these guys know? And was it true? In the typical remission born of desperation, Zed hoped that the FBI *was* following him. But what could the FBI or even the CIA do when he was trapped in the past, a thousand years ago? Or is it *now*?

His thoughts raced, confused, hope alternately rising and falling "—it would have been difficult to account for your disappearance." Frost smiled. Zed saw twitches around the thin lips, tics at the corners of the eyes. Was this guy doing nano-drugs? Something equally destructive?

"*Would* have been difficult?" Zed repeated.

"Yes, but fortunately, when Garcia's man destroyed the hotel, we gained an easy alibi." He sneered at Zed. "You were staying at that hotel, weren't you?"

Zed realized Frost didn't know everything.

"That one across the plaza? No," he lied, "I was at the Holiday Inn, north of town."

"Easy enough for me to check in the morning," Frost grunted. "In any event, you're going to be staying here from now on, until I decide what to do with you." He gulped down the last small portion of wine, setting the glass on the long table. He sat down next to Zed, shaking his head. "Do you know what we're doing, Wynter?" he asked, spreading his arms out as if to encompass the factory. "This is the sweetest deal in history. Don't try to screw it up. I may be able to use you, cut you in for a piece, if you're smart enough to listen to me." Tics and more tics. Zed suspected the man might have had some unsuccessful nano-enhancements of musculature, something to increase strength or endurance. Something that failed.

Zed watched the man's subtle pleading. *I don't think he's very mature,* he thought, *First, he threatens, then he cajoles. Much like a child. That must make Sam the father figure, but a wimpish one. The kid's a brat, all right, and a rich and powerful one. A spoiled brat with a time machine!*

"How did you get a time machine?" Zed asked abruptly, cutting off the disgusting appeal. "And why do you waste it making robots? Why not just take all of the gold here in ancient Mexico? It's yours for the taking." He pointed at the codex. "Why not just codices? They're worth millions in our time all by themselves! "God," he exclaimed, standing up. "A time machine! Here I am, asking dumb questions about a time machine. I'm not even sure I believe you, Frost! What do you have? How does it work?"

Frost started at Zed's outburst. "The laws of temporal displacement were discovered by accident, Wynter. You remember Daviess' Sidespace mathematics work, five years ago?"

"Vaguely," Zed said, not volunteering any knowledge, preferring to sound ignorant. "His work on crystal growths in an orbital station and on the Moon, wasn't it? Something about a modified wave equation?"

Frost nodded. "Well, Dr. Daviess—Steve—was my advisor at Stanford before I dropped out to start up QuanTonics. He was able to develop his speculations enough privately to create an effective temporal device."

Zed had no option but to believe the kid. "But what about paradoxes, Frost? Won't you perturb history by screwing about with this factory in the past? And if not, why did you choose Chichén Itzá? This isn't a very populated area, not much in the way of resources. Why not ancient Egypt? Medieval Europe? China?"

Frost sighed loudly. "Daviess' modified wave equations," he began patiently, "predict the nexi of spacetime. The wave equations, as you know, have solutions at specific periodic intervals—*eigenvalues,* if you will. When Steve solved his equations, he found that the solutions for Earth are widely separated in time and in space." Pulling out a paper of paper and a pen, Frost made a sketch. Instrumentation in the table surface projected the sketches on the wall at the end of the room.

"Here is our plant in Chihuahua City," Frost said as the drawing took form on the wall. "This is a natural solution, a natural eigenvalue, provided primarily from some tectonic fault line strains. From this transition point, by the judicious application of properly pulsed magnetic fields—"

That can fry instrumentation sensors, Zed frowned.

"—we can access at least twelve other spacetime solutions." Frost marked X's around a phantom globe outline. "These are located at predictable coordinates in time and space. Chichén Itzá just happens to be the 'closest' one." At Zed's puzzled look, Frost added, "Closest in terms of energy required to transfer here through time.

"Now, around the world in space and time, we also have Tibet, about 200 B.C.; Zimbabwe, about 700 B.C.; Rome—way back—6000 B.C., roughly; a place in ancient Greece we haven't been to yet, in person; some others near the poles.

"Other times, other places, we can't get to yet. The periodic solutions don't overlap all of history, so there are some times and places we may never be able to visit. Steve is a partner and he's off exploring some of those locations now, in particular checking out that one in Greece."

Zed listened, amused. For all its limitations, Frost had a working time machine. Even with everything he'd seen, all of the direct involvement, his own trip in time, it was still almost impossible to believe. "But paradoxes, like I said. Won't you change our own time by doing things back here?" *Especially a maniac like you?*

"Kill our own grandfathers, you mean? No, I don't think so. You see, Steve's time theories account for paradoxes—they *can't* occur, *won't* occur. Whichever way you want to say it.

"There is a law of time travel—Frost's First Law, we might call it someday; I pointed it out to Steve, after all—that prevents time-displaced matter from impinging on itself. It's a physical law we can measure when we have time to set up a real lab back here, or somewhere else in the past. I figure that it's analogous to the law of conservation of energy."

Zed was not surprised at Frost's sudden academic pose. Nothing the man could ever do would surprise him. *A manic depressive flake like Frost, capable of manifesting multiple personalities, can do the work of many. No wonder he's a billionaire!*

Frost continued, "When an atom or molecule or some packet of energy—I suppose it makes no difference to Nature—is temporally transferred, there is a physical force that prevents the two time-separated aspects from approaching each other. Like the strong force in physics, like two similar magnetic poles, they repel.

"What this has to do with us, is this: if we brought back a Mayan artifact—this Codex, for example—to the twenty-first century, and tried to bring it physically close to itself in a museum, say, there would be a tremendous repulsion force. In fact, if the one suddenly materialized next to the other, we probably couldn't even operate the Daviess field effect generators. We wouldn't be able to go back or forwards between the nexi. Actually, we might see an explosion like matter-antimatter. You remember how that turned out."

Zed gulped; everyone remembered the Third China lunar antimatter explosion; the Moon's latest large crater was still cooling off. But he was beginning to understand, nodding. Frost smiled. "The repulsion force does provide us with one nice extra benefit: the forces involved keep us from ever coming back to meet ourselves.

"So far we have found out these facts empirically. When we have time to experiment, I think we'll find a similar problem with DNA chains, too." He smiled again. "I would expect similar phenomena to occur when specific patterns of thought, other kinds of information transfer, try to impinge on the already-established past.

"So much then for the paradoxes, Zed. You probably couldn't get close enough to harm your grandfather—or mine." Frost bowed and spread his arms. "That's my theory of the *isochronous repulsion effect*, and now you're one of the few to hear my revealed truth." He stood and the projected images faded.

Zed stood, too. "Physical repulsion I can understand," he said, wondering if Frost could catch the subtlety, "But what about written ideas? Diseases? Microbes?"

Frost shushed him. "If it had happened, we would have read about it, Zed. Nothing paradoxical has ever been found, so nothing happened, right?" Frost didn't know of Garcia's discovery of this factory back in the future, apparently. Zed would not say anything about it.

Zed had more questions, but Frost pre-empted them. "We can go back to our own time if we'd like, and arrive at any time we want to. Right now, I've got the chamber set for about two minutes after we left, regardless of how much time we spend back here—years, if we want." Zed didn't like the sound of that. "The repulsion forces keep us from ever returning back to when we were here before. But I should be able to do quite a lot before I use up a thousand years, don't you think?"

Frost stretched languidly, slumping down into his overstuffed chair. "There is one other very interesting effect that we discovered about life here in the past, Zed." His smile was a strange configuration of thin lips and twitches that did not compliment his bizarre appearance.

"You see, I was stuck here for five years when Steve sent me back the first time. And I didn't age!" He jumped up, arms waving, and danced around, laughing, reminding Zed of a crazed Roman Nero in an old flatfilm movie.

"The DNA structures don't recognize aging factors when you're living before your own time, Zed, old man. The death-genes get turned off." Frost stopped the dancing, coming very close to Zed, staring deep into his eyes. "Do you understand me, Dr. Wynter? If you stay here, you'll live forever."

Zed was silent, thinking about Frost's incredible statement. Immortality? Harder to believe than time travel, and unlike the Queen of Wonderland, Zed could not believe quite so many impossible things before breakfast. He was also glad that he had left those Romeo-14 nametags in the engineering office of the QuanTonics factory in Chihuahua. What would have happened if he'd tried to bring them back here in the past, where they originally came from, where they might already exist here in the factory?

Believing Frost's explanations about the anti-paradox forces, Zed trusted that Nature would indeed prevent those problems and preferred not to think about all those strange fields coalescing inside that "robot room." Especially with himself inside.

"Is that why you've been able to build up QuanTonics so fast, Frost?" He asked. "You send stuff back here from our time, take all of the time you need to build it perfectly, using these Indians as slave labor. You ship it back to our time, and it winds up costing you nothing but some electrical power and cheap assembly parts. God," he began to laugh, first at his own thoughts and then at the expressions of the other two men, "talk about offshore manufacturing! This is about as offshore as you can get!"

Suddenly serious, he growled at Frost, hoping to exert some authority over the volatile child-man. Zed didn't want to live in this place, even if —*especially* if—it was forever. "Do I ever get to see what's outside, or am I stuck down in this dungeon?" Frost smiled a friendly smile and motioned for Zed to follow him. Balleen just poured himself another drink and stayed. Zed thought that Sam probably should stay here in the past, because his present age and physical condition didn't promise a long life back home. Maybe that was what Frost had meant by his sarcastic comments to Sam right before this time trip.

Frost led Zed up the stairs that Zed would climb a thousand years later, the Mayan guards bowing as the lighter-skinned man passed. No one dared question why their blond chief was friendly with the taller dark stranger. A door opened onto a long stone-paved trench that pointed toward a group of small pyramids and other stone structures. *This was Chichén Itzá, a thousand years ago.* Zed thought. *And it's all new!*

Zed made a mental note of the relative locations of the trench and the door. If he were ever to visit this place in his own time, he might think of having Filemón excavate the impressive walkway. It must have been covered up during the next thousand years. The reality of time travel, however limited in destinations, still bothered him greatly.

They walked slowly toward the monuments in

the distance. Zed sensed various strange but pleasant smells of flowers, and appreciated the bright blue sky, the luxuriant vegetation, the unusual calls of the quetzal birds. And yellow butterflies in their millions, a virtual snowstorm of fluttering gold, played a complex darting ballet in contrast to the slow swaying of jungle plants. Under other circumstances, Zed would have found the whole experience overwhelming. But right now it was merely excruciating: Frost was unpredictable and dangerous, and Zed liked sure, safe bets.

As they walked, Zed noticed the man's tics and twitches diminishing. Frost said, "I have a map of Chichén Itzá from the '30s, before the war started down here. I've had the natives here start to build some of those structures we see in our time." He chuckled, "I think that's funny, don't you?" He pointed out several small stone structures where crews of Mayans were sweating in the brutal effects of sun and humidity. It had to be at least a hundred and ten degrees Fahrenheit. Zed didn't think it was amusing for people to be slaves to a madman, and said as much to Frost, leaving out direct challenges.

"Zed, they have to get built by these people, either by my orders or someone else's. Otherwise, how did we see them before, back in the 'aught-thirties'? Anyhow, I did think about having them build one with my name on it, in English, a building that didn't show up on our maps, but that would probably be pushing the anti-paradox situation a bit much." The young man took obvious pleasure in the obeisance of the work crews as the Americans strolled through the complex, the bowing and the avoidance of Frost's eyes. "There might be some sort of 'conservation of information' law that could bite me. Don't want to disturb the TimeSpace too much. Might get nasty."

They stopped to admire a goldsmith at work putting finishing touches on an intricate feathered serpent motif. The Mayan bowed and stepped back while Frost took the piece and admired it. "Zed, I would love to take this piece and others back with me, but the amount of gold in circulation at any time is so limited that I'd be bound to run into the isochronous repulsion effect." Smiling, Frost handed the invaluable gold artwork back to the craftsman. The goldsmith held his head down until they left.

"And that's why you saw the aluminum armor and weapons on my guards. Those aluminum atoms came from bauxite mined in our future North America—Arkansas, to be exact—but in *this* time they're hundreds of feet underground and thousands of miles away. There's no repulsion effect to worry about. Similar care in choosing the origins of other materials allowed us to build this modern factory back here without paradox problems."

Zed was beginning to make sense out of the QuanTonics operation. "So that's why you bring back the raw materials from the future—our time—back here for assembly, rather than fabricating robots out of materials here. It would be embarrassing to have a robot that got repulsed from its owner's stainless steel utensils." Frost was caught off guard by Zed's humor, but his smile was not at all pleasant.

"Exactly, Zed. Now you perceive the utility of Daviess' time machine. About all we can use it for is free labor; not that aging more slowly is a disadvantage. But properly used, and with centuries in which to perform, all that free labor and the extended lifespans are quite enough. I've put in over twenty years here in the past, haven't aged any, and I've continued to learn how to build a business. And I've built a real financial empire." Frost pointed to a small pyramid and suggested they climb it.

"Eventually, I guess, this way I could own the whole world. One day, I'll probably retire back here so I can live eternally." Zed considered that statement. What would happen with the repulsion effect when the unaging Frost finally lived into the 2020s when he was being born? Or had that already happened, back "Up Time," as he was beginning to think of it?

They climbed up the pyramid while priests in plumed headdresses backed away, bowing. Frost spoke to the priest softly, smiling. "I try to be benign to these people, Zed," he said, puffing slightly at the exertion of climbing the fifty steps. Zed looked out over a cleared area around the complex, into the jungle beyond. "Over there is the *cenote*, the well. Here in Yucatán there are no rivers or lakes, only the occasional well, and there was already a small village here when I first came back." Frost sat, but Zed continued to walk around the flat top of the pyramid, about ten feet square. Zed estimated the pyramid to be about thirty feet high. He wasn't able to recall any structure this small when he and Filemón were here before. A glance eastward revealed that Zed's favorite Chichén Itzá monument, the observatory called "The Snail"—*El Caracol*—hadn't yet been built.

"How did you establish yourself here, Frost? Just walk in and take over? How come they didn't kill and eat you, or something?" Zed didn't think he himself would be up to strolling in cold to an unknown primitive village and setting up a good business.

"Just like Cortez and Pizarro, Zed," Frost replied. "These guys were just waiting for a white god to come in and take over. Study your history a little bit."

"But why is the factory underground? What's to hide? Not any satellite surveillance out here, not now. No government troops either."

Frost laid back and stretched out to bask in the sun, his balding head resting in clasped hands. "Last things first. There will be no aboveground factory buildings in our home time, so I dared not build one here, now.

"Secondly, it was easier to build the plant where we did. The first probe Steve and I sent back was from a lab at Stanford. A minor miscalculation placed it underground. It tried to coexist with a rock and caused a hellacious explosion—a crater a hundred feet deep and two hundred in diameter. Our next probe brought back video of curious Mayans looking down into the pit. When I appeared out of thin air, Buddhist robes and all, they were all prepared to receive God. Or at least, *a* god. Me."

"Buddhist robes?"

"Yeah, that's all I was able to find on short notice in Palo Alto, at a costume shop. They liked it, though. Seemed to fit in with what they expected."

Zed was glad to hear that the Mayans had not dug out the entire factory site by hand. But the explosion bothered him and he said so.

Frost answered, "You saw how we button up

the transmitting room before each trip? Don't want to bump into anything else when we pop into this time. We've set up similar chambers for our most frequent trips. It's safe enough, we just have to be careful." He rolled over on his side and watched the hundreds of Mayan laborers working on their appointed tasks.

He surprised Zed again. "Frost and Wynter—sounds like a Scandinavian folk tale, doesn't it?" Zed didn't like the kid's tone nor the implication. He frowned.

"Where does Sam fit in?"

"Money, finances. Dealings, contacts, contracts." Frost stood, brushing off his trousers and rubbing sweat from his open shirt. "Sam's a Silicon Valley venture capital genius who helped Steve and me get started."

Zed asked if they could go visit the well; he remembered visiting it once on a vacation. "I don't think so, Zed. You and I are limited to a distance about three kilometers from the factory site." When Zed just stared, Frost continued, "You and I have some atoms from here, from this time, in our bodies. Just the eternal mixing that goes on. Somewhere, some oxygen or nitrogen from ancient Yucatán made its way into our compositions in the twenty-first century. The farther from our natural nexus—the factory site—the more likely we are to encounter those same atoms here this very day, and the harder it will be for us to move. Empirically, this works out to about three klicks. But let me demonstrate. Come on!"

Frost scrambled down the pyramid, Zed followed close behind, arriving at the ceremonial road that led to the cenote. Zed easily outdistanced the younger man, several times waiting for him to catch up, but finally slowed to Frost's slow walk. Zed didn't want the curious Mayans to see their god bettered by anyone else. No telling what their reactions might be. And he wasn't sure that these natives didn't practice cannibalism. Or was that strictly the Aztecs? Why take chances?

Halfway to the *cenote*, he estimated, his vision began to dim and the atmosphere felt thick. The roadway before him took on an *incomplete* look, as if the unreality of watching the doors of the robot room in Chihuahua was kicking in again. Zed found he couldn't—didn't *want*—to move farther. Watching in frustration, he panted while myriads of yellow butterflies danced in and out of the limits of his own reality, uncaring of his plight. The *quetzal* birds *gallup-galluped* in mockery of his inability to penetrate their world.

Zed turned back, defeated

Frost was waiting. "What did I tell you, Zed? Frightening, isn't it? The first time I reached the Barrier, I thought I was dying. And I believe we would die if we physically went further."

"So no airplanes or cars, huh, Frost?"

"Not unless you make them from local materials and use a remote control device. I might do that sometime, when there's time."

"Time!" Zed laughed. "Here you are, a Master of Time, living forever, and yet you don't have time to do anything!" *What a weeko-wacko,* he thought. At the very least, Zed found satisfaction knowing that the nature of Time Itself couldn't be violated by Frost and his kind. There *were* limits, and he took comfort in that fact.

For all the friendliness Frost exhibited during their tour of the site, Zed found himself locked in a cell that night. Abundant food was delivered by an attractive woman, who was guarded by half a dozen warriors. When the contingent left, Zed shouted out the small barred window, trying to locate Cardenas. His voice echoed down stone corridors, but there was no reply from his companion in crime. He could have sworn that there was something … a noise, the mewing of a cat, or a slight whimpering? Zed had counted the stairwell switchbacks, and figured that he was down in the lower levels of the factory. Probably off limits to the day workers.

Finishing the surprisingly good meal of stringy meats and ripe fruits, Zed laid back on a plush cot and tried to make plans to leave the past. Somehow he had to get Frost to push the palm press panel—surely it was keyed to the maniac's palm pattern—and take them back to Chihuahua City in their own time. If his car hadn't been destroyed in the hotel blast, and if it were still there—he recalled that Frost planned the return trip to arrive just two minutes after their leaving, so duration shouldn't be a problem—he might yet make it back to El Paso and safety.

But only if Frost didn't report him to the local police in Chihuahua. Zed sighed. Getting back to the "aught-forties" had to be the first priority; everything else was mere detail. As he drifted off into sleep, Zed wondered if he would dream, back here in the past.

ZED JERKED TO WAKEFULNESS ONCE DURING THE night to the sounds of a woman crying, pleading, followed by a man's shout. Whatever it was quickly died away and Zed didn't know if it was just a bad dream. He wasn't sleeping very peacefully anyway.

Before daybreak the next morning, a guard pounded on the door, waking Zed from troubled dreams. In the hallway he joined the guard cadre and Cardenas, and the captives were taken to eat breakfast, *desayuno*. The QuanTonics owners were not around, but their two involuntary guests ate voraciously. They didn't know what might happen, and they wanted to have enough energy to fight if necessary.

Cardenas acted suspicious of Zed, because of the latter's time alone with Frost the day before. Sensing this, Zed tried to explain, but Cardenas was skeptical. He barely believed the time travel story itself, much less the account of building Chichén Itzá. The Mexican definitely did not buy the concept of the Barrier, that insubstantial things like atoms could prevent a man from going where he wished.

"Hilario, big bombs from tiny atoms grow. Remember the oil fields?" The Garcista soldier shrugged; that atrocity was just one more reason Filemón's support continued to find sympathy among the peasants. Nuking one's own resources to prevent takeover by rebels was one of the century's newest inventions; "Glassed Earth" had replaced "Scorched Earth."

After the two men bathed, they dressed themselves in the modern peasant garb provided. More guards led them up through the still factory and out onto the paved trench walkway. Cardenas tried to speak, but an aluminum speartip and a shake of a grim face convinced him to remain silent. Zed just grinned sheepishly at his friend's discomfort.

They accompanied the guards through a crowd of Mayans up to a group of chairs atop a ten-foot high rectangular structure directly opposite the pyramid that Frost and Zed had climbed the day before. Balleen sat there in welcome, telling them to sit and watch and enjoy. The sun was just beginning to rise.

"Watch this, guys," Balleen said with a grin. "Mike's got something real big cooked up for the locals." He chuckled, and Zed resigned himself to watch the show, whatever it was. He hoped there wouldn't be any human sacrifices, particularly of himself!

Nearly a thousand Mayans thronged the pyramid, chanting low, coached by cheerleading priests among them. *Like cheering sections at an airball game*, Zed thought. Sunlight was just beginning to touch the tip of the pyramid, and the chanting grew louder.

"*Ma-ak! Ma-ak!*" the crowd murmured, the volume rising. Balleen could barely contain his laughter. "That's what they call Mike—'*Ma-ak.*' Ain't that something?" At the sound of their god's name, the guards turned and frowned at the older man. Evidently old Sam wasn't ranked too highly by the locals, Zed decided.

"*Ma-ak! Ma-ak! Ma-ak!*" The volume and the tempo increased as the top five feet of the pyramid caught the golden rays of the sun. There was motion atop the pyramid, and immediately the crowd hushed. What was happening on top there? Cardenas and Zed strained to see.

A bird? A plane? A superman? Zed punned to himself, but he was absorbed by the spectacle: it was Michael Frost, suddenly appearing from some secret trapdoor, strutting around under a brightly-colored microlight hang-glider!

"I just don't believe this, Hilario. What that guy won't do …" Cardenas just stared, as if he hadn't seen hang-gliders before and couldn't grasp the situation. Zed didn't understand the man's shock; weaponized microlights had been used all over in the Central American miniwars. Hadn't this man seen them before? From his awed looks, apparently not.

An awed whisper susurrated from the crowd. "*Ma-ak! Ma-ak! Ma-ak!*" Using a throat amplifier, Frost answered his worshippers with some words Zed couldn't understand. Laser beams flashed in the sky, colored spotlights illuminated Frost and his wings. Music swelled triumphantly from speakers strategically placed around the temple complex: Wagner's *Ride of the Valkyries!* Zed was fascinated by the special effects; *God, what a spectacle!*

As sunlight suddenly filled the one face of the pyramid, Frost leaped from his platform into the open air, the powered microlight glider taking smoothly to the clear morning air. Zed could make out the form of the feathered serpent motif on the widespread wings. The transfixed Mayans stared in silence, then suddenly began to scream, *"Maak! Ma-ak! Ma-ak"*, hysteria that rose to a world-filling screech.

Zed was overwhelmed, impressed. *What a show, what a.way to prove you* are *a god!* The faint buzz of a microprop engine probed its way to Zed's ears through the cacophony of the shouting Indians. *Frost is just too damn intelligent. These people worship him, and why not? A god who comes out of nowhere from a hole in the ground, who builds fantastic buildings, who flies around in the sky. What more could you want?* Zed stood to applaud with Balleen, Cardenas reluctantly joining them. "Hilario, better be enthusiastic. That's some kind of god up there." The Mexican was not happy.

"So how was the show, gentlemen?" Frost asked later as he returned to the conference room. "Impressive enough for the peons around here?" Zed could see the tics and twitches around the man's face again. *Must be a function of adrenalin flow*, he assumed. Frost laughed, "That's a lot of fun to do, even when it's not for profit."

"Are you doing anything at all to pay these people, Frost?" Zed asked.

"I can't bring them back medicines or anything, if that's what you mean, but just learning organizational skills, being a coherent group ought to be enough of a payment. " Frost took a deep drink of the local wine and smacked his lips. "Without QuanTonics, they'd still be tromping around in the jungle, doing nothing."

"But for themselves," Cardenas muttered. "Not for a phony god who is a parasite upon their lives."

Frost paced the room, glancing at the Mexican, then at Zed. Balleen just sat back, drinking, a satisfied glow about him. *He looks a lot more relaxed than usual*, Zed thought. *Wonder what he's been doing since last night?*

Sex? Nano-drugs? Just alcohol?

"I don't really want to exploit anyone, *Señor* Cardenas. And maybe someday you can tell that to General Garcia." The two captives both hoped Frost meant that statement; maybe they wouldn't die back here in the past after all. "I've explained to Zed here how the Daviess time machine works, and how I can't just take things back and forth to our time at will. And I have to be careful about some other things I haven't even talked about yet."

Zed shook his head; more restrictions? Time travel was getting to be too damned complicated!

"But in our time, there aren't many places where you can find cheap labor. The old "offshore' locations—India, People's Taiwan, New Korea, Singapore, the Four Chinas—all priced themselves out of the market for labor-intensive products. The Arab Economic Union, in the last five years or so, has been running into the same problem. You start paying your *fellahin* their fifty cents an hour, and suddenly you're too expensive to build cheap electronics."

Like he's talking to a board of directors, now, Zed observed. *I can just imagine the charts projected on the wall.*

As if in answer to Zed's thoughts, Frost patted the table and charts did appear on the far wall. "Look here, you Mexican revolutionary," he was saying, "robots are still too expensive because the semimorph electronics can only be assembled by hand. To build an assembly robot capable of that level of intricacy—they'd cost millions each, and even *they* would have to be hand-built first." Frost argued persuasively, as if this small audience really mattered. *Do our opinions concern him?* Zed wondered, *Why would he even care?*

Frost went on. "If we can ever get this robot revolution off the ground, say get household robots down to a thousand or two dollars, get the industrial 'brain-arms' down to five or six thousand, then we'll see productivity shoot up all over the world. Even, Cardenas," At that, Hilario shot the youngster a look of pure rage, "even in the poorest villages of México and the rest of the Fourth World." Frost pointed to the color projection on the wall, where a one-wheeled robot tractor went about its business of plowing a large field, while a happy, well-fed Latin family looked on. "Wouldn't you rather see this everywhere,"—suddenly the picture dissolved into a shot of the empty ruins of Cancun. "Instead of this?"

Cardenas softened slightly, his mood less tense, but he said nothing.

"Yes, you soldier of the revolution, this model of robot tractor will receive beamed power directly from the Musk Orbitals and can plow fields for decades. Increase yields! Save the poor backs of the peasants! Damn it, you—you anarchist! What's wrong with using these primitive Indians to contribute something to our own world, or our own time?" Frost stomped over to the door, now shouting hysterically. "This place outside these doors, this ancient Yucatán, it's already dead and gone in our time! I can do *anyth*ing—anything at all — here, and it's of no consequence!" Frost was losing control, Zed saw.

Fortunately no gun was in sight; Zed hoped the guards.wouldn't come running in at the sound of Frost's yelling. "Do you understand, Cardenas, do you *really* understand?"

Balleen laughed evilly, drunkenly, suddenly an ominous presence. "You're right. Guys, you oughta listen to Mike here. Hell, I get to screw all the women I want—every day, and I don't have to take shit from anyone. I've nailed lots of 'em. I'm a god, too! You guys, you could be, too!"

Frost glared at his partner, grunting

disapproval. Balleen cringed a bit, but reasserted himself, the alcohol speaking for him. "Damn it, Mike, I just screw them. The Indians, that 'troped-up American bitch downstairs ..."

Frost pointed a threatening finger at Balleen, and the older man's voice wavered. "But I'm not as bad as you, Mike. With your little boys and the human sacrifices and ..."

Frost screamed and lunged at Balleen, slapping him viciously across the face. "Shut up you damned old fool! This is *my* city! *My* factory! *My* people! I *am* a god, and ..." Gaining control of himself, Frost shuddered, stepped back and looked at the shocked faces of his captives. With a different mood suddenly in effect, he said to Zed, "Sam's just a little upset. I have had to do a few unpleasant things to keep my god status here, but that's no concern of yours." He turned and glared at the shaken Balleen, who was wiping tears from his swollen eye.

Zed tried to recover from the astonishing outburst. *This guy is more complex than he appears to be —a real ayatollah,* he thought. *Alternately threatening and accommodating. Alternately a savior and a destroyer. Must be multiple personalities in that warped brain, a real schizoid. If I just had my wrister going now, my shrink friends in Dallas could psych him quick!*

Zed wasn't surprised at Frost's sexual preferences, nor even at the sacrifices. There was nothing one human couldn't do to another; the horrors from the old videos from the Beijing genocide trials had exceeded anything the human imagination had ever been able to dream up. The former PRC had had hundreds of millions of people to practice on, uninterrupted for nearly a hundred years...

A very unpleasant thread of thought wormed its way into Zed's mind: did Frost's absolute power alone subvert him? Had Frost always been so zane, or did time travel have some psychological side effects? He didn't want to pursue that elusive chain of reasoning, because it might mean that he himself had incurred some irreversible damage.

Cardenas broke his silence, pounding one fist into the other. "Very well, *Señor* Frost, let me return to General Garcia and I will present him with your offer." He eyed the American intently. "There *is* an offer, *Señor*?"

Frost returned to his chair, slumping there as if exhausted by his exertions. "Not yet, Cardenas. And by the way, don't try going back without me. My palmprint alone—my *living* palmprint—is required to operate the Daviess machine. No one else can do it. Except Steve himself, of course."

Turning his swivel chair until his back was toward his captives, Frost was quiet for several minutes. Finally he swung back to face them. "Like your General Filemón Garcia, I try to take advantage of opportunities that present themselves. I did not expect you, Dr. Wynter,"—he looked directly at Zed, sadness in his eyes—"to try to interfere with QuanTonics' operations. I simply dismissed you—too hastily, it turns out now—as a possible FBI or CIA agent, perhaps just an industrial spy. I would have tracked you a while, then had our national databases observe your actions. I had thought your usefulness to your supposed employers to be nil in a few weeks, and I would have forgotten you. I've done it with others, many times, in the course of QuanTonics business. It has been very effective, believe me." At Zed's shocked reaction, Frost commented, "No, nothing violent, Zed. Just destroy your credit, erase your investment accounts, allege your national security risks, that sort of thing."

Sure, Zed thought, *Just the sort of 'non-violence' that would ruin me financially, keep me in poverty. If that was his original intent, I can't imagine him letting me loose now. I wonder if murdering me before I was born is a capital offense.*

"But having you as a part of Garcia's revolutionaries is another matter. That makes you too dangerous, but maybe useful in another way." Frost spoke into his wrister, again in a Mayan command tone. Two large guards appeared, taking Zed by the arms.

"Cardenas, you will stay and talk before I return you to UpTime. But we will let Dr. Wynter remain here as our guest to ensure that General Garcia is reasonable when we negotiate. Back in our century I will meet with Garcia and discuss the security of my factories in Chihuahua, and my position in the future revolutionary government of México. I am certain that General Garcia would like the use of QuanTonics' new battle-rated warbots when his revolution spreads."

Cardenas frowned as Zed was hustled out of the room, but did not interfere. As Zed left, he could see the Mexican approaching Frost as if to discuss the offer in more detail. Zed didn't like the looks of that.

Frost smiled broadly as the door slammed shut.

En route to his dungeon cell, Zed tried to memorize the hallways leading to the robot room—the time chamber. He would escape back to his own time somehow. The guards evidently hadn't had a lot of practice escorting scheming prisoners, and Zed was able to plan a fairly good escape route from his cell to the elevators, and then to the time chamber. This time, he counted ten identical cell doors as his guards turned down the final hallway to his own cell. A light shone through one. There was a face peering through the bars—a woman! A white woman!

Zed stopped, shocked, staring back into pleading eyes. "Please!" she spouted in a choked voice. "Oh, please, get me out of here! Those monsters—!" The face withdrew, sobbing. The guards jerked Zed forward, but a sudden inspiration came. Zed moved his hand obscenely to his crotch, rubbing it suggestively, motioning to the woman's cell. He didn't know if the ploy would work, but hoped the primitive culture here understood such things. And after all, he *was* a guest of the god. His face lit up. "*Ma-ak,*" he whispered, and thumbed toward the door.

Confused, the guards mumbled among themselves. Finally they looked around the empty corridor, then smiled and opened the woman's cell door, allowing Zed to go in. The Mayans chattered a while, standing at the door, taking turns looking in to see if Zed would rape the woman immediately. But he only stood against one wall while the whimpering woman lay curled on her cot. In a few minutes, the guard, disinterested, left the two captives alone.

Zed stood staring at the pitiful woman before him. In the light of the dim LED bulb of her cell, he could make out her reddish hair. Without the bruises she could have been pretty, if not more: the ragged Mayan robe she wore could not hide her voluptuous figure. They would want to keep a looker like this. But why her, a modern American woman? They had millions of good-looking women to choose from in all of the centuries of the past. And why did they treat her so badly, in this rotten, poorly-furnished cell? She was as much a prisoner as any person could be—she couldn't go back to her own time, and the Barrier kept her close to the factory.

"Who are you, Ms. ...?" Zed began, carefully keeping to his side of the room. The woman turned, her tear-streaked face a mass of bruises, one eye nearly swollen shut. There was something desperate about that face, those wide eyes, evidence of—! Zed shut his mouth quickly, recalling Balleen's words about "a troped-up American bitch!" This woman was a 'trope addict? Down in a dark dungeon? A 'trope would do *anything*, anything at all, just for one minute of sunshine!

"Hello, whoever you are," the words were barely audible as she struggled to sit up. "I'm Marina Tanner, and—"

"*Tanner?*" Zed shouted, his voice echoing off the stone walls. "How did you—" He stumbled over to the one chair and sat, stunned. He was speechless.

"—did I get here?" the woman responded. "That weeko, Michael Frost, kidnapped me!" She took her face in both hands and sobbed. "The wacko brought me down here in this factory. Injected me with 'trope ..." Her voice wavered, gained resolution, recovered. "Made me a 'trope addict. The old weeko, that Sam, keeps me as a pet." Her eyes narrowed with remembered pain. Voice wavering, she said, whispering, "That Sam, he—he—rapes me every day. God, how I hate those two!"

Zed shook with confusion. "But you called me

—you tried to call me—weeks ago!" For the moment, his natural revulsion against 'tropes didn't seem important, though a part of his mind wanted him to get out of the cell, get away from her deadly disease.

Genuinely puzzled, she asked, "*I* tried to call you? Not me. I don't even know you. Who are you? I don't know any Mexicans."

"I'm not a Mexican," Zed replied quietly, "Just an Anglo with a nano-carotene treatment." He popped out the dark contact lenses, showing his vapor-blue eyes. "See," he smiled, "a gringo, just like you." The woman held out her arms pleadingly, so in need of comfort that Zed finally overcame the last vestige of 'trope revulsion and knelt before her, embracing her shaking body, accepting the warmth of her arms around him, her face on his shoulder. "My name is Zed Wynter," he said in a whisper. "I'm a metazine editor."

Releasing her hold, the woman reluctantly pushed him back to arm's length and wiped her eyes. Sadly, she said, "I'm sorry, but I've never heard of you."

Zed got up, breaking the embrace, nearly reeling from the repeated shocks to his system. "But, but—you left messages on my computer. You said it was urgent!"

"Mr. Wynter, I've been here for months, I think. But I never called you. I wish I could have." She rose, facing Zed, slight tremblers of muscles witnessing her urgent need for a fix of sunlight, something to take away the withdrawal pains, anything to return the artificial high that sunlight would generate in the nanotech machines in her bloodstream.

Zed accepted her statement on face value. Certainly she hadn't lured him down here, as his immediate suspicions had suggested. No, she didn't know him. Then who had made the calls? And why?

"Zed! Zed! *Gringo! Donde esta?*" Cardenas was yelling from the hallway. Zed ran to the barred window.

"Hilario! Here! This cell! With the light!" he shouted. Footsteps pounded in the hallway, stopping in front of the cell door. Something plumped to the floor like a heavy bag of grain. Cardenas was there, puffing, still bending over whatever he'd dropped. He was holding a flechette in one hand, a ring of large keys in the other.

"Zed! I'll get you out! But look out! Get back!" Shouts filled the corridor, followed by the clank of a spear. A flechette burped, and a gurgling scream drowned in its owner's throat. Zed grabbed Tanner and held her tightly against the wall, out of the way should anyone fire through the open window. When the door swung open, Zed was ready in his *keratsu* stance to take on anyone.

It was Cardenas, breathing hard. He looked at the woman. Without comment, he said to Zed, "*¡Vamanos, amigo!* Let's go!"

Zed held Tanner's wrist. Cardenas grunted, "Bring the *mujer*, too, if you want. But hurry!" Tanner nodded, wide-eyed and trembling. Zed hoped she could hold off the 'trope reaction until they got to the surface. But where would they go then? The Barrier.

"Where are we going, Hilario?"

"Back to the future, *gringo*," his friend laughed as he bent over to pick up a figure from the corridor floor. Cardenas hoisted Frost's limp form over his shoulder, pointing to the unconscious man's palm. "The magic hand; back to our own time!"

They stepped over two bloody Mayan guards who lay dying in the hallway, then left in a run. Pulling Tanner behind him, Zed did his best to keep up with Cardenas, who ran at an incredible pace, even with Frost's trussed-up bulk over his shoulder. "Hilario," Zed panted as Cardenas finally paused briefly to rest, surprised to see that they had arrived in front of the robot room. The time machine! "How did you do this? And where is Sam?"

Between breaths, Cardenas answered, "Frost was in a strange mood, Zed. I was going to be his emissary to Filemón, or so he thought." He spat, sneering at the thought. "As if I could be loyal to this pig. So he let me go with him alone while he was sending Sam off on a trip. I chopped the *pendejo's* neck and knocked him out, just after he pressed his hand to the magic plate. The door acted differently this time, but the glow and the noise were the same as before." He winked at Zed. "I think I might have screwed up Sam's trip. Too bad, but he is on the wrong side, and he is not a nice man when he is drunk. You saw him, *compadre*." Zed nodded; the Tanner woman was enough evidence of Sam's dark side.

Cardenas untied Frost's right hand and experimented with holding it out to activate the hall-side palm press. The young man was still unconscious.

A sudden clattering noise warned the escapees that other guards were on the way to rescue their god. Four Mayans slid around the corner while the

Mexican was dragging Frost through the opening doors into the time chamber.

Cardenas tossed Zed the flechette. Zed gently pushed Tanner into the safety of the room and turned to face the guards. He hesitated to cut down the innocent Mayans, but the first aluminum spear that clanged off the wall, inches from his shoulder, helped convince him. He aimed and fired.

For a moment, the world seemed to stop Time stopped. In extreme slow motion, the flechette kicked. The nearest guard's face peeled slowly away, an awful blooming red flower that opened to reveal splintering bone. The man didn't scream, either, because as he had no face, neither did he have a throat. He just stumbled and fell, gurgling.

The other guards stopped in horror as their comrade splattered to the floor, blood gushing in torrents from his ruined face and neck. Surely the battles of the gods were beyond their mortal control. Zed waved the pistol and squeezed off a flock of flechette rounds that disintegrated a golden mask hanging on the wall next to the guards. Theologically convinced, the three survivors threw down their spears and retreated past the corner. Zed was grateful he didn't have to kill more.

Hypnotized by the ever-growing pool of blood, Zed tossed the gun toward Cardenas, then threw up in the hallway.

Tanner, still dazed and confused, jerked loose from Zed and ran down the hallway, crying, pounding on the doors of the time chamber, finally disappearing around the corner, her cries echoing off the stone walls. Zed could have sworn he heard other chamber doors open, followed by the thrumming of the Daviess effect, but in his excited condition, he couldn't be sure. Recovering from his nausea, Zed started to go after her, but Cardenas shouted at him.

"Hey, Zed! Help me get this *cabrón* over to the control panel!" Zed did, grabbing Frost's ankles. Cardenas retrieved the flechette and then, before Zed could open his mouth to object that he had to go and retrieve Tanner, the Mexican put Frost's palm over the palmpress outline and pressed it hard.

The Daviess Effect plunged them all into the nauseating hysteria of a trip into a hostile Limbo, all the way to the near-Paradise at the other end of the journey.

Time travel ain't much fun, Zed felt. But this time, expecting the worst, he didn't scream at all. He wanted to. This time, the trip was just as disconcerting and nauseating as before, but knowing what to expect helped. Some.

Using the unconscious Frost's palm, Cardenas got the doors open again. The night watchman was still there, staring in shock at the suddenly-absent crates and wondering at the missing Balleen. Cardenas yelled something to him and he ran off quickly. In a minute he came back with a small box. There was a timer on it.

"Hilario, don't kill him!" Zed objected. "He didn't kill us when he had the chance."

"What do you suggest, *gringo*?" Cardenas said as he manipulated the timer control mechanism. "We don't have much time, and I will not let this ... this slaver leave the factory." He pulled the flechette from his belt. "Tell me now, Zed, or I will kill him. Your choice, the fletch or the bomb."

"Wait," Zed said quickly, thinking furiously. "I've got it!" He called the watchman over, described what he wanted, something he had left back in the engineering room where he and Cardenas had hidden, just minutes ago, as far as the watchman knew. It would only take a couple of minutes. The man nodded and ran to fetch. "Let me write a note to warn Frost when he wakes up."

"Why, Zed?" Cardenas shouted, "When he's dead he won't be able to read!" He had finished nano-bonding the bomb box to the chamber floor. It couldn't be removed, and once set, the timer could not be disarmed.

"Listen a damn minute." Zed told Cardenas his plan. Cardenas nodded as Zed talked. Soon, the night watchman ran in, puffing, carrying a sack of metal parts. Zed took one out to inspect it: one of the tarnished metal Romeo-14 nameplates he had brought from Filemón's ancient factory in Yucatán. Maybe they would do the job.

Hope this works, Zed prayed. *Ought to be interesting!* Slipping one nametag into his own pocket, and tying the sackful of remaining ones to the bomb, he asked Cardenas to give it fifteen minutes, enough to clear the factory back in ancient Chichén Itzá. No need to harm anyone there unnecessarily.

Zed slapped Frost awake, pressing the man's palm against the panel at the same time. "Read the note, asshole!" he shouted to Frost as he ran out the closing doors. "Read the note!"

Confused and hurt, Frost pulled his hand back from the panel, a dazed look on his face quickly turning to fear. He jumped for the handwritten note. Zed hoped the man had the sense to understand it in time.

Cardenas slapped him on the shoulder. "Fifteen minutes, Zed. Let's get the hell out of here!" The three men ran out of the factory, the Mexicans screaming in Spanish to warn the guards and bystanders away. The guards ran, too.

Fifteen minutes later, the factory exploded.

The blast—a white-hot fireball bursting like a nova in the center of the building—lifted the tin roof from the factory, spewing fire and flaming pieces of metal hundreds of feet into the night sky, falling like shrapnel over the city. Pedestrians ran for cover, dodging sizzling pieces of steel and robots that fell like fiery manna from a vicious god. Fires spread quickly throughout the rest of the factory building, and the remaining walls collapsed in on themselves, feeding the inferno within. The firemen and the *Federales* arrived within minutes, but too late to do anything but watch the conflagration.

Zed and his co-conspirators also watched thoughtfully as the reflections of flames reddened the smoke-filled sky. Between the campfire haze and the blazing factory, Chihuahua City would have one smoky night. The night watchman told them sadly that now that QuanTonics no longer had a factory in Chihuahua City, he would be out of a job. Cardenas replied that General Garcia would help the man and his family.

At least we didn't kill anybody else, Zed sighed with relief. The boy, Guillermo, had found Zed and Cardenas. A wry smile from an attractive, well-dressed young woman in the gathering crowd told Zed that the Garcista lady from last night could be counted among the living as well.

And at least I'm still alive, he thought, happily, as he made his way toward the beckoning woman. He wondered how fate had treated Michael Frost.

THE NEXT DAY ZED AND CARDENAS HAD BREAKFAST in Juárez. Both men were refreshed after a good night's sleep in the recently renovated Hotel *Camino Real.* Exhaustion had made Zed sleep, but now he was worried sick about Marina Tanner. Was she still stuck back in the past? Had Zed really heard another time chamber in operation right before he and Hilario left? Where would she go? *When* would she have gone? Something about the woman's appearance, her situation, her treatment back in ancient Chichén Itzá, intrigued Zed. And the intense curiosity about the calls she said she hadn't made.

Zed comforted himself that his "time bomb" couldn't have hurt Ms. Tanner, even if she were still in the factory. That little secret he'd kept from Cardenas: after all, the factory was still in existence today, in modern underground Yucatán. Hilario's bomb and Zed's enhancements had not destroyed it, or today it would show severe damage. But there was only that one room with the doors blown off.

Otherwise, Zed felt great. He was a little anxious that the time trips had placed some unnatural strains on his body; he had felt unusually passive the whole time back in the past. The night with Dolores, the Garcista woman, had found him extremely passive, in fact. But, he recalled with pleasure, sometimes passivity has its advantages.

"Maybe, Zed," Cardenas said between sips of his Bloody Mary, "the effects of the nano-carotene drug—you know, you were just becoming a lazy Mexican. And now you are becoming a gringo again—the Mexican just didn't take."

Zed didn't laugh; he still didn't know Cardenas

well enough to make ethnic jokes. *Even though we have traveled together as far as any two men ever did,* he thought. *As far as I know*, he corrected himself.

"But Zed, that was not a humane thing you did to *Señor* Frost. If I had shot him, he would never have known, being asleep," Cardenas said, munching a melon. "You gringos are just too cruel."

Zed laughed aloud. "Hilario, my way at least gave him a fighting chance. My note told him to get away from the factory in fifteen minutes, and to evacuate his workers, before the bomb blew. The bomb was firmly bonded, and I spooked him by saying there was a tamper detonator if he tried to disarm it."

"But it *did* have a tamper device, Zed," Cardenas said tersely.

"I didn't know that, but it sounded good. At least I warned him off, I hope. And that bag of nameplates you brought from Filemón—those Romeo-14s—I figured they would do the rest."

"That part I don't understand, Zed. When Filemón gave me those, he did not tell me the whole story. He only said they were from robots that were never built."

"That's true. I asked Frost that question back in Chichén Itzá, two days ago—a thousand years ago—and he told me that the Romeo-14s were delayed at least two more years. And they had not made the nameplates yet.

"Right then I suspected something and decided what to do if I ever had the chance. When I checked out the Barrier that Frost worried about, I realized that some other forces of TimeSpace must work to keep just one track of reality constant. If we ever ventured beyond a certain physical point, has some kind of nukepak power, long-lasting, thousands of years of operation at current measured energy expenditure rate ... a detection instrument of some kind, synchronized with the energy patterns emanating from those doors ... indeterminate, Sire. That means ... can't determine ... the significance of ... the energy variations." Brighton sounded impatient; impossible! Nothing could interfere with a wrister or with Brighton! Zed cleared his throat with a tugged command for the DI to keep trying to correlate this new data. I *wonder what the hell is going on with that thing.*

Marina was visibly anxious as Zed stood and tried to rock the cylinder. It didn't budge. It must have weighed at least five or six hundred pounds. "And this thing came out from those doors?" he asked again. Marina nodded, saying that she had heard lots of noises behind the doors, and finally pushed the palmpress to open them. "Uncle Steve's instructions said to press it only in an emergency, like if I was running from danger, or there was a war, something that bad. But those noises—"

"What kind of noises," Zed interrupted. "Human noises? Machines? What?"

"Low, rumbling, first, like an earthquake. Then a couple of screams, like people. Some animal sounds. I was afraid somebody was locked up in there, maybe even an animal, so I grabbed this rifle and came down and opened the doors." The remembered trauma was coming back, Zed saw, as if she were experiencing it all again. *Maybe she is? Stay on the job, Brighton! No more surprises, please. She still has a gun!*

Marina said shakily, "This cylinder was standing alone in the center of the room on the we would have to overcome a kind of time inertia, the inertial forces that keep TimeSpace together. Frost's theories—"

Cardenas shrugged; he hadn't understood Frost's theories at all.

"—were only one part of the properties of TimeSpace," Zed continued. "That's why I thought that sending back those nameplates with Frost might cause such a furor. It would take all of the power the QuanTonics plant could draw, and more, to fight Frost's repulsion forces and the other reality track forces. For a moment there, that factory was probably drawing down all of the power of the Northern Mexico fission grid, just to keep that time link open to the past.

"When the bomb when off at the other end—in the past—the unstable connection couldn't be kept up by any amount of power at this end. I'll bet that this end of the link, that robot room, was as hot as fusion reactor. Which just goes to show, you don't want to screw around with Father Time."

Cardenas looked puzzled. Zed smiled, "If ever anything could screw up a time machine, Hilario, it was those nameplates. They were the very essence of paradox. They were never made!"

Two days later, in the quiet safety and comfort of his Dallas office, Zed paused while speaking into his wrister, "That completes my report." Sighing, he welcomed the familiar roomy environment as a respite from his almost unbelievable 'adventures' of the last few weeks. "I don't know whether to hide this report, send copies to the FBI, CIA, and the Adolescent Scouts, or publish it as a science fiction novel," he continued, "Or maybe I should just produce a VR musical of it. Mike Frost's microlight flying scene at Chichén Itzá alone would make the show." The intercom interrupted his dictation.

Simultaneously with Doris' announcement, the two FBI goons, Grant and Farrar, made their entrance. Dramatically this time, Zed observed, what with thin reflective videoglasses, conservative dark red suits and chartreuse overcoats, each with a large vidpad in his right hand. Flechettes still bulged barely hidden over their hearts. Real holo stuff, tough cops! Agent Grant slammed down a filmy print copy of the *El Paso Herald Post Times Journal*. "See here, Wynter, you fool!"

Zed nodded at the headline: "Mystery Explosion Damages Chihuahua Economy," and underneath, "Top Executives Feared Dead in Blast." A sideline story declared: "Garcistas Suspected in Sabotage of Robot Factory. War Coming Closer?"

"What's this have to do with me, gentlemen?" Zed asked coldly. "Why do you have to barge in here unasked?"

Grant fumed. "We can't prove it, because you removed our bugs, but we know you were in Chihuahua City with Garcia's men. We know you're interested in warbot technology, and we think you're trying to help Garcia! That's illegal, if you didn't know. Mexico is a friendly government!"

Zed stood his ground. "Where I go and what I do is my business, and mine alone. I am not a spy for Filemón Garcia or anyone else. I did visit QuanTonics' factory in Juárez, and spent some time roaming my old stomping grounds in southern New Mexico." He knew that the FBI had TT sensors, and he'd been briefed by Mark Donne that telling a near-truth would screw up the TT calibrations. He wouldn't lie, he'd just skirt the whole truth. "As for warbots, I've never even seen one—not in Mexico or anywhere else." Zed was amused that he had found both the QuanTonics and the FBI bugs. He'd just thought Frost was using redundant sensors.

"I would like to think that we can make the U. S. a better place, gentlemen, but not by revolution, and not if you try to protect her from her own citizens." Standing, he jerked a thumb toward the door. "Go and round up some old Marxist mercenaries or something, but don't come to me unless I've done something!"

Muttering threats of future reprisals, the agents folded up their vidpads and left. Zed would have liked to tell them the whole story, but he didn't want any government, not even his own, to have the Daviess time travel technology.

At home, Brighton updated Zed's personal news—his parents worried because he hadn't called them in New Brunswick in a week, worried about rumors of his troubles with the FBI. A friend in Toronto, complaining about an FBI visit. Zed chuckled; he didn't think the Old Canadians would ever accept any police save the RCMP. And of course the Redcoats were restricted to their own diminished, divided country. For himself, Zed had traveled south to warmer parts of the USA after graduating high school in Saint John; he had no remnant patriotism for fractured Canada, and was happy that NB and Ontario had seceded during the last decade's political turmoils. Watching it all from warm New Mexico, especially in the depth of a harsh Canadian winter, had been rather interesting.

Brighton's other news was that his investment program was still paying off extremely well, thanks to his advance instructions to prevent any QuanTonics purchases before he'd left. He wondered if that would be considered an illegal stock tip. Brighton had accessed the various database keywords he had figured would be important. And there were several more calls from Marina Tanner, who never left a forwarding number, never a message.

Zed couldn't shake the memory of the vulnerable woman who had run desperately off into the tunnels in Frost's factory a thousand years ago—*over eleven hundred, actually*, he reminded himself. He wondered if he could ever find her ... it would take a time machine, and he wasn't ready for that experience again. Maybe she had come back to this same time, and would be trying to call? Maybe she came back *before* this time? Was trying to reach him now, even before he'd left to go meet her? It was a confusing thought, but maybe he'd be here when she called again. Disgusted that he hadn't thought of that before, he asked Brighton to put a trace on all incoming calls, starting immediately.

"Sire, I tried that strategy after you left nine days ago, having determined that you would wish that course of action. I have already traced the calls. They originate at—at—" Brighton's voice diminished to a hiss and fell silent. There'd never been a problem with the electronics before, and Zed was at a loss for what to do. He simply stared at Brighton's main panelscreen.

Without comment, Brighton's British accent

clipped the air and he continued on, oblivious to Zed's attempts to find out what had caused the lapse. "Sire, I have evaluated the history files on the sites you requested, at the times you specified. At Chichén Itzá in particular, and in the Mayan culture in general, there are repeated instances of myths concerning white gods in saffron robes, gods who brought technology to the primitive peoples. Some revisionist archaeologists feel these myths describe pre-Columbian visits by Chinese priests. Spurious amateurs credit gods from outer space." Brighton fairly oozed sarcasm, the sage/sagan portion of his DI programming showing through.

"Only one coincidental correlation may be of interest in the Tibetan area of research, Sire... Wait a moment! Priority call corning in, Satellite Service!"

"Let it through, Brighton," Zed said, looking over the hard copy of Brighton's research that continued to spew forth from the 'tex slot. It was Filemón Garcia! "Greetings, Jankee!" the slow scan image slowly mouthed words, far out of sync. "Thank you for your efforts. Too bad about your captivity, and too bad about the—the *machine*. It might have been useful to me. Our friend Hilario told me all about it."

The voice stopped and finally the image smiled. "But I do have a message for you from a—a mutual friend, a *Sr. Escarcha*."—Frost! Zed realized—"Hope you can see it, Zed."

Garcia faded to green and Zed saw the inside of the underground factory—today's version. The slow scan image went from room to room. There had been at least two transfer chambers, Zed now realized, and the one looked like it had been exploded from within, its doors bulging out and the surrounding walls badly cracked. Zed thought he knew what had caused that particular blast. But he wondered about the other chamber. *I'll be damned,* he thought, *what did they use* two *of them for?* Secretly, he hoped that Ms. Tanner had jumped into the other chamber and had come back to the *now.* But how would she have operated the thing? He recalled having heard what sounded like the other chamber. Or was it just wishful thinking on his part? He wanted badly to see her again, under better circumstances. Holding her close, altogether too briefly, had touched him deeply.

The camera stopped its panning and zoomed in on one wall opposite the destroyed 'robot room.' A carved message fairly shouted at Zed: "GO TO HELL, WYNTER. I'M NOT DEAD YET!"

"Señor Wynter," Garcia said a half-second before his lips moved, "A message from the grave? Who knows? Thanks again for solving the mystery, even if it hasn't yet helped save the Revolution. *¡Mil gracias, amigo, y vaya con Dios!"*

The carved message faded from the screen, but not from Zed's memory. He doubted if it ever would. *So Frost got away! But did he get back here? That other chamber? Surely not, or he would have stopped the enormous legal tangle now going on over control of his empire. Could he have lived on, up until this time? Built another time machine? Maybe he helped build this one? But what about Daviess?*

Abandon all logic, ye who enter a time machine!

Zed worried about that other chamber, and wished it were a wreck, too. But of course it hadn't been when he was there. Time travel itself was easier than inventing a language to describe it. He perused Brighton's hardcopy outputs. "Possible correlation 1: Ancient Chinese legends speak of underground cities run by advanced wizards." Zed didn't understand.

"Possible correlation 2: One of the most famous of these was named Shamballah."

Where was that QuanTonics facility in Tibet?

Zed laughed aloud, unable to stop. He remembered a scratchy antique vinyl disc his mother used to play, back when Zed was a small child, from her collection of original old-time rock and roll. About light shining in the halls of Shamballah? *Oh, no, could Hilario have sent Sam to ancient Tibet when he knocked out Frost?*

Sam-Ball-Een? Sham-Ball-Ah? What a laugh! Immortality for old Sam! He wondered what the old man was doing, since there had been no word on his existence since Pisté; Brighton would have uncovered it if Sam were still alive and in the present time. *Oh well, he was a weeko wacko rapist and anything bad that happened to him, he deserves!*

Zed stopped smiling when he read the last sentence. "Possible correlation 3: The ancient chant of Asian religions, a word whose origins are lost in the mist of time: *OM.* Correlates to the business of QuanTonics—O.E.M."

No effect on history? For that one travesty alone, Zed Wynter fervently wished Michael Frost were dead.

FUTURE, TENSE

The Mayan guard runs toward him, throwing an aluminum tipped spear at the American time-traveler who threatens the great god Ma-ak. Zed freezes*: time thickens, flowing slowly, viscous with fear. Infinitesimally, time-tick by slow time-tick, the razor-sharp spear approaches his face, transmuting into a feathered serpent, a rigid, deadly viper searching for Zed's own blood. Nearly paralyzed with fear, Zed painfully pulls a futuristic weapon from his belt and with grim determination aims at the serpent's own face. He pulls the trigger. The serpent only smiles and sails over his shoulder, disappearing into a shimmering blue stone wall studded with golden yellow butterflies. Zed turns to the Mayan. Strangely, the man's head is now a large tropical flower, its petals drawn up tight, a parody of a human skull. Then the flower begins to open...*

"No!" Zed screamed, awakening violently from his nightmare. That damned dream again! He got up from bed and went to the kitchen for coffee, now that another night's sleep was ruined. Zed was irritated that he was losing more sleep over the self-defense killing back in Chichén Itzá. The man was dead for eleven hundred years, would have been dead that long, even if Zed hadn't killed him. He hadn't suffered nearly as much over the first killing, offing that thug back in Juárez that long-ago night with Filemón.

Sipping the strong brew, he smelled the friendly, calming odor. There was something about death in the distant past that upset him greatly: a man from the future killing a primitive in the past. Zed analyzed why this was bothering him so much, and the answer finally came to him like the dawn that was breaking over the Manhattan skyline. *We are all helpless against assassins from the future,* he thought, *that was it! The real problem. This ultimate vulnerability, this absolute uncertainty, will be the painful gift of time travel technology. If time travel still exists in the future, then somewhere, somehow, every one of us living today is a potential target for some madman in all of the millions of years to come.*

This new fear was a lot like the fear of earthquakes—if the Earth itself, Mother Nature, can't be trusted, what can? Not even old Father Time. *Not anymore, that's for damned sure!*

The weeks following his return from Mexico had been pure hell for Zed, as he tried unsuccessfully to adjust to a daily routine work schedule after experiencing the incredible time travel passages to and from Chichén Itzá. Shaken emotionally and philosophically by the mind-warping experience, almost unable to fulfill his editorial and writing responsibilities, Zed finally granted himself a month's recuperative leave of absence from his duties—a sabbatical, he called it—hiring an online gig-editor to fill in, citing mental stress from the bombing attacks during his trip to see Filemón in the Yucatán war zone. His investment income would easily cover his earnings gap, and he knew that he was headed for a nervous breakdown unless he had time to sort out his emotions.

He was aware that he was growing more attracted to the mysterious Ms. Tanner—who had never called again, to his dismay. Zed realized that an emotional attachment to a drugged and sexually abused stranger was probably only some protective instinct coming into play, but his memory wiped away the bruises and the dirt, and removed that Mayan robe, exposing the beautiful body beneath. And there was more, much more, right on the tip of his mind that he couldn't quite grasp. Why didn't he dream of *her*, instead of that guard?

The experience of the time trips was shocking enough, but the awful realization that the nature of reality was infinitely more complex, more flexible, than he had ever thought possible—*that* was the most upsetting aspect of the whole adventure.

So profoundly affected by his crumbling paradigm, his own view of the universe, Zed found himself obsessed with finding not only the strange Ms. Marina Tanner, but the equally mysterious Dr. Stephen Daviess, the man who had started the whole thing. How did Daviess discover the theory, and how did he then go from theory to practical application of the technology?

Brighton accessed social media and commercial databases, but they only discussed some of the popular press speculations, back when Daviess had received the Nobel Prize for his Sidespace theory. Daviess had never really published his work on theories of time travel, had only referred to them in speeches. Zed called up videos of Daviess' talks, but they contained little information. Apparently the scientist had floated trial balloons, found no takers, and the entire subject was dropped by the scientific community with some sighs of relief. A Nobel laureate talking about time travel, indeed!

Having the distinct disadvantage of knowing that time travel was not only possible but practical, Zed wanted to locate Daviess, or at least access his private works. He was obsessed with finding out the extent of Frost's meddling in the past, to give some meaning to his own nerve-wracking experiences in ancient Yucatán. The killing of the guard haunted him excessively still. Pragmatically, apart from any guilt, Zed needed to find out if the weeko Michael Frost could still be a threat to him, hatching crazy schemes of vengeance in that wacko Machiavellian mind, trying to reach out from the past to harm him.

Only one man could help Zed in these important quests—Dr. Stephen Daviess, Nobel Laureate, late of Scotland, professor of physics at Stanford, mentor and partner of the megalomaniac, Michael Frost. Dr. Stephen Daviess, the inventor of time travel.

Zed was finally able to leave *Future Perfect* in the digital care of the new online editor and an able assistant, putting his other affairs in order, before starting the search for Daviess in earnest. Brighton's ongoing efforts were unsuccessful; Daviess had left no information available as to where he was physically located. He seemed to have covered all traces of his activities since winning the Nobel Prize five years before. With Zed's orders, Brighton handled the investigations by more penetrating searches, some of them bordering on illegal, a few on the proscribed UnderNets.

"Dr. Daviess' contact information has been quantum-crypto-sequestered; no public or easily accessible data exists." Brighton paused. "However, through certain algorithmic exercises, I was able to peel through a layer of shell companies, one of which revealed a property of his in a rural area east of San Francisco, near the Castro Valley." Zed frowned at the location, near the infamous Livermore location, but surely it was safe now, after ten years. Then he smiled, knowing that Brighton's findings were not public, that the DI had accessed encrypted data hidden somewhere in the WorldNet system, most likely through the UnderNets. Brighton could never provide him directly illegal data, but its programming allowed unlimited evasions. No restrictive Laws of Robotics for Zed's DI!

Zed knew there could be no way of telling how many under-the-table handshaking routines Brighton's Developing Intelligence persona had set up in its ever-expanding network of computer contacts around the world. In fact, Zed didn't want to know what kinds of DI incentives Brighton employed to obtain information for him. It was better for him not even to know the details. He laughed, thinking, *Corruption, like entropy, only increases!*

On the pretext of wanting to come for an interview about Dr. Daviess' Nobel accomplishments for his metazine, Zed had Brighton arrange a short appointment with an unnamed person who lived in Daviess' house. As usual, Brighton handled the whole affair, synthesizing Zed's voice over the antique audio-only telephone at that farmhouse, filling in Zed himself on the details later.

TWO MONTHS AFTER THE DESTRUCTION OF THE QuanTonics Chihuahua factory,Zed crouched on a brown hillside east of Oakland, California, scanning the house and estate of Dr. Stephen Daviess. *It sure as hell doesn't look like a time machine from here,* Zed concluded, slipping his video field-glasses back into a shirt pocket.

From his vantage point Zed studied the modest white farmhouse, tucked into a tiny valley in the peaceful California countryside and nestled beside a small clump of leafy oaks. From this distance it was a dollhouse in a toy-train landscape, now in afternoon shadow, smack in the middle of a private hundred acres of farmland and hills, in an isolated box canyon some miles south of the old Interstate route between Castro Valley and Livermore. That road now terminated just west of where Pleasanton had once been, and little traffic came that way anymore, the novelty of a fried wasteland having worn off years ago. Furthermore, the dirt road down the winding canyon path to Daviess' place was planted over, the sapling trees effectively blocking anything but hovercraft and motorbike traffic. Daviess had wanted isolation, and had achieved it.

To the east, Zed could make out the blackened hilltops of the Livermore Valley, and on the horizon, the strange colors of Lake Livermore itself. Daviess' farm, indeed the whole Bay Area, had been protected by those hills and mountains when Livermore happened. The blast had been clean, thank God, or northern California might no longer exist. Ten years now, and still no one had determined the origin of the mysterious microseconds that vaporized over a million people. Zed, like many others, thanked God or Whomever that the event hadn't happened during either Cold War, or there might have been a nuclear holocaust afterward. As it was, the event remained a sad and fearful reminder of what could have happened to the entire planet. Conspiracy theorists said flatly that the same mysterious fate that befell Third China's lunar colony had happened to Livermore, that some things were Not Meant To Be Known. Thinking over the similarities of the disasters and of his own recent experiences, Zed wasn't sure the tin-foilers were wrong.

Returning his thoughts to the problem at hand, Zed found it hard to believe that the cozy white-picket-fenced, starch-white clapboard house contained the world's first time machine. "That's it, Brighton," he whispered. "That's where Daviess built his first operating temporal device."

Himself answered, "Sire, datascan reveals that Dr. Daviess turned over operation of this farmlet to a niece just before his disappearance a year ago. She's the woman with whom you have the appointment later today. She refused to give her name."

Accessed on Zed's wrister, Brighton was in constant communication with the various commercial and DarkNet data services that saturated the Bay Area. *For a price, maybe even for free, any proprietary information can be had,* he chuckled softly. *Just like people!*

Movement on the far bald hill, up behind the farm, caught Zed's eye. There were people moving around over there, all in white uniforms or coveralls. Field glasses didn't help; the video images seemed to be wavering. Maybe he was viewing through heat waves? Making out the shapes of several small hovercraft and some tripod-mounted equipment, he concluded that he was seeing a surveying team. *Coming in on hovercraft is a bit easier than bringing in a lot of equipment on ultrabikes*, he thought. Even now, the Castro Valley region was sparsely populated; even though the environment away from the blast had basically renewed itself, the Valley never had never recovered economically. As a result, few people and even fewer roads marred the beauty of the hundreds of small hills and lowlands. A permanent scouring blackness, of course, marred the east side and probably would for hundreds of years to come.

Giving the survey team no more thought, Zed rose from his squatting position and dusted himself off, casually touching his earlobe to silence Brighton's whispered inputs. *I want to handle this interview myself, friend, and don't need your constant distractions.* He sat on the comfortable ultrabike seat, adjusting the handlebar controls until the solid state clutch expanded to tap the energy of the bike's flywheel. Silently the machine and rider accelerated down the hillside toward the small house and outbuildings that Brighton called a 'farmlet.'

Zed halted the ultrabike halfway down the hill. Before going down to find those answers he so desperately needed, he wanted to check the place again, close up and carefully. Both man and DI still distrusted the weeko-wacko genius, Frost. Accessing the wrister's capabilities, Brighton made quick sensor and visual surveillance around the perimeter of the property before approaching. Zed worried that Frost might be setting a trap. That zane Frost was capable of anything! Zed worried when Brighton detected Daviess using only encrypted video in his communications. "Steve's off visiting the Tibet site now," Frost had told him two months ago, DownTime, in Chichén Itzá. Zed hoped that Cardenas, when he'd sent Sam Balleen off to an unknown destination, hadn't brought harm to the scientist, too.

Brighton's scans detected only standard commercial security systems installed around the farmlet, plus a few anomalous microwave emissions. "The Daviess homestead property is registered under another name as an FCC experimental site," the DI said. Zed nodded, there was nothing unusual about that. Except maybe a time machine? He scanned the hill behind the farmhouse once more, hoping for a closer look at the nature of the survey crew working there. No one was there. *Odd that they've moved so quickly*, he mused, *but they're probably planning to put in another subdivision out here, and there* is *a lot of empty land to be mapped. Even if I'm wrong about that, I don't think Frost would be traveling with a crew.*

Zed smiled ironically at the thought of mundane housing projects here so close to the Livermore Event. As he directed the ultrabike toward the Daviess home, in his thoughts he marveled that any technology that could manipulate the once-considered-inviolate stream of Time. *But* I *should be surprised, a science fiction writer at that?* he wondered as the ultrabike whirred to a slowdown at the light touch of his brake. *Here I am with an internal communication system and a Developing Intelligence computer, Brighton, who might really be a sentient being, even though he's just a few files on a semimorphous crystal in my Dallas apartment, and some nano-circuitry in my body. Here I am on a semi-intelligent ultrabike that responds to my body movements and prevents me from suicidal behavior. Why should I be surprised at anything else the human mind can conceive?*

He finally stopped the ultrabike about fifty yards from the house, where the once-cared-for yard did not appear as neat as it had from a mile away on the hillside. As he got off the bike, a darkly attractive young woman appeared on the front steps, dressed in a long green morphsuit. She raised a combat laserifle, spotting its red warning dot pattern over his heart.

Zed recognized her—it was Marina Tanner, the woman from Frost's dungeon in ancient Chichén Itzá.

Zed stood, nearly paralyzed with confusion. The woman was acting very strange; did she recognize him? She was not smiling, but Zed was, nervously, holding his hands up, palms forward, in an assuaging gesture.

"Hi, Ms. Tanner," he shouted across the yard, breaking the awkward silence, "I'm Zed Wynter. I believe we ... we met two months ago?"

Silence. The laser spot pattern didn't move a millimeter. The woman was a cool operator!

Getting no response, Zed offered more information: "I'm the metazine editor who called for the interview—about Dr. Daviess' work. Don't you remember?"

The laser dot pattern didn't waver, but the voice of its user did, ever so slightly. "You—you know about Uncle Steve? You had an appointment?" The woman walked steadily closer, until Zed could see the same brilliant emerald green of her eyes—the same color that had attracted him so much that last night in ancient Chichén Itzá. But why didn't she remember? She was treating him like a total stranger.

Could the 'trope effects have wiped that memory? Maybe the treatment at the hands of QuanTonics' two goons had traumatized her, until she psychologically repressed the whole episode? The laser aiming dots stayed over his heart, rock-solid. Zed decided he'd better play her game, whatever it was, until she pointed that thing away from him.

Her rifle was a Donne Special, and Zed smiled at a private joke. His friend Mark had produced that eponymous weapon—very expensive, limited edition, sold only to very few, very private, citizens. At this close distance, he saw a new version of Marina Tanner, one much improved over the bruised, drugged woman he had helped escape from Frost a thousand years in the past: Her long, smooth hair was a deep, smoldering red, reminding him of dim coals. A smudged green morph suit continually flowed, accentuating her figure. Zed smiled; that was much nicer than her ragged Mayan robes at Chichén Itzá.

Marina stopped about ten feet from Zed, keeping the dots stationary over their threatened target. The rifle had to be computer-aimed, Zed concluded. No one was that steady. "Uncle Steve didn't say he told anyone about our deal," she said flatly, her tone frosty. The laser dots began to smolder Zed's shirt as Tanner squeezed the trigger, increasing the beam's power. Suspicion drew her features together until she didn't look quite so attractive. "You a narcop?"

Zed stepped back and wiped at the hot spot on his chest. "Hey, lady, easy with that beamer!

I'm just an editor, a writer. Not a narcop, not any kind of cop. Just work for a metazine, *Future Perfect*. I'm a friend." Gesturing at his belt-free, weaponless state, he said, "And I don't have anything to return the heat. Will you just turn that thing off?"

Tanner smiled and eased off the trigger, the dots fading away as she lowered the barrel. "If you know Uncle Steve, do you know that weeko-wacko zane, Mike Frost?"

Zed's reaction told her he did know the maniac, but before she could raise the laser again, he spat out, "I met the guy before, a few months ago, down in Mexico. At one of his factories." He waited for some glimmer of recognition, but none showed in her beautiful eyes. *Yeah, lady, we both knew him, a thousand years ago. Why don't you remember? I wish I could forget it!*

Tanner visibly relaxed. "Then thank God you're here. Frost came by last month, demanding to see Uncle Steve, yelling all kinds of crazy things about—the past, the future, I don't know what all. He almost scared me to death with his ranting and raving and threats. He even tried to attack me, but I had my gun and shot at him and he just dis—" She stopped, changing her mind about something, then nodded. Zed could sense she was struggling with the fear. Was it the addiction, or Frost, or something else?

"And those other two, the ones in black, who tried to break in last week—" she couldn't finish; tears welled up and her lower lip curled most attractively. She took a deep breath and continued, "Uncle Steve let me stay here a year ago, part of an agreement we had—"

What Marina had just said slammed into Zed

consciousness: *Frost was here, last month? How the hell—?*

Shivering cold snakes raced up and down his spine, knotting at the tailbone. Frost!

"Frost?" he blurted out, "Here? How?" Marina's shocked expression brought him back to her plight. "Er, exactly *when* did he come? And what other people were trying to break in? Did you call the police?" He kicked himself mentally at that slip; 'tropes never called the cops, and for good reason.

Her emerald eyes met Zed's and she blinked, not answering any of his staccato questions. "I'm Marina Tanner, as you apparently know," she smiled. But she didn't shake Zed's outstretched hand, keeping both of hers on the rifle. The end of the rifle motioned him to follow her into the house. "Come on in and I'll tell you. You won't believe what's been happening."

Casually tugging at his left earlobe, Zed prompted Brighton for inputs as he looked around inside the modestly-furnished *faux*-Spanish interior, its cowhide furniture, *serape* rugs, and all. "Sire, the security system is advanced but could be overcome by professionals, so far as my sensors can determine. Infrared motion detectors, small crawl-bots at the perimeter, emergency door and window closures. No electromagnetic weapons, Sire," his computer whispered. "Just anomalous magnetic fields emanating from below us. High-frequency—gigaHertz range."

Zed nodded and Brighton quieted. "*What's* been happening that I wouldn't believe, Ms. Tanner ... Marina?"

Marina shook her head, as if acknowledging that Zed wouldn't believe her story. "Just sit over there," she motioned toward a well-worn brown and white cowhide sofa, "and I'll fix us a drink. Scotch okay?" Keeping the rifle in hand, she left the room. Nodding, Zed sat and turned his attention to the various archaeological pieces about the room. A full sized *Chac Mool*—the Mayan rain god, he recalled—reclined in divine arrogance in the center of the room, dwarfing the modest fireplace opening a few feet beyond. Small scale copies of the gigantic "Aztec Calendar" framed a ceramic piece Zed couldn't make out. An ancient polychrome vase in Mayan style? Rather advanced for Mayans, he couldn't place it. And the burning incense, its smoky emissions somehow reminding him of the jungles in Yucatán.

Marina returned with the drinks, serving him a large glass of Scotch and ice—no water, his preference—then sat, sipping a large frothy margarita for herself. The rifle was not in sight, to Zed's relief. "So tell me, Mr. Wynter, just exactly how *did* you meet my Uncle Steve and that wacko Frost? And what *really* brings you to this nowhere place?"

Zed smiled and repeated his interview request, adding only enough details to pique her interest. Finally, admitting that he'd interviewed Michael Frost at the QuanTonics factory in Juárez two months ago raised Marina's interest and her eyebrows. "Before the blast in their Chihuahua City plant, of course," he said defensively, in case she may have suspected him. No way could he be traced to that, not even by the FBI.

"I read that Frost had been killed there, but apparently not, if you say he was here last month?"

Marina shook her head, shuddering at the mere mention of that visit. Zed hoped the maniac's appearance meant something else, maybe a visit out of the past *before* the Chihuahua explosion. He'd have to think about that one: the intricacies and twistiness of time travel could be complex beyond belief. "Anyway," he continued, "during the interviews, Frost said that Dr. Daviess had built a prototype temporal transfer device in the basement of his home." He sipped the cool Scotch and watched Marina tense, reacting to that statement. "I wanted to come talk to him—or you—about his invention. Time travel."

The young woman smiled at him, and Zed could swear that she was warming up to him quickly, almost desperately, as if she were fighting to keep control. The 'trope reaction? Marina gulped the rest of her drink and went to the kitchen, returning with the laserifle. "Come downstairs, I'll show you."

They squeezed down a narrow stairwell between the small kitchen to the left and the living room to the right. Zed followed cautiously, hoping her undefended back was a declaration of trust in this newly-met stranger. But she still had one hand firmly on the Donne.

Careful not to make any sudden moves, Zed edged down unpainted wooden stairs into a dimly-lit and musty-smelling concrete block-walled basement. Where he could see through the mounds of clutter, he estimated the room to be about thirty by sixty feet, slightly larger than the house above it. Bare fluorescent fixtures illuminated a sci-tech's lifetime collection of junk—electronic, pneumatic, hydraulic, some unidentifiable—junk that defined a main path from the stairwell to a set of massive steel doors at the far end of the basement. Those doors! Though smaller, they were just like the ones on the time chambers at Chihuahua City and Chichén Itzá. He had found the original Daviess machine!

Barely able to control his excitement, Zed followed the woman to the doors and touched them. They were vibrating slightly, growing cold, then warm, then vibrating again. "You uncle built other sets of these doors, down in México. I saw them operate."

Marina wasn't surprised. "Then tell me, Mr. Wynter, what goes on behind them?" She was chewing her bottom lip, acting disturbed. "Uncle Steve left recorded instructions for me, saying not to open them unless he or some other authorized person were here. But I just had to, once, when there was a lot of noise inside. I was afraid not to."

"What happened? Who was it in there?"

She hesitated, eyeing Zed suspiciously. "That's the problem. It wasn't a *who*, it was a *what*!"

"That's it over there. I don't know what it is, or how it got here." Zed walked over and inspected the device: a tapered, cone-shaped cylinder of highly-polished metal, about three feet high, half that in diameter at its base, six inches across its hemispherical top. Featureless.

Like the doors—in fact, in rhythm with the doors—the tapered object warmed, vibrated, cooled, repeating the same cycle. Kneeling beside the object, he looked up at Marina. "This came through those doors?" Her confused expression prompted him to change the question. "I meant, did this cylinder arrive in that room? *Behind* those doors?" As he stroked the almost erotic smoothness, tried to lift it—*heavy, immovable!*—when suddenly Brighton was all mouth.

"Sire," the bone-conducted whisper came, "it

other side of those doors, and I went in to bring it out. I could tell it didn't belong there."

"You brought it out by yourself?" Zed asked incredulously. "I couldn't even budge it just then." He was growing suspicious of the story.

She noticed Zed's suspicious reaction. "Yes, I did. Alone. At first, it was very light, so I rolled it on its lower edge and it came right out. But then when I turned around, the doors began to close by themselves. The strangest thing, then—just for a moment I thought I saw some figures, but they vanished, faded into nothingness, kind of like those amusement park holographic ghosts. One resembled Uncle Steve," she shivered, "and another one looked like Frost. He just kept appearing and disappearing, like a piece of flatfilm stuck in one of those old time movie projectors. It was really weird."

Marina talked faster and faster, letting the memory flow through unimpeded. Zed was worried about the laser, the way she kept swinging it left and right, as if searching for a target. "And I saw three or four other blurred figures before they faded and the doors closed again. One of them looked like ... you? But darker-skinned." She peered closer at Zed's face, perhaps seeing it for the first time. Zed worried that maybe the 'trope was diminishing or kicking in. "Were you in … that room?"

Zed shook his head. "When did all of this happen?" He had figured out the answer while asking the question.

"Two months ago, the same night the QuanTonics factory blew up in Chihuahua." Her eyes narrowed, becoming steely as she backed away and raised the laser once more at his chest.

"It *was* you in there with those others, wasn't it? I knew, somewhere, I'd seen you before. But you weren't blonde then."

Zed tried to assess the situation. Marina might be unstable, he thought, and this could be difficult to explain. He started to nod. "Marina, Ms. Tanner, you and I did meet before, in an underground factory in Yucatán. Back then I *did* look like a Mexican. And I *was* in Chihuahua City when the factory exploded."

Tears streaked Marina's face, and Zed saw the unmistakable wide-eyed stare of the fully-addicted 'trope. He had to play this out right, or die on the spot. The spot was hot over his heart, getting hotter. It singed Zed's much-abused shirt and began to burn, like a hot match tip touching his chest. He jumped back, yelling, "Hold it, that hurts!"

Marina was shaking, losing control. She shouted, "What the hell is going on? Are you with Frost? I'm so tired of being scared, being attacked, being ... hurt." As if a repressed trauma was taking its place on the stage of her memory and she were watching it, Marina became calmer, eyes looking beyond Zed, into the past. "Were you there ... in that *dungeon?* With Frost ... and that sickening Sam Balleen?"

Zed nodded. "Yes, I was there. I hoped you'd remember, I was the one—-"

"Oh god, you were one of *them!*" she screamed, and pulled the trigger full back. In that instant, Zed saw Death flash its red spear from the end of the barrel.

His shirt puffed brightly, sudden pain causing his knees to buckle. As Zed fell, his body twisted sharply to the right, and the laser burned a deepening swathe up over his left shoulder. The Universe was on fire and pain enveloped him.

Desperate to live, Zed rolled over, regaining some remnant of consciousness, and crawled to find shelter behind stacked crates. "Marina! I saved you! Don't shoot anymore!" God, the pain was beginning to take over!

"Brighton!" Zed screamed. Darkness swept him away.

Awareness of pain, stripes of vertical pain, rods of hot discomfort against tortured skin; then: ease and peace. Sleep. Zed awoke to Brighton's insistent voice. "Sire, wake up! It is most urgent!" There were night birds calling nearby, pleasant sounds. Zed painfully shook off the wispy remnants of disturbing dreams. Outside the bedroom window, a cool dark sky and bright stars beckoned his weary eyes. A hyperjet's bright sparkling contrail stabbed toward the sky, downward toward the Bay Port landing complex. Zed's shoulder throbbed, but—strangely enough—the pain was hardly noticeable. "Sire," Brighton murmured, sensing Zed's more nearly conscious state, "It's good to have you back after your hours of mending. But you must join Ms. Tanner as soon as possible."

Zed glanced around quickly, memories flooding his mind. "Brighton," he said aloud, "Where *is* that crazy woman? Can I get ... up?" Stabbing pains answered that question, but Brighton insisted on sounding positively cheerful. Had Zed really programmed so much into that machine, or were some of Donne's more advanced Developing Intelligence matrices taking hold? Damned if Brighton's presence wasn't almost like having another head!

"Sire, Ms. Tanner regained her composure in

time to treat your burn effectively. Her nano-medicine ministrations prevented permanent injury from your wound. And luckily, in her distraught state, she had not flicked on the laserifle's control to maximum." Zed felt the pain ebb as Brighton demonstrated his convenient neural controls. "Of course, our own onboard nano-dispensers helped speed the healing even faster, more than she suspects. There, I have attenuated pain inputs from the left shoulder, and your sensation of discomfort should decrease accordingly." Zed nodded as the pain diminished and disappeared. "But don't put stress on the wound; the pain was there to tell your nervous system that the damage is not yet totally repaired. I'm working on those repairs. But you must arise as soon as possible."

"Thanks, Brighton, old chap." Unhurried by the computer's sense of urgency, Zed lay back, thankful to be alive and relatively well. He'd been lucky to have had this symbiotic computer installed before this trip. Upon his return to present-day Mexico, knowing he would probably be facing a possibly insane Frost, as well as the hazards of Filemon's war, and the lesser but important challenge of industrial espionage, Zed had wanted access to the latest nano-instrumentation and any other enhancements available. He knew of only one place to purchase such equipment—The Weapon Shops of Donne.

Ensuring that he was not being tracked by the FBI or anyone else, he had visited Donne's secluded shop in a nondescript section of Old Dallas, where his longtime friend ran a small and surreptitious nano-fabber operation that produced barely-legal equipment: ultra-tech weapons, microtech surveillance and anti-surveillance devices, and other advanced tech gadgets that showed up in no catalogs anywhere; Donne's clients were strictly word of mouth.

Zed knew that Mark intended that his innovative products would help ordinary citizens subvert the ever-increasing reach of intrusive governments, criminal organizations, and amoral tech conglomerates. His systems, once characterized by an envious competitor as "revolutions at the speed of bytes," had figured prominently in the liberation of a few now-defunct dictatorships and in the prevention of several more.

"The best thing going for a revolutionary," Mark Donne had said as Zed listened intently, "is our new BTSOTA system: 'Beyond The State Of The Art.' (Donne pronounced his technology *bit-sot-a.)* "Integrates your wrister's picomp system and your body's nervous system via our proprietary nano-structured inductive pickups, the i-tats." Donne's wrister projected a 3D image onto a nearby flatscreen.

"These are molecule-sized machines that can rewire muscles, brain cells, any cells at all, by computer direction, in microseconds. BTSOTA decreases your reaction time; you can even carry linked-in on-board nano-weapons, and on-board sensor systems, if you want." Donne smiled, his grey-speckled moustache bouncing in rhythm to his clipped British accent. "Would have done you some good, back there in old Chichén Itzá, eh?"

Zed nodded thanks for his friend's acknowledgement of the fantastic time travel story, happy to exorcise some of the remnant trauma of the killing back there. Just telling someone else, sharing the knowledge, ease Zed's guilt immeasurably. "Beyond the state of the art, Mark? That means 'still experimental,' right?" Zed walked over to Donne's wet bar, poured a Scotch over ice, and studied his English friend.

An expatriate some twenty years now, having grown weary of the Continent's recurring spillover conflicts into a splintered UK after the E.U. dissolved, Donne had only recently taken American citizenship. At this moment, the Britisher was promoting the latest in a series of highly-successful technical business ventures; his Weapons Shop was only a surreptitious sideline. Donne's namesakes in the world's ever-present shadow wars threatened to replace Kalashnikov as the patron saint of inexpensive but effective personal weaponry. "Master of Lasers, Lord of Light," Zed called him.

Donne grimaced, comically. "All right, Zed, so my BTSOTA stuff is still experimental, but I'm way past lab models. The one I'm offering to install for you is ready for field trial. Try it, it's free. What can you lose? We'll even use your old buddy Brighton as the interface persona, if you wish. He'll keep you company. I'd like to see you have the system. You're into a dangerous business now, traipsing back and forth in time, and in war zones on top of that."

Donne poured his own drink—straight water. Health problems, he said. "And it's masterfully simple, of course. Hell, I'll show you mine!" Donne said, stripping his dress shirt from a broad chest, revealing rippling muscles—and a matrix of strange tattoos. "These are the babies, brother," he boasted, tracing out the fine blue and red lines that marked a five-inch square in the center of his chest. "Control circuitry-picoelectronics, molecular-sized mechanical nanostructures for musculature enhancement, microhydraulics for various other purposes. Everything—" he paused, smiling broadly.

"—but the kitchen synch!" Zed laughed. An old private joke about a business failure of theirs, in an unsuccessful "Home of the Future" exhibit. "With your body building routine, Mark, I'm surprised you wouldn't have room for one of those, too!" Zed sipped his drink and walked around his friend, closely inspecting tiny mole-like attachments, which, other than the "tattoos", were the only evidence of the integrator system Donne was wearing? Wearing? *'Symbioting'* was closer—living in symbiosis with an ultratech computer!

"Symbiotronics," he murmured, as Donne gave him a puzzled look. "That's it, Mark—'Symbiotronics—Living With Electronic Life and Liking It.' Great name for a new metazine, isn't it?" He laughed, but Donne considered Zed's proposal.

"I do rather like the name, chum," Donne said. "Mind if I use it for my new line of onboards?"

"Sure, but don't forget the royalties—old chum."

Donne's technical partner and wife, Jenn, had performed the actual installation at one of the respectable and aboveboard Donne Laboratories over in Fort Worth. *Quite simple, really,* Zed thought as he watched the robot arm assembly trace weird patterns on his chest. Sterile nanobundles were stitch-bonded to the lower surface of the epidermis of Zed's chest skin, with terminations at small dark terminals protruding mere millimeters. *A half-dozen extra tits*, he mused, *but more useful than my real ones!*

"Try it now, Zed," Jenn announced, "Brighton ought to be up and on-line. Symbiotronics' latest masterpiece!" For an instant, Zed wondered if Jenn had her own on-board system in an exposed place, but recalled Mark telling him that the female anatomy was much better suited for nano-enhancement. The circuitry didn't have to show.

Just as well, Zed thought. *Be a shame to stitchbond that attractive chest.* "Brighton!" he snapped.

"Not so loud, Sire. No need to shout," came the whispered reply in both ears. "Try to subvocalize."

"*Hwzss, Bghtnnn,*" the sound croaked in Zed's throat. Both Donnes smiled at Zed's first lesson in re-learning to talk.

"I can read you very well, Sire. Please continue to practice. And, Sire, the access architecture tells me that we now possess many nonverbal means of communication. Please pay attention as I demonstrate." Zed sighed, nodding at his teacher's relentless pace. The session lasted for the rest of the day.

That night, back in the Donnes' luxury condopark, Zed asked about the parameters of Brighton's personality enhancements. "Simple enough, Zed. Brighton's physical location, for the most part, is still in your apartment over in Dallas, in your secure Faraday vault. Your on-board system, Brighton, Jr., accesses the old boy Himself, the mainframe, via the WorldNet, and they continually update each other." He shrugged, "Jr. is on your chest and integrated with your nervous system, while Sr. stays back here in Texas. As long as they are in fairly continuous communication, they're the same machine, the same memory, the same 'personality,' if you will. If they lose contact for any length of time, they will update each other at the next contact, until both systems are in equilibrium once more." Donne smiled and sipped his imported spring water. "The *auld lang syne* protocol, so to speak."

"As for your question," the other Donne said, "we've installed new DI matrices compatible with Senior's software. You're going to get a lot smarter and it won't hurt a bit!" She laughed with the two men.

Zed didn't feel any smarter, but at least Jenn was right about one thing—it didn't hurt, not one bit.

RECUPERATING IN THE BED AT THE DAVIESS farmlet, Zed thanked himself again for submitting to the Donnes' experimental field trial. Although he had allowed himself to be enhanced because of potential troubles with Frost or some other time-traveling weeko, he certainly had not expected the system's first test to come from a beautiful woman with a laserifle. Brighton's quick reaction to Marina's threat had saved Zed from at least a crippling wound, if not his life.

Pain control was one aspect of his new enhancements that Mark hadn't mentioned. The earlobe control system that Zed admired was the least of Brighton's array of talents.

Brighton started to say something, with urgency in his voice, but Zed ear-tugged him into silence as the bedroom door creaked open. Marina's shapely posterior, accentuated by tight micro-shorts, came into view first. She was backing into the room, carrying food on a tray.

"Mr. Wynter," she began, spreading out the bed tray legs for Zed's use, "I'm terribly sorry for the way I treated you, but I have been so frightened for the last year, and I was afraid of you. The prowlers, Frost's weeko attack, then remembering seeing you ... in that chamber, or somewhere ... I just couldn't stand the stress." She brightened up a bit as Zed smiled and thanked her for the appealing snack of link sausage, toast, a fruit tray, and coffee. A vidpad lay to the right of the tray, its flashing news menus awaiting his touch for more detailed displays.

"I seem to be mending properly, Ms. Tanner. You mostly just scared me," he lied. "But I don't like being shot, as I'm sure you can understand." He munched on toast and swallowed coffee as she sat lounging in a morpho chair next to the bed, on his left. She was lovely, he decided, especially when she wasn't lugging that Donne around. Zed's left shoulder twitched, a sharp reminder that the lady definitely had some rough edges to her personality. *Don't let yourself get in too deep, old man*, he said to himself. *She's pretty, but nasty*.

"I guess I owe you some kind of explanation, Zed," she said, standing and stretching. Zed wished she wouldn't do that; too distracting. He looked down at his food and tried not to think of sex. But Marina plumped herself down on the edge of the bed, absently-mindedly stroking his covered legs. "I've been here, nearly alone, for over a year. Hiding, Zed." Between the touching and the nearness of her, Zed wasn't thinking clearly, and she sensed it. "I'm a 'trope, Zed."

Zed started at the news, even though she'd told him about her addiction back in ancient Chichén Itzá. Somehow, in the beautiful California setting, in the modern twenty-first century, the words from that beautiful mouth were more menacing than when first spoken, over a thousand years ago, in a dungeon under ancient Mexico.

'Tropes were the last legacy of some unknown bacteriological nanotechnology lab in Cuba. There, some comrade had made a bold move to suppress various rebel Latino armies by combining the addictive qualities of heroin with a phototropic melanin nano-organism. The nanoes reacted to ultraviolet light to reproduce, spewing their waste products into the bloodstream—a heroin-like alkaloid. It was the ideal combat drug: highly addictive, its primary effect was requiring its users to seek out sunlight in ever increasing dosages, to maintain their heroin high.

By making it physiologically impossible for addicts to remain hidden in the shade of trees and bushes, the drugbug made its hosts easy targets for conventional forces, particularly armed drones and aircraft. There was no cure—the nanoes had been carefully designed to reproduce themselves and to withstand modification. At the very least, the addicts would die slowly of sun poisoning or skin cancer. At the best, they died quickly in the daylight as drones sought out and lasered them. Tens of thousands of 'tropes had died in various Latin American and African wars, and probably an equal number died in the Cuban cities where they originated.

Infected troops returning to most countries were simply shot and burned, sometimes not even shot first. In the United States, 'troped citizens were strictly quarantined and sequestered on the Alaskan island of Kiska, pending a cure or other disposition of the disease. Zed couldn't remember

The scientist nodded with interest. "Why not just try it right now, Zed? I've been formulating a theory here, based on what you've been telling me about your experiences with the repulsion effect, but I need to test it." He waved Zed on. "I think it'll be safe."

"Wynter residence," Brighton answered, "Priority code, please?" Zed recognized Brighton, Sr.'s Etonian tones. "No code? Then, may I be of assistance, please?" Zed gulped.

"Brii—" his voice choked. "Brii—" His vision fading, his thoughts in disarray, Zed turned pleading eyes toward Marina and Daviess, held out his hands and fainted dead away on the floor.

THE VOICE WAS A MILLION MILES AWAY, AT LEAST, maybe even light years. "As I might have expected, Marina," the voice was saying, "what Zed called Frost's Law seems to operate for information transfer as well." *Definitely a real voice*, Zed decided, rising from a drowsy stupor. *I'm definitely alive!* "What I don't completely understand is the physical mechanism that affects the prohibition." Zed recognized the *tap-tap-tapp*ing as Daviess filled his pipe, followed by the acrid sulphur smell of the automatch in the pipe bowl, and the bittersweet odor of protohash. The Scotsman was relaxing with a harmless intoxicant.

Rousing himself at last, Zed rolled his legs off the couch and onto the floor. "Damned if that wasn't just like the physical barrier that Frost and I encountered in Chichén Itzá," he croaked with a dry voice. Marina commented worriedly on his bloodshot eyes and ashen complexion. Noticing if they numbered fifty thousand or a hundred thousand. A lot of tourists and State Department people had got caught up in the various turmoil around the globe in the late 30's and early 40's. Like the early victims in the AIDS plague, those who died before the annual vaccines were developed, 'tropes were just an unfortunate minority, best forgotten.

Until *now!* Zed scratched his earlobe and Brighton responded to the conversation in process. "Sire, *Tropaya Malenkaya*$_2$ or 'trope, is not contagious. The only identified vector is bloodstream injection. The bug does not live in any medium save human blood itself. This observation gives credence that the nanoes were designed as a combat drug. Its designers were very careful that it not spread, except by deliberate use. Of course, as with heroin, cocaine, *druzhba,* and other addictive drugs, the initial euphoria reported by forcefully-injected addicts is usually sufficient to induce others to experiment with it themselves." Brighton's voice sobered, reminding Zed more and more of himself, the way he would have made the same presentation. *I guess my DI does learn.*

"For all its tragic results, the nanobug did not noticeably alter the outcome of any wars." Zed was nodding, glad that such drugs weren't being used in Filemón's Yucatán war. Yet.

"Symptoms of 'trope addiction include irrational behavior when UV light is withheld, as well as periods of euphoria immediately after prolonged exposure," Brighton added. Zed thought about that one, as Marina's caresses took on a more urgent and extremely personal bearing. "The nighttime despair of the victims, their violent and overwhelming physical need for a UV fix, along with the ignorance of transmissibility parameters, account for the hysterical reaction, and the forced isolation of the unfortunates on Kiska today." Thinking of Marina's swings of mood, Zed shuddered. It was no wonder she didn't remember the whole Chichén Itzá episode; he was surprised she had kept any remnant of sanity at all.

Marina said, "I knew Uncle Steve had this little place out here in nowhere, and I called him just a day before he was leaving and he said to come on out and stay. I don't know if he knew about the 'trope, but that's not a problem right now, is it?" Her stroking became more calculated, insistent. To Zed, Marina was eroticism personified, and he was aroused enough to die.

Feeling his readiness, Marina took the snack track and carefully set in on the floor. God, but she smelled great! "I had to hide out during that last sweep for 'tropes last year, but I don't feel guilty, you know. It can't be spread except blood to blood," her voice dropped to a whisper, "and I promise not to bite." Her shirt and shorts were off in ten seconds, revealing a beautiful and tanned body, just perfection. "I never hurt anyone, dear, dear Zed, and I use a little UV tanning booth every morning, get my fix, then do my work."

"Er, what work do you do?" Zed said, gulping at the incredible view.

Marina stood next to the bed, facing Zed in all her nude beauty, a comically hurt look framing her face. "You don't know me? Dr. Marina Tanner, Ph. D., the famous archaeologist? I bet you haven't even read my masterpiece, *Myths of the Mayan Mages?*" Zed shook his head, not believing any of the situation, although the title sounded a little familiar.

She laughed, "And you haven't ever heard of Mick Tann's series of WorldNet novels about sexy shape-shifting shamans in Central America?" Pulling back the bed covers she snuggled her warm body next to Zed's. "Zed, under my pen name Mick Tann, I'm famous. I write science fiction!"

Zed overcame his learned prejudice against 'tropes within minutes, responding to Marina's feverish needs, losing himself in lust and love, purging himself of some of the guilt of the Chichén Itzá killing. After all, hadn't he saved Marina by that action? What if he had never stowed away in Frost's time chamber? She might have spent her life as a tortured sex slave, or maybe have been killed by Balleen or Frost, a thousand years in the past.

In his own way just as feverish as Marina, Zed found a reservoir of self-respect that flowed to meet the caring and sharing and, yes, love. After an hour of intimacy and a mutual release of tensions, Marina was less nervous, positively mellow, and as relaxed as Zed himself.

In the afterglow of a beautiful experience, Marina talked about herself: a native and lifelong resident of New Mexico. Her professional interest in Mayan antiquities—her doctorate was in MesoAmerican archaeology—had led her to meet Michael Frost in Juárez a year ago.

Frost had been well known as a serious collector of unusual Mayan artifacts and artwork, and with her position as a University museum curator in Albuquerque, Marina had wanted to investigate his sources, fearing renewed smuggling of México's treasures by criminals taking advantage of the rebellion in the Yucatán.

"I knew only obliquely of Frost's partnership

with my Uncle Steve. In fact, I only knew Uncle Steve himself by reputation, really. I'd just met him once when our family visited the Scots Republic—my mother was from Inverness; she and Dad met there when he was with the US troops over there during the Breakup. I was just a kid back then, in high school. I knew of Uncle Steve's semimorphous material fame, though I didn't understand it. I was really proud of his Nobel Prize, too, so soon afterwards."

Things had gone well enough during her interview with Frost, and she'd seen a very intriguing collection of the Mayan artifacts in the private museum at the Juárez headquarters. Zed thought it strange that he himself hadn't been shown that museum, but since it didn't relate to robots, perhaps there had been no need. He guessed that Frost and Balleen could have brought unique Mayan materials back one at a time, maybe pieces that had been uncovered in places not known to have been dug up by future explorers. But if Frost dug them up in the past, they never could be found in the future, this present *now*.

Zed knew his time travel logic was missing some significant component somewhere, but right now it wasn't clear what. He guessed that if Frost accidentally tried to bring back some piece that did exist now, the repulsion effect might not be serious if the piece was kept in that private museum, away from all possible isochronous forces. Zed suddenly wanted to see that museum of Frost's for himself. He'd give it some thought.

Marina continued her story. At dinner the second day of her visit, she dined privately with Frost. Somehow her familial relationship to Dr. Daviess had surfaced, and Frost's demeanor

changed drastically. He practically dragged hei a helicopter flight to Chihuahua City, promising show her a treasure trove beyond all archaeologica experience. Half prisoner, half enthusiast, she went.

Cuddling closer to Zed, who loved the smell and the taste of her sweat, Marina shivered slightly as she recounted that trip. "It was the middle of the night, and he flew the helo manually, like a maniac. I was afraid he was on drugs or something. We landed on a building top in Chihuahua City quite late and he took me down into the QuanTonics building there. We woke up the night watchman and he let us past the patrolling robots.

"Frost dragged me up to a door, told me to wait there while he got the access code to a secret underground museum where he kept the really good stuff. I remember taking an elevator ride with him ..." She fought the amnesia, trying to recover the events of that night. "The elevator ride was weird—nauseating, really, I remember ... Must have gone to sleep or something, because the next thing I knew, I woke up in a dark cell ..."

Zed tensed. She was finally remembering the situation. Would she accurately reconstruct Zed's part in the story, the escape? He wanted to know how she'd gotten back here to California.

"It's funny, Zed, because all I could remember about all of that, until tonight, was going to that factory, then an eternity in a cell. Sometimes a UV light in the ceiling would come on and I would feel OK for a while and then I would pass out. The next thing I recall, I was stumbling out of that elevator door, all hurt and bruised, and dressed in a dirty old Mayan robe. It was night, and I wandered past some sleeping gate guards. I ran into a crowd

and passed out. I woke up in an alleyway. Fortunately for me, I had slept in the sun for some hours. I didn't know I had the ... this damned 'trope addiction at first. I just felt unexpectedly exhilarated.

"By the kindness of refugees heading north, I was able to get back from Chihuahua City to Juárez. The hotel where I was staying still had some of my identification papers and an ID chip in their visitor safe. I don't like to carry that stuff on the street, you know, because of purse-snatchers and wrist-cutters. I was surprised that they had kept it—I'd just been gone overnight, they said, but I felt like I'd been away for a long, long time. Months, a year maybe. Certainly not just the one night. It was too incredible, but I was not myself—being 'troped up, terrified."

She studied Zed's face in the faint light, as if the memories were returning. "In a few days I knew for sure I had the 'trope. I was afraid that Frost would find me again, so when I made it back to Albuquerque I didn't go home, but hid out with a sympathetic former colleague of mine. A family member tipped me off about Uncle Steve's place here. I couldn't see turning myself in and going off to Kiska to die in the cold and the dark. So I came here, and I stayed here.

"That was a year ago. But why do I feel that I somehow ... knew ... you back then? Was it just what I saw in that chamber in the basement, all the noises, the figures? Or is there something you're not telling me?"

Zed couldn't answer her question, he was so stunned at the implications of her story. Marina had been kidnapped a year ago, met Zed eleven hundred years ago back in Chichén Itzá, escaped

at the same time as he had, but returned to her own time, a year ago? And never even knew she had traveled in time? It must have happened, but that was a circumstance he hadn't considered: people from various future years meeting together at a common point in the past. *Damn, the concepts are confusing!*

"Marina," Zed stuttered, "I don't know how to tell you this, but—" He stopped, feeling her body tense in expectation of bad news. "Please don't be alarmed, and for God's sake, I hope that laser is somewhere else—but I *did* meet you in that dungeon, in that cell. In fact, I rescued you."

Marina wasn't convinced. "Zed, you don't make any sense. You said you were down in México when Frost's factory exploded. If I remember the news correctly, that was just two months ago. I remember it because I was so happy the maniac was dead. And Sam along with him." Grimacing, she paused. "That's funny, I'm starting to have memory problems. I didn't even realize I hated Sam so much, as much as I do Frost. I just can't remember *why*."

Zed hoped her recollections wouldn't trigger another 'trope mood swing. He had to play this carefully, eliciting memories in the proper sequence, so she wouldn't collapse mentally. "And Zed? I don't remember any cell. Or a dungeon. Are you messing with me?"

"Marina, did you know where you were ... while you were gone?"

"Below that factory in Chihuahua City, of course. I remember going in, taking the elevator, stumbling back out of the building. I told you that already. Why do you ask?"

As Marina listened with eyes wide and mouth

agape, Zed told her in gruesome detail how they'd met in ancient Yucatán, how she was in a small cell, dressed in the ragged Mayan robe. He neglected to tell her what she'd said about her treatment at the hands of Balleen.

Marina disengaged and rolled over to her side of the bed, propping her head up on one bent arm, smiling at him. "Now, Zed, that has to be total nonsense. Even 'trope addiction doesn't make one *stupid*. Time travel, underground factories in ancient Mexico? Mixing up the past and the present and the future? I just don't believe it!"

"I'm sorry, Zed," she continued, coyly running a finger across his lips and cozying up against him again, "But as much as I like your mouth—and all the wonderful things it does—I can't buy your story of Uncle Steve's invention. I don't want to disbelieve anything you say, so just don't tell me anymore, not right now." Her fingers moved to other parts of Zed's body and he was glad to forget time traveling for a while.

He groaned aloud, playfully, "Dr. Tanner, are you famous *only* for your writing?"

LATER, ZED DID REMEMBER READING A NOVEL BY Mick Tann some years back, all archaeological fantasy, heavy in erotic content, dealing with alternate histories and such, not his favorite subjects. With most of his fellow science fiction writers, Zed had always considered alternate universes and time travel in the same league with unicorns and elves. He'd had to adjust to reality and accommodate a few conceptual changes since his trip in time to Yucatán, but he knew that even his relatively open-minded literary colleagues would never believe his story. It was no wonder that Marina didn't believe it.

"Seriously, Marina," he said over drinks at a tiny table in the small kitchen, "how else would I have come here? How could I have known about the ... the … time machine in the basement?"

Dark green eyes surveyed the tattooed rectangle of red and blue lines over Zed's breastbone. She didn't ask about them, but did glance back and caught his gaze. "I don't know that it *is* a time machine, Zed." She put the shot glass down and closed her eyes tightly. "Damn it, if I hadn't been under the 'trope when I opened the doors, maybe I would have known what was happening. Maybe I could remember why it felt like I was in Chihuahua for so many months, when it was just one night!" Slamming her fists against the table, she cried, "Damn the Cubans who built these bugs! Damn Frost and Sam for injecting me! I wanted them to be burnt alive in that factory..." As Zed watched, Marina's anger took some of the pain, loosened itself from her psyche, and departed. He prayed she would recover, at least psychologically, once she recalled the whole truth.

There are weapons worse than nukes, Zed thought. *Much worse.* He thought to steer the conversation to another subject, namely Michael Frost's appearance here last month, but decided to try another tactic first. "Did your uncle leave any records here? Anything we could access? Maybe I could find out what's going on in that room downstairs. I'd like to prove to you what happened, what happens when you start fooling around with Father Time.

"And I'd like to find your uncle, too. I feel very

uneasy with Frost around, especially if he has the freedom to travel in time. I don't think he told me the truth about Dr. Daviess."

Marina said she would humor Zed in his impossible quest, first because she wanted to help, and secondly because she was getting worried about her uncle, too.

THEIR INITIAL ATTEMPTS TO ACCESS THE household picomp system ended in failure. Finally, under the guise of calling in Brighton Sr. by wrister, Zed instructed his on-board system to start the cryptographic algorithms to crack Daviess' security codes. He didn't want to tell Marina about Brighton's full capabilities just yet; he couldn't compromise his own security to a 'trope, no matter how sensuous and beautiful, no matter how earnest she was. A 'trope would do anything for a minute in the sun; that was the conventional knowledge.

While Brighton's DI programs digested, attempted, reiterated, and crypto'ed its silicon opponents, Zed reviewed the physical records Daviess had left in various formats around the house. The written reports in the numerous paper-file cabinets in the basement included many of Daviess' original lab notebooks documenting the plethora of patents and licenses he had obtained in the ten years before his disappearance, accomplishments from which flowed enormous royalties, some of which continued to support the farmlet and Marina. Zed was constantly amazed that Daviess had left his niece here alone to run the estate, and even more surprised that Marina had not been bothered by the drug authorities in the last year. Maybe the government was finally deciding that some 'tropes were harmless. Or perhaps Daviess had bought off some drug enforcement officials. Zed wondered what would happen to all of the denizens of Kiska if they were all allowed to go back home; could they stay as relatively well-adjusted as Marina? And why not? What did it matter if they needed a lot of sunlight every day?

Zed's sore left shoulder twitched in reply. No, their potential mental instabilities meant that the new inhabitants of Kiska had better stay a while longer, until a thoroughly complete cure could be found. While Zed shuffled through a stack of hardcopies of Daviess' theoretical temporal displacement papers, he had a thought. "Marina," he asked across the room from where she sat engrossed in a laboratory notebook, "Did Dr. Daviess, Steve, ever give you explicit instructions on how to escape from here, if the Feds came, or 'if the war happened', as you so carefully told me?"

"Yes, he did, in the holocube of instructions he left." She pointed with her left hand toward an electrical power panel on the wall near the hinged door of the time chamber. "Inside that panel is a bank of twelve switches. I just pick which one I want, then activate the palmpress, walk inside and wait." She laughed, "I think Uncle Steve thought I was some kind of mindless druggie. Can you imagine me, locking myself in that room, when the narkos come a-blazing?" She waved playfully and returned to her reading.

Zed stood, shaking his head. "Migod, Marina, you mean he's got all of the destinations right there on the panel?"

Marina shrugged. "I don't know, Zed. I never looked, because there's only one way in and out."

Zed just placed a hand over his mouth and chuckled.

The panel door opened easily and Zed stared at the dusty hand-written labels covering what appeared to be circuit breaker switches in a standard electrical power panel. The stuff of history, and Marina still would not believe that in her basement was the most fantastic device ever conceived by the human race. He read the names aloud.

"Chichén Itzá," he paused, looking back over his shoulder at Marina, who was not paying any attention.

"Stonehenge." She glanced up. "Giza." Marina stopped reading.

"Chandeleur Island." They both shrugged at that one; it meant nothing to either of them. "Lhasa," he whispered.

"What's that, Zed?" an interested Marina peered over his shoulder. "Tibetan Republic?"

"Yes, Tibet," he answered. "Might be where Cardenas sent Sam Balleen." Marina shivered, then looked puzzled. Zed explained those final moments of the fight underground at Pisté, two months ago.

Zed held her arms in a tight grip. "Damn it, Marina, you saw me, and your uncle, and Frost, and some other people inside this room here. Why won't you believe my story? Look," he said, pushing her up to the panel, "There's Chichén Itzá, where I was, where *we* were. Why would I fabricate a story like that? How would I know Chichén Itzá would be written down inside this panel?"

Marina turned her head aside, refusing to see what she couldn't believe. "Zed, my ... condition's been so unstable since I became ... a 'trope. In the after-fix, or during withdrawal, I can believe most anything, but I can't use those ... hallucinations ... as a rational basis for my sober periods. I just can't accept it."

Looking Zed right in the eye, she admitted, "Zed, if there really is a time machine—this room, here—then archaeology, my real life's work, is a dead issue. Anybody could go back and retrieve all the famous artifacts, interview all the famous people, and recreate the whole history of mankind. The scientific aspects would be gone, it'd just be a media show, like—like the metareality websites." She bit her lower lip. "No, beyond that, as a professional, I know the past is dead. I should know, I dug up enough of it. This —" she looked disdainfully at the control panel labels, "—this is nonsense!"

Zed pulled her, trembling, into his arms, struggling to keep her rational and fearing another episode of a drugbug attack. She submitted to his superior strength, very willingly. "Look at this one label, then, Marina. If you're not affected by this one, if your professional curiosity is not piqued beyond control, I'll let you go and you can believe whatever you want."

Marina reluctantly peered at the one label Zed was pointing to. Her mouth formed a lovely "O" as she breathed a barely audible gasp: "Mt. Olympus, Homeric Era."

Shaking free from Zed, she took a quick, short step back from the panel. "Zed, I ... I ..." She looked at him earnestly. "If you're telling the truth, then we can just throw this switch, push the palmpress, and step back into ancient Greece? Halfway around the world, and three thousand years into the past? Whoa!" Hands atop her head, she waltzed around the crowded basement. "Tell you what, Zed, we can settle this little point real quick."

Zed knew what was coming. "Marina, it's one thing to stow away like I did but—" Ignoring his protest, Marina reached over to the control panel, flipped the "Mount Olympus" switch, and slapped the palmpress. As Zed stood nearly paralyzed with surprise, the two massive doors slid open and a familiar bluish glow emanated from the interior walls, the same ozone odor now returning strongly. Marina stepped sideways into the open room, motioning Zed to come on in.

What to do? Zed instantly calculated that he wouldn't have time to pull her out of the room before the doors closed. On the other hand, if she left him alone, he could never operate the palmpress without her hand. She might be stuck in some dangerous era in the past. *Weapons!* he thought furiously. *We can't go without weapons!* The fear of encountering an armed Michael Frost prompted Zed to a desperate measure.

Faster than he would have thought possible, Zed sprang to the bottom of the stairwell, retrieving Marina's Donne. Knowing he wouldn't have time to run back through the closing doors of the Daviess time chamber, Zed rolled the last yards into the glowing room as the doors shut firmly, mere inches from his withdrawn feet. His wallet and pocket change were strewn across the basement floor. No worry; he wouldn't need credit cards or ID where they were going!

Incongruously, Marina was laughing. "You do move quite fast for an older man, Dr. Wynter, but I still don't think we're going to Mount—-"

The universe vanished.

ZED GRITTED HIS TEETH FOR ANOTHER HELLISH ride into the past.

With a *thrum*, the universe shifted: Zed Wynter's subconscious recognized the *not-there*-ness of the Daviess temporal transfer field as it fought the psychological nausea he'd experienced during the other two trips through time. This occurrence, however, seemed to last longer than the trips to and from ancient Yucatán. The indescribable vortex of time displacement sucked him into unreality, distorted his senses, and convoluted the core of his being. Somewhat prepared by his other trips, Zed resisted the disorientation and held on to his composure. Marina, though, became nearly hysterical, her screams echoing down the twisted coils of time until Reality slapped them both in the face.

Finally, the trip was over. Zed regained his balance and stood to comfort his partner. "Marina! We're okay! You'll be alright!" His tone wasn't a reproof; he'd acted the same way his first time.

"Oh God, Zed," she blubbered thickly, "what happened? What did Uncle Steve *do*?" Ashen-faced, she eyed the doors. In México, the doors had been programmed to open upon arrival and Zed figured they would probably work the same way here, so he wanted to wait. But Marina was impatient. "Let's get out of here. *Please*."

"Marina," he replied evenly, "I'd rather you use the palmpress to get us back to our own time." He was less afraid of another immediate trip back, than of what might be waiting outside the doors.

Hell, there could be an army out there! Glancing around, Zed could not find a control panel inside; there were no selectable destinations here, only the palmpress. Would their initial departure time be the default destination, when they *did* return? Or had Dr. Daviess planned something else for his time travelers?

"Zed, is that really, I mean, on the other side of those doors—?" Zed nodded grimly as he resignedly inspected the condition of the Donne. Fully charged! At least something was going right!

"Let's go outside for just a minute, Zed," she said with only a slight hesitation. Zed still had trouble accommodating Marina's mood shifts, wondering if the 'trope was the sole cause. "I mean, if this really is Homeric Greece, well, we've got a gun, nothing can hurt us." She smiled. "Won't we be safe here?" Her confident shrug answered her own question. She'd decided to see ancient Greece for herself.

Glad he'd risked grabbing the laserifle, Zed stood watching the opening doors. "As long as we're in the neighborhood, might as well take a look," he snorted. "Just stand back."

The doors slid open with a slight *whoosh* and Zed held the Donne at waist height, ready to shoot anything or anyone who threatened. It took him milliseconds to absorb the view outside the doors: Dr. Daviess' basement greeted them—they had not moved!

Zed brought the gun up anyway. They had traveled through time, that much he knew, there was no mistaking the nausea and disorientation. Why they had returned, he didn't know, but he would still be alert. In his mind, Frost was an ever-present enemy, not to be ignored.

How about providing a peep-hole in the next design, Dr. Daviess? Zed thought, *so your customers can see where they're going before they open the doors?*

"Why, Dr. Wynter," Marina laughed, relief in her voice that she wasn't in a foreign country in the distant past, "that was quite a show in this 'time machine'!" She waved her right arm in a grand gesture, inviting Zed to depart the chamber. "Step right into 'Mount Olympus, Homeric Era.'"

Still surprised at their destination, Zed held the Donne at ready, not trusting anything at this point. "I'll go out, Marina, but damned if I know what happened. The last ride I had like that took me a thousand years in the past and down into the Yucatán." He smiled grimly, weakly. "This aborted trip was just as sickening and twice as long. We earned that time trip, but didn't get it." Outside the chamber, the room appeared as it was at the time of their departure. *Wait a minute!* The thought stunned him as he scanned the room. *Where's that strange tapered cylinder?*

Zed whirled to ask Marina, but she was gasping as she took in the differences in the basement she had known so well. "Zed, that machine is gone! So are the file cabinets!" She ran from the chamber and the doors slid silently shut. "How long were we in there? Were there burglars?"

Zed shook his head numbly; the situation didn't make any sense. "Unless we have come back to a different time than the one we left!" The friendly and familiar basement took on an ominous ambience. Were they in their past or in their future? And why the malfunction? He couldn't raise Brighton with his ear-tug or subvocalizations; nothing worked. Something was definitely amiss.

An explanatory concept formed in his mind.

"Marina," he whispered, "can you tell if this is our past or our future?"

A puzzled look was her only response.

"I mean," he continued more forcefully, giving her a stern and commanding glare. "Does this place look like you remember it when you first came, a year ago?"

"Zed," Marina retorted, staying against the chamber doors, "I'm tired of your games. We did *not* travel in time. Somehow, things have just been stolen while we were in that … room." Her sudden intake of breath caused Zed to whirl around with the rifle ready to fire: Standing at the foot of the stairs was a short blonde bearded man, fiftyish, dressed in a safari jacket and shorts. Zed quickly assessed the man as no threat—he was unarmed and standing slack jawed.

"Marina!" the man shouted, looking first at the woman, and then, fearfully, at Zed and his laser.

"Uncle Steve!" Marina shouted back.

Zed barely heard the rest of their shouts as he let the laser-rifle barrel slowly drop. His attention was riveted on the dynamic display calendar above the closest workbench.

The date was five years before he and Marina had left to go to Mount Olympus.

DR. STEPHEN DAVIESS, ZED LEARNED, WAS THE antithesis of the erratic genius, Michael Frost: middle-aged, genuinely friendly and warm, exhibiting nothing like the episodic mania of the younger man. *All in all, a good person*, Zed thought. *How did he ever get mixed in with a zane like Frost?*

To the scientist's credit, he was accommodating

the incredible visitors from his own future with remarkable ease. The three sat in the living room above the basement, all imbibing unblended Scotch nervously, each person agitated for separate and individual reasons. Marina's belief system had been shattered, as Zed's had been after his first trip. Zed was worried about some unknown phenomenon that had made them abort the trip and return to an unplanned destination. And to Daviess.

"I just can't get over this, Marina, Zed," the Scotsman said with some effort. "I have performed some ... other time displacement testing, in another chamber, but I never expected to see—" still unbelieving, Daviess walked over and hugged his niece and turned to touch Zed's rifle. "—two people walk out of that chamber, especially my own niece! Can you tell me from whence you came?"

Zed and Marina exchanged nervous glances. She shook her head and gulped the strong whiskey so Zed took the cue and started to explain.

"Over ... five years ... from now... Dr. Daviess, and right from this ... very spot," Zed answered, struggling to say the words, as if something were censoring his speech. *Frost's warning about paradoxes?* he thought, *Not being allowed to share information from the future?* Careful not to say any more, he smiled at the scientist's easy acceptance of their appearance. On the other hand, Zed wondered, *what else can you expect if you invent a time machine? Unusual things are bound to happen when you interfere with the natural flow of time. If there* is *a natural flow,* he added. He was thinking time might never flow naturally again, after Daviess' tinkering. And his own! "Your time chamber is still ... operating in the future where we left, minutes ago. That is, it *did* operate. But something didn't work as planned."

"Remarkable, just remarkable," Daviess said again, staggering slightly, finally resting in an overstuffed chair. He fumbled with his wrister. Eyeing Zed, the scientist asked, "Mind if I record this conversation on my wrister? Strictly off the record, for research purposes only." Zed shrugged. Marina stayed quiet.

"Marina, my dear, the last news your mother had of you was that you were thinking of moving to Albuquerque, taking a job at the university museum there." Surprised at his niece's sudden outburst of crying, Daviess jerked his attention to Zed, looking for explanation. With a slow shake of his head, Zed motioned him to stop the discussion.

Zed changed the subject. "Frost told me that time paradoxes can't happen because of the isochronous repulsion effect, Dr. Daviess," he said quietly as Marina regained her composure. "Can you explain more about—?"

The scientist quickly interrupted. "Frost? Michael Frost? My most promising graduate student?" He was genuinely perturbed, and Marina turned to stare, upset at the mention of Frost. Zed feared another 'trope attack, but didn't move.

"How did you find out about Michael Frost?" Daviess repeated. Zed felt a sudden subtle shift in the Scotsman's friendly personality, he watched Daviess' eyes take on a hostile glare. Between the frowns of the two relatives, Zed was feeling uncomfortable. "Tell me what you know about that boy, Zed. Has he been talking to you?"

With evasive terms that apparently satisfied the paradox restrictions, and with occasional enforced pauses, Zed explained briefly about his first time trip to Yucatán, as if he had been invited by Frost, from the Chihuahua City factory to the underground installation near Chichén Itzá, conveniently neglecting the details of the young man's eccentricities and the probable involvement in warbot manufacture. Zed also did not mention his own stowaway status, his capture, nor Marina's kidnap and abuse by Frost and Balleen.

Zed also decided not to say that he had contributed to the destruction of two robot factories, the one in ancient Chichén Itzá and the modern one in Chihuahua City. For some reason, the scientist didn't question Zed's implied status as an observer accompanying Frost back for a look at the operation in ancient Yucatán. Maybe Daviess expected such things to be commonplace when time travel was routine, a few years in the future. Zed accepted the role gratefully for now, withholding judgement on Daviess' conclusions about his story. He also was learning that if information from the future was not true, the anti-paradox problems didn't occur. To Zed it was almost an ironic situation: *So it's OK to lie about the future, since no real information is passed. Who would have thought?*

To Zed's surprise, Daviess seemed relieved by the story of the time trip, and his manner reverted to the easy friendliness Zed liked. "Forgive me, Zed, but I'm quite touchy about my relationship with Frost and Balleen." His smile put Zed at ease. "Negotiations have been tricky, but from what you say, our contracts must have been completed. You see, I have already sent Michael Frost back there to Mayan Yucatán twice in the past year. He's setting up that factory even as we speak." Laughing aloud, he continued, "Or whatever the proper tense might be for operations in the past." He edged forward on the couch and gazed at Zed intently. "To tell the truth, I was afraid the young man couldn't handle the job, but I suppose with Sam's help, he must have done all right."

Zed cringed but said nothing more. He made a mental note to warn Daviess of Frost's megalomania, but thought he ought to withhold that piece of information for a while. After all, maybe Frost hadn't yet exhibited the tendencies back here five years in the past. Zed kept feeling an undercurrent of the possible unpleasant side effects of time travel, and he wanted to determine Frost's present condition before discussing the man's future psychological state. Also, Zed wanted to sound out Daviess' intentions, plumb his character, and understand his goals, to be able fully to trust the scientist before passing on such dearly-acquired data. As a technical writer and editor, Zed had learned long ago that privileged information should never be disclosed without some concrete gain or accomplishment.

Zed thought Daviess would be unhappy to know the ultimate fate of the Yucatán and Chihuahua factories. He didn't think of himself as a destroyer, but he was not sorry to see both of the installations obliterated, nor sorry that he had helped in their destruction. Maybe if he knew the Scotsman better, he could talk more freely. He desperately wanted to warn the scientist about Frost's destructive personality, but was afraid that the anti-paradox forces might slap him down again. It was just too damn bad all that work of building those factories, the wasted years of labor of ancient Mayans and modern Mexicans, had to go for naught. Zed's engineering background nagged at the unnecessary waste.

As Zed brought his attention back to the present, the scientist was explaining that Michael Frost had suggested factories in the past as a way of financing their grander schemes of routine time travel to witness all historical events. Reluctantly, Daviess had gone along with the proposal. But unfortunately, the mathematics of the time travel equations allowed only certain times and locations to be visited, within the limits of commercial power available.

"It's an inherent limitation in the infinite-series solution of the modified wave equations. Some places and times we can get to relatively easily. Others will require enormous amounts of energy, some will be impossible to achieve, regardless of power. Of course, when they bring the solar generating panels of the Great Southwestern Solar Sea online, with the satellite power redistribution systems, I can buy enough energy to visit almost everywhere and every*when*, especially non-nodal points." Daviess nodded in deep thought. "The Crucifixion lies between natural nodes and I'm determined to record that event." He motioned to a crucifix over the fireplace. The reverence in the scientist's voice surprised. Zed thought it strange to find a religious Nobel Prize winning scientist.

Daviess returned to the subject of time paradoxes and outlined some of Frost's contentions that paradoxes were conceptually impossible in time travel. Only after Daviess was convinced of these limitations had he completed the initial full-scale time chamber downstairs in his basement. There was another, one-person sized chamber at the Berkeley campus itself, from which initial experiments had originated. But the chamber in the basement was built for commercial purposes and was Daviess' private property.

Zed concluded from the scientist's dissertation that Daviess had contributed most to the theory of isochronous repulsion, and his faith in the man made him more confident than he'd been with only Frost's explanations. But there were so many other factors about time displacement that Zed wanted to hear about; how had Daviess come upon the phenomenon in the first place? What led to the development of the equations? What technology was employed in building and in operating the time chamber? How did they determine the destinations? Could he, Zed, build one himself?

But the paradox question wasn't his first priority at the moment. "What's to prevent Marina from contacting herself by telephone? Or even me ..." His voice trailed as the implications struck home. Marina *had* tried to call him, even before he'd left for Juárez, two months ago in his own time. Would that be a *future* Marina, trying to warn him? He'd have to tell her to be careful. Did that mean she would travel in time again? Or ...? He shook off the thought, not wanting to try to sort out the time tenses again. He went on.

"I recall that Frost mentioned something about paradox forces possibly preventing information transfer as well, but what could be the possible physical mechanism? The isochronous repulsion effect I can comprehend, physical forces and all, but interfering with information strikes me as downright mystical." Smiling uneasily, he touched the voice-call button on his wrister. "What prevents me from just telling the phone to call me—myself —in Dallas, right this minute?"

her concern, he said, "No, I'm ... I think I'm alright, but still puzzled. How does Nature conceivably know not to allow an information paradox?" Daviess was nodding, speaking softly into his wrister. "And, Dr. Daviess, I'll bet that if you tried to tell my present self about this, that wouldn't be allowed, either. Damned weird!"

Daviess let a leg hang over the arm of his stuffed chair, relaxing as the smoke took effect. "I'll wager that a subconscious realization of this information prohibition—this *paradox denied* phenomenon, if you will—is what has kept you and Marina from discussing more details of the future with me. Had you attempted such, you would have passed out sooner. An unexpected property of time travel, but now that we have observed it, it is probably logical.

"I would like to ponder these phenomena, Marina, Zed. Meantime, please do not subject yourselves to any unnecessary dangers. No more phone calls, don't mention any future events to me, and —" he shifted his legs and stood straight, his friendliness enhanced by the contents of his prote pipe, "—for God's sake, don't try to leave the house. I want you two safe. Tomorrow we'll attempt to determine the extent of these paradox forces, the parameters, the boundaries. Perhaps we can extract *some* information from the future in a perfectly allowable and safe manner." Daviess bowed slightly, smiled, and strode off to his bedroom.

"Marina," Zed said in a low voice after they closed the guest bedroom door, "I think we're both in danger just being here. Maybe putting your uncle in jeopardy too."

"Why, Zed? Who could possibly find us here?

We've got the only time machine there is. Why not just stay here for a while?" Zed sighed. He wanted to explain the possibilities of all of the time machines that would exist in the future, but thought better of it. Marina had taken a hit off her uncle's prote pipe and the smoke made her eyes widen in anticipation. As she stretched languorously on the bed, Zed could think of no other arguments.

After all, it had been a long, long day.

TIME LAG? ZED WONDERED AS HE POPPED AWAKE hours before daybreak. Marina made occasional cooing noises in her sleep but otherwise nothing broke the silence save an occasional faraway rumble of a hyperjet descent. *Is my biological clock still set to the future,* he thought, *Pacific Standard, Pacific Daylight, or Pacific Future Time?* He laughed silently, his mind racing with the incredible events he'd experienced since first arriving at the farmlet.

Brighton! Zed grabbed his chest, felt the minute ribbing of the micro-tattoos, the implanted circuitry, the extra tits, and tried to raise his onboard system again. No response! He remembered his initial surprise upon stepping out of the time chamber earlier that night. Why wasn't Donne's interface functioning now? An earlobe tug brought no answer: Brighton, Jr., was not functioning, he had no access to Brighton, Sr., and no access to the WorldNet. Another manifestation of the "paradox denial" forces? Or merely incorrect interface channels? He tried to think back, to remember Brighton's operational system status five years ago. Maybe Donne's interfaces wouldn't work with the old systems.

Zed mentally reviewed what he knew of the paradox denial forces. One aspect of those forces was the isochronous repulsion physical forces, a literal force. But what would stop information flow? What would interfere with the human nervous system? Whatever it was, it was a second kind of force. And, could there be some entirely different mechanism operating on his onboard electronics, something affecting hardware and software, a third force? Might there even be hierarchies of paradox forces, what could travel in time and still work, and what couldn't?

Zed's mind seethed with the possibilities. At what point would the Universe, Nature, intervene, if he tried again to communicate with himself via wrister? While he planned it? During the electronic exchange? As he received the information? Zed couldn't begin to answer himself, and at last the fog of sleep began to drift into his mind.

Some kind of force had limited Marina's and his trip to five years, instead of their programmed destination of ancient Mount Olympus thousands of years ago. The Sidespace equations were distorted somehow, and they had landed in the first available "port," the largest or nearest temporal well.

Zed's last thought before sleep was to wonder if TimeSpace had infinitely many laws that protected its being, laws to be encountered one at a time. He hoped none would be fatal.

His dreams were heavy, ponderous: long, silent walks in solitude, finding himself dwarfed between rows of large marble columns that stretched to infinity in all directions. Ominous twilight—the usual twilight in his dreams, he remembered with another part of his mind—thick, dusty twilight that threatened him, slowed his motion, stifled his breath. The deadly dreamscape frightened him; he turned to run but the columns grew thicker, he could barely squeeze between them. His brain quickened, he was trapped! Stuck between two columns that crushed the breath from his lungs. His heart pounded until the sound filled his universe.

Thump! Thump! Thump! Thump! Zed awoke, startled by the sound. The door! Someone was pounding on the door! He tried to move but a partial paralysis gripped his limbs. He tried to shout to Marina for help but only faint grunts escaped his mouth. As Zed struggled vainly to gain control over his body, the door burst open and Daviess almost fell into the room; he'd broken open the door with the force of his shoulder and the momentum took him almost to the bed.

-

"Marina! Zed! Get up!" With the room lights on, Zed's motor control grudgingly returned and he slowly forced himself up off the bed and onto the floor as Daviess picked up his niece. Both Zed and Marina were nude, but the scientist didn't comment. "Down the stairs with you both," he ordered. "It's dangerous for you to be here." Zed's dull expression exasperated the man. "Damn it, Zed, move on to the chamber! I'll try to explain everything down there!"

Daviess already had Marina lying on the time

chamber floor by the time Zed staggered through its doorway. Marina rocked from side to side, woozy. Zed plopped down beside the trembling woman, trying to comfort her, trying to comfort himself. "What's up, Doc?" was all he could say, feeling stupid as he said it.

Then, catching himself, Zed added, "Steve, this ... lassitude, dullness. I ... felt it in ... Yucatán … the Barrier ... tonight ... the wrister call. What's happening?"

Daviess was quick with his reply. "Zed, I called your Dallas number a few minutes ago, and finally wrangled out of your DI that you were arriving in the Bay Area tonight, coming out to a symposium in Hayward. Your hyperjet is approaching even as we speak." Zed's sluggish mind compared the nervous scientist to a flighty terrier, stalking yet fearful of its prey.

"I did ... come to a robotics … conference at Hayward, years back … you think I'm getting *too close* to myself?" It was becoming harder to think of the past, and for an instant Zed was afraid he might be suffering a brain injury.

"That's it, Zed. You've got to get back to your own time, away from here, or I believe, you may die of paradox effects." The Scotsman stepped outside the chamber doors, motioning for the others to stay inside. "I'm going to operate the outside palmpress and send you back to your own time."

"But—" Zed tried to object as the doors began their slide. "What's happening? Tell us before..."

The doors were closing as the scientist shouted, "I've set the arrival time for twenty-four hours after you left." Then: "Look inside the basement wall, Zed, I'll—I'll paint a cement block red. Look inside the wall!" The doors shut, but Zed thought he heard Daviess' attenuated voice through the thick barrier: "*Memes*, Zed. It's *memes*!"

What in the hell were *memes*? Zed wondered as the universe died and reconstructed itself around his battered body. Time travel was a bitch!

ZED HELD HIS EYES TIGHTLY SHUT AND RODE OUT the gut-and-mind-wrenching *shift* relatively unscathed. As the distance receded and the world came together again into an understandable form, he found he'd only bitten through one lip, his lower one, this time. Marina, still lying on the chamber floor, trembled convulsively, gasping between her screams. *Time travel won't ever be a tourist attraction, not like this*, he thought sarcastically, helping Marina to her feet. As Zed held the rifle at ready, Marina weakly pushed the palmpress then stood back waiting for the doors to open once again, hopefully back in their own time.

To their mutual relief, the familiar overcrowded basement presented itself, this time complete with the tapered cylinder and the file cabinets in their proper places. Zed checked their arrival date with a subvocal request of Brighton, Jr., praying for a response:

"Brighton, what time and date is it? How long have we been gone?"

"Sire," Zed let his breath go at the sound of his familiar friend, "you've been out of touch behind those doors for approximately twenty-four hours and eighteen seconds. I will inquire in the databases to determine the kind of shielding that was used in the construction of that room. I completely lost contact with your onboard system and there is no data from that period. Most interesting."

"Take all the time you need, old friend," Zed said aloud, smiling. "Meanwhile, check out the house for bugs, possible intruders, that sort of thing." He wondered if Brighton would be able to access anything at all from the onboard system, Brighton, Jr., any passive data collection. He was sure the computer would update him at once.

Marina wandered around the basement; from the look in her eyes, Zed wondered if she was in shock. Time shock? She wouldn't question anything for a while, so he'd felt comfortable in addressing Brighton openly. Zed helped her upstairs to the bedroom, where she collapsed on the unmade bed. Within minutes, she was groaning and undergoing muscle spasms. Zed figured that the time trips must have triggered her 'trope addiction. He scooped her up gently and took her to the tanning booth in the adjacent room.

An hour later, with Marina satiated from the waste products of her unwanted nano-parasites, Zed tucked her in bed and returned to the basement to search for a red-painted cement block. He hoped that Daviess had remembered the promise.

It was midnight when Zed finally located one cement block, barely tinged with faded red paint, just one course above ground level behind a massive tool cabinet. The paint looked like a paint spill residue, and only a dedicated searcher could have found it. But Zed was desperate for explanations; he had looked for any red coloring at all.

With tools from the nearest shelf—a hammer and chisel—he removed soft caulking from around the block and pried it out slowly, until he could grasp the entire piece and remove it. Inside the fake block was a small metal safe with a fingerprint access door. Zed shrugged, trying his fingertips against the pads until the door sprung open. He guessed Daviess must have taken his fingerprints from the drink glasses to use for the lock. Zed pulled out a sheaf of papers and a small datacube player.

"The concept of memes," Dr. Stephen Daviess' voice was saying from the video screen of the datacube player, "arose in the 1970s. Briefly, memes are theorized to be mental analogs to genes —that is, they are precise thought patterns, definite ideas, which manifest themselves in human minds and propagate by spreading mind to mind." Daviess' image smiled. "Memes were proposed as a way to explain the madness of crowds and mobs, each individual of which seems suddenly swept up in a frenzy over some idea or symbol, some cause that rationally seems absolutely insane. I believe that such a theory can explain the physical phenomenon that affected your ability to call Dallas, Zed." Zed couldn't make any mental connection at all; he wasn't sure what memes were, physically, and how could an idea, a *thought*, have physical substance?

"If we accept that memes are a sort of mental virus," Daviess' playback continued, "we may speculate that they may take the form of electrochemical potentials in the brain, by means of which the memes are stored. A given meme may form a three-dimensional structure unique to the thought it expresses." Zed could hear the scientist pause, as if to give the listener time to take a mental breath. Zed was particularly interested in this aspect of Daviess' long exposition: He suspected that the unexpected physiological aspects of time travel might severely limit the exploration of the past. *Maybe I've already done irreparable damage to myself,* he worried. *And to Marina?*

"A meme replicates itself from mind to mind by causing the same train of thoughts to run rampant through the brain, over and over again, until its physical structure is ingrained and permanent. Chants, rituals, discipline, repetition—these are the means by which the meme is forcibly propagated. Once in place, however, this holographic-like electrochemical construct in the human brain might be the physical basis of an isochronous repulsion effect for mental processes.

"MUCH LIKE THE TIME-SEPARATED ASPECTS OF THE same atom generate the physical forces you encountered, Zed. No wonder the effect on you was similar—the forces that prevented you from talking to yourself on the wrister last night were identical to the forces you literally ran into in the Yucatán."

Zed stopped the datacube playback right there and restored the system to the beginning of the section on memes, listening to it once more. This time it made more sense: the scientist was telling him that the Universe recognized that his future self was trying to pass on information to his past self, and the physical constructs already in his own brain could not be allowed to approach themselves in the past. *Sounds good*, he thought, but it sounds incomplete. *But what if I try to pass the future information to someone* else's *brain? Are meme configurations exactly the same, person to person, or is some fuzziness allowed?* He let the datacube play on, but since Daviess seemed not to be converging on any other important conclusions, he stopped it. There were other more important tasks at hand.

By then Brighton had broken into the house's picomp system and was operating it as an extension of his own network, and Zed figured they were as secure as possible under the circumstances. He checked on Marina—sleeping rather soundly, thankfully—and scouted the farmlet property, finding all systems secure. All this accomplished, Zed decided to check the datacube library for Daviess' reports on the origins of time travel theory. He sat in the living room this time, with the Donne resting within easy reach. Something was keeping his nerves on edge, but *what* he couldn't say, just a general feeling of unease.

Daviess' image, life-sized and 3D, appeared on the wall screen. "I uncovered the basic physics behind temporal displacement—'time travel', in the vernacular, Zed—while I was doing my other studies with graphenes and semi-morphous materials." Zed remembered some of the more speculative WorldNet reports at the time, but mostly he remembered the other uses of that series of discoveries—the Nobel Prize in physics had been awarded to Daviess not for any theories of time travel, but for the discovery of Sidespace. Still only a theoretical proposal for the physical reality of alternate universes, it had found no practical application. *Unless time travel is it?* Zed concluded.

As if in answer, Daviess chuckled on the screen. "I know that the possibility of time travel was one of the more speculative considerations that arose from the Sidespace experiments, but I didn't encourage those. You might remember that I had been doing strictly commercial experiments at a lunar lab up in Musk City, trying to find substitutes for expensive graphenes and other proprietary two-dimensional materials, using existing semi-morphous compounds. My Moon work was only semi-successful, so I took the materials and went to a zero-G orbital lab to continue the tests.

"Renting lab space on the Third China Station, I was fortunate to come across some recent advanced Finnish Labs semi-morphous matrices to add to my own materials. Then I hit upon the idea of testing those new compounds with the 'time torque' data suggested by the Russian, Kozyrev, way back in the 1960s. That set of circumstances —coincidences, really—proved fortuitous."

Zed stopped the playback, thinking of Daviess' last statement. *Fortuitous?* Think of Lennon meeting McCartney. Think of Jobs meeting Wozniak. Think of Su-jin meeting Loh. Here was the one man in whose mind two disparate laws of physics had melded, mixed, yielding fundamental advances in human knowledge. Zed stroked the playbar and watched as Daviess continued.

"The next day, after I had recuperated from a terrible bout of space-sickness, I found that some of my semi-morphous gunk mixture had oozed out of its container and contaminated my adjacent Kozyrev micro-torque experiment. I was furious! But because I had no opportunity to re-do the Kozyrev data and use only clean materials, I analyzed the results anyway.

"The data were anomalous and I thought at first I had wasted an entire orbital laboratory rental period. But I found that the results could only be reconciled with known physics if the graphene and semi-morph mix were considered to have a Sidespace component, that is, if ultrathread forces were present. What used to be called the 'string' theory of Universal structure, and what are now called ultrathreads." Daviess laughed. "I lumped all those thirteen ultrathread dimensions into the one term, 'Sidespace', mostly because I was beside myself trying to explain ultrathreads over and over again to an ignorant bunch of media reporters."

Zed was aware of the public interest, and of what had followed: Daviess had founded the new technology of semi-morphous electronics, recognizing the industrial potential of his findings. After that, everything electronic, from computers to Zed's own ultrabike to DI systems like Brighton, owed their genesis to Daviess' days of discovery in space and on the Moon.

Zed ran the datacube fast forward to see if Daviess had left any closing statements. To his dismay, the indicator panel showed ten more hours of recording remaining. Zed placed the datacube in a drawer for future reference, yawning as physical stress caught up with the mental stress of the last day. "The last *millennium!*" he laughed aloud.

It was time for bed.

NEXT MORNING, MARINA WOKE REFRESHED AND aroused from her tanning booth fix and several hours of sleep. She kissed Zed, waking him. After a very pleasant interlude, Zed made coffee and a light breakfast.

Zed looked at his love's eyes. *Red, white, and green*, he thought, like the Mexican flag, *like Filemón Garcia's flag*. Filemón's rebels used the same flag at the Federales, just with a Mayan pyramid motif in the upper left corner. He shook the thought off as Marina asked, "Zed, can you please tell me what happened to us yesterday?" She closed her eyes and rubbed them with her right hand. "I just can't believe we went backwards in time and saw Uncle Steve five years ago, and today," she waved both hands, palms out, at the kitchen walls, "today, we're back in our own time again. I can't … accept it."

"Not quite 'our time', Marina," Zed responded between bites of his fried eggs. "We came back twenty-four hours later than when we left." To her shocked look, he just laughed. "I think Steve did that to demonstrate to both of us that we can just as easily travel into the future."

Marina flinched in alarm. Zed hoped the 'trope wasn't continually affecting the woman he was coming to care about. "I ..." she stammered, "I guess that this *is* the future, at that." She paused. "Time travel! Okay, Zed, I said it! *Time travel!*" Smiling at him, she took both his hands in a warm grip. "I do believe we traveled in time. I finally do believe your story about Yucatán. But, Zed?"

"Yes, what else, Marina?" He was afraid her memory about Yucatán might return, given the mental shocks she was accommodating so easily.

"I'm confused about ... well, you. I seem to remember seeing you ... in that chamber, or somewhere else. You said once that you helped me escape from Frost. Can you rescue me *now*, from this 'trope addiction?"

Zed shook his head sadly and shrugged, kissed her, and left her quietly sobbing and he went outside to scout the property once more, the Donne a warm and familiar friend in his trembling hands. Right now, he wasn't sure about their intertwined trips in time, what was actually going on, what effects TimeSpace was having on both of them. He was just disgusted that Marina had been forced into an unwanted addiction and that he was helpless to do anything about it. All he could do, at best, was to try to protect her from the weeko wacko zane, Frost.

Outside on a nearby hillock, Zed used his video field glasses to scan the surrounding hills for unwanted visitors. The bare California countryside sported occasional outbursts of rangy green-topped greasewood, and the dry elephant grass waved like miniature wheat fields in the March wind. The breeze from the west carried hints of sea-smells, of salt water. He saw no people. Turning to walk back to the farmhouse, he accessed Brighton. "Well, Himself, what's your DI programming say about the security of this place? Why am I worried?" As he walked downhill toward the house, the sweet smell of dry oak smoke from the chimney indicated that Marina had stoked the fireplace to take out the morning chill.

From a quarter-mile away, Zed saw Marina as she appeared at the window, waving at him. Zed waved back, knowing she was welcoming the bright sun as much as she was him, as it was feeding her 'trope compulsion. As if Marina sensed his thoughts, she pulled thick curtains and shut off the sunlight entirely. Zed sighed. Soon she'd have to go to the tanning booth, surrendering for the ten-thousandth time to the whole-body craving that otherwise would engulf her intellect in a silent, uncaring scream.

As the curtains closed, Zed began to jog back. "Brighton," he said, subaudible, "remind me to tell you about that time machine in the basement."

"Sire, the Daviess temporal transfer device? My banks already have all of that information. I retrieved it from the household system, per your command, some minutes after you and Ms. Tanner went into the chamber." Between the effort of his jogging and his concern for Marina, Zed barely caught Brighton's sarcasm. "Is that where you were for a whole day, Sire? Off time-traveling again?"

Zed ignored the DI's remarks and touched his earlobe to silence his garrulous onboard companion. His alarm system would let him know if Brighton detected danger, but just now he felt an urgency to get back to Marina. Breaking into a dead run, he reached the door in seconds. In the darkened living room, Marina's sobs racked the usual silence.

"What's wrong, Marina? Is the 'trope acting up again? I thought you didn't need a fix so often." He knelt by the couch, clutching her closely, but she was uncontrollable.

"Zed, it seems worse, much worse." In the semi-darkness he saw her jaw clenched tightly, felt the convulsions that traveled, wave-like, over her body. "It's ... worse ... a lot worse … since our trip in time."

"God damn it! What is time travel doing to us?"

Zed picked Marina up gently and took her to the tanning room, opening the coffin-like ultraviolet chamber. He slowly removed her loose robe and laid her inside with infinite care. She managed a weak smile.

"Zed, dear, I do remember now. You rescued me. Somewhere, somehow, you ... saved me."

Stunned, Zed just smiled. "Dreams, Marina. 'Trope dreams." He kissed her and closed the lid. "Here you go, darling, but only at low intensity." A bottomless pit of sickness opened in his stomach as he dialed in a setting that would once more stimulate the hideous nano-parasites that demanded ever more and more of her will. He vowed she would never travel in time again.

LATE EVENING TWILIGHT WAS DARKENING THE small valley, plunging the farmhouse in shadow, by the time Marina came out of the chamber. This time she was not relaxed; her eyes were dry, dead-looking, she walked as if in a daze, stumbling. In a dry, raspy voice she asked for a drink and Zed gave her water first, then opened a can of soup. She couldn't keep down any solids. As the sun finally set, Zed punched up the maximum security mode of the house alarm system and told Brighton to keep especially alert through all means at his command—the perimetric crawlbots, intensified sensor scans, the works.

Satisfied as much as possible with the security set-up, Zed turned his attention to Marina's health. She seemed to be getting steadily worse: cold sweats, muscular twitches, incoherent babbling. He hoped that the damned nanoes hadn't been mutated or stimulated by their trips through time.

Making sure Marina was tucked under the bed sheets, a cool cloth on her forehead, Zed went back into the living room to play back more of Daviess' long discourse on time travel. Maybe something in the cube could help with the 'trope addiction? Only a long shot. He weighed the decision on whether to call in a medical emergency craft. If he did, Marina's symptoms might be treated and the immediate crisis might pass. But just as surely she would spend tomorrow night, and most likely the rest of her life, untreated, on the hell-hole island of Kiska. The authorities dared not ignore a discovered 'trope.

If Zed didn't call in medical help, Marina might die. What would he himself want, were his and Marina's roles reversed? To die tonight, rather than suffer life as a 'trope? Stroking the wrister's playback, he hoped that something in Daviess' experience might help the Scotsman's niece. If time-traveling made the 'trope worse, maybe there could be ameliorating circumstances, too.

Zed searched on, praying. He tried to keep up with Daviess' theory of time travel, but eventually it took the expected technical turn and the scientist departed from his Nobel-winning mathematical treatise. Somewhere between the eigenvalues and the ultrathreads, the effects of physical stress from the time trips and the emotional stress over Marina's condition pushed Zed into blissful sleep.

Meanwhile, Brighton kept trying to extend its security range to detect the activities of a newly-arrived group of human figures in the hills, just outside the reach of the perimeter crawlbots. Based on his programmed judgement, the DI chose to wait until the figures moved toward the house or otherwise threatened the occupants. Monitoring Zed's and Marina's conditions, Brighton recognized that the humans needed more rest. No doubt, Zed would have to be awakened sometime during the night if trouble arose, but for now the haunted man was allowed to sleep. And to dream.

IN *THE PERPETUAL TWILIGHT OF HIS PERSONAL dreamworld, Zed Wynter walks alone down deserted streets. Not even his footsteps make a sound to penetrate the total, ominous silence. Devoid of advertising neon, dark buildings nonetheless exude rusty orange light from dim windows, punctuating Zed's path with keystoned squares of illumination.* The usual place, *he notes, his dream-memory calling up relevant information about this frequent destination.*

He finds himself inside a crowded department store where not one person turns to look at him, though he now realizes that he is wearing no clothes at all. Covering his crotch with one hand, he sprints up the molasses-slow escalator into the men's department and slips on a pair of bright red bikini briefs. Ready to contend with the sullen crowd, he turns slowly. The room is vacant now, just a slight impression—a vibration, really—that an aged Indian shaman has just departed not long before. Dry red petals of a flower stir in a soft breeze, blowing away as Zed tries to understand their meaning. A hallway, there, on the right!

His dream-self wanders down that endless white hallway, wondering which of the infinity of white doors on his left or on his right he should open. He chooses the first. In a transparent coffin lies his mother/Marina/his first lover, Mildred, amalgammed into one woman, naked, convulsing, crying. She awakens, turns over and her eyes meet his: they are raging white fires, and she screams, loudly/silently, pounding on the inside of the coffin lid, trying to escape, trying to get out. Suffocating!

Paralyzed, Zed's once-more-naked dream-self stands in

shock. Should he help her escape? Should he run? He can't run! He tries to scream! He can't move!

"Zed!" The changing creature in the coffin finally found her voice. "Help me! They're in here!"

"I can't, Mom/Marina/Mildred," Zed mumbled. "I ... can ... not ... move!" *What's wrong? Who's in there?* Zed thought, his mind clearing from sleep. "I don't see anyone in the casket but you!" Suddenly realizing that he was awake, Zed leaped from his chair, knocking over the coffee table and lamp. The house was a cacophony of noise. Alarms were sounding, Brighton was shouting in his ear, and Marina was screaming. It was not a dream!

Zed shook his head to clear his mind for action, noting that the Donne was not where he'd left it. Someone—!

"Zed!" Marina shrieked from the bedroom, and Zed's mind was made up for him. He ran to her, hoping his long neglected *keratsu* training and his on-board nano-enhancements would be enough to save Marina, and himself. For the moment, he gave no thought that his opponents might be armed.

By the sparse illumination afforded by the open bedroom door, Zed saw a dark figure bending over Marina, some kind of pencil-like cylinder in its hand, pushing that device up against the back of her neck. Another dark figure whirled to meet him. In the milliseconds before he attacked the two intruders, Zed noted gratefully that he saw no guns.

The closer intruder dodged as Zed plunged forward, and Zed arched over him, toward Marina's assailant. But Zed's enhanced reflexes brought one foot straight down, catching the man in the face. As Zed tackled the cylinder-wielding figure, he heard a *"whoof!"* and the clatter of the cylinder as it bounced off the wall and onto the floor. Zed and his tackled target slammed against the wall and he felt the man go limp.

FEELING DONNE'S NANO-ENHANCEMENTS TAKING effect, speeding up his perception, was much like watching the world in slow motion. Zed clambered back to meet the first intruder, who by now was standing and rubbing his head with both hands. Zed drew back both hands in *keratsu* fashion. And for brief microseconds, he hesitated. Memories of the street fight in Juárez, of Filemón Garcia, of the hoodlum Zed had killed in justifiable rage. But he still carried some guilt, even after all these years. In a corner of his mind, Zed welcomed this long-festering guilt, as he would welcome an old friend. Not at all as ragged a wound as his killing of the Mayan guard in ancient Yucatán. Not at all as bad.

Zed knew intellectually that both of his killings had been necessary to save both himself and others each time, but the regret remained. Microseconds ticked off as he deliberated whether to add two more burdens to that load of regret. His gaze flicked to Marina, who was holding both her hands on the back of her neck, her back to the man near the door. *Hell, they're the bad guys*, he decided, *and my woman's been attacked!* He edged forward, ready for the confrontation.

In a surprise move, Zed's opponent held up his hands in a gesture of surrender and backed toward the door. Zed jumped closer, and the startled man fell backwards into the living room. Zed glanced back at Marina. The other intruder was still slumped against the wall, their totally-enveloping clothing a dark mass against the slightly illuminated wallpaper. "Marina, come here!" Zed commanded. "Get up. *Now!*" Between glances in Marina's direction and toward the prone figure in the living room, Zed saw that Marina was able to move from the bed on her own.

As Zed walked warily around the man on the floor, he motioned Marina over to the couch. Zed stared in awe as the man's head-to-toe suit was trying to adjust to the parallel stripes of bright colors of the *serape*-like rug beneath him, finally settling itself into a solid black. *A dynamic camouflage suit!* Zed thought. *Like a chameleon.* He could see no seams anywhere. The suit seemed to absorb all light, as if it were a black hole in space, cut off from the Universe. The surface of the whole-body suit seemed to possess a shimmer, as if its surface were slightly fuzzy, having a weird *not-quite-there-*ness about it. Technology was progressing much too fast for Zed to keep up, but he'd never even heard of a fabric or plastic or any other material remotely capable of such a feat.

"Get a weapon, Marina. I think there's a pistol in the coffee table drawer." Zed cursed himself for forgetting his earlier preparations, when he'd stashed weapons in various places around the house. He could have saved the theatrics, and his shoulder was beginning to hurt.

The lying figure didn't move as Marina brought Zed an old six-shooter Colt .45. "Let me see what they were doing to your neck, darling." He glared at the prone man. "I'm mad enough to trash them both if they've hurt you."

Marina's neck showed only a reddish spot

about a centimeter in diameter. Pressing the spot, he asked, "Feel any pain? Doesn't look like a puncture. More like a pressurized injection."

The dark-suited figure on the floor grunted. Marina drew in a sharp breath, but Zed placed the end of the barrel against the cloth-covered face. "You'd better talk now, weeko, or we'll see if your chameleon-suit can deflect a .45 caliber slug!"

The man on the floor moved his hands into a pleading gesture, shaking his head. Zed grunted. "Please, don't? That's all you can do, mime? Get the hell off the floor and face me, you wacko!" Zed withdrew the pistol from the man's face and roughly jabbed it into the ribcage. "Up! Now!"

Slowly, his arms never moving threateningly, the man got to his feet. "Off with your suit, zane," Zed commanded. "Let me see your face!" The man shook his head quickly, urgently. What was wrong with the guy? Zed couldn't imagine such defiance in one who had such little choice. Zed repeated the demand, this time prodding the man in the abdomen with his free left hand while keeping the pistol in the right. "Now, do as I said. You want to die?"

"Hmmph!" the other blurted. "Nuh ... no!" Satisfied that the man understood English at least, Zed told Marina to bring him rope, and they tied the intruder hand and foot to the heavy couch, flat on his back. They found the second figure still unconscious in the bedroom and Zed brought him out into the light, Marina holding the pistol at ready if needed. They tied the smaller intruder to the leather chair across the room, facing his partner.

Keeping an eye on the safely-tied-up figures, Zed backed into the kitchen to rummage for another gun while Marina stood guard over the pair. He carried on a heated subvocal conversation with Brighton. "Damn you, Brighton! Why didn't you wake me sooner? Those goons could have killed us both!" In his anger, it was difficult to keep his voice down, but he didn't want anyone else to know about Brighton just yet. Not even Marina. "You must have known they were coming in, you must have sensed them at a distance, in the house, in the God-damned *bedroom!* Why didn't you do something?"

Brighton did not respond for a full ten seconds. Zed wondered if there was an interface problem between his onboard Brighton persona and the mainframe crystals back in New York. But finally one of the DI personae answered, slowly and in measured tones, a cadence Zed didn't recognize at all.

There had to be conflicts within the DI programming matrix. "Sire, I received ... contradictory inputs ... that inhibited action." The voice slowly gained confidence, it seemed to Zed, and he recognized the inflection outputs based on less conflicting programming. "These two people disarmed the entire outer perimeter of security crawlbots and sensors. I was aware of their progress and began to initiate countermeasures when suddenly—" The pause surprised Zed; Brighton's present behavior was totally new. What was happening?

"—Sire, for just a microsecond I penetrated their antisecurity defenses and I picked up ... information ... from one of them." Zed frowned. What the hell did that mean? His mind raced with possibilities. "Sire, the ... information I received ..." The voice faded.

"Brighton?"

"Sire, I ... can't... respond ... to any questions ... about that communication." Brighton's tone was solid. Final.

Furious, Zed commanded, "Brighton, Priority one! I order you to respond immediately!"

"Sire … they are ..." Zed could tell Brighton was straining to keep the voice output activated. It reminded Zed of his own battle to stay conscious at Daviess' back in the past. Could it be...? ".... from ..." Tremendous effort. Could Brighton do it? "… the *future! ... bzzzzz ...*"

The DI's voice trailed off into noise.

The future! Zed staggered against the kitchen dinette table, knocking over dirty dishes from dinner, smashing them on the tile floor. Marina yelled out a question, but Zed couldn't respond immediately. He ear-tugged off Brighton's buzzing sputters.

I'll be damned, Zed thought, trying to absorb Brighton's information. *Brighton's been zapped with that same repulsion effect, so he can't share any of that information from the future. Wonder what the hell it is? And who the hell are these guys?* Zed visualized his DI's datachips, semi-morphous meme-constructs, nobly fighting off the forces of the future-memes. But wouldn't that mean similar constructs, semi-morph versus-semi-morph? And that meant ... a *future computer, a future DI!*

The mental twists were more than he could handle, and to retain his sanity, Zed laughed, guffawed, uproariously. In this near-sickened fearful state he re-entered the living room to face the time travelers.

Marina was alternately swinging the barrel of the .45 from one to the other of the intruders, and started to ask Zed about the smashed dishes and his laughing. Holding up his forefinger for silence, first to his lips, Zed touched the end of the pistol barrel. "Don't shoot, Marina." At her puzzled glance, he made a broad sweep with his right arm, in introduction. "Marina, my dear, meet two travelers from the future." Marina's eyes grew wide and she held the gun steadily on the pair. Zed hoped the trembling she evinced was from fear and not the 'trope.

Zed bowed toward the black-garbed intruders. "Dr. Marina Tanner and Dr. Zedediah Wynter, two of the first time-travelers, at your service!" *We're a pair o'docs*, he realized, but only grinned at the grimly appropriate pun.

"You're—you're serious, Zed?" Marina blurted out, her expression begging for a negative answer. She sidled next to Zed, finally accepting his prognosis with an uneasy smile.

The figures were not moving. "Hey folks," Zed said, forcing unfelt cheerfulness, "Brighton says you're from the future. Are you?" No response. He repeated the question. "How about simple shakes or nods? You can transfer that much information from the future safely, now can't you?"

The smaller person—intruder *Dash Two,* Zed decided to call him—nodded. Finally, intruder *Dash One* also nodded. "You're really from the future?" Marina asked, still stunned. Reluctant nods.

In sudden inspiration, Marina popped a bold question. "Did you come from the future to ... help us?" Zed thought that she didn't waste any time. *Dash Two* made shrugging shoulder motions to be released from his bonds.

Dash One was pointing at his own chest, then

holding out his own palms from under the ropes that held him to the couch. A question? Of course! Let Brighton and *Dash One's* onboard computer communicate, for Zed was sure that onboards must be standard issue for future time travelers—hadn't he himself started the trend? If they could. If the repulsion effect didn't take out Brighton again. Trusting his own judgment, Zed told Brighton, out loud, to set up communication with the onboard computer or computers of the future folk. Marina looked on, at first quizzically, then in anger as she realized that Zed had not told her about his onboard picomp. Seeing her reaction, Zed bit his lower lip.

Damn! He had meant to share Brighton's existence with her, but the time hadn't been right. An inspiration born of desperation helped soothe Marina's injured feelings. "Brighton, talk to me out loud, use the house speakers," Zed said.

"Sire," Brighton's voice boomed from every speaker in the house. *Thank God that Himself has not O.D.'d on the repulsion effect!* Zed thought. "I've got a link with a very sophisticated ... symbiotronic—" Zed smiled upon hearing his own coined word used "—onboard DI. This is ... the DI ... that contacted me ... immediately before the ... future visitors … entered the house. … I have been assured that ... its programming takes into account … the manifold aspects of isochronous information transfer and repulsion. You may *ask* any question, but ... not *all* questions ... may be answered, for safety's sake."

Marina listened, fascinated, her anger temporarily assuaged. She blurted out, "Brighton? Can you hear me?"

"Certainly, Madame."

"Then ask them who they are, why they attacked me. Are they the same two who tried to break in last week? Why did they have to break in? If they're from the future, why, why didn't they scout out the place in advance? Or did they intend to do us harm?" The query took Zed by surprise. He'd been wondering what to ask first, but Marina's logic fit in quite well with the concepts of time travel.

And yesterday, she hadn't even thought it was possible!

Brighton delivered the answers from the future folk. "Madame, Sire, the events of the interval of several weeks around this day, past and future, are not reliably documented anywhere, so errors were made in the visitors' planned arrival time. Yes, they did ... attempt to ... enter last week, thinking the house would be empty. Upon ... detection ... by the house security system, they ... departed.

"The physical interactions, for the most part, were not supposed to occur. There were cases of mistaken identity, crossed schedules. No harm was intended, and no harm came."

Zed thought about Frost's visit to Marina last month, before he himself had come here. Was this farmhouse becoming a backwater time-transit bus station, always a little off schedule?

These two intruders had broken in without invitation, causing Marina and Zed unnecessary fear and a dangerous fight; Zed could barely move his sore shoulder. But he decided to drop the matter for now, maybe he could find out the details later. After all, he and Marina held the upper hand —their 'visitors' were still bound and Marina still had the gun.

"Brighton, what is that tapered machine in the basement?" Zed asked, happy that he'd been able to think of a relevant question. He had trouble accepting the absurdity of the situation, especially considering that only ten minutes ago he had awakened from troubled sleep and then fought a major battle with two chameleon-suited men from the future. No wonder he wasn't as brilliant an inquisitor as usual.

"Sire, the device is called an 'Anachroscope.' Its sensors are actuated by the anachronic energy that is generated when any out-of-time matter is embedded in another time. It operates on much the same principle as the Ĉerenkov Radiation effect, when particles in non-vacuum media travel faster than light does in that same medium; the isochronous effects can be detected and measured.

"Some ... an ... authority ... in the future utilizes the device to ... monitor ... excursions into the past. It arrived here ... by accident ... because of an unknown anomaly in the ... Sidespace temporal field."

Whew! Zed breathed, *There's another whole world of temporal physics just waiting out there! Publication after publication, phenomenon after phenomenon! Is there no end to it?* He was getting another headache.

Marina didn't wait for Zed to follow up his line of questioning; she was hot on the trail of something else. "Your—these, *uniforms, coveralls,* they protect you from the effects of time travel, right? The nausea, and all that?" Without acknowledging the nods from the tied-up intruders, she plowed right in. "You wanted to come in and get that Anachroscope, and then leave without us knowing about it, right?" Again, Marina was jumping on the train of thought without waiting for an answer. "But for some reason you decided to visit my room, put something in my neck.

"What were you doing to me?"

"Madame, Sire ... I ... cannot ..." Brighton began

"Enough! Stop, Brighton!" Zed said abruptly. To Marina: "You've got to be careful, Marina, some questions can't be answered." To the intruders: "But that particular one must be answered, somehow. Otherwise, you two don't get to leave." Thoughtfully, Zed took the .45 pistol from Marina, trying to think of a safe way to obtain the information he wanted. What had they done to Marina?

"Brighton said you didn't have good records of these few weeks, but—" he pointed between the two of them and laughed "—we're right here now, and I doubt if we'll ever forget any of this! We could write the history down and make it available in standard reference databases, so there *will* be records." He smiled. "Then you won't have to come here and bother us."

Dash One's covered head shook, slowly. Brighton chimed in, "Sire, the future computer says that no documentation exists of these events. Many … *significant* … events … occurred … between their time ... and ours ... that may have altered or erased such records. Particularly, electronic records ..." Zed caught himself. *Damn! So much for free will!* Philosophers would have a field day, if and when they ever got wind of temporal physics. *TransTemporal Logic 101*, he could see it all now.

Zed eyed *Dash One* and frowned. Marina was chewing her lip, thinking of another question, and wasn't paying attention to his interrogation right then. "How far in the future, I mean, *my* future, the real future, my, er…" Zed stumbled, stuttering, searching for meaningful language. "From *when* did you come back here today?"

Brighton's reply was slowed because at that moment Marina thought of the one concern bothering her the most, and asked it in another way. "What you were doing to my neck—was it to help me? Because I feel wonderful!" She waltzed around the room, spinning, laughing. "The god-damned 'trope is gone! Gone! I don't feel the high anymore, the withdrawal, the craving! Zed, I think it's—*gone!*"

Brighton spewed forth both answers at once, one atop the other, barely separated in time. "Sire, these ... travelers ... came from ... about two hundred years ahead ... to retrieve the Anachroscope ... to prevent it from … falling to ... a gang of adventurers..." Zed was astonished. *Two hundred years!*

"Mistress Marina," Brighton continued in a lighter tone of voice, surprising both her and Zed by his choice of address, "these ... helpers ... detected your ... addiction … as they monitored ... the house ... last week. They brought an antidote, not knowing if the ... repulsion effect ... would prevent its use. It did not, and so you are now cured."

Marina smiled, crossing herself in Catholic fashion, and grabbed Zed, kissing him strongly. She walked over to the visitors and began untying *Dash One*. Zed started to object but realized his debt to these people. Bad guys or good, future folk or not, he could never repay them. He put the pistol aside and undid *Dash Two's* bonds.

If they have compromised Brighton's system, we are dead meat anyhow, Zed thought as the time travelers stood and massaged their limbs. The visitors indicated by gestures that they couldn't use any medicines, nor did they want a muscle massage. Brighton relayed information that the bodysuits had to remain on at all times, and in fact could not be breached at all. The wearers, however, were subject to momentum transfer, so that high-velocity impacts and even some lasers were dangerous. The suits did attenuate some amounts of energy by absorption, raising the fabric's temperature, but laser weapons were a risk to the person inside. Zed was perversely comforted by the fact that not *all* laws of physics could be circumvented by the magic of technology.

Brighton continued on for several minutes with the information downloaded from the future computers. "Sire, these people do not have much longer to spend here," the DI said, unaware of the irony of that statement, "and they wish to impart as much information as permissible during that time.

"The Anachroscope is used ... primarily in ... police work ... to detect illegal tampering in the past. These two ... *people* ... have come to retrieve it, but they will require your physical assistance in moving it from the basement to their vehicle outside." Zed shrugged his shoulders at Marina; why would the visitors want the thing outside? Why would they want it at all?

"The device," Brighton continued, "was temporally displaced from the future to monitor certain ... temporal anomalies ... occurring in the past, back beyond this period. Malfunctions of an unknown nature truncated its journey, causing the machine to stop here. Presumably ... the same malfunction has prevented its return to its own time in our future. Others ... want to claim the 'scope for ... their own purposes. Illegal purposes, you may conclude.

"These two ... future time travelers ... came with weapons ... because they feared … interference by the ... criminal elements. They had to proceed ... even though ... you two were here." Brighton stopped.

Lights dawned in Zed's mind. "Aha!" he interjected Brighton's pause. "In the future, Daviess must be famous as the inventor of temporal technology, and future folk all know where and when he lived, I'll bet! But can you imagine all the time machines in the future? They won't be able to keep track of all the time trips ever made, and they can't possibly know every destination that was ever visited by all those travelers. Our own chamber, downstairs, might not even be in their records. Maybe Daviess kept it a secret, maybe *we* never tell anyone until it's dismantled, Right?" Brighton was silent and the *Dashes* didn't comment, body language or any other way. Zed felt he was getting close to an answer. "So there's a little unmarked detour, sometimes, when things are zooming up and down the super timeways of future time travelers, and occasionally things get stuck in an uncharted place." How close dared he get? Zed stopped that line of speculation, fearing some repulsion feedback forces.

"While I'm at it, Brighton, tell our visitors we want some kind of hint about who the bad guys are that the Anachroscope is monitoring. Are they related to Michael Frost in any way?"

"Sire," Brighton said softly, "I am allowed to say ... that the analogy of the uncharted detour is indeed a close approximation to the ... actual events that transpired for our visitors to arrive here.

As to their ... opponents ... the future folk have merely hinted that the ... gang … tries to change the past for profit, in spite of the ... repulsion effects. Their activities are extremely dangerous, and many past and future disasters have been caused by imprudent tampering. Some of them in recorded history."

Zed nodded. The damnable thing about Daviess' temporal displacement was that you never knew what you could do until you tried it; you had only the barest hints about Father Time's fatal taboos! The technology of the future time travelers, as Brighton described it, impressed Zed: the coveralls were made of an advanced form of semi-morphous fabric that utilized Sidespace technologies, attenuating some of the repulsion forces, physical and informational. Zed thought, *Good for protection against genes and memes!* He guessed that the Sidespace component of the material was a shield against the fields of paradox forces inherent in TimeSpace. Probably the shielding and the paradox forces themselves all originated out there in the Corkscrew somewhere. No further information was forthcoming, and Zed didn't dare ask.

Their visitors had used the opportunity to help their involuntary hosts by ridding Marina of her drugbugs. Marina begged them for more serum, more data on the cure, so she could help the other 'tropes, but she was denied with silence. Zed couldn't help but feel bad for the tens of thousands of addicts living in Kiska's hell, victims that these future folk couldn't help. But he mused that he himself could envision a similar situation, were he to visit 14th Century Europe during the Plagues. Could he afford to risk the vengeance of the antiparadox forces by passing out penicillin and vaccines? Then another thought transcended that one: given their extensive capabilities for time travel, the future folk may have indeed already encountered the exact problem.

The technology of the Anachroscope itself was obviously a future secret, but he wondered about the change in its weight. Brighton replied after a moment, "Sire, they answer that the increase in mass is part of the anomaly, perhaps the reason for the malfunction. One of the reasons it must be taken back to the future for evaluation. They suspect some kind of yet-undiscovered repulsive or attractive forces." Zed flinched—*attractive* forces? He felt like an ancient alchemist trying to understand modern physics—no matter how much he thought he could comprehend, there was always some other aspect of temporal physics that staggered the imagination.

"You—" Brighton's voice stopped and then returned with a note of urgency. "Sire! There is danger! I detect the materialization of strangers outside the house! Emanations from other time-travelers! Three hovercraft ... the riders ... are *carrying weapons*! Prepare to defend yourselves!"

Zed shouted, over Brighton's continuing second-by-second updates, "Marina! Get more guns from the weapons locker downstairs!" She nodded and ran toward the basement door. Zed looked at the two visitors. "You are armed, my DI said?" The dark figures nodded and pulled some rifle-like devices from inside their close-fitting suits. Zed marveled at the apparent magic, weapons from nowhere. One more shocker from the future!

Within a minute Marina had brought back four Donnes, precariously tucked under one arm. A couple of smartguns hung under her other arm, and she explained that the flechettes were probably too lightweight to work, if the new intruders were garbed like the *Dashes*. Lasers and smartbullets packed more momentum, more energy. Zed smiled as the *Dashes* acted stunned at Marina's remarks. "She keeps a small arsenal down there. Remember that one for your history books: Dr. Daviess was not a pacifist!" *Remember it*, he thought, *if we live through this mess!*

Communicating through Brighton and the visitors' onboard computers, the four worked out a defensive strategy and positioned themselves, one at each door and one at each end of the house, near the windows. Zed figured that the attackers wouldn't risk vaporizing the whole house with one bomb if they were indeed after the Anachroscope.

If they just wanted to eliminate the four defenders, Zed's hunch was that they would have already done it without any warning at all, given future weapons technology. Vaguely through his fear and anxiety, Zed wondered what future time this bunch was coming from. And if Frost were in any way connected with the attack.

Zed's proposed tactical retreat, should his side start losing the imminent battle, was to withdraw his team to the basement, then as a last resort, go into the time chamber and depart. But *Dash One* had made it clear that he didn't want to do that, because apparently the *Dashes* used other means of time travel that could not be divulged. Zed had figured as much: Daviess' chamber was the Model T, so the time travel devices of two hundred years later would be Tesla Flyers by comparison.

Brighton warned that only thirty seconds remained before the first of the hovercraft would arrive at the house. Zed ordered, "Brighton, contact the incoming visitors. Ask them if we can negotiate, if we can talk instead of fighting."

Dash One shook his head, but Brighton attempted the commanded contact. "Sire," the answer came, "they gave a response in one Spanish word: *Daguello!*"

"Translation to English?"

"'*No quarter*,' Sire. No one will be spared."

"Oh shit, the God-damned Alamo all over again!" Zed spat with disgust. Were these some kind of Mexicans from the future? Frost's troops? Future *Federales? Carteleros?* With all eternity out there in the future, who the hell knew?

Time travel, Zed thought, *is a real bitch!*

Zed thought over his options, considering the disposition of his own "troops" and the fact that the Mexicans probably didn't know about his reinforcements, the Dashes, and their own future weaponry. Defiantly, he said, "Send 'em this message, 'This time, Crockett has a rocket.' Then nuke 'em!"

"Sire?"

"Do it, damn it!" With that coded command, Zed authorized Brighton to do everything in its power to eliminate the attackers. Brighton's programming switched to total offense/defense, throwing all resources at its disposal at the incoming enemy. At that, thousands of miniature sharp-fanged crawlbots, earlier rendered inanimate by the *Dashes*, activated themselves: small, dumb, robots the size of mice, programmed to attack and hold on to anything human-sized that approached the house. They crawled, leaped, flew, propelling themselves against the flying craft and the new intruders. Zed warned everyone to stay inside, no matter how the battle went. "Those little guys are nearly brainless, no smarter than a Chihuahua but just as vicious, and they'll chomp onto us, too, if we go outside!

"Everyone pick a target!" he yelled as the hallway monitor showed the hovercraft just yards from the house, closing fast. *Colonel Travis, is this how you felt back then?* Zed thought. But the historical comparison fell short; piteous screams rent the night air as the attackers faced creatures even Santa Ana would have feared. Crawling, whirring, steel-toothed creatures sensing body heat, tearing at human flesh.

"A couple of them are bot-meat," Marina shouted from her end of the house. "Good for our side!" A small part of Zed's mind was grateful that Marina hadn't loosened the house's defenses upon him when he had come here, two days ago. There was no calling off the little devils, not as long as the target's body heat was higher than the surroundings. Zed grimaced to think of stainless steel mice—*rats!*–at his throat. Briefly, he was puzzled that these new guys didn't have the same technology as the *Dashes* did, that they hadn't deactivated Brighton's defenses in the same manner. Maybe they were not as advanced as the *Dashes*, maybe from the not-as-distant future? Maybe they'd be more vulnerable!

Boom! Wham! Crash! Something like a mini-grenade exploded against the front wall of the house near the front door, scattering pieces of clap-board, thick wooden door splinters, and chunks of brick trim inward into the house like shrapnel. *Dash One*, near the kitchen door, turned to see to Zed's safety and was caught full force by the flying wavefront of debris. Thrown bodily against the kitchen cabinets, he slumped and lay still. *Dash Two* spun around in panic, but Zed motioned for him to stay at his post. "*Dash*!" Zed yelled out, "I'll help him! You just shoot anybody that comes in!" But before Zed could move, a snowmobile-sized hovercraft carrying two white-suited figures shot through swirling smoke through the breached wall, coming to a halt a foot above the living room floor, its fans kicking up whirlwinds of dust.

Zed's nano-enhanced adrenaline rush kicked in and the world slowed again. In painfully slow motion, he saw *Dash Two* raise his future weapon toward the hovercraft. Almost simultaneously, the enemy driver aimed a pistol-laser at *Dash Two*. The backseat rider on the hovercraft, meanwhile, rolled off, pulling up a laserifle in Zed's direction.

Zed made his choice in a split second. *Dash Two* would either live or die depending on the luck of the draw, but Zed would kill at least one attacker first. The Donne, set on full power penetration, spat out untold quanta of laser energy at the rider. Then Zed turned and rolled hard to the left, behind the ruins of the couch, hoping to get a shot at the driver.

In that slow-motion universe, Zed saw the hovercraft smash upward against the ceiling. His laser shot had enveloped the hovercraft rider, who tumbled off the craft, his legs tangling in a stirrup-like attachment, leaving him dangling. The man's white coveralls sparkled in crazy-quilt colors as it absorbed the horrendous energies of the Donne. *This one dies upside down, like an animal in a trap,* Zed thought grimly. Idly, a part of Zed's mind noted the four crawlbots still chewing on the man's legs.

In the instant that followed, Zed saw that *Dash Two's* initial shot of—what?—a cone of yellowish light, had killed the driver. *Instantly,* he hoped. The dreadfully hot bodysuit, occupied but unmoving, was wedged between the ceiling and the joystick controls, a crawlbot still dangling from the dead man's ankle. Zed smelled cooked meat. *Dash Two* gave a thumbs-up signal, then pointed through the gaping hole in the front wall: another hovercraft was just seconds away from entering. The dark figure indicated that he was going across the room to help his injured comrade, then stepped over the scattered remnants of drywall to *Dash One's* side.

Zed jumped back from the hole in the front wall, just as laser fire lanced from outside, under the first hovercraft. Marina was yelling from down the hallway. "Zed! Get down! I'll get this son of a bitch!"

Zed flattened himself against the floor, but pointed his Donne toward the hole for a quick shot. The second driver, anticipating a frontal attack, slid his vehicle sideways through the air, filling the entire hole in the wall. Both riders unslung their weapons, craft-mounted and handheld, for broadsides into the house, directly at Marina. However, neither rider was expecting shots from the floor, and Zed's wide-beam caught them unaware.

The remaining energy in Zed's overheated weapon was not enough to kill the attackers, but it was enough to hurt them: They threw up their hands to shield against another shot, which was a fatal mistake. Marina's smartgun, launching tiny explosive rockets, belched and farted pellets of death. Zed rolled again, back toward the *Dashes*, as the smartbullets smashed into the hovercraft occupants. Fancy suits or no, the high-velocity energy transfer pummeled the men a thousand times in one second. Hand weapons clattering ahead of them, both fell to the floor. They made no sound. Their hovercraft whined to a stall and fell atop them, effectively plugging up the hole in the front wall, leaving no room for another craft to follow them through. *A real deadman switch*, Zed noted grimly.

"How many left, Brighton?" Zed yelled out as he helped *Dash Two* pick up his large friend. Marina crept into the living room, smartgun still at the ready. Cautiously, she leaned against the wall, stepping out quickly to take aim at any other attackers. She didn't see any.

"Good shot, Marina," Zed puffed as he pulled *Dash One's* limp form over to what was left of the couch. "That's two I owe you!" Marina scowled, looking at the dead men. It was always hard for civilized people to see the bodies of those they killed. For all that these guys were totally covered in bodysuits, they were still dead. Zed hoped his lover wouldn't have to go through his own killing-traumas. *This is war, my lover, not murder*, he thought, but said nothing. Marina knelt over one of her unmoving targets and gently touched it. Zed turned his head.

"Sire, two more craft are approaching the house. Now ... one has stopped twenty yards out, but the other is attempting to breach the south basement wall!"

Damn! Zed thought. At that moment the far end of the house exploded, knocking all three defenders to the floor. From his new vantage point directly under the first hovercraft and its dangling crew, Zed idly wondered why the vehicle continued to bounce against the ceiling like a frustrated insect, its dead crew now dangling like puppets.

Bad deadman switch? He figured his side might use the machine later in the battle, if there were to *be* a later.

The thought had not completed itself when the roof fell in.

In panic, Zed pulled Marina and *Dash Two* from the wreckage, saw they weren't bleeding, as far as he could tell, and yelled, "Everyone to the basement! They're coming in down there!" *Dash Two* obeyed instantly, while Marina scrambled through the ceiling debris to dig out weapons.

Dash One was still out on the couch, so Zed left him there, grabbing one of the fully charged Donnes Marina had retrieved, and struggled to get around broken beams and chunks of plaster to the basement stairwell. Marina was right behind him, *Dash Two* was already down the stairs.

Chaos roared from the basement. Shots and screams filled the air, laser blasts and rifle fire, the symphony of battle. Zed hit the basement floor in a roll, but withheld his fire until he could tell where his allies were. A quick glimpse to his right showed *Dash Two* leaning against the time chamber door, one arm hanging limp. To Zed's left, at the destroyed basement wall, two white-bodysuited attackers were climbing over chunks of concrete blocks and clods of earth. The hole wasn't large enough to maneuver their hovercraft in. Good! Three against two.

Marina stayed in the stairwell. Good move! She would take out the first baddie who appeared in front of her position. Zed rolled to his feet, grabbing the injured *Dash Two,* pulling him over behind the file cabinets, away from the time chamber. If the bad guys wanted that chamber, Zed didn't want to be in front of it. And he didn't want his brave comrade from the future shot dead.

These two guys can't be the leaders, Zed thought furiously, *there's another craft out there. But they were professional enough*, he conceded. One against each wall, the two worked their way steadily toward the end where Zed and *Dash One* waited, staying behind machine tools and cabinets, not presenting Zed with a clear shot.

Brighton popped in, "Sire, these two are carrying ... ultra-smart, nano-tipped weapons. One shot has injured ... *Dash Two* ... even through the bodysuit. One hit could easily kill *you*."

Zed was afraid for his life. He leaned *Dash Two* up, the one good arm still holding its future rifle, trigger finger twitching to show he was still operational. Zed nodded, then crawled between two cabinets a few feet away. He would get at least one shot in, no matter the outcome of the battle.

Without warning, the world flashed yellow. *Dash Two* had stood up, spewing laser flames against both walls in a desperate attempt to get the enemy to show themselves.

The surprise tactic worked—one man stepped out from behind a workbench and aimed his weapon at *Dash Two*, a slow, deliberate maneuver. Puzzled, Zed spun around to see—there he was! The other one! Zed stood up behind the filing cabinet, screaming in fury at the top of his voice. Both attackers swung around to face him. Again, it was pure chaos: swinging his Donne like an ultra-tech sickle, Zed lashed out with full beam power, left and right, left and right. When both men fired back, Zed knew he was a dead man. But then *Dash Two's* yellow laser cones filled the basement, illuminating the area like a low-rock concert hall.

Somewhere in the melee, amidst the shouts and the screams and the lights and the blasts and the sizzles, Marina's smartgun added its obscene grunts to the cacophony.

This is pure holy hell! Zed's mind screamed at him. Then a jolting pain jerked him violently around, slamming him to the floor. Finally, darkness took him somewhere warm and safe.

ZED AWOKE TO A BURNING *BEAT* IN HIS CHEST, A *beat* pain keeping *beat* time with his heartbeat. A splitting headache accompanied his chest discomfort, a hellish parody of a sadistic orchestra. *Beat! Throb!* He couldn't bear to open his eyes against the brightness he knew was waiting to stab his tortured nerves. *Beat! Throb!* "Brighton, why am I hurting?" he asked quietly in the darkness. Himself didn't answer, just the constant beating pain:

Beat! Throb! Beat! Throb! Beat!Throb!Beat-throb! beat!-throb! beat-throb! The symphony of pain increased in pitch, built higher, spreading from chest and head, deep into all the known and unknown regions of his pitiful body, reaching a crescendo. Zed passed out again. His dreams were blood and fire and screams and pain. Finally he awoke again, this time forcing his eyes to accept the unwanted light. Thankfully, there was mostly dark, just one concentrated light source near him. A dark figure—*Dash Two*, it looked like—stood over him. A hurricane lantern supplied the only light in the ruined basement. Zed smiled weakly, gritting teeth against the throbbing pain in his breastbone. "Did we good guys win?"

Dash Two was silent, just shaking his head slowly left and right.

"No? But I'm alive, and you're—*where's Marina*?" The pain in his heart matched the pains in his chest as he screamed out her name. "Oh, God, is she…dead?"

Dash Two shook his head, vigorously this time, and pointed out through the missing end of the blasted basement, making a spinning trajectory with his fingertip. Then he clapped both hands together.

"She went outside? Chasing the Mexicans?"

Dash Two shook his head again, grabbing one arm, resisting with the other, as if trying to drag himself away. Zed groaned.

"She was—taken away? Kidnapped?"

As Zed knew he would, *Dash Two* nodded, slowly, sadly. "By the Mexicans," Zed stated flatly.

Surprisingly, *Dash Two* shook his head again

"Then—" the worst possible scenario suggested itself to Zed's battered mind. *Dash Two* held himself with both arms, shivering as if in the cold.

"Shit. It was Frost. Michael Frost!"

Dash Two nodded, turning his head as if in shame. Zed could not accept the emotional overload on top of his physical pain, and though he struggled to stand, he toppled over into unconsciousness once more.

IT WAS MORNING, THE BIRDS WERE CHIRPING, AND the rising sun greeted his eyes. Warm sunshine and a gentle breeze caressed Zed's skin, reminding him of the morning when he and Marina had—

Marina! Where was she? He tried to jump out of

bed. There was a bed under him, and he was—? He sighed, opening his eyes. It was Marina's bed, cleared of ceiling debris, but there was no ceiling over the bedroom. *Dash Two* helped him sit erect. *Dash One* lay on the bed next to him, either sleeping or still unconscious.

Dash Two pointed at himself and Zed, a waving finger and mime actions indicating that they were to go to the basement, pick up something, carry it to the yard, and then the Dashes would—there was that hand-slapping gesture again. Zed reasoned that *Dash Two* meant they, the future folk, were going to leave, back to their own time.

"But—you meant last night that Marina was taken—somewhere in time—by Frost?"

The dark *Dash* nodded, holding his hands palm up in a gesture of helplessness. *Oh God,* Zed thought, *these guys can't help me, won't help me. If I could just grab whatever portable time machine they're using..* The thought passed.

He was in no shape to confront the *Dash*, and wouldn't expose himself and his ally from the future to the paradox forces. It might be fatal. It might even be impossible to strip off that suit, use whatever technologies were built in.

Built in? Where was Brighton? "Brighton! Are you there?" No response. To the *Dash*: "Did they take out my computer?" A nod, accompanied by a mimicked pistol shooting Zed. "They shot me there, huh?" Another nod. *Shit!* He thought. Disarmed, dis-computered, disgusted. Why hadn't he stayed with Marina? What happened? He doubted he'd ever know, unless this *Dash* could somehow communicate.

Dash Two sat next to his larger companion and pulled out a cylinder, pointed it at Zed, shrugging his shoulders as if asking a question. "You want me to take a shot of that ... stuff? Will it help me?"

Two nods

Ah, what the hell, Zed thought. *Dead, I couldn't be much worse off.* "Go ahead, Mr. *Dash Two.* What's to lose? Future knows best."

He barely felt the *puff* of the injection into his neck. He'd wait to see if he passed out again, or if he got better. In any case, he understood that no doctor of the present time could treat his plight. If his wounds were not life-threatening, he would not stir up questions. *God knows, from the mess the house is in, there are going to be enough questions from the authorities.* "If I can maybe get a line to Brighton, Sr..." His voice trailed off. It was not information he needed, it was new hardware in his chest! Zed had gotten used to the back-up intelligence, his "other head," and he suspected that Brighton's DI programming was actually developing into his own alter ego.

Losing the computer was like losing a brother, maybe worse. A Siamese twin? He chewed his lip, considering his plight, his options.

Where, *when*, was Marina this very moment?

Over the next half hour the pain of his injuries subsided, and Zed guessed that *Dash Two's* ministrations were taking effect. Why didn't that man help his own comrade?

Of course! The bodysuit. That fabric wouldn't allow a pressurized injection into the body of *Dash One.* But *Dash Two* didn't seem too worried about his partner's condition, otherwise, why didn't they just leave Zed alone and return to the future after the battle? Or even before the battle? There was no accounting for their sense of duty, and their mission had been to retrieve the—

The Anachroscope! Was it still there, or had the Mexicans taken it, as they—as Frost—had taken his beloved Marina? He gestured downward to the basement, describing the shape of the device to the Dash. The dark figure nodded, pointed again at Zed and at himself, made the motions of carrying, his fingertip finally resting in the direction of the front yard.

"OK, I see. You and I, we carry that machine to the front yard, so you and your friend can scoot back to your own time?" A vigorous nod.

The visitor from the future left the open-air bedroom and in a minute, Zed heard the whine of a hovercraft. *Dash Two* led it—one of the Mexican vehicles from the attack the night before—down the hallway, a foot off the floor, like a child leading a gentle pony. Zed stood to watch as the *Dash* mounted the craft and rode it out the blown-away south wall of the house, turned it around, and lowered it into a large hole in the basement wall. At least they wouldn't have to drag out the damned Anachroscope by themselves, manually!

Flexing his arms, Zed felt almost all the soreness, all the pain, miraculously gone. *I could sell that spray injection potion for a billion dollars*, he smiled. *Fat chance, though!* Groaning, he headed for the stairwell to meet the time traveler in the basement.

The basement was a total wreck, two walls gone, all the equipment scorched and still smoking. A quick glance revealed that the time chamber doors were intact. *Dash Two* was pulling off floor joists that had wedged the Anachroscope against the concrete block wall. He weighed in to help, lugging against splintered timbers, hoping that the pains would not return.

They labored an hour to free the tapered

cylinder from a ton of concrete shards, blocks, and dirt. *Dash Two* took great care in removing all debris from the Anachroscope, peeling off and discarding various scraps of metal that stuck to the device, then spraying it with some kind of polish. As Zed continued to be amazed at what the man could produce from that magic bodysuit, the futureman pulled out yet another article, a spool of fine wire. Following mimed instructions, Zed lashed the stuff around the cylinder, then stood back as the Dash operated some kind of wrist computer. The fine wire glowed and dimmed. *Dash Two* tested it, then Zed pulled. *Damn!* The stuff was stuck somehow adhering to the cylinder. *Dash Two* straddled the hovercraft and goosed the future flyer slowly, until the heavy cylinder finally budged and with seeming reluctance, began to slide through the ruins of Dr. Daviess' basement toward the open end. Zed helped keep the device dragging straight behind, occasionally putting a shoulder behind it to help shove it over a pile of broken bricks. Coughing from the dust of concrete and earthen residue, Zed finally guided the 'scope through the wall as *Dash Two*'s craft jerked the device free of the basement.

Once the cylinder stood erect in the front yard, *Dash Two* just as magically unstuck the wire and the fine filament rolled itself back onto a spool as Zed stood in awe.

Dragging the device through the piles of junk in the basement and across the yard had not affected it in any way. Zed thought he'd like to have some of that polish that *Dash Two* had sprayed on the machine; it kept everything away, dust, dirt, scratches. Finally *Dash Two* handed the rolled wire to Zed, the spool no larger than a spool of sewing thread. In fact, the wire itself was finer than any thread Zed had encountered. The dark figure indicated to Zed that the stickiness, the welding, was actuated by pressing both ends of the metallic spool. *Handy stuff*, Zed mused. Not feeling any imminent danger from Father Time's surprises, he stuffed the spool into his pocket. "Thanks, Dash," he said.

Zed helped bring out *Dash One's* barely moving form out, placing him with his back leaning against the Anachroscope. His friends were leaving, probably forever, Zed knew. Then he'd be alone as never before. At least when he got back to Dallas, he could get another implant from Mark, and an update from Brighton, Sr.

Dash One had gathered up all the bodies of the attackers, their hovercraft, and their weapons and piled them some yards from the wounded *Dash Two* and the 'scope. A hand-waving circle that took in all the future equipment told Zed that the *Dashes* would remove all the evidence from the Daviess property. He nodded. Good idea, the police were going to be after him enough, without strange magical devices and un-suitable dead Mexicans to explain. He smiled at his cruel pun.

Dash Two came to say goodbye to Zed, but instead of the expected handshake, the dark figure threw his arms around Zed and gave him an affectionate embrace. The feel of the black Sidespace suit was warm and erotic; through the soft clothing, Zed could have sworn *Dash Two* was pronouncedly female. *A woman,* he realized, most definitely. He was shocked. That magic suit concealed more than future tools and toys, it covered up one voluptuous female, one tough woman, tough enough to be—sadness intruded upon his thoughts—Marina's sister.

And there's a fortune to be made in marketing that erotic suit material, Zed sighed to himself. Any reference to warmth, to eroticism, and he couldn't keep the comparison with Marina out of his mind.

Dash Two ran back to *Dash One* and the collected bodies and equipment. He (she?) tugged at the bodysuit where the right ear would have been, then dropped a hand to his (her?) beltline. Instantaneously, a translucent thirty-foot diameter hemisphere, wispy and golden, enveloped the future folk, the living, the dead, their weapons, vehicles, and all. They blinked out of existence, had never been. In the bright sunlight, dry grass danced with iridescent eddies of convoluted Sidespace, soon dying down to bare sparkles, tiny star-points, then nothing.

The display of advanced technology didn't impress Zed; he expected such progress in temporal transfer technology in the next few hundred years. And though grateful that his physical pain was gone, *Dash Two's* injection had not improved his emotional state. Even future technology wasn't that good. Marina was gone, maybe forever, and he wasn't sure he could handle that pain, that emptiness, for the rest of his life.

Zed was alone. Desperately alone.

But, something asked him, (his mind's voice?), what was *Dash Two*'s ear-tugging business about? Absently, he tugged his own earlobe, copying the gesture.

"Sire," Brighton answered cheerfully, "Welcome back to the living!"

Zed nearly fainted at the computer's sudden

intrusion. "My God, Brighton, is it really you? What happened?"

"Sire, in the flesh, so to speak. I have been reactivated by ... the visitor *Dash Two.* I, and you, suffered damage from a smartround carrying a nanotech warhead, during the battle in the basement. I do not recall the details. But the ... visitor ... defeated the nano-tech infection and then reconstituted me from downloads from Brighton, Sr."

Zed asked, "Brighton, were you ... your components ... part of that injection that the *Dash Two* gave me?" He was uneasy, thinking about the possibilities. Brighton in his chest was one thing, but in his bloodstream? He shivered.

"Sire, you are correct. My constituent components now comprise nano-elements that course your bloodstream and lymphatic system. Nanotechnology is the safest and most efficient means of achieving onboard capability. It is quite common in ... the future ... and easier to maintain than the quaint picoelectronics the Donne company installed in your chest."

Brighton's tone changed slightly, taking into account Zed's visceral reaction. "The ... visitor ... knew that you might feel some ... invasion of privacy, but part of the medicinal injection has provided a ... buffer ... to attenuate your psychological ... discomfort." Zed sighed. His long lost Siamese twin had returned, but with a vengeance. He hoped the *Dashes'* buffers would kick in soon.

"Sire, if you wish to reverse the injection, I am programmed to accept your decision. I can deactivate and be eliminated as a part of your regular bodily excretions."

Zed's first thought was, *Then piss off, ol' buddy!* But that momentary revulsion passed. Overall, he felt relieved. Given the free choice, he'd wait, see if he could accept the new technology, and overcome his prejudice. *If this is commonplace in the future, surely I can do it now*, he thought. "Brighton, my old friend, you can stay; at least unless I change my mind." He smiled. "It's good to have you back, old buddy."

ZED NEEDED PHYSICAL EXERCISE, SOMETHING TO work out the residual soreness in his body, something to work off the mental and psychological pain. The warm brown California hills, Daviess' acreage, provided just the right balance of energetic walking and reassuring calmness. He walked the perimeter of the farmlet property once more, surveying the house from the hills. It was pretty much a total wreck, with holes in three walls, parts and pieces of wall construction strewn all around inside the ruined house. He didn't know whether to call in a demolition company to remove the mess, or a contractor to repair it. Maybe both.

But without legal title, and with both Daviess and Marina gone God knows where, Zed couldn't get the permits or the money for the work. But, he hated just to leave the whole place open to the elements, especially with the time chamber there. He'd have to check whether the device still worked. It might be his only access to ... Marina. Frost had carried her off somewhere in time, *Dash Two* had said. *Damn!* If only he had stayed with Marina, if only he hadn't been so heroic in saving that *Dash*...woman.

He couldn't win, in his own mind. He'd thought Marina was safe and capable, that *Dash Two* was the one who'd needed help.

"Brighton?" he queried, hoping his friend might have more information about Marina, "is there any information at all about how Frost came in and grabbed Marina? Can you help me find out where—*when*—he might have taken her?"

Brighton answered with a sober tone; Zed concluded the DI's programming must have been enhanced—he himself had not programmed it to sense emotion and respond accordingly. Or else his friend had learned some wisdom lately. "Sire, my downloads include video monitoring of the household security system. The entire fight and abduction are available for playback."

"Why didn't you tell me right away, damn it?"

"Sire, your emotional state was ... *is* ... highly variable. I had to wait for your request." The voice was understanding, patient. Then: "I am your friend, Sire, not your mother."

Zed found a working video monitor in the wreckage of the living room, and sat on the battle-scarred couch to watch Brighton's replay of what happened after Zed had been shot. He had turned down Brighton's offer to replay the video directly into his optic nerve; he wasn't ready for the full-blown array of future capabilities the *Dash* had given Brighton.

The video caught the basement battle in full swing, multiple images simultaneously appearing on the screen. Zed hadn't known there were so many cameras following his every move. He grinned, thinking, there might be some good ones of Marina and himself in her bed... He let the thought drop. There'd be time enough for those, after he found her. *If* he found her.

Zed saw: himself, erupting like a horizontal volcano, spewing laser fire like a sickle, washing the two whitesuited Mexicans again and again with lances of pure energy; a yellow bloom blossoming in another corner of the screen, *Dash Two's* cones of yellow light scouring the walls, peeling paint, igniting wooden workbenches, blistering cabinets; and in a third corner of the screen, Marina crawling out of the stairwell at floor level, blasting the intruders with her smartgun, the tiny tracers of the smartloads impinging on the white bodysuits like pinprick meteorites; from the other quadrant of the screen, the attackers firing bursts of their weapons, their shots emerging from the clouds of energies that surrounded them, at first a swarm of fiery pellets, diminishing to nothing as the two men crumpled under the combined assaults. From a floor-level vantage point—Marina's, he realized with a start; how did the security system record that one?—Zed saw himself jerk backwards, holding his chest, and disappear from sight between two filing cabinets.

Marina ran to him, "Zed, darling! My God, don't die!" Zed's eyes filled with tears as his lover approached his video image. Little did she know she'd be gone, with Zed living on behind in agony. He forced himself to watch the rest. Marina cradled him in her arms, kissing his face, her hand searching out the flowering red obscenity on his chest. *Dash Two* looked around for other attackers, then placed his *(her?)* weapon aside, kneeling beside Zed. He (*she*) pulled out the magic wand cylinder, pulled open Zed's bloody shirt and gave him an injection directly into the bleeding wound. Another injection to the heart area, then another in the neck. Watching the video, Zed nodded. *Dash Two's* injections had saved his life from the smartround that blasted him. So he'd made the right decision after all; had *Dash Two* been killed, Zed himself would be dead right now.

He frowned; but at least dead, his heart wouldn't be hurting so much, missing Marina so much. But dead, he would be of no possible help to her. Grimly, he kept watching the video.

Suddenly, on the video sound channel, Zed heard what he knew was Brighton speaking to Marina. How could that be? Did *Dash Two* also inject her with a Brighton clone? That shot in the neck that cured her 'trope addiction? Good God, so Marina would have one of those future nano-tech onboard DI's too?

He was surprised that the paradox forces hadn't intervened, but then, he himself had had the same treatment, the same computer, hadn't he? He figured there must be some exceptions to the repulsion forces. Would he ever learn the rules of the damned game?

On the screen, Brighton was saying, "Mistress! Be warned! Temporal energies are coalescing! Another person is materializing in the front yard!

"What's it doing, Brighton?" the image of his lover asked. Zed was right, she did have an onboard Brighton. This was interesting; if Frost didn't know, perhaps she would have some advantage, and maybe could escape. He was determined to clear away the entrance to the time chamber downstairs, in case Marina had the opportunity to come back here. Damn it, if he knew where she was, *when* she was, he could go there himself in that same chamber. That would wait. Maybe the video would give some clues.

"Mistress," the screen said, "the one person has materialized. Another time traveler."

"What's he doing?" Marina asked, giving Zed over to the care of *Dash Two*. Zed knew she would go for her weapon and confront this new arrival, certainly the leader of the hoodlums. He hoped the video would follow her, then realized that part of the video was what she herself had seen, from the vantage point of her version of Brighton.

Outside, Marina stood with her smartgun aimed at the single person standing next to his hovercraft. Zed could tell that it was a man dressed in casual clothing, khaki pants and blue work shirt, no semi-morph protective clothing. From the lack of any repulsion forces as the figure approached Marina, Zed figured that the man was not part of the family. From thirty feet away, Zed saw that the newcomer had one misshapen leg, much shorter than the other, giving him an almost belligerent natural stance. The man was barefoot, too. Short, not over five foot six. Then Zed saw the man's snarling face and his heart nearly stopped.

Michael Frost!

"I'll be go to hell," Marina said under her breath.

She kept the gun pointed directly at Frost's head, her eyes not moving from the object of her hatred. In fact, she walked right up and stuck the smartgun right into his stomach.

"What the hell are you doing here, weeko?" she demanded. Zed watched as Frost's perpetual petulant scowl turned itself into a grin, somewhat grotesque now, in an older, aged face. For all the bravado the man appeared confused, uncertain.

"I enjoyed your body so much all those years ago, Ms. Tanner, that I had ... to come back for more," Frost snarled. "How long has it been, Dr. Tanner-Wynter? Just a month ... in your ... time ...? Or a ... century? I keep ... losing ... track ... of the ... *time*." Calmly he glanced down at his wrister. "You might want to … put down that gun, by the way. My Mexican *cartelero* reinforcements ... will be here soon." A crooked smile vipered across his wrinkled face. "You don't want to ... get hurt, my ... dear."

"It's been at least a *thousand* years, wacko," Marina answered, spitting out the words. The smartgun was now right in the small man's face. "Zed and I thought you were blown to hell in the Chihuahua explosion." Zed could almost feel her rage, her twitching trigger finger, her desire to hamburger this piece of human filth that had caused her so much misery. Zed studied the man's face. Frost looked positively ancient, sixty or seventy years old, at least, his face drawn into a disfiguring sneer, his eyes bloodshot and rheumy. What had happened to him? Had Zed caused that horribly mangled leg with the Chichén Itzá bomb?

Marina continued, "I seem to remember you liked boys better. I'd like to send you back there with your Mayan slaves, let them know you're not any kind of god. They'd know how to treat you!" Zed was somewhat startled at her words, but then recalled all the revulsion he himself had felt for Frost's human sacrifices and child abuse. And Marina's treatment from Frost and Balleen had been personal and extensive, essentially their sex slave for a year or more. She had every right to be furious!

In view of all the disasters since his return from

ancient Yucatán, Zed found himself wishing he'd let Cardenas kill the megalomaniac and end the whole mess back then and there.

On screen, Frost put his hands on his hips in the defiant stance Zed remembered from the Yucatán, but it was rendered somewhat comical by the misshapen left leg Frost favored. "Oh, but Marina, I—" he cut short his own statement as her words sank in. "You said ... a *thousand years* ... ago? In the ...Yucatán?" Looking closely at her face, he screeched, "Oh, *shee-ite nights and sunni days!*" Zed didn't recognize the terminology, but knew it was a curse. "How ... old are ... you, Ms. Tanner-Wynter? *When* ... the hell are you?"

"Frost, you should know, you wacko," she replied somewhat taken aback by the demeanor of a weeko with a gun in his gut. "Zed destroyed your God-damned factories just two months ago. I got out of your dungeon fourteen months ago, *with* your little 'trope gift, you bastard!"

Frost's eyes bulged and Zed thought the little man would die of apoplexy right there. Instead, he took a step back. Zed was surprised that Marina didn't shoot him on the spot. Instead, she taunted, "And, we killed all of your Mexican terrorists an hour ago, right here, you son of a bitch!"

Frost held up his fists in rage, screaming, "They came ... *earlier?* No! No! We were supposed to sack … Steve's records and equipment … from his empty house! We had it all timed ... *Aarrghh!*" As his anguished cry of fury and frustration faded, the hysterical man exploded in a whirlwind of fists and feet, knocking Marina's weapon out of her grasp. Before she could react to the unexpected assault, Frost pummeled Marina's body and face with a volley of blows.

Finally Marina responded. Faster than Zed would have thought possible, she whirled from Frost's reach, just as he was turning to hit at her chest. Marina's right heel hit solid on Frost's incoming forearm and there was a satisfying *crack*! Screaming and holding his broken arm, the man rallied to attack with his feet. Zed reasoned that the man must have received some nano-enhancements of his own, to fight so fast and furiously. Zed hoped Marina would hold her own, then realized that whatever she did in this video, she had ultimately lost the fight, had been taken captive. *I hope she maimed the wacko more, at least!* Zed thought in anger.

The view changed, and Zed saw both fighting figures from a camera somewhere outside the house. Marina parried Frost's unshod kicks with her hands, getting a few significant bruises along her arms, but giving as good as she got. With an effort she bypassed Frost's swinging right foot and landed a kick on his right knee, bending it backwards, the wrong way. A sickening crunch rewarded her effort and the man tumbled with a shriek.

Marina's resistance paid off: Frost broke off his attack, rolling to his bruised feet some yards from her. Marina jumped to retrieve her smartgun, but Frost pulled a pistol from somewhere on his body and told her to stand still. She hesitated.

As Zed watched in horror, Frost fired a greenish beam at Marina. She crumpled into a heap. Frost returned to his feet, walked until he straddled above her, and fumbled with something at his belt. He disembarked, kneeling to fondle under Marina's jumpsuit. Frost yelled out to the house, directly to the camera, which zoomed in on his bleeding face. "Screw you ... Zed Wynter ... wherever ... you are. I've got ... your woman, and will I have ... fun with her! Some of my men ... just love ... gringo women!"

Zed's blood boiled at the sight of his lover being molested by the weeko wacko creep. He knew the scene was being staged just for him, and that enraged him even more. Through pain-filled eyes, in purest agony, he watched the final scene on the video screen. A golden hemisphere formed around the unconscious Marina and the triumphant psycho Frost, glimmering in the night sky. As the bubble coalesced, Zed heard Frost shout something inaudibly. With a soft *pop*, the bubble vanished, leaving the video camera and Zed alone, vacant air sparkling and twinkling like lonely stars in a vast empty galaxy. Zed could feel Brighton staying away from his thoughts, withdrawing to leave the human alone in his grief.

Zed wept.

THE GENERAL IN HIS UNDERGROUND

Afterward, Zed camped out in the wreckage of the Daviess farmhouse, sweeping out an area to sleep in, taking time to clear the time chamber door of the residue of the battle. Outside the house, the cool ground offered him a respite from the warfield atmosphere, away from the bedroom he and Marina had shared and its attendant memories. His emotional state was rock-bottom, feeling hopeless in the face of superior technologies from God-knew what future time. A grim smile accompanied the memory that at least he and his small band of defenders had kept off most of the band of gangsters. If only he'd been there to face Frost at the crucial moment...

He had dredged up the fortitude to function partially normally in those first few hours after the *Dashes* had left, before the loneliness of the dark valley closed in around him. In the databases that Brighton had copied from the household computer before it was destroyed in the violence of the previous night, he'd found a message from Daviess for Marina, giving the name and phone number of a building contractor, a personal friend of his, in case any maintenance was ever required. Zed quickly made contact with the man, stressing the urgent need for confidential repairs, giving as a reason a gas furnace explosion and passing on to the man an agreed-upon password. The man laughed, saying he'd been told by the Scotsman to take care of any and all repairs for his niece. The contractor took Zed's word that the niece had let him stay there while she was gone, and was reassured when Zed gave him the proper password. The contractor said he'd be there the next day with his crew, to clean up the whole mess.

As Zed fixed himself some supper on a campfire outside the house, he felt that he needed information before deciding upon action. Anything to keep his mind off Marina's fate. He asked, "Brighton, do you have any idea about the temporal anomaly around this place? Why the time travelers, even Marina and I, couldn't achieve the destinations and arrival times we wanted? Frost screwed up at least twice, the Dashes arrived at the wrong time, the Mexicans didn't rendezvous at the right time with their boss, Marina and I only went back five years, not to ancient Greece. What could be going on?"

Brighton did not respond for a full thirty seconds, though Zed sensed the DI's energies in full swirl. The human realized that his DI was rapidly adapting to Zed's own thought processes; Zed wondered if his 'symbiotronic' relationship would someday produce a chimera of electronic/man, a being with accelerated thinking capacity yet still human. *As long as I maintain control*, he thought, *as long as I stay myself, then infinite knowledge and lightning thinking will be very handy*. But if he had those powers, would he still be Zed Wynter? *No time for such thoughts now, not when Marina is still lost.*

"The anomaly, sire," Brighton finally answered, "had to do with an out-of-time artifact located here at the farmlet. Acting on information downloaded from ... the future visitors ... and their Anachroscope data, I have come to this conclusion."

Startled, Zed tried to think of any anachronistic 'artifact.' Could Dr. Daviess have recovered something from the past and brought it here? Could it be one of those vases that used to be in the living room before it was all destroyed in the battle? And, even if there were some old Mayan carving, what kind of power would it possess, to disrupt the smooth trajectories that the future folk routinely traveled?

He queried the computer once again, "Brighton, what is the nature of that 'out-of-time' artifact? Something Daviess brought back? And why would anything screw up everybody's time traveling, why would it grab the Anachroscope and make it weight more?"

A minute of silence while Brighton's nano-components coalesced, caucused, integrated the accessed information. *It tickles a little,* Zed said to himself. *Kind of sensuous, though.* Finally the computer said, "Sire—Zed. I have tentative answers, though still somewhat speculative. The anachronistic object was possessed of an intense field of 'temporal embolism,' to use a future-word. This object, when brought to this place, near the first operational Daviess chamber, caused a severe distortion in the temporal potential of the chamber, analogous to an intense gravitational field."

Zed followed Brighton's logic, though it still didn't explain much. "The temporal Sidespace components of the chamber here were extended backwards and forwards into time, diminishing with distance from the initial event."

Like the inverse-square law of gravitation, Zed noted. *Very analogous to Newton's Law.* "This distorted field was sufficient to alter, to 'screw up,' as you most colorfully put it, planned trajectories through Sidespace. You and Ms. Tanner were physically closest to the disturbance, using the most primitive and inefficient temporal technology, hence your journey was prevented. You could not escape the temporal potential well."

Zed saw where the discussion was leading; it was like listening to himself explain to himself. Brighton was really becoming his 'other head.' "The temporal potential well disturbed even those more sophisticated time travelers, affecting their arrival times, making them almost unpredictable."

"I can accept that, I guess. But what about the Anachroscope? Its change in mass, its own stop here?"

"Zed, the Anachroscope fell into an unexpected eddy current of Sidespace, attracted by the anachronism here. When the 'scope and the object were finally physically intimate, the nature of the device's Sidespace components locked it into local TimeSpace coordinates. This manifested itself to you as an increase in mass."

"But—when did the anomaly arrive here? Physically?"

"Three days ago, Zed."

. . .

"It—it came here when *I* did? How could that be?" Sudden realization struck Zed and he patted his pockets. "Oh my God," he breathed, almost prayerfully, "I know what it was." In Zed's brain, Brighton played back a video scan image: *Dash Two* prying off a small rectangle of metal adhering to the Anachroscope, tossing it casually to one side, not knowing or caring what she had done. As the image zoomed in on the metal piece, Zed knew from memory what the camera would show:

Model Romeo-14, Serial Number 002-35-101RR.

Manufactured by QuanTonics, S. A.

Hecho en México

The QuanTonics nameplate!

Zed cursed himself, slapping his forehead with an open palm. "God damn it! I brought one of those things with me when I came to see Marina. The stupid thing must have fallen out of my pocket! And then was somehow attracted to the surface of the 'scope." Suddenly he was thankful that he had dropped the thing before entering the Daviess chamber with Marina—that could have been an even worse disaster.

Zed visualized his nameplate souvenir as a gaping chuckhole in a great temporal highway, bouncing and jouncing great vehicles until they wrecked. On the other hand, something inside him seemed to say, Who's to say that it wasn't better that the *Dashes did* come, *did* treat Marina, *did* implant the new Brighton? And Frost; what if he had arrived on time with his Mexicans? What if Zed hadn't come here at all? The Anachroscope might be in Frost's hands, like some future equivalent of a nuclear weapon.

"You're right about the 'intense temporal potential', Brighton. That nameplate is an anachronism to beat all anachronisms. A part that was never made, a loop in time all by itself." Zed stirred his pork and beans and doused the fire. "I'd better go down there and find that thing, dispose of it out in these hills somewhere. I have a feeling I might want to use that time machine in the basement, and next time, the God-damned thing better work!"

The nameplate turned up easily, Zed following the pictures in his mind, in a pile of smashed electronic equipment. Fingering the plate through his hand like a magician with a gold piece, his mind flashed on a possibility. *What if Frost and the guerrillas were after the* nameplate, *not the Anachroscope? What if they'd tried to work out the knot in TimeSpace themselves, maybe get a hold of the anomalous piece, use it as a weapon to hijack yet other time travelers?* The possibilities were endless, he sighed. At the moment he just wanted to be shed of the tiny piece of metal that had caused so much disruption in TimeSpace, and in his own life.

Zed hiked the hills a mile east and buried the nameplate in an arroyo on the scoured side of the mountains. A few tons of boulders rolled down the hill on top of the anomalistic rectangle ensured Zed that the thing was well hidden, and well away from his basement time machine.

His work done, Zed sat and watched the strangely-sparkling waters of Lake Livermore, a blue-black shimmering jewel, set in the unlikely scoured hills surrounding it. Perhaps with the notoriety of the site, it would be years before anyone even bothered to walk to this place again. He returned back to the ruined house and cold food and tried to sleep.

Later that night, lying awake with his turbulent memories, Zed reviewed his plans and his resources. There was no need to return to Dallas; his "sabbatical" still had weeks to go. He didn't need Donne's implants anymore, either, not with the future-folks' nanotech Brighton in his blood. He smiled, his DI "blood-brother" was perfectly welcome now.

Really, he couldn't tell the difference between the extra-tit Brighton and the new nano-Brighton. Except the latter was much more of a person, more sensitive to his needs, a real partner. A *soul,* perhaps. *Hmmm.* Given that Brighton could access all of Zed's memories, all of his brain structure, and that the improved Brighton could exist without Zed's organic body, could that mean that in a fashion Zed would be living forever? He didn't buy that, not at all, on further reflection. Brighton himself might stay around for centuries, but ol' Zed, without the guts and the gray matter, would not be aware of the DI's immortality. No, Zed would surely die. But the thought of Brighton living on intrigued him. He'd think of the implications of *that* later.

Right now, he wanted to find Marina. Could he? In all of Time and the whole planet, would there be some way of narrowing the possibilities? He turned to Brighton with the question. "Old friend, brother Brighton, I want you to collate all of the known information about time travel, all of Daviess' papers, cubes, computer files, everything. I want you to review the video recording you showed me last night, of Frost's comings and goings through time. And try to answer the question: is there any way of telling where and when he has taken Marina?"

For the first time, he *felt* Brighton's machinations, as if some of the computer's internal workings were as available to him as his were to the DI. *Is that possible?* He asked himself, *Can I feel inside* him *as he feels inside* me*?* Clearly that would be an even more effective integration of man and machine, an advance far beyond mere implants or nano-machines. For a moment he wondered if there was more to the nano-Brighton/Wynter interface than he had been told. But now he had more important things to worry about, namely Marina's when-abouts.

"Sire—Zed. There is information about Michael Frost's immediate temporal destination as he left here last night."

Zed sat up sharply. "Tell me, now!" There was hope!

"Zed, a survey of the instrumentation on Frost's control belt, done under extreme magnification of the images you saw, gives an indication that he intended to travel to Mt. Olympus, Greece. The exact time destination is unclear, however, because of the anomalous behavior of all temporal transfer devices during the interval of plus and minus two weeks about yesterday."

Zed heard only one of Brighton's statements: *Mt. Olympus!* The destination that he and Marina had attempted, only to arrive at Dr. Daviess', five years in the past, and in the same chamber. Would it hurt to try it again, now that the anomaly was far removed from the chamber? Zed jumped to his feet, found a laserflash and a fully charged Donne, and made his way through the scorched stairwell, down into the jumble of debris that was the basement. The time chamber waited, the path clear, the path he had made for Marina's return.

With any luck, he would bring her back that same way, down the triumphal path, surrounded by Stephen Daviess' scattered equipment. Grimly, he pressed the button labeled in Daviess' hand, "Mt. Olympus, Homeric Era," and stepped inside the chamber.

The doors slid shut silently, but nothing happened. For a moment Zed feared a power shutoff, something to prevent his passage back in time. But as the familiar blue glow finally enveloped the room, Zed sighed in relief, realizing what had transpired in the few seconds of hesitation. Brighton had foreseen that Zed's palmprint could not start the temporal transfer, and had reprogrammed the chamber to respond to his hand.

Reality *wavered* as temporal potentials from the Sidespace components of the chamber wall fought to reestablish themselves in accordance with the sudden surge of power. Dancing in rhythm to relationships first discovered by Dr. Daviess, a few cubic yards of the Universe burped into Sidespace and resettled itself *elsewhen*, satisfying new constraints of TimeSpace. Dr. Zed Wynter, by now a collection of indistinguishable electrospatial constructs within the volume of oscillating TimeSpace, was reconstituted, along with his clothes, laserflash, and Donne weapon, at another point in Time and another point in Space.

Zed came to consciousness, aware of a pounding on the door of the time chamber. "Get out, Zed! Hurry! It's dangerous!" He didn't recognize the muffled voice, but its urgency was unmistakable. Taking no chances, he flipped the Donne onto full penetration power, then slapped the palmpress and stood to one side, ready for anyone. He hoped it would be Frost.

The doors slid full open and Zed nearly choked. There, blocking the view of a sloping muddy walkway leading to the surface, a silhouette framed against bright moonlight, stood possibly the last person Zed ever thought to see: Hilario Cardenas!

Cardenas stood watching as the time chamber doors slid open, laughing loudly as the American stumbled out into bright southern moonlight that flooded a steep upward staircase. Zed smelled seawater and mold, an unpleasant combination. "And you are wondering what century this is, Dr. Wynter? You are wondering why the Garcista *bandido,* Cardenas, stands ready to welcome you to an island off the coast of the state of Louisiana?" In answer to Zed's astonished look and numb nod, the Mexican laughed and put his arm around his *compadre,* leading him up the stairs from the underground chamber to the surface. Water sloshed around their feet and Zed saw with dismay that the time chamber stood to be flooded by rapidly-rising seawater. He held onto his Donne.

Stunned, Zed protested, "What the hell is this, Hilario? You said *Louisiana*? What the hell century is it, anyhow? I was on my way to ancient Greece!"

By this time the two men were at the surface, evidently a small island, Zed could tell by the moonlight on a wide seascape of tiny waves just yards away. They were surrounded by perhaps a dozen people, some dressed in Garcista battle fatigues. Cardenas looked at the glowing face of his wrister. "*Señor* Zed, it is still Wednesday night, and you left your California farmhouse just microseconds ago, as the ether flies."

"But how—?" Zed didn't know which question to ask. "Filemón wants to see you, *immediamente*," Cardenas said flatly, as if his General's wishes were the law of the Universe. From the way the General had intervened in Zed's intended time travel, Zed figured the Universe might indeed take account of Filemón Garcia's wishes.

A fast motorboat took the entourage from the coastal island through moon-flecked Gulf waters to a dark ocean-going ship. Small lights at either end defined the length of the vessel, some hundred feet or more. Zed guessed it to be a destroyer or frigate of some kind, judging from the missile batteries and cannon silhouetted on its superstructure. *Filemón must really be serious,* Zed thought, *to arrange for this ship to be here. And how the* hell *did he arrange for my time chamber to be hijacked?* By now, Zed was accepting almost any kind of strange occurrence as normal in time travel. Like the repulsion paradox forces, if it happened, it was allowed, and that was the only rule.

INSIDE THE BLACKED-OUT VESSEL, ZED WAS TAKEN to a paneled office, complete with a four foot by twelve foot oaken staff officers' table. Cardenas introduced him to half a dozen or so Garcista officers, some in Mexican Navy uniforms.

Looks like Filemón's getting some support from the Mexican armed forces, Zed noted. His friend's revolution might have a chance after all. Cardenas raised a glass of tequila to his American compatriot. "*El Señor* Wynter," he said, "*¡Salud, dinero y amor!*" Eight men and a woman joined the toast, and Zed responded with one of his own: "*¡A el General Jefe*, Filemón Garcia!" Amidst cheers, Zed took his shot glass in one heroic gulp.

"And we have the benevolent neglect of your Coast Guard, *Señor* Wynter," one Mexican naval officer was saying as Zed relaxed on an overstuffed chair, "to account for the ease of our entry into your country." The man paused and licked his lips, his full moustache moving jauntily. "Your own government wishes Filemón to accelerate his victories and so re-establish stability in its little brother of the South." Zed heard a significant sneer.

"Peace, stability, what's wrong with that, *Señor*? You don't sound happy about it."

"*Señor* Gringo," the man said, as the other Mexicans grew quiet, sensing a confrontation, "you have perhaps heard the saying, 'Poor México! So far from God, so close to the United States.' Some of us think your country, so big and so rich, has caused much of our pain."

Zed sighed and countered the argument, pointing out that the pre-capitalist feudal system Mexico had inherited from Spain was the root cause of most of México's problems, whereas the United States had adapted the relatively free British economic and political systems and flourished. He contended that the once-colonized nations of the Pacific Rim, now the richest per capita countries on the planet, offered the best model for Mexico's eventual destiny, a pathway to free enterprise and free societies.

"Ah, so the ministrations of capitalists like our

Mr. Frost offer salvation for México, *Señor*," the Mexican wagged his head. "I wish so, but I cannot believe it. You may wish to study the course of Mexican economics of the early 21st Century." Zed was getting tired of the man's arguments. What was this leading to? Mexico's economic debacles of the 2020 and '30s had nothing to do with free enterprise, they were the last gasps of a dying monopolistic one-party system being parasitized by drug cartels, one that ultimately failed to go down with the worldwide collapse of dictatorships.

"*Señor,*" Zed said, standing to give his opinion, "Your own General Garcia advocates a free-enterprise libertarian economy, the one way proven to help the poor. Why do you take issue with your own leader?"

"There are discussions in the leadership that you know nothing about, Yankee—" the Mexican fairly shouted at Zed. In back of the officer, Zed saw Cardenas flinch, preparing to draw his holstered pistol. *For me or for this crazy Mexican?* Zed wondered.

Someone raised another toast at the mention of their leader, and Zed and his antagonist dropped the discussion. Clearly, one more revolution in Mexico was not going to erase a few hundred years of ill feelings. Not while the Marine Hymn and the Heroes of Chapultepec continued to be hotly contested holy causes on either side. The American shook his head; could some other Mexican group be the ones that sided—*will side?* —with Frost, and come back from the future to attack us last night?

Around the room, the tension gradually eased and energetic discussions about wartime missions and the postwar system abounded. Garcia had advanced significantly in the past few months, taking effective control of several southern Mexican states and much of the Pacific coast. Though *El Jefe* himself continued the struggle in Quintana Roo and in the Yucatán, his free-enterprise rebellion had touched the souls of millions of Mexicans. Particularly those with direct experience in new technologies. Guadalajara itself, with its productive ultra-tech industries, was in open rebellion, though the Federal troops were keeping the factory workers going by brute force. *That's one region too important financially for México City to lose*, Zed thought. It seemed to him that the entire country was on the verge of a successful revolution. If only the *Federales* didn't decide to nuke their own cities as they had their oil fields.

Looking around the room at the Mexican sailors and soldiers, Zed wondered if some of these very people could be the ones he, Marina, and *Dash Two* had killed—*would* kill?—in the foothills around Livermore. Time travel had a way of screwing up tenses. During the drinking, Zed kept trying to pry the reason out of Cardenas—and the how—he had been re-routed to a tiny island off the Louisiana coast, rather than being allowed to continue on to Mt. Olympus in ancient Greece.

And how did that chamber ever get out in the Gulf of Mexico, anyhow?

"Ah, but that terminal no longer exists, Zed," Cardenas said at last. "My men dynamited it soon after we left." Watching Zed's shocked reaction, he said, "It was situated at a convenient but temporary time and location for the Daviess machine to easily access. It was flooding anyhow, my friend, and we could not afford to leave evidence of its existence behind. You see, that terminal was built to be used only once." The Mexican grinned widely as Zed stood puzzled. "And today was that time!"

MUCH LATER, ZED POUNDED A FIST INTO AN OPEN palm and wrinkled his forehead, staring right at Cardenas. "So, Hilario, all of you Garcistas, this is what I am asked to believe: Your people received a message engraved on an aluminum plate found inside the old underground factory site in Pisté. Right?" The Mexican nodded. Others stood and listened to the story for the first time, overawed at the concept of the interlocking trajectories possible in time travel.

"And this message was supposedly from Dr. Stephen Daviess, telling you I would be arriving at this particular place, this Chandeleur Island, on this very night." He paused, gulping down more tequila to calm his frayed nerves. "And that you had to hurry to fetch me because the temporal chamber was only temporary, and I had to be dug out first and then the chamber destroyed after I left." He looked at the faces of all of the Mexicans. *Do they really understand all of this?* he thought. *I sure don't!* "Am I correct?" Nods from most, and blank stares from a few, confirmed his retelling of the information.

"But did Daviess say what you were to do with me? Why I was brought here? Why didn't you just put me on a plane and fly me down here?"

Cardenas held his palms forward as another Mexican, (Herrera, Zed remembered) whispered in his ear. Cardenas shook his head. "My *compadre* here, Zed, has just confirmed what we suspected."

"Which is?" Zed asked, irritated.

"The Daviess farmhouse is no more. It was obliterated in a large explosion earlier tonight, probably seconds after you left, Zed. Nothing remains but a crater." Cardenas listened to more of Herrera's whispers. "Holy mother! Zed, they think it was a micro-nuke!"

Zed fell backward on his chair, stunned. Steve's house, destroyed, nuked! But why?

"In answer to your unspoken question, Zed," Brighton told him subvocally, "unknown agents, possibly Mexican Federales, possibly another group of future terrorists or guerrillas, in the surrounding hills, mortared the farmlet with some kind of clean sub-kiloton weapon."

Damn, the waste! Zed cringed, but grateful to have escaped his intended vaporization. Someone, some*when*, had decided to put an end, once and forever, to whatever anomaly had existed at the Daviess farm. Suddenly Zed felt gratitude that Frost had grabbed Marina. He scowled. *Or did he come back to finish me off? That son of a—*

"Brighton, old friend! You made the time trip O.K.?" Zed subvocalized. "Are you all right?"

"Sire, you must remember that I am now distributed in nanosystems in your body. I am also backed up in innumerable mainframes and subsystems scattered around the world and in space. I have ... provisions ... for countering my own paradox forces. I am independent, I am well. I can travel with you anywhere, any*when*." Zed nodded, acknowledging both Cardenas and Brighton. He hoped these Mexicans did not suspect anything about his onboard DI or his nano-enhanced physical capabilities. Not all of these men were friendly, not in the least.

Cardenas had been saying, "We do not know who destroyed your base there, but Dr. Daviess did say in the engraved tablet that you would be away when the farmhouse was destroyed."

Zed thought back over the convolutions that time travel allowed. Had Steve deliberately included the Gulf Island terminal as a refuge from an attack he had known would occur? If so, why didn't he know about Marina's abduction, and warn them to leave two days before? And which time-displaced aspect of Daviess had sent the message? How had he gotten back to the Yucatán factory to deliver the engraved warning? Did that mean the Yucatán chamber was still in operation?

"What I still don't understand, Hilario," Zed said, trying to sort out some meaning from his situation, "is why Filemón pulled me out, what he wants."

The Garcista only shrugged. "*Quien sabe, Sr. Zed?* We are just following the instructions left for us by Dr. Daviess. So far they have been accurate and very helpful. Why not continue to believe that they will be of utmost utility?

"And also," he grinned evilly, "Filemón wants you to come with me to Yucatán. By sailboat."

"A sailboat?" Zed wrinkled his forehead with suspicion. "I'm supposed to get to General Garcia in Yucatán with a *sailboat? Un poco loco, no?*" He laughed sarcastically, tossing back the sheaf of sailboat drawings and photographs to the stunned Mexican guerrilla.

Eight men and a woman sat around the meeting table in the naval officers' paneled room. To Zed's left sat the one other Anglo who had arrived just minutes ago, a young Dr. Bill Lorenz, a semimorph expert who hoped to evaluate Daviess'

Yucatán time travel chambers. Four Garcista officials sitting opposite them were frowning at Zed's rejection; they spoke in rapid Spanish. Zed knew they weren't happy.

One man, a naval officer whose rank Zed couldn't determine, stared at Zed directly and after a significant pause addressed him in flat uninflected tones. Zed read nothing at all in the man's expressionless Mayan face. "*Señor* Wynter, our man Cardenas tells us of your fantastic trip from *Ciudad Chihuahua* to Quintana Roo." Zed didn't blink. He could play the flat-face, too. "We believe Cardenas. We acknowledge and applaud your actions in destroying the installations, factories that were producing warbots for the Federal Government of México." Smiling, Zed nodded.

"However, we want to utilize this technology, this instantaneous travel machine, for—" the Mayan scanned the faces of his countrymen, "—for military purposes, to hasten the conclusion of our Revolution, to reduce the casualties that must occur when we lay siege to México, D. F." The man stood, walked to the wall, and accessed a full map projection of México, the rebellious provinces showing dark red, Filemón's Guatemalan bases in dark green. Pointing to the rebels' provisional capital in Mérida, the Mayan finger-tipped a circle around the city. "For this reason, for your technical help with the time travel technology, General Garcia wants you to return to Mérida immediately." He turned to Zed and nodded. "I must convince you to go."

Zed sensed the solid determination in the man's mien, his facial expression, his body language. It was the same dedication, the same resignation he'd seen in Cardenas, in a thousand other Garcistas in the Yucatán: *I will do anything to satisfy Filemón and the Revolution!*

"*Señor* Wynter," the Mayan smiled, "I believe you will want to go."

The Indian explained that General Garcia wanted to tell Zed that the Revolution was in its final phases, but there was still significant warfare ahead. Cardenas and one man had come from México to meet with sympathizers in the U. S. to appeal for whatever support could be sent during this crucial period. Garcia, having heard Cardenas' time travel story in full detail, thought there might be a way to use the Daviess chambers to transport troops across the front lines, directly into the Capitol, ending the Government's resistance with one quick wave of assassinations and communications facility seizures, proclaiming victory from Government headquarters in one surprise move. All Federal forces would lay down their arms, and much bloodshed and destruction would be avoided.

And your side would win for sure, Zed said to himself, *whether a majority of Mexicans wanted you or not.* Aloud, Zed argued that he did not have access to Daviess' technology, that he barely understood the physics. He didn't want to return to the war zones, wanting no part of the massive civil war now brewing across México. But during his discourse, Brighton reminded Zed that there might be other reasons for going to México.

"Zed, recall that General Garcia has received messages from Dr. Daviess. Remember too, that the one remaining operative time machine may be located in the Yucatán factory." Zed absorbed that information. Brighton was telling him that

Marina's only chance was for Zed to return to the Yucatán, and use the remaining time machine to find her. Zed wondered if Daviess had left other instructions for Filemón. His determination wavered, and his Mexican friend caught the scent.

Cardenas wrinkled his mouth in a half grin that quickly became a scowl. *"Compadre,* for this I dig you out of a submerging tomb on a deserted island? Zed, you must be brave, and help us in our war. Why, if you had stayed home in California, you would now be ionized gas, floating in the stratosphere." He bowed, smiling, "Come with us, help us."

Just then, a uniformed naval officer came up to Cardenas and whispered in his ear. The Mexican agent stiffened. "Zed, more bad news. Your Dallas apartment was also bombed tonight!"

Zed sank into his chair, realizing that much of his life's work, all his collections, maybe all of his possessions, were gone, destroyed without reason. His patience exploded; out of control, he jumped to his feet and grabbed Cardenas by the shirt. "Damn you, Hilario! Is this how you get volunteers for Filemón? Blow up the Daviess farm? Blow up my apartment? Leave me with no place to go, no choice but to come with you?" Cardenas was surprisingly compliant and offered no resistance to Zed's hysteria. Through his rage, Zed realized that the Mexican could have beaten him, *keratsu* or no. The man was a trained warrior. Zed relaxed his grip, stepping back from Cardenas. It was just as well, for six weapons were pointed at him. One Mexican had already grabbed Lorenz as well. In such a confrontation, all Anglos were suspects.

Zed broke off the situation. "I'm—sorry, Hilario. I've been through so much—this was just the last straw." He crumpled into the chair. The one Mexican released Lorenz and half a dozen pistols slipped back into uniforms and holsters.

Cardenas said sympathetically, "Zed, *compadre*, I won't deny we would have bombed your house, your office, anything at all, if such had been our orders, but I assure you we did not. And, no one was in the farmhouse when it was nuked, and first reports say that no one was killed or injured when your apartment was blasted." The aide, Herrera, eyed the two Anglos while he sidled up to Cardenas and spoke in a low voice to his boss. "Zed," Cardenas continued, "our own surveillance teams in California and Texas think there may be *Federales* after you. Our spies in the Mexican embassy in Washington report that the United States and México are both trying to apprehend you."

The FBI again, damn it! Zed swore to himself. Of course, an ostensibly "friendly" government like México's could request intelligence information about suspected agents acting in its territory, probably a routine computer inquiry between intelligence organizations. Zed hoped that the bombings of the two places had been Federales, not the FBI. He wasn't too worried about the failing Mexican government, it was not likely to be a threat too much longer. But Washington, that would be another matter entirely; the FBI had never fully recovered from its political scandals of a few decades back. Zed decided not to mention Brighton's assessments or his own, that the bombers were likely Mexicans from the future, possibly even linked to Frost.

"Looks like I have to have somewhere to hide,

until this thing is over, Hilario." He stood and offered his hand to shake. "When do we leave?"

"WHY A SAILBOAT?" ZED HAD ASKED. THE Mexicans convinced him that the boat was probably the safest way now to return to Yucatán. "Satellite surveillance and intensified patrols hinder us now, and unfortunately, Chile has proclaimed neutrality," Cardenas was explaining. Zed could understand Chile's position. Politically, it was unwise to antagonize a cornered Mexican government that possessed nuclear weapons. The world had learned that lesson very well when several dictatorships collapsed, some in self-destructive nuclear fire.

Having outfitted Filemón's rebels early on, the Chileans had decided that it was up to indigenous Mexicans to carry through the final *coup de grâce* on their own. So Filemón's side would receive no more anti-satellite jamming equipment and no Chilean Navy support, would have to rely on their own ingenuity for the duration.

It must be getting very close to the end, Zed concluded. *Very serious now, for both sides*. He hoped there would be no nukes where he was going. He very much wanted that Pisté factory to be in one piece. He needed that time machine.

MORNING BROKE OVER THE GULF OF MÉXICO. A red ball of sun broke through layered clouds. There was no wind, the surface of the Gulf being as smooth as a Midwestern lake. Zed stood by as a crew of sailors hoisted their sailboat over the side of the frigate. A Mexican, dressed in a pink leisure morphsuit, was instructing Zed and Lorenz on the operation of the boat.

UNDER OTHER CIRCUMSTANCES, ZED WOULD HAVE taken the Mexican, Antonio Medina, for a Juárez shopkeeper. But the man was an electronics engineer, and a good one. "The boat we have for you men," he said, sweeping his arm to include Zed, Lorenz, Hilario, and a small dark man named Francisco Marquez, "has a set of sails for show, but an electric semi-morph peristaltic jet for primary propulsion. It can be sailed under computer control or manually, if necessary." Medina punched up a handheld display that showed various views of the sailboat, the *Chica Negrita*. It was made in Hong Kong, Ltd.'s, Cheoy Lee shipyards, back before the Four Chinas split, she was fourteen meters long, three in the beam, with an adjustable keel. And the phony sails. A veteran only of bay sailing, Zed asked about crew responsibilities. "*Señor* Wynter, do not worry," Medina said, laughing, "These three able seamen here will be able to carry you through, even if all else fails."

Cardenas asked about the boat's weapons, and Medina showed them closeups of the small laser cannon and the complement of robo-torpedoes. Inspecting the latter devices, Zed noted the Donne logos—Mark's weapons were supporting Filemón's revolution, as they had so many others. He was simultaneously impressed with the boat's defenses, and worried that such an arsenal was deemed necessary. As Hilario had told him the night before,

Zed was willing to put his trust in Filemón's instructions, but stayed uneasy as the necessities of warfare stood out in stark reality. He continued to wonder what information Daviess had passed on to Garcia.

The *Chica* would make thirty knots under power, Medina explained, and the peristaltic jet would remain silent, nearly undetectable by most sonar and electromagnetic sensor devices possessed by the Mexican Navy. The hull, superstructure, sails, and ropes had been treated with nonreflective semi-morph derivatives that minimized visual detection. Zed asked about the Mexican minisub defenses around the Yucatán, but his new crewmate, Marquez, just shrugged. It was apparent Garcia's men weren't worried about that eventuality. Zed wasn't so sure.

They expected the eleven hundred mile trip to take about forty hours, given the currents and the careful maneuvering required between Yucatán and nearby Cuba, where they thought the loyalist Mexican Navy patrols would be the most intense. The plan was to make for Progreso, the port nearest Mérida, Filemón's provisional capital. There was no longer any reason to make the much longer trip around the peninsula to Cozumel; the rebels now held much more area than during Zed's last trip, and almost all of the Yucatán peninsula was theirs. Garcia planned to meet the crew back at Pisté, at the factory site, if possible. Otherwise, the four-man team would survey the factory again for more technological clues, and await further orders from the General.

When he thought about it, Zed was amazed that one of the time travel chambers might still be operating in the ancient factory. *Or, if it's a far future*

Daviess we're dealing with, he thought, *maybe he's got one of those portable jobs with him?* Zed hoped for the latter, an advanced version he could acquire that would let him chase the madman Frost into any corner of TimeSpace, and let him find and hold Marina again.

Zed held onto his hopes, hopes of finding Marina, of meeting Daviess again, maybe even this time strangling that God-damned Frost with his bare hands. But first, he'd have to stay alive during the passage across the Gulf of Mexico on a tiny sailboat, in the middle of a war, trying to elude the whole Mexican Navy.

At least maybe they could hide, given the stealth technology of the *Chica* and the size of the ocean. The Gulf was a vast expanse, but crossing it on a sailboat, was that a half-vast idea? The sea was rough, twelve-foot waves, precursors of an inbound tropical storm, tossing Zed's universe and his stomach past the limits of acceleration vector tolerance. The earpatch medicine didn't help. He threw up the heavy breakfast and the intemperate celebratory champagne, returning it back to the sea from whence it had originally climbed eons ago. The other three crewmen smiled as the landlubber's stomach settled into a routine just a little more sedate than the sea around them.

"Hey, Zed," Bill Lorenz chirped up cheerily, "Aren't you a sailor? I thought all of us with English blood took to the sea quite easily." Zed found it hard to accept the man's instant friendliness, but agreed it was better than the opposite. Lorenz, like all of them, wore darkened wet-weather gear, head to foot. They were not making much headway; the storm impeded their forward velocity, and even with sails down and the jet engine at full throttle, the *Chica* barely held her own against the elements.

Marquez, the captain appointed by the Garcista naval officers, turned off the automatic pilot and fought the winds and the sea by hand, but fatigue finally forced him to relinquish control back to the boat's computer. All four men stayed below decks as the waves and salt spray washed the small craft repeatedly, smashing first from one side, then the other. Zed was glad to strip off the clammy plastic gear, appreciating the chance to luxuriate in the cabin's dry warmth. If you can luxuriate,, he thought ruefully, *in a tossing sailboat in the middle of a hostile sea, on the way to a war!* But he decided to take whatever comforts he could and enjoy the moment.

"We're not going to make our schedule, *compadres*," Cardenas said, speaking for the reticent *capitan el jefe*, Marquez. "Just the luck that this storm hit us after we got to blue water." He glanced at his wrister. "When our satellite link is up, I'll send a coded message to Filemón so he can change plans accordingly." After that, Lorenz offered to fix supper for the crew, as first in rotation. Zed politely declined any food, instead popping another dramamine tablet to augment the unsuccessful ear patch. In a few minutes, he was asleep.

"It's watch time, Zed, gotta get up on deck," the voice said. *Helluva dream,* Zed thought, his brain hazy, drugged. *Wonder why Marina's...* A lurch of the boat brought him to full awareness, and he awoke to see Lorenz awkwardly attempting to don the wet weather gear as the boat tossed from side to side. Zed steadied himself as best he could and began the laborious process of pulling on his protection against the wet.

Zed and Bill Lorenz shared the 0200 to 0600 watch the first day, taking turns sleeping two hours while the other stood watch. The storm seemed to be subsiding a bit during Zed's two hours, for which he was thankful. Watch duty consisted of looking out for tankers or warships that might knowingly or unknowingly ram them. Not that intent would have made much difference to a dead crew.

Two hours was a long time to stay alert looking for the dimmest of light on the horizon, waiting to hear the warning ping of the radar gear. Two hours alone, to think, to plan, to rehash memories. To experience the inner self. Zed's thoughts kept turning to Daviess' tampering with temporal forces. He was of two minds. First, he wished that the principles had never been discovered, but then he wouldn't have met Marina. His thoughts bounced back and forth. With some advanced future equipment, could he hopefully find Marina, find Frost's trail through time, track him down, and…kill him? He didn't know if he could do that in cold blood, even after the weeko's depredations. Knowing Frost as he did, Zed figured that their final showdown, if it came, would be violent. He hoped so; he wanted the wacko dead.

Zed's mind was somewhat dull; the effects of the sea-sickness drugs, he figured. He had felt a blandness, an unfocusing, the entire trip so far. He really didn't want to learn much about the intricacies of sailboating, he experienced no desire to operate the satellite navigation system, to scan the video about the peristaltic propulsion equipment. Totally unlike himself. During the enforced leisure time in the daylight hours, he hadn't wanted to read or watch the video player—nothing! When he did venture to let his mind loose from the hypnosis of the incredible vastness of the open Gulf, he kept thinking back to Marina and Michael Frost. Where had that son of a bitch taken her?

Was he right now—raping her? Torturing her? Why had he even taken her at all? Just to spite Zed? If the bastard had left her in California, Zed would have had no reason to chase him through TimeSpace. The thought came: if Marina had stayed in California, she and Zed would both have been vaporized in the blast the next day. Did Frost know that? Or, did Frost *cause* that?

Zed had Brighton call up and replay the last scenes of Marina, hoping he would catch some insight or nuance that would ease his pain. He left off the audio portion, unable to bear the sound of Marina's voice. But Frost's aging interested him. Why did he look so old? Zed recalled Frost saying to Balleen in the Chihuahua factory, "...hundreds of trips, Sam. It's safe." Zed was beginning to suspect that the trips were not all that safe, just look at the man! He hoped Marina—and himself—would not suffer from their few time trips. Idly, he wondered just how many trips it would take until he finally traveled in time no more.

Zed nodded off to sleep occasionally, welcoming the cessation of thought, but duty brought him back again and again. Again and again, to the pain of Marina's kidnapping, to morbid fears of Frost's insanity, a raving ghost haunting the dark night of the sea.

Behind him, in the *Chica*'s wake, swirled streamers of phosphorescent eddies, the luminescence of trillions of destroyed bacteria, their brief lives given up in pale bluish light. *How beautiful*, he thought, *like galaxies of tiny stars as our great craft plows the universe of these tiny creatures. Do our own souls emit such beautiful lights for higher beings, when Their vessels pass our way? Do we die for Their pleasure?*

That night he laid himself down and dreamed strange dreams of the sea.

THE NEXT MORNING THE REMNANTS OF THE STORM subsided and the winds eased off. Marquez kicked the Chica up beyond forty knots, hoping to make up for some of their lost time. As the bright day wore away into the early evening, Lorenz told Zed below decks he was worried about Marquez straining the engine. "Wasn't meant to be run flat out, you know. Cooling and all that. And we're still three hundred miles from the nearest land." Zed nodded, hoping that *El Capitan* knew his business. Zed was about to reply to the scientist's concern when he heard Cardenas yelling from above.

"*¡Ola!* Hydrofoil approaching! *¡Federales! ¡Ayudame!*"

The two Anglos scrambled up the hatchway to their rehearsed battle stations, Lorenz uncovering the forward laser cannon and Zed flipping up the built-in torpedo control console in front of the helm. Behind Zed, Marquez steered the boat directly at the warship to present a minimum target area, then shifted the engines to reverse to reduce the closing speed. The sun was at their back. Cardenas, for his part, hefted a shoulder launcher into place and braced himself against the mainsail mast.

"At least it's a beautiful day, *amigos,* no?" Cardenas shouted above the noise of the hydrofoiling enemy ship. He glanced at each of the other three, nodding. "Now we do it, *compadres!* To the death!" Their target was at five hundred yards and closing. Zed activated Brighton, hoping the nano-enhancements and the improved computer would help him survive the battle to come. The world slowed down for Zed; the battle would last a long time for him.

Furiously, Zed trackballed the robo-torpedoes into lock-on, pressing the "*Fuego*" button. Four miniature torpedoes, less than half a yard long, leapt from their barrels slightly above the *Chica*'s waterline, plunging into the Gulf to their fates, hopefully carrying doom to their target.

Cardenas hesitated only the barest moment, surprised as he was by watching Zed's inhumanly quick reactions. The rocket launcher bucked, sending its deadly charge toward the hydrofoil craft. Then, Bill Lorenz's laser cannon squirted a ruby-red dashed line of coherent energy at the water line of the hydrofoils, the very air sizzling in ionization as the energy density barreled its way at the speed of light.

Almost simultaneously, bright lights flashed at various points on the dark shape of the menacing gunboat. To Zed, in his enhanced battle mode, it appeared that everything happened at once, in heart-wrenching slowest motion.

The *Chica*'s laser cannon carved the enemy vessel from the stern through hydrofoils to the waterline, gouging out chunks of red molten steel that spiraled lazily above the wake of the gunboat, ending their brief trajectories in sizzling spouts of steam.

In rapid succession, Zed's robo-torpedoes exploded one at a time along one arm of the forward hydrofoil of the fast-closing ship, lifting it momentarily, sustaining the appearance of levitation before the unstable doomed craft began tilting to port.

Simultaneously, Cardenas' superbooster warhead disintegrated the superstructure amidships, the gunboat rolling, spewing debris and unfortunate sailors across the surface of the Gulf like flat rocks thrown by small boys.

The *Chica* wasn't safely away yet. Marquez cursed, revving the jet engine controls, turning the *Chica* to port, trying to dodge a free-flying hydrofoil plane that sliced through the air towards them. Lorenz and Cardenas were pointing at the incredibly large foil structure and shouting. Zed reacted instantaneously, spinning the trackball and targeting the incoming piece, firing half a dozen torpedo drones at it. The tiny weapons connected with their target only ten yards from the sailboat, showering the craft with shrapnel. The explosions heeled the *Chica* sixty degrees, throwing everybody but the captain from the deck into the Gulf waters.

The universe turned in slow motion as Zed felt the sailboat slip away from under his feet. To his right, Bill Lorenz described arcs in the sky, head over heels. Cardenas went headfirst into the sea, cursing. Zed could not help but notice that the deepwater Gulf was a dark, peaceful blue.

The impact pushed Zed ten feet under the surface and he spread-eagled to slow his descent. He swam back to the surface, shaken and hurting, and looked around for his companions. A quick look showed that the *Chica* was righting herself. *Good,* he thought prayerfully, *'cause there's no other way out of here!* Taking Marquez' hand, he tied himself with a safety line and then tossed out life preservers to the other two.

"*Hijo*, what a close one!" Marquez shouted as Lorenz clambered aboard, last. *"Muy bien, Zed, muy bien*!"

They circled the smoking wreckage of the Mexican gunboat but found no survivors. At Zed's insistence, they launched one of their two inflatable lifeboats, tossing a first aid kit on board it.

"Just in case, *amigos.* It's not really my war, and I don't want any more deaths than necessary in my conscience." Cardenas shrugged and went below for beer, bringing up a case of small bottles of golden brew. Those *Coronitas* were the best beer Zed had ever tasted. Though the battle left him with a strange feeling, it was great to be alive and drinking beer. He hoisted his bottle and toasted his friends.

As their boat left the battle scene, however, Zed kept watching for signs of life of the enemies he had helped destroy in the heat of battle. The last he saw of the area was the lonely lifeboat bobbing on the disturbed waters, its locating light flashing *red-red-red*, the color of blood, washing the waves.

An hour later their jet engine quit and the boat was dead in the water. Lorenz nodded at Zed, but Marquez was cursing the shrapnel that had gouged the water intakes. "The surfaces are eroded from small particles in the water and the pounding we took in the battle." The Mexican's long, dark fingers brushed the vertical water intake "gill" on the starboard side of the *Chica*. "Cavitation," he said, shaking his head sadly. He explained that the peristaltic engine required laminar flow near the intakes, and that the roughened surfaces prevented the engine from operating efficiently. Consequently the semi-morph walls had overheated and frozen in place. "Cannot be repaired at sea. *Necesito* a drydock."

All four sailors looked at the sails. There was no wind.

THE DISTORTED DISK OF A CRIMSON SUN STRUGGLED to emerge upward from layered clouds as haggard gray dawn greeted Zed Wynter's bloodshot eyes. Fog was beginning to lift from the mirror-still Gulf waters. The air was absolutely calm. Zed frowned at the limp sails overhead, cursing his luck. Morning in the Gulf of Mexico and he was stuck, dead in the water, a hundred miles from land.

Zed's watch was nearly over. Barely awake, he tugged at the overboot of his co-watch, Cardenas, who was sleeping on the deck. "Hilario," he whispered, not wanting to wake the other crew members below deck, "time for your watch."

The Mexican struggled to awaken. Zed smiled. *"Buenos días, compadre,"* he said.

"*Su madre*, Zedediah," Cardenas muttered, shaking off sleep. "Another day in the stinking Gulf." He sniffed the air. Zed agreed—it did stink of dead algae and fish. "Any wind today?"

"*Nada*, Hilario," Zed replied. "Not a damned breath." He handed over control of the large helm wheel to Cardenas then lay back on a makeshift bed of life preservers. At least there was no ocean spray, no rough seas, like their first day out. "Better luck to you." The Mexican snorted. Though Zed's mind fretted about his circumstances, fatigue fought a successful battle, and he was soon asleep.

Bill Lorenz roused him for lunch and Zed found his luck improving. The other crew members were in a good mood because the wind had picked up to ten knots and in a favorable direction. With sails full and the engines responding ever so slightly under Marquez' skilled touch, the *Chica* was heading straight for the Yucatán peninsula and the captain expected to make landfall the next day. Riding the wind-driven waves, all four men, including their captain, swigged *cerveza* and sang songs, ancient Willie Nelson ballads, new *salsitas*, some regg & roll. It was joyful.

A wind shift halted the sailboat's progress during the night, and the crew had to hastily reef the sails in the pre-dawn hours. The jet engines, however, kept their speed at eight knots, better than the sails alone could have done. They made coded radio contact with the Garcista shore batteries an hour before landfall. Garcia's forces launched a diversionary bombardment fifty kilometers up the coast, firing at Mexican patrol boats at sea, drawing attention away from the tiny boat that docked at Progreso under clear skies and a full moon. *The water is absolutely clear*, Lorenz said, *like sailing on air.* Zed had felt the same way, the first time he had arrived at the Yucatán, years ago. All four crew experienced heartfelt relief that nobody dared express openly in front of their mates.

The western horizon flashed intermittently with the battle lights of lasers and rockets and cannon fire. *It's May Day*, Zed recalled with irony as they stepped onto the dock and were greeted by Filemón's men. *What better way to celebrate the old discredited socialist holiday,* he thought, *than with a pitched battle between a corrupt one-party government, and an army of free-market libertarian guerrillas!*

Progreso was in ruins. Zed could tell that, even in the blacked out wartime condition. Everywhere, the violence of Garcia's sieges and the Federales' counterattacks were in evidence. Moonlight reflected from ruined docks, looming hulks of burnt cruise boats projecting from the transparent water like skeletons of prehistoric monsters. The full moon illuminated the sea floor, revealing the remains of ships, dark debris that blotted the bright sand bottom.

The scene on land was just as disheartening to Zed. Aside from the occasional murmuring song of a sentry watching the seafront, and the humming sound of their own electric vehicle, the city was dead. Zed and Lorenz exchanged frowns as they proceeded toward Mérida, toward the man who had brought such destruction to a once-beautiful corner of Mexico. Each man wondered if he were on the right side. Cardenas and Marquez kept their gazes straight ahead the whole time, never once turning to acknowledge the ruination of their beloved country.

THE NEXT MORNING DAWNED BEAUTIFUL IN Mérida. Most of the city had been spared the ravages of war, and in fact appeared to be a normal Mexican city going about its daily business. Marquez had left during the night without explanation and Zed never saw him again. Maybe he was going back to sea, another mission for Filemón. He'd been one hell of a fine sailor in Zed's estimation, surviving through the sea battle, getting them to their destination with sails and a wounded engine.

Cardenas arrived to tell the Anglos to get ready to leave the modest hotel where they had spent a few restful hours. All that first night, Zed's body felt as if it were still riding the waves. He woke several times, afraid and sweating, from a dream that replayed their battle at sea with the Mexican ship. *Dr. Wynter*, he told himself, *you're becoming quite the bloodthirsty warrior. Watch out that you don't become another Michael Frost!*

"After *desayuno* we drive to Pisté, *compadres*," Cardenas said during breakfast at a pleasant sidewalk cafe across from the burnt-out provincial capitol building. "Filemón's orders; he will meet us there tonight or tomorrow if possible. Meanwhile, he asked me to show you one other archaeological site en route."

"Archaeological site, Hilario?" Zed asked in surprise. "Which one?" Lorenz's expression was as if to say, "Sightseeing, in the middle of a war?" Zed just laughed at his Anglo shipmate. "Why not, Hilario? *Como no?*"

"THIS IS *DZIBILCHALTUN*," CARDENAS SAID AS HE pulled the electric jeep up on a small mound. "A city that was inhabited continuously by my ancestors for more than three thousand years." Zed wondered if Cardenas could substantiate that ancestry, or if, like Filemón, merely claimed whatever genealogy suited his cause. It was impressive, if true.

Before them stretched miles of scrub jungle, punctuated here by the occasional mound, there by the rare restored temple.

A wilderness, Zed thought. *Where's the great city?*

And then it came to him as they began to hike down a narrow trail toward a rough-cut monolith atop a stone dais. "These mounds out here, Hilario," he said, waving a hand at the jungle, "each one of them is a temple, a building?"

"That is correct, Zedediah. At one time, almost a hundred thousand people lived here, worked here. Died here."

"But for three thousand years?" Lorenz popped in. "What in the world happened to the city, then?"

By this time they had arrived at the monolith and clambered up on its pedestal. Directly north of them was a beautiful restored temple, its brownish stone made golden by the rays of the morning sun coming in from their right. Cardenas pointed it out to the Anglos. "This is the so-called 'Temple of the Seven Dolls,' friends. Excavated over a hundred years ago, restored to only a small part of its original beauty." He turned to Lorenz. "When the Spaniards arrived in the 1500s, they decided to make a city at Mérida, where we just spent the night." The Mexican waved at two jungle-covered mounds to their left. Tumbled blocks in the underbrush showed them to be ruined buildings. "Most of *Dzibilchaltun* was torn down and moved away in pieces, for construction materials. As simple as that." He jumped from the pedestal and began to jog toward the Temple of the Seven Dolls.

Lorenz followed, and Zed ran beside him,

speaking in short bursts, catching his breath between words, "Don't take it—for the complete truth, Bill. I read—that the modern Mexicans themselves—plundered this place—as a quarry—until the gringos came and declared it archaeologically valuable!" Lorenz turned, grinning. The Anglos caught up with Cardenas at the top of the temple stairs.

"'Temple of the Seven Dolls', Hilario?" Zed asked, puffing. "Was this a brothel, then?"

"No, *Norteamericano,* this is not your homeland," the Mexican chuckled. "Small figurines were uncovered here during the excavation, so the name."

They all sat, catching their breath, and talked about the plans for the day. Zed wanted more explanation. "Exactly why did Filemón want us to come to *Dzibilchaltun*, Hilario? We've got important work to do at Pisté. I want to—to find Marina, if I can. And besides, if I'm going to play tourist, I'd rather it be at Chichén Itzá."

Cardenas replied softly, "As always, your old friend Filemón wants you to learn the lessons that México has to offer, Zed

"You, too, Sr. Lorenz. Here is an ancient city that once was as important as any in the New World. Strangers came here with new technology, alien social systems. Life changed, the city died, a new country was born. Now the ancient ways are less than a memory." He stood, opening his arms to the quiet jungle, as if conducting the swarms of yellow butterflies that flitted over the trails. "Let us succeed in our Revolution, so that all of México may not become so."

He turned, stern-faced, speaking without

expression. "It is time to depart for Pisté, for the factory. For Filemón."

Behind Cardenas' back, Zed just shook his head in sad surprise. "I'll bet Garcia had another lesson in mind," he told Lorenz under his breath. "Mexicans can destroy themselves without foreign help."

DARKNESS WAS CREEPING ACROSS THE SCRUB jungle when the three men finally reached Pisté that evening. Above the dark trees, Zed was happy to see once more the familiar monuments of Chichén Itzá, *El Castillo*, the largest stepped pyramid, immaculately restored, and his own favorite, the domed observatory, *El Caracol*, "The Snail." So far as he could see, the last few months of warfare had not touched the ancient monuments. He prayed a silent *thanks*.

A kilometer down the cratered highway from the main site, toward the ruins of the village of Pisté, rose an encampment of olive-drab tents and a veritable industrial park of tanks, trucks, armored personnel carriers, artillery, and various other military equipment and vehicles. *Surrounding the factory entrance like ants around an ant hole*, Zed mused. There had been massive changes since his visit a few months back. The opening was now clear of a thousand years of dirt and debris, and even in the moonlight it was still as impressive as when Zed had walked it back in 903 A. D.

Damn, he thought, *if that doesn't just seem like a weird dream now*. But somewhere in that dream was a nightmare, and his beloved Marina was trapped inside, with a raving maniac. He shivered. Zed let his hand slide against the rough textured surface of the descending passageway, recalling the same surfaces when they were new and smooth. An ancient mustiness seemed to come right from the stones themselves.

As the entourage entered the humid factory, they found the lights on and a dozen men sitting about, some playing cards, others listening to a Mexican radio station. A sergeant spoke briefly to Cardenas. No one bothered to speak to the Anglos, so they wandered around, under the suspicious eyes of watchful soldiers. Zed showed Lorenz where he had first entered the factory a few months before. "Or a thousand years ago, if you wish." The scientist's expression showed Zed that he wasn't accepting all the time travel stories, not just yet.

"I am impressed with the restoration General Garcia has done on that walkway, Zed. It's wide enough to drive a tank—" Lorenz stopped short as he realized the logic of his description.

"I wouldn't be surprised, Bill," Zed responded, thinking the obvious. "Materializing tanks inside the Zocalo in México, D. F., would be the kind of coup Filemón would dream of."

"Can he do it? I mean, transport tanks, men, guns, from here into the Capitol?"

"I think he means to try, Bill. Since I don't know all the limitations of temporal physics, I honestly don't know what can be done." He showed the scientist the set of time chamber doors that Hilario's men had blown open months before.

"So that's the place where all of this began, huh, Zed? Not too impressive, not a bit." And Zed agreed. The plain concrete walls, the skid marks on the floor, a corroded control panel hanging from a rat's nest of ancient wires. *Not impressive in the least,* he thought soberly, *but it damn sure made some history!*

The Anglos wandered alone while Cardenas stayed with the other troops. Zed found the first chamber, the one that was already destroyed when he first arrived with Filemón. "This must be the one that Frost returned in, the one that Hilario's bomb exploded in. I figure that bomb—plus my bagful of anachronistic nameplates—must have melted the electrical power system back here and stopped the whole place." He smiled. "I'll bet it was an interesting time when the Mayans saw their little tin god screaming down the halls, trying to get out!" Even Lorenz laughed aloud, imagining a panic-stricken Frost running for his life, in the dark. Since Filemón's men had not found any skeletons in the factory, Zed concluded that the bomb had not killed any of the workers.

Of course, Zed grimaced with the memory, *there was one Mayan guard...* He let the image go. Nothing could be done.

Around the corner in the hallway Zed and Lorenz found evidence of recent excavations. Stepping inside they discovered another flight of stairs that led down to two more sets of time chamber doors at the end of a dead-end hall. Zed was astounded. "I'll be go-to-hell, Bill!" he blurted. "These must be escape chambers that the little son of a bitch prepared here, all along." He shivered. Zed knew that somehow Frost had found his way back to Zed's own time, at least twice. The zane had visited Marina a month before Zed had even met her UpTime. Then after the weeko's Mexican guerrillas, wherever or *whenever* they came from, had attacked Daviess' house too soon, Frost had still managed to fight and kidnap Marina.

Zed thought he'd marooned the maniac in the distant past, but right here in these rooms, the weeko wacko zane had escaped to torment Zed, to abduct Marina.

"Time machines, Zed?" Lorenz asked, moving his hands over the finely-machined surfaces of the chamber on their left. "You know, this one feels like it's vibrating." He turned to Zed, puzzled. "Are these things operational?"

Zed started to yell, "They're dangerous—" but the warning went unheeded. He and Lorenz were witnesses to events, as surprised as any two humans since Adam and Eve.

The doors of the time machine chamber glowed blue, did their little *waver*ing dance, and slid open. There were two men inside.

"Dr. Daviess!" Bill Lorenz exclaimed

But for Zed, the surprise was even greater. *Filemón Garcia!*

In the center of the open time chamber stood Dr. Stephen Daviess, hands on his hips, wearing his standard uniform of safari shirt and shorts. He was smiling broadly. Zed thought that the man looked quite a bit older than when he had met him—when? Five years ago or yesterday? Time tenses continued to confuse him.

Beside Daviess stood General Filemon Garcia, dressed in battle fatigues but once again wearing a broad gold-braided white *sombrero,* bowing low to his guests. "*Señores,* welcome once again to México."

"Filemón, I—" Zed tried to speak, to say anything, but the words wouldn't come. His guerrilla friend, arriving in a time machine with the great Dr. Daviess? It was too incredible to believe, yet… With Daviess' help, he could find Marina!

Daviess looked at his watch. "Just as scheduled, Filemón. There are no extraneous temporal anomalies here in the factory. Nothing to worry about." He turned. "Hello, Zed. Great to see you. Is Marina with you?"

Zed's heart sank. The scientist didn't know about his own niece? The sudden joy of finding Daviess alive evaporated, and Zed felt the long journey was at once worthless. "Filemón and I were just trying out my timebelt version. We traveled from his base in Guatemala to Yucatán, here, in a fraction of a second." The scientist was beaming. "This man, your general, has used my invention for real-time temporal transfer, Zed. I never would have envisioned such a use. Just incredible!" Zed nodded. It was going to be incredibly useful, that was certain, one more use for the technology that was going to screw up TimeSpace beyond belief.

Footsteps behind the Anglos belonged to Cardenas, and the agent greeted his chief, chatting in rapid Spanish that Zed couldn't quite follow, something about setting up the factory to build—time belts? Garcia came over to Zed, sensing the American's despair. Zed nonetheless greeted his old friend.

"Good to see you, Filemón. I'm glad you're here. But I need your help."

Garcia gave Zed a puzzled look. "I'm glad you made the trip safely, *compadre*. But Cardenas told me about your Marina. And of course I will help you. What can I do?"

Garcia escorted them all to relatively luxurious living quarters in the reclaimed office areas of the factory complex. The General promised he would explain everything to Zed and Lorenz the next morning, but that he was suffering from extreme fatigue, and would have to be excused. He said that he had enjoyed traveling in the time machine. "Speedy Gonzales had nothing on me, *amigos. I* am the fastest Mexican alive. *¡Buenas noches!*"

The next morning, however, *El Jefe* was off on the more urgent business of running a war. Dr. Daviess offered his own version of the astounding events in the lower time chambers. Zed had not mentioned Marina's kidnapping yet. He wanted Daviess to be at ease before enlisting his aid to find Marina.

After a Mexican soldier's breakfast of tortillas, beans, and coffee, the Scotsman and the two Americans sat alone in Zed's room, sipping coffee from steel cups. A lone pitcher sat on the small table. Zed relaxed on his cot, while Daviess and Lorenz occupied the two spindly wooden chairs.

"It all started a day or so after you, Zed, and Marina, came back to meet me." Zed shrugged; he didn't understand.

"Our old friend, Michael Frost, came calling," Daviess said, sipping the distasteful coffee. "He had left the Chihuahua terminal after the first day of your visit there, a few months ago, and went back some five years, to my home in Castro Valley." At Lorenz's reaction, the Scotsman tried to explain. "Michael had known for several years that I was gone, and let it be, suspecting it was on company business. You see, all I'd done was to leave a brief note on our computer net, where I told him not to worry, that he would eventually understand where and when I was. The word, 'when', was our code for trying to avoid paradoxes as we traveled forwards and backwards in time."

He laughed. "We figured that our paths might cross up in the tangles of TimeSpace, and we did not want to encounter some fatal paradox errors we might have overlooked." Daviess was in top form, taking naturally to the mode of professor, leading his wards through the intricacies of temporal travel. Zed hoped he could follow, but he was anxious for Daviess to finish. Explanations, for all their interest, didn't help find Marina.

The Scotsman rose, pacing in front of the table in the twelve-foot-square room. The place was a refurbished engineering room, probably where Frost himself had made schedules and budgeted time for his slave laborers. Green factory walls, recently painted over with the ubiquitous cream color that Mexicans everywhere seemed to prefer for their interiors. A very grimy whiteboard was still attached to the wall.

Daviess continued his expositions. "So, I was sitting in front of my computer, trying to think of what else to add to those commentaries, Zed. You know, the ones I put behind the red brick in the basement of my house the day after you left me?" Zed nodded.

"I had just put the cubes away when I heard the temporal displacement chamber operating. Then out stepped Michael! You folks missed him by just a day!"

That would have been some meeting, Zed thought,

meeting the weeko at Steve's place, and him not even knowing I had—would!—blow up the Chihuahua factory!

Daviess lit a pipe, tamped in some odiferous protohash, inhaled deeply and went on. "Well, I was surprised, but Michael hurriedly told me I was needed at the Tibetan facility he was working on. He'd come back from five years in the future to get my assistance with an emergency of some kind. Said that Sam Balleen needed me, right away. Of course, I didn't tell him about yours and Marina's visit; even then I knew you were keeping information from me, whether because of paradox issues or other concerns, I was unable to tell. I suspected that Michael had not voluntarily taken you back to the Pisté factory, but beyond that, I did not wish to speculate

"I didn't have time to add more notes to my cubes. From your visit just the day before he arrived, I did know that Marina would be coming to live at my place in a few years, so I arranged with my home picopmp to simulate my image and give her access to the house and grounds, and to explain anything else in my absence. The maintenance minibots would keep the place shipshape for years, pending my return." The scientist took a drag from the prote pipe, savoring the smoke, and blew a smoke ring. Zed often wished the tobacco industry had been able to make the smoke as tolerable to non-smokers as to smokers. Cancer-free or not, it could be a damned nuisance!

Daviess stared at Zed. "Of course, I had no idea I would be gone for so long. I didn't know that Michael was verging on insanity. But apparently he had suspected you from the first day you visited, Zed. He came back to get me out of the way, to prevent you and me from ever meeting. He should have known you really can't change the past. So I went with him to near Lhasa, Tibet, circa 200 B. C., to our factory there. While I was out of the chamber looking for Sam, Michael left, stranding me there. I could not get the machines to operate. He had disabled them for transmission. They still received, as I found out."

"How long were you there, Dr. Daviess?" Lorenz asked.

"Five years, William, both in the past and in this UpTime. My home DI took care of all my business affairs, such as they were, while I was away. Allowed Marina in, as you discovered. Synthesized video, you know, using my own persona as avatar."

All of that time travel must account for Steve's apparent aging, Zed thought. *But Frost said you don't age in the past. Another mystery.* "How did you survive?" he asked, shaking his head at the scientist's incredible ordeal of imprisonment.

"I wasn't alone the whole time, Zed. Sam arrived a day later. He told me the story of how you, Zed, and Hilario Cardenas had stowed away in the Chihuahua chamber. It was then that I realized Michael was psychotic and intended to maroon me there in ancient Tibet forever. I suspected, too, that Balleen was coming unhinged.

"There we were, 'timejacked' in the past!" The scientist drew another puff from his pipe. "Funny thing, Michael was sending Sam to Tibet when Cardenas ambushed him, so old Sam wound up where Michael wanted him to be, anyway. Between the two of us, Sam and me, we decided that Frost wanted him there permanently, too.

"At first we didn't trust each other, but over the

months and years that followed we decided to operate the factory with the trained personnel Michael had already chosen. We didn't like each other very much, but there was nothing much else we could do while remaining sane." They had chosen to produce low-tech manufactured goods rather than robots—cured leathers, milk additives, farm implements, even weapons. But most of the time, Daviess had devoted the available engineering tools and equipment to research and modify the temporal transfer devices.

"I dismantled the semimorphous walls of the chamber and used the material to build a personal timebelt, Zed," Daviess said, showing the four-inch wide belt that shimmered around his waist. Controls and display panels were upside down to Zed and Lorenz, but appropriate for the wearer. While Zed and the other American looked, Daviess pulled another belt from inside his safari jacket and handed it to Zed. It was fantastically light. *Like holding a spider web*, Zed thought.

The device looked familiar. Silently, Zed had Brighton call up the image for comparison; the belt was an exact copy, or the same one as Frost had had. How did Frost get one? He said, "Steve, Frost was wearing that identical belt when he…abducted Marina."

The scientist took a step backwards, almost stumbling in shock. "Michael—with one of these? How—?" The other part of Zed's revelation sank in. "Marina abducted? By Frost? How? Why? Oh lord, help us all." Shaking, he slumped down in his chair. "Zed, we've—got to get her back. She's all the family I have left..." The Scotsman bit his lip, his eyes full of fear. Zed knew the man would be concerned, but this seemed like an overreaction.

Hadn't he and Marina only seen each other twice, ever? What did the man know that he wasn't telling?

Zed related the whole story of his relationship with Marina, from the dungeon in this very building, up to Marina's capture by Frost. He skirted any mention of Brighton, not wanting to reveal his own capabilities to anyone. He neglected to mention the role of the future folk, too, for fear of invoking the paradox forces. The less said about the future, the better, as far as Zed was concerned.

"So you see, Steve, my main reason for coming down here was not just to help Filemón but to get access to a time chamber, and there are a couple of operational ones here, right now, so the trip was worth it. But," he pointed at the belt in his hand, "with one of those things, I can go after the weeko wherever he is." His eyes pled with his lover's uncle. "Let me have the use of it, and I'll do what I can to find her and bring her back."

Daviess nodded sadly. "That one is ... for Filemón, Zed. He controls the transmissions and the destination." He sensed Zed's confusion. "Other than my own, Filemón doesn't want the belts used by anyone but himself. He's afraid of counter-revolutions, or a coup. He's had me building some more, here in this factory, for use by ..." The scientist shook his head slowly. "For use by his troops. For a quick attack into México City. At least it will be a quicker affair than this guerrilla war that goes on and on. And a lot less bloody, too."

Zed nodded in sympathy with the Scotsman. He, too, was getting wrapped up in a war not of his own doing. But if Steve was already producing "timebelts" for Filemón, why had the General nearly kidnapped him, Zed, to return to Yucatán? He guessed he'd know, eventually.

"I'd like to look over your design closely, anyhow, Steve. Filemón brought me down here to help, so maybe he wants my manufacturing expertise? Maybe build these things more rugged, cheaper, whatever. And I'm sure Bill here would like to talk to you about the TimeSpace physics involved ." He had a thought; *maybe Daviess' quick design was vulnerable to Brighton's hacking?* "All the trip parameters are in one commercial chip, Steve?" The scientist nodded absently, his worried face showing his concern for his niece. Subvocally, Zed told Brighton to start reprogramming the belt's software for his, Zed's, access. No way would he let this opportunity slip by, not while Marina was out there, timelost.

"Zed, Sire," the familiar voice whispered into his audio nerve system, "wet your right index finger and touch the neural input mesh wire on the inside of the belt—yes, now I have … contact ... with its ... rather primitive smarts." A pause. Zed pretended to be scrutinizing the belt controls while Brighton did his magic. "It is now accomplished. Merely strap on the belt, or hold onto the neural mesh and we can operate the controls."

Satisfied with Brighton's hacking, Zed had the Scotsman teach him the belt controls. "Because it has very limited power, Zed, the belt only travels between significant temporal potentials. Rather like ice-skating on a surface filled with smooth, tapering holes. You only have a little power to kick you along, so you can just coast. To arrive at a destination, a 'hole' or temporal potential well, you skate down the hole's descending conical surface, coming to a rest at the bottom. The belt's energy source has just enough power to kick one or two people up from the 'bottom' of a typical hole, to that free-energy surface. Unfortunately, the traveler cannot yet choose which 'hole' he will arrive at.

"For example, just now Filemón and I traveled from his staging area at Tikal, where we have built a full chamber, to the other full chamber here at Pisté. The chambers have a lot more power." He frowned, chewing on his lip. "In fact, when I finally escaped Tibet with the earlier prototype of this belt, I was actually trying to return to my own chamber at home, but instead I popped in here. As if something pushed me to this place, rather than allowing me to return to California the night after I had left."

"When was that, Steve? When did you get here, I mean?" Zed asked. He knew that soon the tangles of time would be beyond his comprehension, but he might find clues to Frost's location in time, while the stories were fresh. "Two and a half months ago, Zed, just after your own trip to ancient Chichén Itzá, here. When you and Cardenas destroyed my—Frost's—Chihuahua factory," he added ruefully. Zed just stared. Another time travel anomaly revolving around the Chihuahua explosion. What chaos had he caused with that bag of nameplates? He was beginning to suspect it was far beyond his ability to understand.

"About these controls, Zed, maybe Filemón would allow you to—"

"*God damn you, Steve!*" a voice boomed from the hallway. In the strange slow motion that his nano-enhancements endowed in times of panic, Zed saw a small man in a dirty white robe plunge through the doorway and attack Daviess with a flurry of fists and feet, knocking the scientist to the floor.

With a triumphal gesture, made grotesque by the figure's tilted stance on a shortened leg, the man held up Daviess' time belt, spinning around to face Zed.

Michael Frost! Here in the factory! In this *time!* Zed pulled back his arm in a *keratsu* motion, ready to chop the little wacko—

"Sit down, Wynter! I'll blow you to all to shit!" Zed drew back the arm in the face of a flechette Frost had pulled. Zed thought the man was totally insane, his eyes glazed, maniacally pop-eyed.

"I've got the damned timebelt at last. The Mexicans said I could snatch it here! Now to go change the past..." The man's gaze returned to the other two men, finally resting on Zed. "Wynter, god damn you, why are you always after me?" he screamed at the top of his voice, "Chihuahua, Pisté. You trapped me back there, back *here*, for years! You mangled my leg! Ruined my life! Just leave me alone!"

Zed's voice was cold steel. "Frost, just give me back Marina and I *will* leave you alone. What have you done with her, you piece of filth?"

Frost was genuinely confused. "Marina?" He snarled, waving the pistol closer in Zed's sweating face. "Oh, the twat that Sam had in the dungeon? Hell, man, you took her away years ago? I—" That same glaze fell like a shutter over Frost's eyes, the last remnants of rationality dimming with it. "Wynter, why don't you leave me alone? Pisté, Chihuahua—oh shit!" Looking to Daviess with pleading, Frost wiped sweat from his forehead. "Steve, I—The Mexicans told me ... this belt ... need it ... I can't get where I try with the chambers ... don't know what's happening. My mind. Please

—" Frost alternated between rage and grief, between rationality and insanity.

Though Zed's mind felt that it was irrational, part of it accepted Frost's story about not knowing Marina's whereabouts. Did that mean the guy had not yet gone to California? Zed's mind raced: *Logic be damned, if I can stop the Frost here and now, he can't get to Marina! I will stop him!*

Fumbling with the time belt, Frost somehow actuated its controls, overriding the built-in safeties, all the while raving at the three dumbfounded witnesses. Fear possessing his expression, a shimmering golden sphere materialized around Frost and the maniac began slowly fading from view, on his way to some unknown destination in Time

Zed acted. He shouted, "Brighton! Now! Lock on to that wacko!" Daviess turned to object, but Zed held tightly to his reprogrammed timebelt and ran toward the fading ghost of Michael Frost, hoping his desperate gamble would succeed. But when his arms reached out to seize the zane, there was the merest tickling sensation. Zed's golden bubble, barely formed, merged with Frost's, and Zed felt the world turn blue.

Together, they vanished.

Something was wrong, again! Zed swirled down uncharted trajectories of TimeSpace, just bare yards from Michael Frost, as if a thick layer of smoky quartz separated them. At times the younger man faded to no more than a remnant image, like an old faded 2-D print. This trip, this time, outside the familiar and protective Daviess chamber walls, Zed experienced the raw, swirling forces of TimeSpace, his senses naked to the raw physics that slammed him some toward some unknown destination.

Frost didn't seem to be aware of Zed, the maniac looking like a statue of a crazed Caesar, unmoving, wide-eyed. Zed himself could not physically move, but felt as if he were spinning in a gaseous blue whirlpool, sensing resistance in myriads of contra-rotating threads of indeterminate colors, a holo regg-rock concert gone wild. Squeezing his eyes tightly shut didn't help; what he was experiencing was not sight but direct stimulation of neurons by unknown energy fields

Zed fought sheer panic as long as he could. The trip was longer, much longer than his other ones. What was wrong? Just being outside the usual chamber walls? No, Steve hadn't reported any such problems. Had his timebelt's field locked into Frost's? Were they now two of the "ice skaters" Steve talked about, but spinning around each other out of control? If so, what kind of "hole" awaited them?

He gritted his teeth and tried to fight the whirlwind.

MUCH LATER *(HOURS? DAYS? WEEKS? YEARS?)* THERE was a slowing, a palpable deceleration, and Zed welcomed it gratefully, not even knowing if he was still sane, for all the abuse his body and nerves had taken. *At least something is happening*, he concluded, glad to be able to think coherently, *and anything is better than this—this Dorothy in Oz tornado!*

He didn't see any munchkins, however, when the Universe returned from its blue hurricane.

Interlocking golden globes gradually materialized around himself and around Frost, amoeba-like auras that gradually separated like cells in mitosis. As the outside world took on familiar shape and a heart-warming cessation of motion, the two globes touched only tangentially, barely a kiss. Zed wondered if Frost would use the flechette on him when everything came to rest. He was prepared to jump out of the wacko's way.

The world stopped. Frost's globe disappeared. Zed's globe, though—by now a ten-foot diameter hemisphere straddling a flat, open patch of grass—flicked in and out of visibility, as if it were stuck between worlds. Instinctively, he slapped the timebelt controls for a way out, anywhere, any*when.* Nothing happened.

Oh shit! Zed groaned, trying to press against the shimmering, compliant surface of his golden prison, *I can't get away, I can't even get out, I'm trapped in this God-damned globe, and there stands Frost with his flechette!* He waited for the little man to turn his way, waited for the inevitable evil snarl, waited for the pain to tear away his flesh.

But Frost only glanced his way once, as if not seeing Zed or the globe. He stuffed the flechette into his belt and turned to walk toward a tidy farmhouse framed by a white picket fence.

Holy shit! Zed said to himself, but so loudly that Brighton asked what was wrong. "Brighton," he gulped, "that's Dr. Daviess' farmhouse! Marina's place! And it's still there!"

"As it should be, Zed," Brighton calmly noted, "because we have traveled back in time." Zed tensed, continued trying to push his way out of the hemisphere, but nightmarishly the energy field refused to yield. The globe was holding him, an insect in amber. But not for eternity, he prayed. *There's got to be a way out.*

"Brighton, what's happening? Why doesn't this timebelt work? Why am I stuck here?"

"Zed, *we* are stuck here because of some untoward interaction between Michael Frost's timebelt and your own. Analysis of my ... future information ... shows that overlapping Daviess fields are not amenable to mathematical analysis, even by the fully developed DI computers of ... two hundred years hence."

"So, how do we get out of it?"

"Zed, I frankly don't know."

Zed groaned

FIGHTING HIS FEAR, ZED WATCHED IN THE DISTANCE as Frost limped toward the front of the farmlet house. The door swung open. "Brighton, let me hear this, what are they saying?" Immediately, newly-enhanced hearing brought the conversation from a hundred yards away.

"You God-damned scum, what are you doing here?"

Marina! She was alive, and well! *Damn,* Zed reminded himself, *it's a whole month ago, now*. Marina had told him about Frost's visit.

"Ms. Tanner, is it?" Frost replied politely. "I just left a friend of yours down in México. But—this is Steve's house," Zed heard him stumble, beginning to sound like he had in México before this crazy flight started. *He's going over the edge again,* Zed thought. *These flights are doing something to his mind! And my own mind?* He shivered.

Marina spoke in cold, flat tones, "Frost, you

kidnapped me. You raped me, you weeko. And then the 'trope ... I hate you, detest you. Leave now or I will kill you." Zed couldn't believe she'd been in such control of herself.

Years of hatred, dreams of revenge, and she just stands there talking, even when she was 'troped. His admiration for her, his love, increased. Why hadn't he met her years before? Why had so many years gone to waste?

Frost held out his palms apologetically. "Ms. Tanner, I am most sorry about ... what happened, but I didn't think of it as rape. If that's what it was, then my apologies. But 'trope? I am not… deranged, Miss."

He sounds so damned sincere, I could almost believe him myself, Zed thought. But the memory of the beaten, ragged Marina in the dungeon surfaced, and Zed fought back rage.

"Ms. Tanner, did Sam do those things to you?" Frost continued, self-confidence returning as Marina pondered his statements. "Well, I sent Sam ... away. For life! He ... won't be bothering ... us anymore."

There he goes again, Zed thought. *The weeko's pausing, losing his train of thought.*

Frost shook his head as if to clear it. "No time to waste, Ms. Tanner. I've got to find Steve, talk to him ... tell him ... ask him ..." The man's voice trailed off to nothingness. Then he screamed, "Where's goddamn Steve Daviess?"

"Leave," Marina barely whispered. "Or I'll kill you." Frost bounded the five yards that separated him from Marina, screeching insanely. Surprised by the sudden attack, the woman stood for a few seconds while Zed screamed, unheard, for her to shoot.

Frost almost closed the distance before Marina sizzled the air above his head with a wide-beam spray of laser fire. Frost rolled quickly to one side, firing his flechette wildly, peppering the house with hundreds of tiny needles. Zed gulped. He hadn't known it was so close. Marina hadn't told half the story.

Marina slammed the front door, and Zed heard the large hydraulic deadbolt slam. *Now, Marina,* Zed thought, *sic the crawlbots on the weeko!* He stopped the thought short. No, Frost had gotten away that time. Right now, he just wanted Frost to return and turn on his time bubble. It was Zed's only hope of springing the trap. *Let's hold hands, old fellow ice-skater, and get the hell out of this hole!*

From the window, Marina fired blast after blast at the retreating Frost. *Good,* Zed grinned, *he's coming back out here. Closer, now, old buddy. Closer*. But Frost stopped only halfway to Zed's own bubble, still screaming at Marina, ineffectually wasting his flechette ammunition over fifty yards.

This homestead is going to be a valuable salvage yard for metals someday, Zed noted. Then he remembered the nuclear blast that in one more month would vaporize this part of the valley. This event, just one month away, was entirely too close for Zed. "Let's go, Frost! Get out of here!" he said aloud.

As if in reply, Frost's golden hemisphere lit up the afternoon shadows of the valley, and Zed felt himself jerked up and away. "Where to, Brighton?" he managed to squeak out before the world turned to a bluish maelstrom.

"Somewhen in time, Zed," his computer answered. "I wish I knew."

THE HEPHAESTUS MISSION

Again, TimeSpace rushed by in a swirling vortex, battering Zed's psyche and his soul. Knowing now that he would arrive wherever and *whenever* Frost was going, in his controlled panic state Zed still tried to plan what to do when he got there. Trying to think rationally in the midst of a Timestorm, Zed finally focused his thinking. "Brighton, are ...you ... functional?" Zed's mental communication with Brighton seemed strained, strange, as if he were thinking to himself.

"Yes, Zed. I am here. But unusual energy fields surround me. They are most ... you would say, *erotic*, to me."

Oh God, Zed thought, *not a sensuous computer. Not when everything around me is—turbulent!* "Brighton! Forget ... the energies. Where … are we ... going?" Zed could see Frost's frozen image, just yards away, like the first leg of the trip. "Any ... way ... to get ... away from … Frost's belt?"

"It is ... beautiful, Zed. The visible spectrum is ... different ... here in ... TimeSpace.

"Brighton! ... listen ... disconnection ... possible?"

"Of course … Zed … I will … turn … off ... our ... belt … and ..." Brighton said, and Zed's timebubble separated from Frost's. The universe wrenched, and Zed felt an actual, physical velocity increase.

Brighton's voice quavered. "Zed ... Zed ... we are ... oscillating ... in ...Time! Future. Past. Future. Past. Future. Past. Future.Past. Fu.pa...."

Brighton was going zane! Zed shouted mentally as loud as he could "Brighton! ... Help ... us!" He felt Brighton struggling to regain its composure, felt it prevail. "Brighton ... turn on ... the belt!"

Another *thrumm*, and the swirls of TimeSpace slowed down to a relatively smooth ride. *Not much worse … than a hurricane*, Zed thought. "Where are we bound to this time, Brighton?"

"Oh, of course, Sire, Zed ... following ... Frost's latest ... destination ... we are … traveling to ... last week … to the Daviess farm."

Last week? Zed thought. *Where was Frost then?* "My God, Brighton!" he screamed aloud, his voice a mere croak, "that is when he last came to California!"

"That ... is correct ... Zed."

"But, damn you, I was at the house when he arrived! The repulsion forces!"

Brighton responded cheerfully, "But ... Zed ... he arrived .... will arrive ... safely then." Brighton stumbled over the English tenses just like humans did, Zed noted with irony.

"You idiot," Zed said, "you and I might both be killed when he does arrive. Have you thought about that?" Zed's fears expanded to meet the onslaught of the vortices of TimeSpace, and he lost consciousness.

MEMORIES ... TORNADOES ... LOST IN A BLUE SEA. Zed loved the deep bluewater depths of the Gulf. *He could swim down here forever, never surface, never any more worries. But ... a noise? Down here in the deep, deep bluewater? Yes, an engine, a roar. Watch out! He must save himself, must dodge the oncoming throbbing propellers of the large ship that will overrun him! Swim! Swim! It is too late ...*

Zed woke from his nightmare sweating, throat tight and dry with unscreamed fear. Opening his swollen eyes, he saw a dark, thick mist. It was either late afternoon or right after dawn, wherever and whenever he was. Underneath, the ground was rocky, barren, just bare sprigs of greenery. He was sitting on a large flat stone. He was cold, alone. Looking around, the golden hemisphere was gone. "Thank god for small favors," he murmured. "At least I'm not trapped in a damned bubble."

"Brighton, what was all of that, the dreams, the roaring, the blue...?" he whispered subvocally, hoping not to call Frost's attention to him, if the insane man was anywhere out there in the darkening fog.

"Sire, Zed, we experienced some sort of ... near collision ... during our ... temporal transfer," Brighton whispered back. "Unusual energy concentrations. Our destination was ... aborted. We ... were detoured ... to somewhen else."

"And that *when* is?"

Brighton hesitated. "Zed, without the timebubble around us, my sensors are much more sensitive. From the language being spoken a quarter-mile from us, I would conclude that we are now in a Greek-speaking location. From the archaic pronunciations, it is ancient Greece, actually" Brighton continued. "On the western slopes of Mt. Olympus."

"ANCIENT GREECE..." ZED'S MIND ABSORBED THE information slowly. Was this the place—? "Marina!" he shouted, "Is she here, Brighton? Is this the place we tried to go before?" Cursing his incaution, he remembered to subvocalize, "Brighton, can you sonically scan this area? Is she near? Is Frost around?"

"Zed, out to one kilometer, I do not sense either Marina or Frost. But ... wait! There are transmissions." Brighton paused. Zed hoped the computer wasn't going to have any more paradox force phenomena limitations. "Zed, I am ... detecting ... anomalous ... very weak ... electromagnetic radiation ... from … *myself*? I don't understand...?"

Zed chuckled, "Old boy, I understand. It's Marina's version of you, her onboard Brighton, you're receiving. By God, she *is* here!" He stood, flexing strained arms and legs. "Home in on those signals. Let's go find her!"

The mist stayed dark, but Zed could tell that the sun was rising and it would soon be dawn. He hoped that Marina wasn't too far away, or he would be going after her blind if the mist didn't dissipate. "Not blind, Zed. I can enhance your infra-red retinal sensitivity, and we can go on searching even at night."

Zed hadn't thought of that. "Do it, then, my old friend. And, Brighton?"

"Yes, Zed?"

"How about just enhancing every little old sense of mine that you can, so I don't have to be continually surprised at what you can do."

Pause. "Very well, Zed. Here you are."

As the full force of a new complement of senses emerged upon his consciousness, Zed stumbled. Enhanced vision was incredible, the mist there/not there. A mountain rose in the distance in front of him. To the left, clearly visible through the infra-red sense, he guessed, were campfires in a small group of huts. Women were cooking. He sensed the odors of cooking meat, of boiling vegetables, even the sweat of the several cooks. He stopped walking, not wanting to disturb these people. He expected to see temples, togas, intellectual philosophers. Instead, as his vision zoomed in on the details of the village, there were earthen-roofed stone huts, emaciated babies, wallowing pigs. And as they walked out of the village, near a series of shallow holes, overriding the pleasant smells of the cooking pots was a stench of human and animal waste, so gross that it almost caused him to vomit. "Brighton," he ordered, "cut out the new olfactory enhancements, pronto!"

Surveying the primitive condition of the village and the awful health of its inhabitants, Zed observed, "This is ancient Greece? What a dump!" He saw scrawny adults, scrawnier children, and crumbling huts. And worse than the odors, a reeking sense of despair, lassitude, hopelessness. Fear.

Zed bypassed the small village; he estimated its desperate inhabitants numbered maybe a hundred on a good day. This time of day, nearing daybreak, the weather was cool, but the village children, he saw, were all barefoot and most were naked against the chilling breezes that blew down from the ragged mountain that dominated the misted horizon. To his far left and far right, the sky seemed to be lightening; only the middle was still dark. He had been in the shadow of the mountain the whole time. Now he would find Marina in the light. But would Frost be there, too?

"That is indeed Mt. Olympus, Zed," Brighton chirped cheerily. "My sensors detect ... myself … there. Overlapping signals … confusion. I cannot communicate ... Also Frost. And Marina." Zed's heart leaped. For a moment there he'd been prepared to censure Brighton for reading his thoughts. But perhaps he had better get used to it.

"Thanks, Brighton," he murmured, hoping to keep his voice low enough not to attract the villagers. But he was disappointed; first a child spotted him and ran back shouting to other children. Then the sullen adults emerged from the dissipating mist to watch him suspiciously. Zed didn't want hostility from anyone; the sad stares of fear and envy were keeping him upset enough. *Do they stone wizards in these days?* He wondered.

"I detect your troubled thoughts, Zed," his onboard friend said. "But, we are able to converse in many variations of classical and primitive Greek, should you desire." Zed checked his memory; sure enough, in his "other head" resided nearly a hundred Greek dialects and accents. He figured that Brighton would hear the locals speaking and adjust his speech accordingly.

"Not now, Brighton, just keep quiet." But he had unwittingly spoken aloud, in one of the Greek dialects. The increasing crowd, perhaps twenty by now, murmured. There was rising excitement in their voices, and alternating waves of fear and awe. Had he endangered himself? But no! They were pointing beyond him, at a figure coming down the mountainside.

Zed recognized the limping silhouette from a hundred yards away. "It's Frost," he hissed between clenched teeth. "And now we end this whole mess!"

"Without weapons, Zed?" Brighton warned. "Be cautious."

"Certainly, Mother Brighton," Zed snapped.

Michael Frost limped down the remainder of the stony slope to face Zed Wynter, the man's god-like hauteur evident even to the amazed crowd of ignorant Greeks. The short man was dressed in a gold-trimmed white tunic and wore golden sandals, the elegance of his clothing accentuating his flawed leg. At this time—in this TimeSpace—Frost did not appear to be as gaunt and drawn and distraught as he had in the factory in Pisté; Zed felt that this must be Frost at an earlier time than that, which he found confusing. But Zed still felt the man's rage across the ten yards between them.

"This is *my* domain, Dr. Wynter," the amplified voice boomed, startling Zed and villagers alike. "What have you come here for?" *An onboard loudspeaker system*, Zed concluded. *What else has Frosty got up his sleeve?* Looking back over his shoulder Zed saw the Greeks taking cover behind the corners of their miserable hovels, cringing at the awful voice of their small but wrathful god.

Zed tried hard to keep in mind that Frost still held Marina captive. He'd have to be patient, get Marina free first. Time to neutralize this weeko later. "Frost," he smiled, "we meet again. How about we drop this adversary business? Just give me Marina, and we call it quits. I go back to my century, you go wherever the hell you want." Zed knew he was lying to the false god. No way would he let Frost terrorize these primitive people. But that could wait.

He did keep Brighton's sensors up to warn him of any attack from the rear. Though he was sympathetic to the plight of these local people, he didn't want to be rushed by them if they were indeed Frost's worshippers. And he didn't want to create any issues in TimeSpace, or mess up History as We Think We Know It. What if one of the scraggly villagers was Homer?

Frost drew a few yards closer and spoke in an unamplified English, "Zed, you and your greaser friend Cardenas ruined my leg in Pisté. Your woman, Marina, is my woman now. She came willingly. Let's call it even, OK? My leg for your woman. Now just leave me or I will kill you."

Zed felt the Greeks coming closer to him from behind. Would Frost give them an order to attack? "Brighton," he thought—*loudly enough, I hope!* —"can you operate this timebelt like Filemón did? Just zap us over close to Marina in a real hurry?"

"Yes, Zed, I can, but—"

"No buts—when I say GO, we go—but just a few microseconds in the future, OK?"

"As you wish, but be—"

But Zed's attention was already on Frost's next words. "So why don't you just leave ... now, Wynter, while you're ... still alive?" Frost was sweating now, even in the cool breeze, his voice beginning to lose its continuity. *Another attack of the crazies*, Zed thought. He'd have to clear out before the guy went totally zane. "Is it these Greeks, Zed, is that ... your problem? Well, you can ... just go now. As I told you once before ... in México, these people—"

he wimped a loose hand toward the cowering villagers, "—are already … dead … in any terms … you can conceive of. You can't … save them, and I can't really ... hurt them." Without warning, he pointed a bony finger in Zed's face and shouted powerfully:

"Again, I order you, in the name of Hephaestus: Depart Mount Olympus!" As the thunderous voice echoed around the countryside, Zed realized the man was speaking in Greek; Brighton was giving a running translation only milliseconds out of sync with Frost's moving lips. *Like an old cheapie flatfilm movie,* Zed thought, *dubbed with improbable English.* Only this time it was too real. *Why would Frost use Greek?* Zed wondered furiously. The stirring of the crowd behind Zed told him that the god Hephaestus—Frost—had issued a challenge, one that the villagers were expected to help answer.

What to do? Behind him closed the innocent Greeks, some now toting mean-looking scythes and hoes. In front, the insufferable Frost, beaming with victory.

If Zed touched their god, the villagers would tear him apart. Merely to vanish in front of their eyes would increase Frost's power here. He hated to leave Frost alone with power over these poor villagers. But Brighton reminded him of the lock on Marina's position.

"Shall we go, now, Zed?" Could a DI sound worried?

But—no, Zed decided, *It's here and now, or never!* He mumbled more commands to Brighton. Then, aloud, he shouted in precise aristocratic Athenian: "No! I, Ares, say you are a misshapen son of a she-goat!" Mouths of the peasants dropped, followed by the clattering of weapons. Who would dare attack the God of War? "I call on you, you filth-ridden crippled monster, to bow down before *me* and acknowledge this, Mount Olympus, as *my* domain!"

Frost paled, taking a step backwards. In stumbling English he replied, "You speak Greek, Zed? What? Oh, of course, your onboard parasite, Brighton!" He cackled, stepping forward, craning his neck to face Zed as close as possible. "I copied your ... damned system ... Dr. Zed ... from Steve's farmhouse ... but I used it for ... something better than ... a silicon vampire!"

Zed didn't follow the peripatetic speech, but figured he should make his move, then find Marina while he could. "I, Ares," his voice rolled across the hills, drowning out Frost's incoherent ramblings, "shall return to the summit of Mount Olympus and there bring down *my* great powers upon you, false god!" Smiling, 'Ares' gave 'Hephaestus' "the fig", the thumb between two fingers of a clenched fist, a gesture of ultimate insult, well-known even in ancient Greece. "Hit it, Brighton," he said.

As Zed vanished in a golden bubble, confusion shaped the faces of the villagers. The God of War had departed. What now of their own Hephaestus; did he lose the battle?

For Zed, the blue maelstrom was short-lived this time, and he popped back into reality an arm's length from a hobbled, handcuffed Marina. They were inside a primitive stone-walled hut. At first, she jumped, seeing Zed's bubble materialize beside her, but she quickly adapted to the situation. "Oh, Zed, thank God. How did—?" The question died as Marina's pragmatism shifted into control. "Let's just get out of here!"

Zed looked at the spare furnishings of the hut, snorting, "Always the best accommodations from our Mr. Frost. I'm going to kill the son of a bitch!" He grabbed Marina with one arm. "Hold on, dear. Brighton, get us back to 21st century Mexico!"

"Wait!" Marina insisted. "Frost has a workshop not far from here, in a concealed cavern system. He bragged about it to me. He has been coming here for years working on a specialized warbot all by himself. It's a big brass-colored thing with long whips instead of guns or lasers. It looks like it was made for terrorizing ancient Greeks or somebody, people without guns to fight back, instead of the jungle warfare going on in our time's Mexico. If we leave him here with it, no telling what he'll do with it. He could attack us before we even leave, or he could wipe out a lot of ancient Greece, change our history."

What a woman, Zed groaned to himself. *Instead of saving herself, she thinks about the madman running rampant through Time, savaging others. Well, she's right. Time to stop the little shit, once and for all.*

"Stop, Brighton. Just take us outside the door there." Zed had hardly stopped speaking when there was a flicker of blue light. He and Marina were outside the wall. "How did you do that number, Zed?" she asked, mouth agape.

"New technology, Marina. I'll tell you about it later. But first, let's find the weapons."

"Over there." A plastic backpack against the wall bulged with armament. Zed took out a hand laser and cut Marina's bonds.

Arming themselves each with a laser pistol, they chopped up the remaining weapons, leaving a smoldering mass of metal and plastic. Marina spat on the simmering trash. "Now, we can leave. The weeko won't have an arsenal anymore."

But it was Zed's turn to hesitate. "No, Marina, Frost is over there, a mile away, with helpless villagers who think he's a god of some kind. As long as he has that timebelt, he's free to travel and cause more mischief. I think the time trips are beginning to make him more psychotic than he was. We can help a lot of people, ourselves, even Frost, if we just take away his time traveling ability. You can stay here if you like, but I'm going after the guy."

Marina put her arms around Zed, but carefully held her pistol vertically, at ready. "Let's go, lover. We've got him outnumbered."

"Let's go back, Brighton!"

But nothing happened. No blue mist, no flicker of light. Nothing. "God damn it, Brighton, where are you?" Zed yelled. But there was no answer.

"Marina," Zed groaned. "Somehow, Frost has jammed Brighton, or else some kind of paradox force has zapped him. We're stuck!"

Marina tried to raise her onboard computer without success. She sighed. "Well, if we have to stay back here, we have to stop 'Hephaestus' to be safe. And he's also got a portable time device we could use, hasn't he? He brought me … back here with one."

Zed nodded grimly. They trudged in the direction of the village. The sky was much lighter now, and the collection of rude dwellings a distant splotch on the bare, rocky hillside.

To Zed's surprise Frost was waiting for him exactly where he had been, half an hour before. Armed, two people to one, they had decided to face 'Hephaestus' in front of the villagers. "I thought you'd ... be back ...Wynter. Hero ... saves the girl. Now ... comes back ... to save ... the ... innocents." Frost's speech was in amplified English. Zed saw the crudely-armed villagers cowering in the clear morning shadows of their huts, afraid to leave the presence of their insane god, but afraid to stand too close to him. They were, however, murmuring and pointing at the comely Marina, whose long red hair must surely grace the heavenly halls of Olympus.

Frost spoke to Zed and Marina in English. "Rather more difficult being a hero, with your damned silicon soul out of commission, eh?" He patted his belt. "But don't worry; I've got my own version of old Brighton, just dying to meet you!" Hephaestus' voice boomed out again, in Greek. "I ... Hephaestus, call ... upon … my creation ... Talos! *Attack!*"

"Talos?" Zed repeated, puzzled.

"The first mechanical man, Zed," Marina replied. "Frost envisions himself as the old Greek god who invented robots. He's totally weeko!"

True, Zed agreed, but a genius wacko at one time. Who sure as hell *did* build a lot of robots!

Grinding, crunching noises, like a semi truck on gravel, emanated from the low-lying fog in a nearby gulley. Whatever it was, it was getting closer. Marina queried aloud, "What weapons do we have, Brighton, old boy? Or old boy and girl, I should say?" She smiled, patting her chest. Zed thought he'd like to do that to her, too, if they got out of this one alive.

"Marina, ask your Brighton if we have any heavy artillery? Bazookas?" Suddenly the laser pistol in his hand felt very small against the noisy monster coming his way.

Over the hill rumbled a golden giant, an enormous fighting machine, its tank-treads spewing up rooster-tails of gravel and dust. "*She-ite nights and sunni days!*" Zed whistled, remembering Frost's curse. The thing was tremendous. A vertical cylinder, six feet in diameter, at least twelve feet in height. A medusa's nest of whiplike tentacles, twenty to thirty feet long, emanated from its midsection, whipping the air with evil intent, spiraling in deadly snaps! The main body itself was mounted on a circular pedestal driven by independent tank treads, giving it track-powered drive in any direction, and inhumanly rapid rotation. A cacophony of screeching mechanical sounds completed the horrific scene, amplifier or machinery, Zed couldn't tell.

Terrified of the oncoming behemoth, the engineer's part of Zed's mind admired the fearsome appearance and the battlefield utility of the fantastic robot. Glaring from atop the central body, evil red lamps glowed like the eyes of a fire-demon.

Taking steps backward, terrified, Zed pushed Marina on farther back, motioning for her to seek shelter in the village. For whatever good it would do. Marina had said that Frost modified this monster, this warbot, from one of his future designs. Originally it must have been one of the military robots Filemón was worried about. It had enough awesome appearance and weapons, here in the past, to conquer the whole world. *Hell*, Zed thought grimly, *the sight of it alone would panic entire ancient nations!*

Zed spun around to bring his weapon to bear on Frost, to call on the warbot, but the little man was zig-zagging around a corner into the village center. No villagers ran after him, Zed saw. Fear, or loathing? Both?

"Zed, I'll try to get Frost, you take care of this *thing*," Marina said, kissing him quickly before running into a crowd of Greeks, disappearing through their hastily-parting ranks into the tangle of huts and pigsties. At least she was temporarily safe. Even if she found Frost, she was armed. But Zed himself couldn't back up; he was afraid the excited villagers would kill him with their farm implements, god or no god, if they saw him retreating from a mere metal creature.

Zed gulped in fear. *It's hard to be a god!* He wished Brighton was working again.

Even though the onboard nanotech Brighton was not functional, Zed felt the residual nanoes from Mark Donne's muscular micro-enhancements kick in and time slowed. *At least one advantage Frost hadn't figured on, thank God.*

What to do? The robot was less than twenty yards away now, coming at Zed like a runaway train, slicing the air with its whiplike tentacles. Zed calculated his chances: small to none.

The villagers, innocent or not, were going to have to take their chances along with their war god, Ares. Zed ran at the crowd, firing his laser over the heads of the terrified villagers. Between the fire-throwing god and the golden metal demon creature, the primitives threw down their tools and ran for their own cover.

For Zed, it was still a slow-motion war. Behind the corner of a massive stone wall, he fired directly at the laser-eyes of Tales, was rewarded with sputtering and crackling as one lens shattered. "Poor design, Frost, you shithead!" Zed cheered. He was answered by a sizzling blast of laser cannon from the warbot, scorching the air around him, slagging most of the wall he was hiding behind.

From behind him came a shout: "Oh, hey! Dr. Wynter!" It was Marina's voice. Turning, he saw Frost behind him, laughing, stomping the ground in joy. Marina was behind the wacko, holding the timebelt up over her head in triumph.

"Marina! Does it work?" Zed was desperate. No way could he defeat Frost's warbot, not without major weapons, not without his onboard computer friend's help. He needed to get away, and quickly.

"Not yet, Zed," she yelled back. "I don't know how!" The warbot was closing in. One more volley of laser fire, one kiss of a whip-tentacle, and Zed would be dead. "Hold on to its inside surface, tight. Try to raise my Brighton!" His voice died under the noise of the onslaught of the monster machine. A fantastic battle scene unfolded, a sequence of events never quite understood by the awe-struck Greek villagers. In pure panic, a frantic Zed Wynter tapped his hysterical strength, ran the ten yards to where Frost stood laughing, and swept up the chortling man in his arms. Marina stood in shock.

"Try the damned belt, Marina! It's got to be the way he's jamming my Brighton. Some kind of button, somewhere! Something he added—something crude! Try something! *Do it now!*" he heard himself screaming. It seemed to work; Marina squeezed the device tightly, her mouth moving in an arcane chant Zed couldn't hear. Maybe she was screaming at him.

He ran, carrying Frost, right into the path of the banshee warbot.

Talos stopped, its treads reversing, crunching

rocks. Its screeching died down until Zed heard only the idling of the semi-morphous tread motors. His gamble had paid off, he had guessed right; Talos obeyed the one law Frost would have built into a combat robot: don't hurt your Creator, no matter what!

Zed breathed a prayer of thanks to the memory of one John W. Campbell, Jr., an old science fiction editor who had first suggested the Laws of Robotics that the writer Asimov had put in print. *Thanks, Lord John! Dr. Asimov!*

"Zed, Sire?" Brighton was back! Marina's diddling with Frost's belt had worked.

"Brighton, what?" Zed almost cried for joy. He wasn't dead yet, though the warbot's body was rotating left and right in short jerks, as if it were looking for a clear space between its tightly-held creator and his nemesis. Its tentacles coiled menacingly around its cylindrical torso, throbbing as if in anticipation.

"Zed, that robot … its DI computer is a copy that Frost ... remotely downloaded ... from Dr. Daviess' house." Suddenly Brighton said excitedly, "Zed, it is *me*! *Before* my future download!"

Zed hesitated, holding the struggling Frost tighter in his grip. He told Brighton what to do, then spoke to his captive. "Frost, if I let you go, will you call off your hell-hound?"

"Fuck you, Zed, you can't …hold me ... forever. Talos will ... pull off ... your arms ... and legs." The ravaged face turned, spitting in Zed's eyes. "And I'll ... have ... him ... rape ... your bitch ... until she ... dies!"

Zed saw red. All his repressed rage, all of the fear and fatigue of the past months focused on the scrawny wretch who was trying to kick and bite him. "Nuke 'em, Brighton!" he roared, raising the small man up over his head in one swift motion. In a herculean toss, a nano-enhanced-hysterical-strength Zed Wynter launched the flailing Michael Frost right into the medusa's maw.

As Zed suspected, knowing of Talos' Three Law programing, the warbot swung to fulfill its prime directive, whipping its tentacles around to save its master from injury. Zed took advantage of those few seconds and ran the intervening distance, jumping aboard the robot's track drive platform.

Zed was along for the ride, but just barely. Brighton was utilizing electromagnetic interference, attempting to bollix Talos' semimorphous brain operations, trying to take control of the robot's braincase computer. Talos responded, and the resulting battle in the radio spectrum stormed inside Zed's own brain: crackling, sputtering, megaHertz shrieking, digital-to-digital combat in his head. The human was right on the edge of unconsciousness, but there was nowhere to go, nothing to do but to hold on. Brighton's memory space, impinging on Zed's own, was pure pandemonium, a raging battlefield of inhuman intelligences. A mere human had no place to hide.

What the Greeks saw was this: the god Ares threw the god Hephaestus toward the sky, and the crippled Olympian beckoned his metal man, Talos, to come save him. Ares then wrestled with the giant, and the outcome was in doubt.

Could mere metal, even God-forged metal, withstand the rage of the War God, Ares?

Laser fire sizzled the air above Zed's head and he flattened himself on Talos' platform. Marina was firing her laser pistol, flashing coherent energies at the pulsing red lamps that were the robot's demon-eyes. The Greeks saw Hephaestus' mate, beautiful, red-haired Aphrodite, casting lightning bolts at the metal man.

Talos' final "eyes" shattered as the continuous fire from Marina's laser overheated the lenses. "Sire, my Marina version adjusted the laser wavelengths to overload the robot's lenses." The Greeks saw the metal man blinded by the bolts of the Goddess.

In the seconds while Brighton/Zed and Brighton/Marina were attacking Brighton/warbot, Talos sat Frost down gently behind a hut, out of harm's way. The warbot spun around to face its tormentors, flailing its sharp-edged tentacles toward Marina. Brighton/Zed kept up its E-M attack on the robot's DI system as Zed's laser carved the tentacles from their mountings. Marina ran for shelter, and Talos rumbled into action after her.

With his laser, Brighton/Zed hacked through a tentacle and watched it fall behind them, writhing until it hit the ground. Time after time Zed ducked as the robot flagellated its own body to rid itself of the unwanted passenger.

The unceasing roar of the electronic warfare in Zed's head reached a frenzy, and Zed himself neared collapse. The warbot was overtaking Marina, and her laser fired wildly, more danger to Zed than to Frost's killing machine. Tentacles whipped the ground near her feet. In seconds she would be cut apart, dismembered. "Brighton," Zed croaked aloud, "Save her! Stop this goddamn thing!"

The war inside his head stopped; the noise ceased.

Brighton had eliminated the giant's external sensor circuits. The blinded behemoth lashed out, missing the retreating Marina. Zed judged the creature's timing, then jumped from the platform and ran beyond its reach. The blinded behemoth, quiet now that its amplifiers were dead, merely rattled and clanked, moving through the village with its remaining whips slicing out in frustration at unseeable enemies.

Zed felt Brighton easing full control back to him. "I think purely human responses will be adequate now, Zed. Your turn." Zed motioned for Marina to follow him, and they caught up with the blinded warbot. It was a great pleasure to carve up the tank treads. As a final present, Marina carved out a hole in the robot's main body and deposited a mini-grenade inside. She and Zed jogged back behind a stone hut and waited.

Talos exploded, showering the village with assorted robot brains, gears, wheels, and electronic assemblies. *For those who survive this twilight of the gods, there will be the rewards of scarce metal, pure and finished, ready for other uses.* Zed reflected. *Just hope they can work the stuff into useful tools. Or weapons, if they need them!*

Zed caught his breath, waiting for the adrenaline to stop pounding his overwrought heart. He finally asked, "Marina, is your Brighton still working, too?"

"Yes, Zed. My boy—my little assistant—is fully functional."

"Is that Frost's time belt?" She nodded. "Does it work, can it get us out of here?"

"Yes, Zed it can." Zed let out a long sigh of relief and was happy they weren't stuck in Greece. "Brighton?"

The DI hesitated. "Yes, Zed?"

"What's wrong? You don't seem to be very active right now. Aren't you relieved to be going back to Mexico, to our own time?"

"Zed ..." the man didn't recognize the computer's tone. What was wrong? "Zed ... I had to reflect for a minute. You see ... destroying ... Talos ...was like ... killing my own clone..." Sadness, melancholy, in a *DI?* Zed was certain, now, that his Developing Intelligence partner was now a Fully Developed Intelligence.

They couldn't find Frost. The onboard Brightons, all the DI sensors, everything, all scanned to no avail. They searched the village, the complex of simple huts and workshops that constituted the "Halls of Olympus," even quizzed the villagers about their crippled god. But there was nothing. Frost had escaped, unseen, during the battle. "Either he had another time-belt, Zed, or a chamber somewhere back here."

"A chamber, I'll bet. This place was on Steve's list in your—*his*—basement, when we tried to come here, weeks ago! When Steve wrote that list, he had only constructed the large fixed chambers. The timebelts didn't come until afterwards." Zed told her how Frost had appeared in the underground factory at Pisté, seizing Daviess' timebelt, and how he had followed Frost using another timebelt to lock on to Frost's.

Marina thought for a moment. "The man time-jaunted from ancient Pisté, to modern Pisté, in a chamber, right?" Zed nodded. "There he seized a timebelt from Uncle Steve?" He nodded again. "And from there—?"

Zed kept looking around the Greek countryside, its ruggedness beautiful now that it was no longer threatening. "That much I know, I was with him then, connected to him somehow, stuck in a timebubble. I saw you, but you couldn't see me. He visited you last month in California. You shot at him, and he attempted to go forward in time, to the time after his Mexicans—after we killed the Mexican assassins of his. But something stopped that."

Marina shook her head. "No, Zed, *you* were stopped, you couldn't be allowed to visit your past self, so you were thrown back here." Zed watched her emerald eyes, her face screwed up in deep thought. "So ... Frost came to the house, we argued, he disarmed me, brought me back here with that 'timebelt', the portable time machine like the *Dashes* used."

Zed nodded again. "Marina, I later saw the video of what happened when I was out cold. I guess you're correct. The paradox forces let him go, but I couldn't go there to visit myself, so I got knocked for a loop." He smiled at the pun. "A real loop. In Time."

Marina just laughed, shaking her head. "Always the comedian, my lover. But look." A few brave villagers were approaching the smoking ruins of the Talos warbot. One or two picked up the mysterious gears and machined parts and marveled over them. *From here to Antikythera*, Zed mused, thinking of the two-thousand-year-old geared computer uncovered in a Greek museum in the last century. Actually, he had no idea of *when* he was, and no way to tell.

Marina reminded him that they were supposed to be gods. "We don't want these poor people to suffer any more, Zed. We can't change their superstitions with modern arguments, because of the paradox forces. But we should at least give them some comfort before leaving, and do something in keeping with their expectations. Don't add more complexity to their lives, they have a hard enough time just surviving here."

Zed agreed. "Thus the great Ares defeats false gods," he bellowed in Greek, the amplifiers carrying his boasts to the very foot of Mt. Olympus. "And the great goddess—Aphrodite?—will accompany me back to our home. Farewell!"

Before leaving, Zed held Marina close and surveyed the villagers one last time. Most of them were prostrate, worshipping the powerful gods. A few were just running back to their homes, Zed saw. "A hopeful sign, those people. Running from powerful gods instead of worshipping them, is the smartest thing to do," he murmured in English. Only one Greek, a small boy, dared stand with his face raised, looking up at Zed square in the eyes.

The boy pointed toward the ragged peak overlooking the village. "Back to your holy Olympus, holiness?" the brave little one replied. Nodding, Zed stared at the boy, a courageous soul whose eyes contemplated Zed with as much interest as awe. Zed was reminded of himself at that age, and a fleeting thought flickered. Had Zed set off a mythology of his own, created something that hadn't existed, wouldn't have existed? He couldn't follow the logic, but one thought remained, one question: Could this boy possibly be Homer, chronicler of the battle of the Greek Gods of Olympus?

"Homer? Ye Gods," Zed moaned, "oh ye ancient Gods!"

Zed's final thought before using his timebelt was, *Where the hell did the weeko-wacko zane go this time? How far?* He shivered to think of Frost showing up again and again throughout his life. Zed didn't want to travel any more in time until at least he had one of those bodysuits the *Dashes* had worn. Long trips via timebelt were not any fun, and losing your mind would be even worse. Gritting his teeth, with Marina holding him tight, Zed jumped once more through TimeSpace.

Marina Tanner and Zed Wynter plunged into a vortex of blue mist. His only thought was, *Something's wrong, again, every damned time!* The forces of TimeSpace were angry, vibrating, and blue. The doors of Hell and Time opened and Zed and Marina fell through an endless tunnel, feeling actual, physical pain. Zed tasted Eternity and knew it to be Hell. Something existed in TimeSpace, something pulling him inexorably toward it; something *wanted* Zed Wynter.

Abruptly, infinitely many years later, it seemed, the journey ended. Shaken and dazed, the couple stumbled from the temporal transfer chamber in Pisté. Marina collapsed into the waiting arms of her uncle Steve Daviess. With the help of a Mexican guard, Zed swallowed a slug of tequila, choking on the strong brew. Two guards helped him to a room, and he fell, exhausted, on the cot as Daviess came in to see him.

"Zed, old boy, we heard the chamber actuating and came to see who our visitors might be. Looks as though you and … my niece fell into our strong temporal well." The older man surveyed Zed's condition. "Frankly, my boy, you look like *cacada.* The ancient Scots word is 'shit.' You must have had an extremely wearying journey. Where did you go after you tackled Frost? And where is he now?"

Wearying? Neverending was the way Zed would have described the return trip from Olympus, but he was totally exhausted and fell silent after the briefest of answers to Daviess. The trip had been a manifold trauma, and Zed was drained of all energy. He just couldn't talk any more.

He slipped into and out of sleep, nausea and diarrhea taking their toll almost hourly during the night. When he was finally wholly conscious, Zed asked after Marina's condition, but the Mexicans said nothing and he was too tired and too sick to pursue the matter. He awoke with a throbbing head; a skull full of dirty cotton between his ears and a nauseating coating on his tongue. Across the room, as his eyes wearily focused the wan lighting, Zed's vision condensed into the form of Daviess, who was puffing his stinking, damnable prote pipe. "Hullo, Zed. Welcome back to México, once more. First off, Marina had a bad night, similar to yours, but she is now recuperating in the emergency room upstairs. Now, I hate to bother you, but Filemón is anxious to know about your trip, about the operation of the timebelt. Can you talk?"

Zed stayed silent for a moment, making sure that Brighton was functional again, then breathed a deep sigh and told the scientist about his lock-on to Frost's time belt, the first visit to California, and the forces that knocked him backwards to Olympus. Daviess whistled at the story of the fight, "You are the stuff of legends, Zed, my boy. Ares, indeed!" He laughed. "And Marina, as Aphrodite! I'd always imagined the goddess as blonde, for some reason, but red-haired Greeks, what a joke!"

A soldier came in with a tray of breakfast,

which Zed gratefully accepted. His system was empty, and the tortillas and fruit were welcome fuel for his wracked body. "Steve, there's something out there in the time stream, in TimeSpace, that is dangerous. This last time, I could feel the energies of the thing, like I was looking into the jaws of Hell itself."

The scientist was somber. He began sketching on the white board in Zed's room. First, a horizontal line with various dates written above it. "I have attempted to track Michael's trajectories through time. Here," a dot labeled Rome, "is the farthest distance back in Time we had set up chambers, Michael and I. Next in line, coming toward our time, is Mt. Olympus. It is the place from whence you just returned." Prote smoke swirled around the Scotsman's head, and Zed frowned as the smell whisked toward his bed.

"Cut out all smells, Brighton" he ordered his DI friend subvocally.

Daviess said, "And this point, at the far right, is the farthest point we know Michael traveled in the future. That was yesterday, here in Pisté."

The scientist continued a zig-zagging, overlapping series of marks, to and from the past. "Here's Chichén Itzá, here's Tibet—*Shamballah*," he chuckled at Sam Balleen's namesake "—here are the times Michael visited my California home." Daviess stopped. "My *late* home, Zed. Hilario told me about the battle and the bomb. Oh well," he shrugged, "I have other properties, other houses. But I will miss that one.

"But back to my point. You see how these trajectories seem to alternate back and forth, as if there were some concentration of mass in TimeSpace at a recent time, something drawing

Frost—and you—to it. Like my analogy of the ice skater, if there were one very large, deep depression in that ice surface, one that you had to skate past every time you went from one end of the lake to the other, you would lose some energy, just trying to skate around its edges. Enough passes, enough lost energy, and you would be drawn into that hole, never to leave."

The professor cracked his knuckles and looked nervous. "I have compared my estimates to some particular eigenvalue solutions of my modified wave equations." Zed pictured Frost bouncing around in time, but why? How?

"Without going into the spaghetti-knots of all possible temporal transformations, I have concluded that Michael's use of the timebelt is dangerous. Furthermore, Zed, I advise you and Marina not to use the belt for any more travel. The human body and nervous system are not as protected by the belt's field as they are by the walls of the temporal chamber." Zed could certainly vouch for that.

"As for Michael, it would be wise for him to avoid any further journeys through Time at all. For you see, he is doubly dooming himself. The equations will show you what I mean, and I will explain.

"First of all, Michael must have lived extensively in the past when you and Cardenas sent him back here with the bomb in the chamber, the one that injured his leg. You see, I believe Michael was wrong about not aging in the past, before you are born. I believe the usual aging effects are just not apparent when one remains embedded in a different time, maybe just postponed for a period. These aging potentials, we can call them, are only made manifest, unbound as it were, by repeated travels. So some of Michael's mental problems are caused by the effects of rapid aging." The Scotsman drew in a long deep breath of prote smoke and frowned, shaking his head.

"But there is another component of Michael's psychosis, one that grows worse with every trip, by timebelt or by chamber, although the chamber attenuates the effect."

"And that is?" Zed asked, worried that he and Marina might be victims of yet another phenomenon of time travel.

"The isochronous repulsion effect prevents us from popping in on ourselves by accident, that much we know." Zed nodded as Daviess paced in front of the white board. "But when we do arrive at a different time, some of our constituent atoms are displaced out of our bodies, by that same effect. Essentially, they themselves are popped out of our bodies by suddenly being too close to their past or future selves.

"We don't notice the few thousand or even millions of atoms we lose each time because they are so few as to be insignificant to our body's operations. And of course, we absorb other atoms at our destination."

Zed didn't like the sound of the scientist's argument. It meant that he and Marina had lost atoms the same way, many times now. Was it that dangerous, maybe fatal? He shuddered, he didn't want to wind up a zane like Frost!

"Food, air, the more we take in at our destination, the worse the problem when we return, because those atoms have become parts of our functioning biological system. Losing atoms at each end of our temporal transfer, they are literally knocked out of us by temporal forces. Not only do they exit, but they can take along other atoms with them, disrupting molecules of which they are a part." Daviess' face grew very grim. "As I said, a few trips are not harmful, it seems. I haven't noticed any changes in my own condition, and I have experienced at least a dozen transfers."

Good, Zed thought. He and Marina were far behind that number of trips. He breathed easier as Daviess continued. "However, for hundreds or thousands of trips, the accumulated deterioration begins to affect macrocosmic operations in the body. And because the neurotransmitters that affect information storage and transfer in the brain are of molecular size, they are the most sensitive to the removal of individual atoms.

"I believe it is these neurotransmitters that are affected first. The manifestation of this condition is unpredictable brain damage, mental instability." A sad frown. "As a result of his many temporal transfers."

"But, Steve," Zed objected, "yesterday he mentioned something about Mexicans telling him where he could grab a time belt."

Daviess snorted. "That is true, Zed. Maybe our friend was visited in the distant past by other time travelers from our own future? It is impossible to tell." Garcia stiffened at the mention of other Mexicans with time machines, but Cardenas touched his arm, and the moment passed. Zed saw the reactions, but made no comment.

The scientist went on, "Zed attached himself to Frost's TimeSpace field and accompanied him to California, just a month after the QuanTonics factory in Chihuahua City was ... destroyed." Sorrow in the man's voice told Zed of Daviess' sad resignation over the destruction of one of his prized projects. Hundreds of millions of dollars lost; that much money, that much work, would be important even to a billionaire like Daviess.

"Michael then came forward to a more recent time, just five weeks back, to my home in California, with Zed's timebubble attached. Then he came forward once more, where he abducted Marina. Zed had detached himself from Michael's timefield by that time, fortunately. Zed, of course, could not visit himself there because of the temporal paradox forces, and was propelled far, far, back in time, back to the Homeric Era, in ancient Greece.

"Zed, the time you spent with the timebelt power off tells me something interesting—you were 'coasting' in TimeSpace, Brighton called it 'oscillating,' you said, from Past to Future and back again, like you were out of control." The Scotsman drew Zed's journey in a red color, all the way from near the far right end of the horizontal line, to the extreme left. "This was almost as if some large mass had imparted energy to Zed as he passed by it, analogous to the 'slingshot' effect when a spacecraft is propelled past one planet, taking advantage of its gravity field to increase its kinetic energy for a further journey."

Daviess sketched in another timeline for Frost. "Michael then departed California and took Marina back to Olympus himself. Then and there, as you know, Marina and Zed fought with Michael's robot and then returned back to here." The red line traced all the way back to the farthest right point, representing the present day.

"And this Frost, this warbot genius, *where* is he?" Cardenas demanded, glaring at Zed. The

American thought, *Yes, Hilario, you were absolutely right. We should have killed the wacko that first time we had the chance. Look at the mess he's made.* The whiteboard was fairly covered with Frost's zigzags through time and space; even Zed had not kept track of it all. Daviess grunted in response to the Mexican's question, making a few more in his series of criss-crossing patterns.

"Based on Michael's statements of yesterday, right here in Pisté, when he grabbed the belt, plus what Zed and Marina have told me about his other encounters, it seems that he's jumping back and forth across some obstacle in the TimeSpace field. Something very strange, within the last year or so, I'd say." Daviess paused and puffed his pipe.

Zed wondered, *Could Frost's 'origin' have something to do with the Chihuahua explosion? How? Why?* But his subconscious (or was it Brighton? He couldn't tell anymore) whispered that the bag of anachronistic nameplates, strewn through TimeSpace during the factory explosions, could have wreaked havoc with the orderly flow of Time.

"To answer your question, Hilario," the scientist said, "I don't think Michael will come this far forward in time again. He seems to be jumping closer and closer to this mysterious origin, this 'Black Hole' in Time, if you will, which lies several months back in our own past. He can't get past it often, if at all. I think Michael and all time travelers from any*when* will have difficulty scaling the powerful TimeSpace obstacle that seems to have arisen from nowhere."

Satisfied that they were shed of the psychotic genius Frost, the Mexicans said goodbye and left. They had a lot of war to do. But the engineer and the scientist pondered their interpretations about the convoluted causes and effects of the madman's time trajectories, adding their own journeys to the chaos. Dark marker dust covered their hands and joined the collection of stone dust that dirtied the floor of the ancient room. By this time, the whiteboard was thoroughly marred by alternative explanations, and the two men were thoroughly confused as well.

Zed said, "Something must be yet to happen, then, that enabled you to tell Filemón to pick me up at Chandeleur Island?"

Daviess nodded. "It was you who told me, right after my arrival here. You left a written message here, in this chamber, where Filemón's guards brought it to me. I don't know when the message originated, so I can't begin to draw that loop here on the board."

Zed was weary of time-loops. "Too many loose ends, Steve, but let's drop it. All I care about is, if Frost can't get back to us, he's harmless now." Zed erased one of the dots along the Time-line. "It's all in the past, it can't concern us anymore."

Daviess was disagreeing when Marina came in. "It's good to see you both. Zed, what *was* happening during that awful trip? Brighton said there was a 'hole' in the TimeSpace field." Waving her hand at the rat's-nest of colored markings on the whiteboard, she commented, "That's what you're working on, right?"

"Brighton?" Daviess asked, but neither Marina nor Zed elaborated; still their secret for now. The scientist didn't ask any further questions. "Not really, my dear Marina," he said, erasing the board. "Zed was just congratulating himself that Michael Frost is at last stuck in the past. I, however, am not quite so complacent."

"What's that mean, Uncle Steve?"

"You two have said, Marina, that you were attacked at my—*late* house—in California, by time-traveling Mexican assassins hired by Frost. Michael mentioned Mexicans when he was here yesterday, our time. I fear that he must have encountered these future Mexicans, perhaps time-traveling tourists, perhaps the gang your *Dashes* mentioned, during his tenure at old Chichén Itzá. After all, this temple site would be—*will be*—a marvelous place to visit, when temporal tourism happens." Marina and Zed agreed. That situation assumed that future time tourists could—*will?*—easily bypass the big anomaly. Better technology could explain a lot, and Zed had certainly witnessed his share of future magic.

"Further," the scientist said calmly, "Filemón's encampment at Tulum, on the coast, was attacked last night by a wave of hovercraft-borne, bodysuited Mexicans." At their dropped jaws, he continued. "Filemón thinks they were from the future, coming back to stop his revolution!"

General Garcia summoned the three *Norteamericanos* to lunch in a fairly comfortable, well-appointed dining room Zed hadn't seen before, somewhere in the underground factory complex. Finishing a sumptuous meal, Garcia and Cardenas and another Mexican officer toasted their guests, and received toasts in return.

During a toast to the future Garcia government, Daviess hesitated, and the General commented. "Dr. Daviess, believe me, I understand your concerns about becoming involuntarily involved in my revolutionary struggle. I sympathize. But my sympathies and my friendship cannot be factors in the final battles to come. Zed," Filemón nodded at his Anglo friend, "you and I have shared adventures, experiences, even our souls, I would suppose, but even that closeness would not influence, in the slightest degree, do you realize, harsh and impersonal decisions I might have to make, were you, or Dr. Daviess, or Marina, to become impediments to our victory." The guerrilla leader put down his empty glass, the toasting now a hollow gesture.

Garcia stood and rubbed the back of his neck in a gesture of indecision. "You see, *amigos*, I am not the *Filemónito* from New Mexico any more. I am *El Filemón, El Jefe,* an embodiment of the aspirations of my people." He slapped at the dining table and a full color projection of México filled the end wall. *Just like Frost had,* Zed noted, impressed. Garcia-controlled areas, red splotches, grew in area as Garcista columns moved on Federal positions in a dozen areas. Yucatán, by now, was a red shield. Red daggers pointed at Guadalajara, Monterrey, Torreon. Coastal beachheads at Tampico and Mazatlán were red amoebas, shifting shapes with the progress of battles. Filemón was happy. "This display shows our progress in the last weeks, up to this very moment." The red columns froze.

"But now, I must go here!" The display showed the brown arches and columns of the Zócalo, the traditional seat of Mexican power. "This is my next target, my final target, where I will miraculously appear, make my *grito,* my shout of victory, right in *Ciudad México* itself. And then my country will change."

Garcia put both hands on the table and leaned forward to face the Anglos. "I know of your uncertainties now, afraid of the violence and bloodshed to come. But you need not be part of that, you may stay here until the final victory." Zed saw armed Mexican guards coming into the dining room; he and Marina and Steve were prisoners! "Someday," Garcia whispered, dramatically, "I will be old and, perhaps, a venerated elder statesman, hopefully even a retired *Presidente*, truly and freely elected. I want to be surrounded by real friends, old friends, *compadres* with whom I can relax, and once more share my soul. Then I will be the old Filemón again, *amigos*, and I don't want to die alone." He waved the five guards back to the wall where they took up positions, rifles still on their backs.

Pacing the floor like a Mexican version of Napoleon, hands behind his back, Garcia continued his oratory. "I will make you this promise, Dr. Daviess, Zed, Ms. Tanner—we will use the timebelts only once, to seize the Zocalo, and then I will destroy them all!"

Daviess rose in anger from his chair. "You can't do that, Garcia, these belts are the answer to the world's transportation system. It would be like trying to destroy the wheel!"

Rifles clicked to "ready" as Garcia left his chair and strode around to the scientist, waving the guards to lower their guns. "But, Estevan, this belt is not the wheel at all. It is my Mexican A-bomb, you know? I compare its use against the *Federales* with the Americans' use of the atomic bomb against Japan in the Second World War."

"Or the Mexican Oilfield Bombs," Daviess shot back. Even Filemón grimaced at those memories.

"Whatever," Garcia continued, "they each solved the problem of their day. Against an uncompromising enemy, one must utilize unbelievable technological advances, no? And what could be more unimaginable than this tiny piece of paradox, eh?" Zed wondered how much Steve had revealed about temporal physics. "So, it is a very useful weapon, but only while you have sole possession, correct?" Zed saw what the general was getting at, remembering the conversations he and Filemón had years before, during the collapse of the old socialist systems worldwide. They had speculated on a world in which the U. S. had kept sole possession of nuclear secrets in 1945, in which the world might have been spared more years of Marxist repression and terror. Zed heard, in his friend's present exposition, echoes of those previous discussions.

"Once the secret of fission bombs got out," Garcia was saying, "the Pandora's Box was opened and we all lived under its threat until Cold War One ended. Well, what if the U.S. had somehow kept its secrets, either by imprisoning or killing all enemy atomic scientists? What if there had been no headlong rush to build bombs worldwide?"

Zed interjected, "Tens of millions more would be alive in the Middle East right now."

Garcia stared. "And, too, in northern California? On the Moon? Maybe in other places? Who knows? But let me summarize quickly, you are educated people. I want to destroy all of these timebelts and keep them a military secret after my revolution. The peasants and officers I will take with me know nothing of the technology represented here, much less how to reproduce it. I personally have the greatest incentive to keep these devices out of the world's armament market." The General smiled, relieved that his proposals were sinking in on his guests. "I sure as hell don't want any other revolutionaries to have these belts, to use them against me!"

Zed frowned. *Good luck, Filemón,* he thought. *But we know for certain that some Mexicans from the future will ally themselves with Michael Frost and sure as hell will use some kind of time travel device to come back and try to kill Marina and me, and will attack your post at Tulum!* Daviess, even Garcia, must have been thinking similar thoughts, but no one said anything.

"Of course," Garcia murmured, "if anyone from the future dares to attack me, it must be because my revolution will be successful. And so I welcome such attacks!" He swept from the dining room, motioning his guards to go with him. The door, Zed heard, was bolted shut from outside.

Daviess was shaking. "God, Zed, you heard what Garcia said: 'if the Americans had killed or imprisoned all those atomic scientists.' Can he mean to implement such a threat against us, you and me? And what about Lorenz? He's out there somewhere in the factory, doing something with Garcia's troops." More calmly, he added, "But Bill does not know the details of my work. Only Michael would."

Zed nodded grimly. "Who knows what goes on in the mind of a revolutionary sensing the blood of a victory? But never mind that, do you have another belt, one we can use to get out of this god-damned dungeon?" Zed could not bear to spend any more time in the place where Marina had been treated so brutally. Maybe it was the aftermath of the bad time trips, the battle with the robot, or the battle with the future Mexicans, but Zed felt totally weary, not ready to have any more violence around himself or Marina. He wanted to go somewhere away from time machines of all kinds, away from the Yucatán. Away from war.

Daviess whispered. "I've been worried about this eventuality for days, Zed, so I took precautions. What you want is in the adjacent kitchen. In the fridge." He smiled broadly. "Frozen in the ice compartment! But it won't operate right away. We'll have to get the components up to their nominal operating temperature range."

"We'll let it thaw out, Steve, and then we can all escape," he whispered. Marina left for the kitchen and the clatter of ice trays soon followed. She was more than ready to leave.

"But Zed," Daviess said, stroking his goatee, "I have said that traveling by timebelt right now is not safe. Whatever the anomaly that is affecting temporal transfer around this date, it still influences unprotected travelers. Maybe even those in chambers, too."

"Steve," Zed snorted. "Do you think it is safe to stay here, when Filemón is planning his final assault on México City, and we're the only ones who know how he plans to do it? At best, he's going to keep us prisoner here, a long time, to protect his secrets. And at worst ..." Zed's frown conveyed his conviction that execution was likely to be their most probable fate. Daviess remembered the old cowardly terrorist's words, too: *We don't have a revolution to make friends!*

"So, Uncle Steve," Marina said as she returned from the kitchen with a time belt secured around her waist, "I'm doing my best to thaw this thing out. I heard you say it was dangerous to travel 'around this time.' What did you mean?"

Daviess explained to her his theory that some kind of temporal anomaly had perturbed normal temporal transfers, causing Zed's and Michael Frost's wild spirals through time. "My own inability lately to get beyond two months back convinced me. That, and Zed's description of his temporal travels since that time. The trips a few months ago were smooth, if frightening. The trips since? Bad and getting worse. So, located sometime in the past few months is a dangerous perturbation, an anomaly in TimeSpace that disrupts the smooth flow of temporal energy."

"Steve, those anachronistic nameplates I threw into the chamber in Chihuahua. Did they ... cause something to happen?"

The scientist gasped. "Of course, Zed. That had to be a contributing cause. Let me think." The Scotsman played with his wrister, sketching display after display on its tiny screen, a screen that to his lens-augmented eyes appeared as large as the wall. The man looked comical, making drawings in the air. Zed bid Brighton access the wrister's outputs for himself and Marina. Immediately Daviess' hand waving took on solid form in open air. As Zed's gaze followed the equations and the sketches, the scientist stopped abruptly, looking at Zed and Marina. "Onboards, hmmm? Your Brighton?" They both nodded. "Very well, follow this."

Daviess drew some nomenclature Zed didn't follow. Marina just shrugged. The scientist said, "Hmmph! Well, if you don't know the mathematics of TimeSpace, listen to my verbal explanations: I believe—and the evidence seems to bear me out—that at the instant of the explosion of Cardenas' bomb back here in the chamber downstairs, the anti-paradox repulsion forces were thrown out of kilter by the anachronistic properties of the nameplates themselves. A singularity in TimeSpace existed for a brief, yet eternal Moment.

"My temporal chambers operate on the principle that the interior volume is plucked out of normal TimeSpace, and during the temporal transfer interval, exists within the dimensions of Sidespace. Like the ice skaters I mentioned before —" Marina frowned; she hadn't heard this analogy "—or like a bubble that falls from one height to another.

"Without enough power, the chamber's detached volume merely follows a trajectory that terminates when the closest temporal potential well is encountered, like that ice skater skimming down into a tapered hole. The trajectory is complex, yes, but governed by well-understood laws. And nonetheless, still falling.

"To do more than merely fall, one's time machine must be independently powered. The subtleties of my temporal chambers include the palmpress, which adds directed power, much like a mid-course trajectory correction in a spacecraft, to ensure that the time traveler arrives at the chosen destination, the desired TimeSpace coordinates, not merely the closest one. You can skate past one temporal well and seek another one."

Marina seemed to follow her uncle's explanation well enough. Zed preferred to think of the "ice-skaters" as spacecraft in trajectories out to the planets, and so began to understand his own time travels better. His own initial trips in the chambers had been powered. The timebelt trips were more like falling unpowered into whatever hole in TimeSpace opened up first. *And a damn sight more uncomfortable!*

"Back to that bag of nameplates," the scientist

said, bringing Zed up from the well of his own thoughts, "the bag here at Pisté was only the past-time half of an entity I call a 'timepair.' When the objects entered the Chihuahua chamber, they reacted with the temporal transfer field, the 'timefield', if you will. The amount of 'past time' matter unbalanced the equilibrium of temporal forces that has to exist for my chamber to operate properly. This excess of past matter created a potential well so powerful that nothing could escape from it, a well that could not even exist in our own TimeSpace." The Scotsman paused and lit his prote pipe. Zed grimaced at *that damned protohash, stinking crap*! But he said nothing; the scientist was shaking, in need of calming, and barely croaked the next words.

"The resultant condition, the singularity, is a Black Hole in TimeSpace!"

Marina looked at Zed. Zed didn't completely understand the scientist's conclusions, but had expected something very bad.

Daviess, the smokedrug taking effect, looked relieved. "My theory calls for a 'timepair' to be created at that instant in Time. Or else for TimeSpace itself to collapse. The latter obviously didn't occur, fortunately. I could not begin to calculate the extent of such a catastrophe upon the whole of TimeSpace." Zed was in shock. Was it possible that he had nearly ended the Universe with a bag of metal plates? He couldn't believe it.

Daviess held up a hand to silence his friend. "Wait, Zed. The most probable reaction did occur, and we're all still here. Nature took the path of least resistance, creating one 'future matter' bag of nameplates that shot forward in TimeSpace. The other bag, 'past matter', shot back to the factory here, where they were found a thousand years later by Filemón's men." He let that statement sink in, sucking some more satisfaction from his heady pipeful.

"I think," Daviess said, "that what we have uncovered is the temporal analogy to Hawking radiation from normal-space matter entering a spatial Black Hole." The name rang a bell; a famous theoretical physicist from decades back, Zed remembered.

"No questions yet? Then let me finish. I suspect that at a quantum level, all of the matter in Michael Frost's body, the very quarks and quanta themselves, were impressed with the coordinates of that singularity, that Black Hole, during the Chihuahua Event. I mean Frost himself is *part* of that singularity, was there at the instant it was formed. He was lucky to have escaped at all. But as a result, Michael's very atoms are entangled with that Black Hole."

Daviess looked up at Zed sadly. "And Zed, I am afraid for you also. You were physically close to the Chihuahua Event, and you, too, may be at risk when you travel unprotected in TimeSpace." He touched the warming time machine belt that circled his niece's waist, ready for operation. "That is why I fear for your travel by timebelt. You may be drawn into that Black Hole of Time, Zed."

At that moment, the lights flickered and the walls shook. A loudspeaker announced, in Spanish, that the underground complex was under attack. The hallways suddenly filled with shouting, and there was banging on their door. Continuous concussions rang the ancient structure; ceilings and walls crackled and popped with the stress of artillery explosions.

Lorenz, of course, had been somewhere outside the room, somewhere with Filemón and the other guerrillas. Zed winced. At least *that* guy had made a voluntary choice to be down here; Zed couldn't begin to save him, now. Not and risk Marina and Steve. And himself.

The banging on the door increased. Zed idly wondered why they just didn't unlock the damned thing; after all they were the ones who had locked it.Panic does strange things to the mind, though. Holding that thought, Zed asked, "Is the belt ready to go, Steve?"

"But Zed, we don't know where and when the destination can be," Daviess protested, his voice rising as the doors began cracking under repeated attack. "We don't know where to go!"

"Brighton," Marina said aloud, calmly, "Give us your best shot. Can you detect the nearest operating time chamber?"

"Certainly," Zed heard the computer reply. There was a pause. "According to ... my information, the nearest one is in Juárez, Chihuahua."

"Then, let's go!" Marina shouted, grabbing Zed and her uncle by the arms. "To Juárez!"

This time trip was the absolute worst: the vortices of blue mist seemed to thin out, revealing a Presence nearby, something large and ominous, the Thing that was a Black Hole in TimeSpace. The nearness of Marina and Daviess did not help Zed's paranoia; the hole was out to get *him*, personally.

The landing, this time, was rough, too. Zed felt as if he were being crushed. There was no room! What was happening? Zed came to consciousness with Marina and Daviess pressed against him so tightly that ... the pressure was increasing. Were they inside a coffin, all three of them together? Daviess breathed a groan. "I … know ... where we are. Exhale ... let me ... *there!*"

The pressure vanished as all three people fell outward from a tiny closet-sized chamber, into a large museum-like foyer. "What was *that,* Uncle Steve?" Marina gasped, lying prone.

"Yeah, Steve," Zed wheezed, gulping down air, "why such a small chamber?"

"We are in the basement of the QuanTonics office building in Juárez, in our private, hidden museum. That chamber was a small one Michael and I used for—for artifact transport only." Daviess pulled himself up with a chair leg and rubbed his chest. "Thank God it was no smaller. There should have been a mass or volume override." Helping Marina up, he chewed his lip, "Could have been fatal."

"Brighton," Zed asked aloud, "*When* are we?"

"Zed … I am ... checking the computer nets ... we approached that TimeSpace anomaly again." Brighton's tone was somber. "And although we have arrived in *Ciudad Juárez, Chihuahua,* we did not make a direct trip. You have not yet arrived in El Paso, the first time, less than three months ago."

"I came to this *same* building?" Zed exclaimed. "Oh shit!" Marina and her uncle were mouthing those same two words.

They were underground in the QuanTonics factory in Juárez, the same place Zed from the past would be visiting, just weeks from now. While Zed sorted out possible plans, Daviess said, by way of explanation about their private museum, "Michael and I thought it not unethical, Zed, Marina, to bring back pieces that were never going to be found. We were very careful about that."

Zed didn't want to point out that if the pieces had been brought from the past they couldn't very well have been found since. But he didn't say anything at all. He was too worried about Zed-past and Zed-present, and what would happen when the two came close

For the moment, Daviess assured them that the vault was well protected and that they were in no immediate danger of discovery, being several floors underground. "Michael only rarely visited this vault, and certainly would not come here during business hours." Besides, the scientist said, he could operate all the door locks with his palm and they could easily escape during the evening when no guards were around. "Patrolbots, Zed. They all recognize me and will let me pass. And you two as guests with me, of course."

Marina could barely speak. "But where would we go? I mean, Zed, Zed-past, is supposed to arrive, will arrive, in a couple of weeks, and will come to this very building." She eyed Zed with fear. "If that happens, will one of you be—*destroyed*—by the paradox forces?"

Zed shook his head. "Listen, I *did* come here weeks later and I didn't die then—*won't* die then. So, it will be the now-me, old Zed-present, who gets the axe." He blew through clenched teeth. "If I just hadn't made that trip, none of this, this damned Black Hole, these crazy back and forth trips in time, would have happened." He closed his eyes, thinking, *and I would never have killed those people!*

Zed walked around the museum a bit, stretching his strained muscles, trying to get some flexibility back. He damned sure didn't want to be stuck back here in his own past, yet he had to leave Juárez right away or die. Or worse. The thought of that Black Hole in Time, waiting there for him like a giant spider in a web of TimeSpace, scared him shitless. He had better get back to his own time, he knew, or that Thing would always be there, patiently biding its Time. Zed's skin crawled.

On the other hand, using the timebelt again, so soon after this last trip, was marginal at best. That might be the fastest trip to the Time Spider, pulled down by the same tidal forces jerking at Frost. He outlined his fears and observations to Marina and Steve, whose logical conclusions paralleled his own.

"What about Frost, Uncle Steve?" Marina asked thoughtfully. "Do you have any idea what is happening to him, right at this moment? Any forces that could help Zed and us get over this Chihuahua Event, and back to our own time?"

"There is this time chamber right here," the scientist said, patting the coffin-sized, wooden-covered chamber. *For all the world, with that red paint, it looks like a Tardis from Doctor Who,* Zed thought, smiling grimly at the memory of an ancient 2D video show. "This box was to be a 'receive-only' system, but I can easily re-program it to 'transmit' as well. Perhaps we could send ourselves, one at a time, using its energy to boost us 'over' the potential well that will initiate three weeks from now."

Such fame I've earned, Zed scowled, *to have precipitated a Capitalized Occurrence, for all Time. And a roadblock for all Time Tourists?* He could see it now, two hundred years in the future. First, the nameplate at Castro Valley—*"Ladies and gentlemen, this is 'Wynter's Chuckhole.' And a little farther back down the line, we have 'Wynter's Bypass', constructed by the infamous weeko who almost destroyed the whole Universe!*" Shaking off the thought, Zed shuddered.

Daviess asked Brighton to do the energy calculations to estimate their chances of making it across the anomaly that was yet to be formed. "Zed, please tell Dr. Daviess that I do not know the parameters of the problem, that even *he* cannot predict the 'event horizon' of the temporal Black Hole."

"Your conclusion, then, Brighton?" Zed asked.

"Send one person at a time, with maximum power, to a known temporal coordinate."

"My buried nameplate in California?"

"That is the one safe coordinate, Zed. I would suggest we arrive the day after the farmlet was destroyed. We were all down there in Yucatán then, so the paradox forces on our bodies shouldn't be so severe up in northern California. And it's a good time to re-establish our time lines, I should think. But ..."

"Yes, now what?"

"Dr. Daviess and Marina are to go. Not you."

Brighton explained its proposal to Zed. It took half an hour of argument, mostly from Marina, before all three agreed to the plan. Zed was to see the other two off to the future. "Then, Zed, you may use the time belt plus the power of the time chamber, in an attempt to use the extra energy to boost yourself over the C.E. Since you are the person here who is most intimate with the original Event, your atoms, your energy fields, will be the most affected by its tidal forces. You are in the most danger."

Finally, Marina huffed off into another room, refusing to speak further with Zed. Her uncle explained, "She is extremely upset with you, Zed. Thinks you are exhibiting male *machismo*, irrational behavior, totally testosterone-induced visions of grandeur." He smiled, puffing his prote pipe again. "Of course, I think it is because she loves you and does not want to leave you to the tender mercies of TimeSpace anomalies."

Zed patted the scientist on the shoulder. "Steve, she knows I love her, too. But Brighton's way is the best idea we've got. I have to get out of here, we all do. That chamber is large enough for only one person at a time comfortably, and we can pull down enough electrical power tonight, when the place is practically empty, to push you and Marina into California, at the right time, and safely.

"I'm the one that's got tainted and entangled atoms. I'll pull down max power in the chamber, having Brighton synchronize this belt's field with the other chambers. If that doesn't kick me through ..." The alternative was an unspeakable descent into an eternal black hole. There was an old folk song, Zed recalled, about a place where "...not even God could find me."

Daviess gave Zed a comradely hug, patted him on the shoulder, and went to find his niece.

Eyes red from crying, Marina came in, scowling at Zed. "Damn you, Zed Wynter, I tried. I've got my wrister calling you …"

"You *what?*" Zed cried. "Your wrister is doing *what?*"

"Zed, I tried to call your Dallas office but you weren't there. Brighton answered at your home." Zed slapped his forehead, but Marina continued, "So I called my home system in California and had it record my voice message and told it to keep on trying your numbers, to tell you not to come to Juárez."

Light dawned in Zed's mind. "So *those* were the calls!" Laughing, he told them about the mysterious calls the days before he came to Juárez. "All I could get was your name, Marina." Zed thought of all the horrors of the last few months, all because of his trip at Filemón's request. *Can't blame everything on your old friend*, his conscience reminded him. *It was your* own *curiosity!*

"And so is completed yet another loop," Daviess muttered. Zed knew the man was mentally constructing yet another paradox-denied scenario.

Over her protests, the two men saw Marina off first.

Zed kissed her passionately. "Hon, check with your Brighton when you get there. If it's not the proper time, then get to a downtown hotel—the Hyperport Hilton—and wait." Whoever arrived when, if no one else came, they would each check a safety box at Daviess' bank? If there was no note, the arriving person would leave one.

"I'll find you, Marina, *whenever* you are. Goodbye."

Daviess held his niece closely and stepped back. A blue halo surrounded the 'Tardis' box and when they opened the door, Marina was gone.

ZED WAS ALONE, FINALLY. DAVIESS HAD BEEN transmitted somewhen, without incident as far as Zed could tell. Now, once again, Zed was on his own. But doubt raged. What would be the hurt in just leaving the factory and getting away from Juárez before Zed-past showed up?

Well, he argued with himself, first it would be the cowardly thing to do. Then, he would always be out of synch with his Time, and any perturbation in TimeSpace might warp him back into the loving arms of that Chihuahua Time Spider. Besides, Marina and Steve were waiting for him a few months hence. All he had to do was get over the Chihuahua Event. "Wynter's Folly" future generations would call it.

Before Zed screwed up enough courage to open the time-box door, the whole chamber began glowing. Migod! One of them hadn't made it! They were being forced back! Marina? Oh no!

The time-box door flung violently outward, and a small man stumbled out, falling on the floor. The figure was wrapped in material much like the bodysuits of the Dashes, but with no head covering. Then Zed saw the ravaged face, made ancient by incessant abuse from TimeSpace, and nearly retched. In a body old beyond its years, its eyes raging furnaces of mindlessness, lay the crippled thing once called Michael Frost.

"Frost," Zed whispered softly, gently, surprising himself with his compassion for the ruined human being at his feet, "Why?"

With gnarled limbs quivering and a face erupting with fury, the image was made gruesomely comic by the tinny voice that slithered from the contorted mouth.

"Zed Wynter, you ... shit," Frost mouthed, the words barely audible. "I tried to ... find you ... after Olympus." Wizened lids closed over bulbous, vein-streaked eyes. "The Mexicans ... from ... next century." The voice gained in volume, rasping words that grated Zed's ears.

"THIS ... SUIT ... COULD GET ME ... PAST ... THE Thing ... but ... I'm going back ... and forth ... something ... waiting ... out there ... for ... me. Can't ... get ... out. Looping."

Frost struggled to his feet. *My God*, Zed thought in horror, *the wacko zane's shrunk a foot!* Frost was bent, crooked, his limbs shaking, and his hideously knobby knees evident even through the bodysuit.

"Frost, you were supposed to be totally covered in that suit, it doesn't help otherwise." Zed found his sympathy swelling for this pitiful little man. Whatever evil he had done, he had paid for in spades.

The gnome twisted for a poignant look at the towering Wynter. "Took ... headpiece ... didn't work ... I'm flatted over ... bad, Zed. Here ... help ... me. Please ..." Frost held out a hand, a quivering claw swathed in bodysuit material.

Calmly, Zed took Frost's hand. What else could he do? But Frost suddenly seized Zed's hand in a death grip and with his other hand, slapped at his time belt. Triumph lit his ravaged face and he spat at Zed, "Got you ... piece ... of sh—"

In ultimate horror, Zed felt the world turn blue, and he plunged into the maelstrom of temporal transfer, hand in clawed hand with an insane Michael Frost.

THIS TIME THE TRIP IS ENTIRELY DIFFERENT, ZED Wynter told himself calmly, *this time you're a dead man, in the death-grip of a time-zombie, going to the Hell that is the Black Hole.* Around him roared the naked energies of TimeSpace, hazy swirls, bluish whirlpools of temporal potentials coalescing into a cavernous Blackness, a maw that was far, far beneath him. But growing closer.

"Remain calm, we'll get out of this, Zed" Brighton told him.

"*Help me, or shut the fuck up, Brighton*" Zed screamed silently, fighting the taunting, prickling energies that buffeted his body, his mind, wanting to suck him down into Hell forever.

"Frost is doomed, Zed, get away from him."

"*How*, my brilliant friend?"

The universe of TimeSpace was belching, bellowing, screeching. Like a spaceship's frictional re-entry into the atmosphere, Zed thought. Or into a Black Hole.

"First, remove his hand."

Across light-years of dark crystal, Zed saw Frost, eyes bulging mindlessly, face transfixed in rage, mouth moving, insect-like, in a silent scream. At Brighton's urging, Zed operated his own hand as if by remote control, feeling nothing. After infinite time, Frost's hand disengaged.

Zed felt his own sanity disengaging as well, neuron by neuron. *I'm losing brain cells. In a few minutes I won't even care. A mercy.*

There were doors. Zed saw the insides of Daviess timechambers, flickering in and out of his vision, felt them lashing him, slamming him.

There were other creatures, too, not human, too far away to distinguish. *Other lost souls?*

He stared at the TimeSpace Tornado, a dark, whirling, nexus of nothingness. His mind was slipping.

"I hope I'm crazy before I go down to that!"

"Zed, we will use your timebelt."

"Sure, Brighton, why not?"

"We will exit Frost's timefield and return to Juárez."

"Why bother?"

"We will utilize some of Frost's temporal kinetic energy and slingshot to where Marina is."

"Marina? Sure, I love …"

In a violent explosion of pure white light, Zed felt himself be kicked away from the Black Thing, velocity increasing without bound. Whether in imagination or by direct sight, he saw Michael Frost spiral in toward the Black Hole, the blue haze around the mangled figure turning shades of rainbow hues, blending into colors his brain had never experienced.

In a flash of less-than-black void, a silent scream on his maggoty lips, Michael Frost disappeared from this Universe.

Zed *saw*: a flash of purest white light, jerking suddenly to deepest blue.

Zed *felt:* a *slam!* into the coffin-like time-box in Juárez.

Zed *saw:* a whirlwind of blue, overarching a dark void far, far beneath him. A tiny speck of blackness orbited it at unbelievable speed.

Zed *felt*: Nausea. Disgust. Hate. Sorrow. Pity.

Zed *saw:* Marina and Steve standing over him. A bright blue sky over familiar brown California hills.

Zed *felt*: The odor of fresh rain. Cooling winds. Diminishing pain. Relief. Love. Darkness.

TIME TELLS

Twenty-four hours later, Zed and Marina were in a freshly-made bed in a motel in nearby Hayward, satiated with seafood from a nearby fishery restaurant. "Uncle Steve is back at his Stanford office," Marina said, smiling as she clicked off her wrister. Stretching languidly, she jumped into bed beside Zed and nuzzled in his neck. Zed yawned. "What's this, lover? Bored already? Already an old married couple?"

Zed bopped her with a pillow. "If you ever start thinking that, you know just what to do." His eyes narrowed with the memory of pleasure.

Miraculously, all three of them—Daviess, Marina, and Zed—had successfully made the time transit from the time-box chamber in Juárez, nearly three months back, over/through/around the Chihuahua Event, arriving within minutes of each other outside the crater that was the remains of the Daviess farmlet. Zed credited this feat to Brighton's precise control of temporal energies, and maybe to something else.

"Brighton, answer both of us, please."

"Sure thing, Zed, Marina. What washes?"

Zed frowned. "What is this with the slang, my old buddy? And aren't you losing your nice, aristocratic British accent?"

"Trying Americanisms, Zed. Your question?"

"How did you get us through the Chihuahua thing, and have us all arrive so close together? I thought we might have landed days, even months, years, apart. Did you have—future knowledge?"

Brighton paused and the old voice and inflections returned. "Sire, Mistress, I cannot tell a lie. Although the future folk—the ones you called *Dash One* and *Dash Two*—downloaded much future information when they injected me into you two, they also downloaded the laws of temporal transfer. Two hundred years from now ... they have —will have much accumulated ... unbelievable experience … in ... time travel. Thus, I was unable to impart much of this information to you, even though I ... desired ... to, exceedingly so.

"Part of their data related to survival around temporal anomalies, including this most infamous one, the Chihuahua Event, or 'C. E.', as it is known, UpTime."

Zed breathed a sigh of relief at that appellation. At least it wouldn't be "Wynter's Folly," as he had feared. The DI continued, "I did not think it wise to use such knowledge during the previous trips, but the enormity of the situation when we were in Juárez was such that I deliberately acted against my programming."

Zed's jaw dropped; how could a DI—?

"Because you, Zed and Marina, and Dr. Daviess, were in danger of death or worse. My Campbellian Law ethics overrode the potential damage of paradox repulsion forces, and I adjusted the 'time box' and your timebelt, Zed, so that you three would arrive intact. Not to mention myself.

"Unfortunately for Mr. Frost, our slingshot boost pushed him into the singularity even faster."

"Brighton, what is a few seconds more or less when he has all eternity to spend there? He *did* die, didn't he?"

The computer paused. "No. He was screaming incoherently as he passed the event horizon. If Dr. Daviess is correct and the TimeSpace singularity acts as a physical Black Hole, then Frost's last conscious moment will endure for all Eternity as he descends into the Hole."

Zed gaped. "You mean, eternally insane? Screaming? Raging?"

Brighton answered simply, "Yes."

Marina gasped. "The ancient vision of Hell: an eternity of torment. How awful."

Zed formed a mental image of the younger Frost as he had appeared just a few short months ago, in México: blonde, balding, not yet aware of the damage he was even then doing to his mind and body. And then, there was Frost stuck on a gigantic web, his panic-stricken gyrations *thrumming* the web-lines of TimeSpace, beckoning the Time Spider to devour him, an eternal feast of damnation.

"Just like Prometheus," Zed whispered in awe, "he brought a new technology to Mankind and he suffers eternally for it. Michael Frost, Prometheus of Time!"

Zed shivered, and Marina came to him, crying.

Dr. Stephen Daviess, Marina Tanner, and Zed Wynter stood on the hillside overlooking the new construction that would soon become, once again, the Daviess household. Six months had passed since their troubled voyage from Pisté by way of Juárez.

Zed knelt and spread a picnic lunch over the brown grass on the hillside, enjoying the fall coolness. "Think they'll be finished before winter, Steve?"

Daviess, bringing out his pipe, sat on the blanket Marina had brought, and admired the three-story house the crew was erecting. "Zed, with the on-site additive manufacturing techniques that California building statutes require, my place will have walls in two days, a roof the next, and all internal utilities, being modular, the next." He laughed. "All the work so far, this last month, was just digging out and disposing of all the junk from the original place. I wanted to be damned sure nothing remained of your nameplates, nor of my own temporal chamber." He grew very sober. "I do not want any temporal technology anywhere near me, not for a long, long time." Zed could tell the man was very wary of more experimentation, now that they all knew what had caused the final blast here.

It hadn't been someone's nuclear device at all. Daviess himself had explained, after analysis of all the similar mysterious "nuclear blasts" around the world. "It must have been the moment in TimeSpace when Frost's mass entered into the singularity, Zed. For it occurred at all of the chambers we had built, everywhere." Marina said nothing; she had seen the video from the blast centers at Pisté (Zed was grateful that Chichén

Itzá, though seared, had survived more or less intact, and Juarez (minor damage), Mt. Olympus (no loss of life), Zimbabwe (a few farms had vanished), Tibet (fortunately, also buried under centuries of rubble and so far back in time that the blast was mostly attenuated), and finally, the Daviess basement chamber itself.

"I think my own house exploded first, just because of the many, many instances of anomalistic incursions. Think of it as the repeated scars of TimeSpace. Or else, it exploded last, if you view it from the origin of the explosion in TimeSpace coordinates.

"It could have been so much worse, had we not built underground. So much worse..." The hundred or so innocents in Africa who had died would remain on Daviess' conscience the rest of his life, Zed knew, but neither he nor Marina commented.

Marina broke the tension by speaking of the message she'd received from *El Presidente* Filemón Garcia of México. "You know, he didn't even realize we had escaped until he saw Uncle Steve on the WorldNet interview last week."

Zed frowned, "Yeah, Filemón timebelted away to México City with most of his elite troops when the Pisté stronghold was being attacked. Luckily for Lorenz, Filemón took him along, even though his fate was not necessarily better, being the only foreigner who witnessed the actual assault by time-belt. No telling what will happen to him. Filemón thought *we'd* been conveniently eliminated when the place was vaporized, a few minutes later. Everybody, Filemón and us, were just lucky things didn't go off sooner."

Daviess commented that he didn't think the

paradox forces would have allowed Zed to die "before" he had jumped to Juárez and around the Singularity with Frost. A few attackers—future or present Mexicans, Zed never had been able to determine, as the media didn't yet know about temporal transfers—had not been so lucky.

Marina and Zed sat, an arm around each other, taking in the beauty of the hills and valley. Zed said, "You know, Steve, even after questioning our Brightons, we still haven't figured out how I was able to warn you about the Chandeleur Island visit."

Daviess shrugged, lighting the prote pipe. "It must mean you are yet to travel back and leave me that message. Or else, there are other ramifications of the technology we don't yet understand."

Brighton chimed in. "Now that you have brought up the subject voluntarily, I can tell you, Zed, Marina, Dr. Daviess." The DI's voice even chirped out of the Scotsman's wrister. "*Dash Two* wrote that note addressed to you, when Zed was sleeping here at the farmlet. She sent it back to Pisté to arrive at the appropriate time so that Zed would be rescued."

The three humans stared at each other. "How did she know to do that, exactly when Zed would arrive there?"

Brighton paused, then explained, his British accent even crisper than before, "Some things are well documented in the future, Ms. Tanner-Wynter. It was you yourself who wrote that note and sent it back in time. I merely ensured that Zed would make the jump on schedule."

Light dawned on human faces. Zed choked out, "Then — *Dash Two*—was *Marina*?" He already knew the answer.

Marina smiled, her lovely hair now a frond of fine copper wire, "And, of course, *Dash One* was—"

"*Zed!* Be damned!" Dr. Daviess blurted, spitting out his pipe. "You will come back to visit yourselves from two hundred years in the future! What a damned circle in TimeSpace!"

Two hundred years from now? The final irony, Zed thought, *a never-ending fate for me, too, although the smile on Marina's face promises it to be an interesting one.* Maybe he'd been wrong before; it appeared that one day he *would* get the hang of time travel!

"What hath Daviess wrought?" Zed asked quietly.

END

Milton Keynes UK
Ingram Content Group UK Ltd.
UKHW030856111124
451035UK00001B/1

9 781946 419668